The Tartarus Transfer
By James D. Eate

For Jeanie,
who always believed I'd finish
one someday.
So sorry it took too long.

With special thanks to Lynn Gittings
for her help, encouragement and continued friendship.

Table of Contents

PROLOGUE

Why did they want to meet here of all places?

Meet by the steps just before the amusements at midnight they said but was that this end of the prom or the other? The instructions had been far from clear. He should have clarified them at the time but the lateness of the unexpected call had caught him unawares, confused him. Why did they need to meet at all? What could possibly be so important that it couldn't wait until the following day? And if it was so important couldn't they have met at the barn as usual? Why go all the way to Bridlington for god sake and why so late at night? He was still annoyed with himself for not asking; annoyed that he always jumped when told to jump. At thirty two years of age he was still being bullied, still not asserting himself. His overbearing father had derided him, mercilessly mocking his only child as being an invertebrate; he'd been encouraged to stand up for himself but he always backed down; always avoided confrontation of any kind.

His father's dominating personality had driven his mother away when he was only thirteen years old. She should have been stronger. Should have stayed and protected her only son but she abandoned him. She didn't have the courage to stand up for herself either. He hated her for that. Bitch. As far as he was concerned he was an orphan.

The feeling of frustration at having been standing there shivering for almost twenty minutes was slowly transforming into angry resentment. He sunk his head below his upturned jacket collar; gloveless hands were thrust deep in to shallow pockets; the sharp wind whipping in off the North Sea forcing the prevailing moist air to penetrate the flimsy jacket he was wearing. What was it someone said? *There's no such thing as bad weather only inappropriate*

5

clothing. Certainly his jacket wasn't suited to the conditions; much too lightweight to keep out the cold damp night air of the East Coast but then he hadn't expected to be exposed to the elements when he left home. God he wished he was back in relentless heat of Thailand. Holidays were never long enough. Never mind, one day he'd be out there permanently. It couldn't come soon enough.

He was cursing himself for having arrived early. He always arrived early; it was yet another compulsion drummed into him by his late father. Ironically dying was the only reason the adjective late could ever be applied to the old man. It was very bad manners to keep people waiting, his father had hammered home to his son; it showed disregard for the value of their time. Weren't they now showing disregard for the value of his time? He'd give them a piece of his mind when they eventually arrived; no he wouldn't; he knew he wouldn't and he hated himself for being a milksop.

He checked his mobile for messages; it was set to vibrate but he hadn't felt any movement, maybe it had gone unnoticed in the shivering of his body. No messages, no missed calls. Perhaps he should make a call. Check that they were still coming. No, they'd ring if there was any serious delay.

He checked his watch. Midnight they'd said. Ten minutes late.

At last he heard footsteps approaching. Peering, half faced, around the stone sea wall he could just about determine the outline of two people. As they passed under one of the inadequate sodium lights, lining the promenade he caught a glimpse of their hi-vis patrol jackets. Police. He slipped into the shadows and held his breath as the two uniformed female officers strolled past stepping around the pool of piss and vomit deposited by a drunken youth and his urinating companion twenty minutes previously. He was confident the officers hadn't seen him, just as well because there was no plausible reason why he was loitering there at that time of night.

He checked his watch again. Each minute seemed more like ten. Then he heard a voice coming from the bottom of the steps.

'Tom, we're down here.'

6

'Is that you?' he called back in a whisper. What a stupid question; who else would be calling him at a quarter past midnight on the promenade.

'Yes, down here.'

He looked over his shoulder to check that nobody was around then made his way gingerly down the barely visible first flight of steps towards the darkness of the beach. Once again he questioned why the hell they wanted to meet here and the need for the cloak and dagger arrangements.

The answer became clear as he started to descend the second block of steps.

ONE

Doctor Denise Morrison, the duty pathologist, decamped from her estate car fully kitted in her all-in-one forensic overall. 'I'm getting too old to be on call at five-thirty on a Monday morning,' she moaned to DCI Pullman.

Humberside's most experienced pathologist was approaching fifty years of age from the wrong direction but even without make-up on at that early hour she could have passed for being ten years younger.

'Nice to see you back Mike,' she said. 'How are you coping?'

'I'm not, at least I haven't been but I'd rather not talk...'

'Of course I understand.' She noticed immediately that he was looking gaunt and tired. She changed the subject. 'What have we got?'

'A problem,' said Pullman unhelpfully.

Morrison drew back the flap of the white forensic tent and stepped inside to join the FSI recording the scene on a digital camera. The freestanding arc lamp illuminating the victim projected both their silhouettes onto the side wall. Pullman stood outside watching Morrison's shadow examining the body.

The fully clothed corpse of a decapitated white male, age unknown was found by an angler on his way home from night fishing on the pier. At first sight he thought he was going to the aid of someone who had collapsed or been mugged but the reality when he approached the victim caused him to involuntarily retch and vomit over the victim. No attempt had been made to hide the body which was laying in full view; a stream of blood flowed, from the neck, like molten lava seeping from an erupting volcano. It had started to solidify creating a Takeshi Kawanoke like sculpture cascading down the second level of concrete steps leading to the beach.

Denise Morrison exited the forensic tent. 'Nasty,' was all she said.

Pullman blew hot breath into his cupped hands. 'Deni take fingerprints and DNA as soon as the body gets back to the lab then run a check as fast as you can please.' A completely unnecessary request, she would have done so anyway. 'Let's hope the poor sod's got form.'

Twenty five years in the police assured that Pullman was no stranger to murder but this was the first time he had been called upon to deal with a headless corpse. If the victim's DNA or fingerprints were not held on record then it could be a nightmare trying to identify him.

DS Lynne Sperring, standing to Pullman's right, emerged from the chrysalis of her forensic suit; despite the 5am call out the newly born butterfly looked immaculate in her black trouser suit with a feint pinstripe, crisp white blouse; she removed the white plastic overshoes to reveal well-polished shoes with a low heel. In the seven years since leaving university she had amassed an extensive shoe collection and an even more extensive wardrobe of designer label clothes.

'Lynne as soon as forensics have finished, get a local uniform team scouring the area for the head.' Killers have been known to collect fingers or ears as trophies but if this victim's head has been taken as a trophy it was unique in Pullman's experience. 'If it's been discarded then we need to find it before the gulls do.'

DS Sperring nodded. 'It could have been thrown in the sea,' she said.

'The tide's been coming in for the last few hours so if it had of been the chances are it would have washed up on the beach by now.' In his youth, Pullman had spent many hours sea angling off the pier at Brid, as Bridlington was commonly known, so he knew that the incoming tide tended to drift in towards the pier. 'Start this side and work back this way and up as far as North Beach to start with, maybe we'll get lucky.'

Pullman hadn't expected that his first case on returning to duty would be quite so challenging but he was glad he got the shout.

9

Not that he derived any great pleasure from viewing mutilated corpses but the job diverted his thoughts away from Jane. Three months of enforced compassionate leave and sessions with well-meaning bereavement counsellors had not helped. Thoughts of Jane filled every second of his down time. He had allowed himself to wallow in self-pity and like quicksand it had threatened to engulf him, suck him down into a pit of dark despair.

He needed the job.

He needed the distraction of the job to fill his every waking hour; to relieve the pain; absorb the heartache. He had been lying in bed, eyes wide open staring through the darkness, thinking of what might have been when the shout came. Jane was beside him. He couldn't see her; he couldn't touch her; he couldn't speak to her. Jane existed only in his memories; memories that seeped through the cracks in his consciousness and spread like the cancer that took her from him.

The shout provided temporary respite from the self-inflicted mental torment. He'd responded to the call from the new Chief Constable immediately; he'd showered, dressed and got behind the wheel of his car within fifteen minutes. No time to think. No time for memories. For the time being his mind was focussed on the gruesome scene before him. The murder victim deserved his full attention.

'Have a word with the local nick, we'll need to set up an incident room,' he said to his DS.

'Already had words with the local Inspector sir,' Sperring nodded in the direction of a senior uniformed officer supervising constables. 'He says he hasn't got enough room for his own people let alone us. You could have a word…'

'Nah, I can't be arsed to argue with anyone today. Get a mobile set up. You can get it in there or up top. I'll clear it with the CC later.' Pullman indicated the area where the fairground attractions were housed in the summer months. In the autumn the rides were dismantled and removed from the site for routine maintenance, some were destined never to return. There was something inherently depressing about a British seaside resort in the autumn/winter period, after the last of the school half term holidays had finished, when rides, amusement arcades, cafes and the like were closed down, especially if, as with Brid, those closures rendered the central seafront area a ghost town. The only thing missing was the tumbling tumbleweeds.

'What about the CCTV?' he asked, meaning have you checked it out.

'I've sent a uniform over to the council security offices to requisition the tapes for last night.'

'And the surrounding area?'

'Yes sir.' Lynne Sperring was being her usual efficient self. She was glad her boss was back on the job. She had spoken with him several times on the telephone and had exchanged texts during the preceding three months but had not physically seen him since the funeral. He was looking tired she thought. The sparkle had gone from his eyes; the sepia bags under them looked more like bruising and he was badly in need of a shave and a haircut if it came to that. She remembered how inconsolable she had been when Rocky her pony was put down after a bad fall, not that it was any comparison to the loss of a spouse she imagined. She resolved not to mention Jane or his feelings unless he did so first. 'Good to see you back sir.'

Pullman just nodded a silent acknowledgement then stuck his head inside the tent covering the body. 'Found any ID yet?' he asked the Scene of Crime Officer who was now examining the body for non-medical purposes.

'Nothing at all. No wallet, no jewellery, no phone. Looks like someone didn't want him identified. Gang killing?' proffered the SOCO.

'Doubt it, they'd have chopped his hands off too so we couldn't get prints. In any case a gang would have had to come from outside the area; in Brid there's just the usual amount of alcohol fuelled crime, vandalism and drug dealing; there's one or two dodgy families they keep an eye on but this is way beyond their sphere of activity. This guy's more likely to have been a comfort.'

'Sir?'

11

'A comfort,' he said before adding in his best Yorkshire accent, 'comfort'day,' a visitor, holiday maker.' It was his dad's pet phrase and Pullman smiled, as he always did, when passing it on to an unsuspecting new audience.

Pullman left the young man to finish his search. He shook his shoulders in a violent shiver, his hair still damp from the hurried shower. Removing the thin anti-contamination gloves he rubbed the palms of hands together rigorously to create friction; the transient heat generated did little to overcome the creeping chill biting into his fingers. He sighed deeply, expelling a stream of warm breath in to the cold air like the exhaust from a cold car engine.

A dank, autumnal sea fret was hanging over the Bridlington coast compressing the temperature. The tide was high but the murky visibility combined with pre-dawn darkness rendered the shoreline obscure. Mewing herring gulls and the occasional kark of a crow could be heard above the sound of the North Sea lapping gently, unseen on the sandy beach just a few feet away. Reflections of flashing blue lights illuminated the surroundings.

What a dismal location to die thought Pullman. There were no good locations.

It would take an hour or two before they got the body back to the mortuary in Hull where Denise Morrison could properly establish the exact time of death.

According to PCSO Carol Lingard, being interviewed by DS Sperring, she and a colleague patrolled Alexandra Promenade along to Royal Prince's Promenade about ten minutes past midnight and had not seen or heard anything at the murder spot. They did break up one fight involving four females, further on down by Jerome's café but they were all so drunk they could hardly stand up. This meant that the murder probably happened sometime between midnight and five o'clock that morning when the body was found.

Aside from signs of residual sand from the promenade the victim's clothes were smart and clean. On first glance Pullman ruled out the death being a result of a turf dispute between vagrants frequenting the shelters along the prom; they'd fight each other over a bottle of cheap supermarket cider but were unlikely to go this far.

It was too extreme to be a street fight between the drunken hoards that turn out of the clubs and bars in the early hours of the morning. Since deregulation of licensing hours Bridlington had developed an unenviable reputation for being the worst place to be in Yorkshire after dark. Police resources were drawn from surrounding areas every night to deal with the brawls between drunks and junkies that populated the streets towards the dawn.

Pullman looked up at the wall above the promenade, then at Denise Morrison then back at the wall. 'I don't suppose it could have been dumped here. Maybe thrown over the top?'

'No way.' said Morrison. 'The killer would have to be super human to throw it this distance from the wall. No, the splatter patterns clearly indicate that it happened right here; having said that, the gulls webbed footprints all over the place and the finder's vomit haven't exactly helped preserve the scene.' She was stripping off her plastic overall. 'Mind you, it took some doing to hack his head off; the neck area is a complete mess and there are several cuts to the shoulders and back where the implement appears to have missed its target. The killer would have been covered in blood.'

'Well at least we don't have to worry too much about the cause of death.' said Pullman.

****

Unlike the state-of-the-art CCTV control room in Hull, with which Pullman was familiar, the Bridlington security monitoring room was little more than the size of a broom cupboard; made even more cramped by the obesity of the security operative monitoring the screens. Stale air was further tainted by the aroma of cigarette smoke on the man's clothing and coffee breath. There was insufficient room for all four of them to huddle around the monitors so the uniformed police officer had to wait outside; Sperring wished she could have joined him. The aging non digital system consisted of a total of just

13

eight live monitor screens. The cameras were currently focussed on the approach to Bridlington railway station; two on Quay Road down to Prospect Street; keeping an eye on illegal parking mainly, since the introduction of the local council's new restrictions. One was located on Chapel Street where the market was held every Wednesday and four along the sea front promenades covering the Forum bar and cinema, fun fair area and harbour.

The spot where the body was found was in a poorly lit part of the prom made worse by the contrast of the shadows deepened by the new moon; being in mono did nothing to improve the clarity of the pictures.

They watched the tape from a starting point of 11.30 pm. A sporadic array of pedestrians passed by the spot, some as expected were the worse for drink including what was possibly two of the girls who had the fight further down the promenade; one man stopped to relieve himself while his companion threw up.

Then what appeared to be the victim appeared; the tape showed the time as 11.50. With his back to the camera he could be seen to walk to the edge of the concrete steps where he stood motionless except for occasionally swivelling his head, owl-like, through ninety degrees; apparently expecting someone to join him.

'Maybe he's looking for a prostitute,' said Sperring.

'Wrong part of town for one of those,' said the security man. 'So I'm told,' he added quickly.

At 12.11 the subject checked his watch, then looked over his shoulder and just seemed to vanish into the shadows. Two uniformed officers, presumably PCSO Lingard and her colleague, walked through the frame.

'He's obviously nervous of uniforms,' said Pullman. 'What the hell is he up to?'

'He's waiting for someone and judging by the number of time checks whoever he's waiting for is late.'

'Who would you arrange to meet at midnight on the prom?'

'A drug dealer,' suggested Sperring without any conviction. 'Or maybe he is one.'

'Yeah that had crossed my mind too,' said Pullman. 'Could be he was a rent boy meeting a client.'

'Or a mugger who got more than he bargained for,' suggested Sperring.

'If he was a mugger he was bloody unlucky to pick a target that just happened to be carrying a meat cleaver.'

At 12.12 the man reappeared, his back still turned towards the camera; he was clearly aware of the camera and didn't want to be recognised.

At 12.14 he walked back towards the steps and disappeared again. They watched the tape for a further twenty minutes; the subject never re-appeared.

'I'm guessing that our victim has been hacked by now. It's probable that the killer approached the steps from the beach, there's no CCTV down there; the sand would make for a pretty silent approach and the tide would obliterate any footprints. Clever bastard, whoever he is.' said Pullman. 'It's pretty clear that the victim knew the killer.'

He patted the security man on the shoulder. 'We're having a mobile incident room erected sometime today, about where camera six is sited; I'd like you to pan around it as best you can and capture the inevitable gallery of spectators that will gather. Keep this one on the area of the incident too.'

Pullman's thinking was that killers frequently return to the scene of their crime, drawn back by a morbid fascination to see what activity is taking place. If that happened this time it could help a future prosecution if they could later identify the accused at the scene of the crime.

Pullman stepped outside and instructed the uniformed officer to go back in and sit through the rest of the tape. He was to watch the tape from around ten pm to midnight to make sure the killer hadn't arrived early and concealed him or herself before the victim arrived. He was requested to make a note of anything unusual, in fact to make a note of anything whether unusual or not. Then he was to get the rest of the tapes from the surrounding area and bring them back to the incident room where researchers would spend as long as it took to view them all. Pullman wanted to know if there was any footage of the victim elsewhere in the area immediately before he was murdered.

Pullman and DS Sperring returned to the promenade in the hope that the mobile unit had arrived. It hadn't.

TWO

By three pm that afternoon; the forty foot long mobile incident room had been set up about fifty metres from the public toilets on Royal Princes Promenade. It may not have been the most attractive of locations but it was convenient in every sense. The installation team had located a power source and wired the unit to mains electricity to power the computers and electronic communications equipment on board. As expected the large white construction, with yellow and blue chequered stripes along its length, drew considerable attention.

Pullman had spoken to Pauline Crompton the Chief Constable who was not happy that he had organised a mobile unit without authority. The budget was very tight and she didn't want to give the newly elected Police and Crime Commissioner any ammunition for a battle.

Inside the brightly lit unit, DS Sperring sat at a desk reading the first of the reports from the uniform team who had been busy questioning local business owners; conducting a door-to-door of the apartment blocks overlooking the promenade and quizzing passers-by. Not one person had so far reported having heard or seen anything in relation to the murder. No surprise there then.

Pullman sat at another desk reading the emailed autopsy report. He had not attended the examination. He'd never developed an appetite for seeing cadavers sliced open; never seen the reason to be in attendance and had only ever reluctantly done so when ordered to by a superior officer.

EXTERNAL EXAMINATION:

The victim wore a pale blue button down collar, cotton shirt; Navy blue Chino trousers with black simulated leather belt; Navy blue lightweight zip-up jacket. Black socks and lace up black brogues; all garments including underpants are from M&S. There are no other belongings or items on the body.

The body is that of a normally developed white male measuring approximately 186 cms (73inches) allowing for the missing head and weighing 78.1 kilos (12st 4lbs) , aged approximately mid-thirties.

Upon removal of the victim's clothing, a stab wound was located between the third and fourth rib under the heart. A second wound was located under the chest cavity and piercing the duodenum. From the depth of the wound these would appear to have been caused by a 6 inch serrated blade, possibly a kitchen knife.

A small single colour tattoo was identified on the inside of the right forearm (see image 3) this appears to illustrate the letter H in a circle 2.5 cms across its widest points formed by a snake's body. The forked tongue of the snake is entwined around the letter.

The hands are clean. No callouses or ingrained grime would indicate that the victim is not a manual worker.

The genitalia is that of an adult male and there is no evidence of disease or injury. Limbs are equal, symmetrically developed and also show no evidence of injury. The fingernails are medium length and fingernail beds are blue. There are no residual scars or markings.

INTERNAL EXAMINATION:

HEAD—absent.

SKELETAL SYSTEM: The missing head was severed at the Epiglottis and jagged edges to the vertebra would indicate that the victim's neck was struck several blows from behind with a sharp, heavy, straight bladed implement before the head became separated from the body.

Deep cuts to the shoulders have severed the right clavicle.

Pullman already knew that from the comments Deni made at the crime scene. He skipped through the pages detailing the internal organs; there was nothing requiring his attention nor was there amongst the evidence exhibits collected from the victim; apart from the clothes he was wearing, there was nothing found.

OPINION

Time of Death: Body temperature, rigor and liver mortis, and stomach contents approximate the time of death between 11 pm on Sunday 06.10.2013 and 2 am on Monday 07.10.2013.

The CCTV showed that he was still alive at 12.14 so that narrowed it down a little further.

Immediate Cause of Death: I am unable at this time to categorically determine if the cause of death was the stab wounds to the chest or stomach or the severance of the head as it is likely that the wounds were separated by a very short period of time.

Dr Denise Morrison FRCPath

Senior Pathologist

Pullman sat back in his chair, clasped his left palm to his forehead, and ran it down his face to his chin; he rubbed his stubble and realised that he hadn't shaved since Friday. Since Jane's death he no longer worried about his appearance at weekends, he rarely ventured far from the house, except for the occasional visit to the local convenience store.

'Well what does it say?' asked DS Sperring.

'Do you want the short version or the lon......?'

'The short one,' she interrupted.

'It's a dead bloke with no head,' he said.

'And the long version?'

'It's a dead bloke with no head and two stab wounds,' said Pullman.

'Stabbed as well?'

'Yep, in the chest and stomach. There probably wasn't much delay between stabbing him and chopping his block off so Deni can't tell which one killed him but if you're gonna stab someone why go the extra mile and hack his head off too. Bit extreme. Has it been found by the way?'

'No sign yet. Probably in the middle of the North Sea on its way to Denmark.'

'Call Deni and see if she's had the fingerprint and the DNA reports back yet. If not chase them. We need to know who this guy is – was.'

That night the two detectives, along with a DC assigned to the investigation and a team of uniformed officers, mingled with the Bridlington night hawks on the off chance that they would find a reveller who remembered seeing anything suspicious the night before. Those that had been out and about on the Sunday night would have had difficulty remembering their own names and were seemingly proud that they had been so drunk they had no recall of what they had done let alone seen. Even at 8 pm on a Monday those who still had the funds to be out were already partially inebriated on supermarket wine and own brand spirits when they arrived to start their night on the town. Pullman's team were getting little co-operation; it was however more co-operation than their colleagues wearing stab vests would be getting come closing time in the early hours of the morning.

He and Sperring called it a day and went their respective ways. It was only as he turned into his drive an hour later and saw the house that he realised he had not thought of Jane for sixteen hours; he felt guilty. He felt he should be wearing a hair shirt. He poured himself a drink as the pain filled his mind.

The grief he felt when Jane died was almost more than he could cope with at the time; if he could have joined her in death there and then he would have done so. They knew she was dying but that didn't lessen the heartbreak when death came. He wept unashamedly for days and nights; there were still days and nights, when the tears would well up.

Little things triggered the sadness; a piece of music; a scene in a film or TV programme; places they went; the empty seat on the sofa. The only way he could stem the tears was not to think of her; not to invoke happy memories; then he'd feel guilty for not thinking of her; for not remembering their happy times together and he would well up again.

He'd lost both his parents but that was different type of grief. He missed them, of course, but he hadn't lived with them for over twenty

20

years. They got on with their lives and he got on with his so when they were no longer there it did not affect his day-to-day existence. When he lost Jane a huge void opened in his world; she had been by his side for over twenty years. He'd always believed that he'd be comfortable in his own skin; content with his own company. But when she died he realised that they weren't simply two people sharing their lives they were conjoined. Now he was alone and for the first time in his life he was frightened. His life support system was gone.

They had planned so much for the future. He would retire at fifty. Just five more years; Jane would be forty-two, they had no children so would be free to travel, to see the world. To do the things their working lives prevented them from doing. So many dreams shattered.

For the first time in the past three months he did not drink himself to sleep. A good sign he thought.

Previous Saturday 5th October
Katonah, Lower Hudson Valley, New York

Despite the chill night air, the long haired brunette, in her early thirties, was wearing only a tight fitting, short black leather skirt and a skimpy, low cut, white tee shirt that barely concealed her 36c boobs. She swayed from side to side hardly able to balance on her stiletto heeled, patent leather shoes that matched the capacious red bag slung over her shoulder. From a window above his gift shop, insomniac, Clark Meridith watched the woman stagger across the deserted street towards a UV with darkened windows parked opposite, in a bay alongside the thicket of trees and shrubs that ran the length of Katonah Avenue. He shook his head; surely she wasn't going to attempt to

21

drive. If she did he'd call the cops. She was either loaded or as high as a kite. Or, in this day and age, he thought to himself, both. The woman made no attempt to get into the vehicle but stumbled forward towards a two hour parking restriction sign mounted on a round aluminium pole; she made to lean on it for support, missed and locked her arm around the pole in a swinging movement and, as if in slow motion, spiralled to the ground where she sat nodding like a toy dog in the rear window of a car.

Meridith couldn't recall seeing the woman before; then again he didn't know everybody in the community but drunken women in Katonah at 2am in the morning was a rare, if not unique, phenomenon. His innocent voyeurism was at strict odds with his staunch Methodist beliefs but more than that he didn't want to get involved. She got herself into that state; she could get herself out of it. He closed the curtain and returned to his book. Unaware that he too had been observed.

With some difficulty and a great deal of physical determination the woman grabbed the pole with both hands and pulled herself to a standing position. Then uncontrollably loosened her grip and lunged two steps forward before steadying herself on a yellow fire hydrant which she hunched over whilst resting with both hands on the domed top; still she swayed as if being buffeted by a strong wind.

In the shadow of the trees, Raymond Hospic watched her every movement through narrow eyes. Beads of perspiration trickled down his forehead and into his eyes, he rubbed them with the back of his right hand to ease the stinging while simultaneously squeezing his stiff cock with his left hand through the purpose made hole in his trouser pocket. He lowered his right hand and swiped the back of it across the damp, dark stubble from his left temple, across his chin and up to his right ear in a continuous movement. He bit his lower lip and the tempo of his breathing increased rapidly. This would be easy; this hoe was so drunk she wouldn't put up any fight at all. It would almost take the fun out of it. He liked the struggle; the feeling of power as he forced himself upon these whores. This one was asking for it and he'd oblige.

22

He hoped she wasn't too drunk to attempt to scream; he liked them to try. He got high on the look of fear in their eyes when they realised what was about to happen; it was the control of forcing them to submit that stimulated him to orgasm not the penetration; usually within a few seconds he was withdrawing and ejaculating over their stomachs. He wouldn't plant his seed in these whores.

His chosen target was facing away from him. He glanced up at the window above the gift shop to check that the old boy had gone. Now was the time. Hospic moved stealthily behind the woman, silently lowering the zip of his fly as he went. He habitually kept his genital hair closely cropped to ensure that in the heat of the moment he didn't get any strands caught in the zip. Hospic was primed and ready. The frenzy inside him built to a crescendo. As he raised his arm to grab her by the hair, she sprang up from the hydrant, spun round quickly to face him, her eyes wide and alert. The surprise as her hair piece came away in his hand caused him to gasp then gag as the six inch blade of the knife in her steady hand penetrated his rib cage. Hospic's eyes widened further in disbelief and he clutched his chest with both hands as he began to slump to his knees. Before they touched the ground a second woman stepped quickly out of the parked UV, clutching a razor sharp machete which she swung horizontally in a well-practised movement cleaving through the cricoid cartilage in his neck and severing his C7 vertebra. It was a powerful, single clean cut. Not until his lifeless body slumped forward did his head separate from his torso, hit the grass and roll three metres from his body, over the kerb and onto the tarmac parking area. It came to rest staring up at the night sky, the look of surprise fixed forever.

Hospic's body had collapsed in to a praying position; his neck resting on the ground as a pool of blood formed. The 'drunken' woman repositioned her wig and raised her head towards her accomplice, nodded, as if to suggest that the job was done, then picked up the severed head and dropped it in to her bag. They quickly looked around to make sure that they weren't being watched; the two assailants then climbed into the metallic grey UV; as they drove off towards Bedford Village the brunette threw the wig into her bag and ran her fingers through her short blonde hair. Clark Meridith never heard the vehicle drive off; he had fallen asleep in his armchair.

There were no witnesses to the night Raymond Hospic lost his head.

THREE

Tuesday morning was in complete contrast to the previous day; firstly the clear blue sky afforded perfect visibility all around the bay from Flamborough Head on the left, across to the distant Spurn Point on the far right and secondly, there was no decapitated corpse on the promenade.

Contractors were busy erecting a semi-permanent structure around the crime scene to protect the integrity of the site for future examination by both the police and possibly by the appointed defence counsel when the perpetrator was eventually caught. The beach had also been cordoned off for thirty metres in each direction; not to protect the scene, neither the tide nor the seabirds recognised the blue and white tape but to stop the public ghouls getting too close. Along the promenade pedestrians were required to walk up the incline, used by the Spa Light Express Land Train, to street level and re-join the prom by the incline leading to the toilets just beyond the mobile incident room. Since the breakfast news was first broadcast, rubberneckers had turned up in their droves to view the crime scene.

The fingerprint report was negative as was the DNA report. Whoever the dead man was, he was not known to the police. They did however find the victim's head. At least at this stage they presumed it was the victim's head; it would be one hell of a coincidence if it wasn't.

'York! For Christ's sake how did it get to York?' asked Pullman incredulously.

Overnight the decapitated head of a male had been placed on a five foot high, one and a half inch square, wooden fence stake driven into the lawned area outside York County Court; the head itself had

25

drooped to the left and the eyes were open. The gruesome display had been deliberately sited in full view of early morning commuters and incoming court staff.

The scene was being examined by forensic officers but digital photographs of the scene emailed over to the incident room by York police showed the letters S O C had been written in black permanent marker on the victim's forehead.

'What the bloody hell does SOC mean?' Pullman said to no one in particular. 'A message for our SOCO boys perhaps? The killer's initials? SOC, SOC? There's SOCA – The Serious Crime Agency - could be a finger up at the law I suppose but it just says SOC no A. Can't think what else it could be.'

'Maybe you're right sir, maybe it is the killer's tag, like graffiti painters use to identify their work,' said Sperring.

'Better see if Banksy's got an alibi for Sunday night,' said Pullman facetiously.

Sperring gave a forced smile. 'Or perhaps it's some new texting abbreviation that I haven't come across like OMG or LOL. Something like Sod Off Coppers.'

Pullman was not about to join in the guessing game. 'Whatever it means, we need to find out pronto. Get the computer artists to retouch a photo, get rid of those letters and clean up the cut line, then get it out to the media in the next two hours; no mention of it not being attached to a body though. Someone other than the killer knows who he is.'

'There must be CCTV outside the court,' said Sperring, 'I'll make sure they're checking that.'

****

The editor-in-chief, news editor, researcher, senior crime reporter, chief investigative journalist, picture editor, chief cook and bottle washer of Newzferret, a cult independent investigative news internet site, sat in her London office reading the email release from Reuters and studying the accompanying image of an unknown male.

Missing Person

Police have issued a request to all media to publish/broadcast the attached image of an unknown male aged approximately 35 years old, six feet one inch tall. Anyone who may have information about the man's identity should contact their local police station. All calls will be treated in the strictest confidence.

***Editorial Note:** Our sources suggest that this image is the head of the murder victim whose decapitated body was discovered yesterday in Bridlington on the East Coast of Yorkshire, England. Further updates will be issued as available.*

Caroline Nichols saved the email to her 'Look at' file and temporarily put it out of her mind. She had three pending files depending on how she perceived the urgency of the matter: the *Look At* file was for issues that could lead to a story but with no particular urgency, such as the current email; *Do It Now* was for issues that were hot and needed her rapid attention and the *FFS!* file was for issues that she knew needed immediate attention but for which she had no enthusiasm and kept putting off.

Nearly everyone who works in an office has a similar filing system. There are problematical or boring matters that need dealing with that initially seem easier to ignore; the longer they are ignored the worse the problem becomes. Procrastinators get a mental block about getting something sorted to the point where it causes them extreme anxiety; even sleepless nights. The irony is that if an issue is dealt with promptly it is usually easily resolved, proving the anxiety to be pointless and unnecessary. Modern communications just exasperated the situation; emails, texts and mobile telephone calls are so intrusive that most recipients cannot resist responding immediately to the intrusion at the expense of whatever they are dealing with at the time. Caroline though, was not a procrastinator.

She had built Newzferret's huge international following by reacting quickly to stories that the conventional media wouldn't, or couldn't, touch for political or legal reasons. If this particular email had stated that the image was that of a decapitated head of a murder victim, found forty miles from the crime scene, she may, just may, have related it to a news item she had picked up on the American Fox News channel. The story concerned the discovery of a severed head in White Plains that was subsequently found to be the head of a murder victim in Katonah in the Lower Hudson Valley, New York. To an enquiring mind like Caroline's that may have seemed more than a mere coincidence but the email didn't tell the whole story, if it had, she may well have promoted the item to the Do It Now file. Instead she returned her attention to the missing banker story she had been researching.

Peter Ebingdon, the forty five year old, erstwhile head of DFZ, the global investment bank, had disappeared whilst attending the G8 Financial Symposium in Germany. Her research had so far indicated that there were no financial problems in his personal life or with his company. In 2004 he married, South African born, socialite Tamara Bell-Sampson then only nineteen years old and a full seventeen years his junior. Her family owned Bell-Sampson Publishing and BS Communications Network now re-branded as the BSC Group. The police were no longer treating his disappearance as suspicious nor were they looking for him. His credit cards had been used in Belgium and twice in Germany since his disappearance; checks on CCTV at the ATMs where the cards had been used, clearly identified him as the user. So if he did not want to go home that was purely a domestic matter; of no interest to the police.

The bank, on the other hand, was very concerned and employed a firm of investigators to locate their missing CEO.

Caroline was rapidly coming to the conclusion that there was no story to be had. Just another overpaid banker who had decided to take an unannounced sabbatical and to hell with the consequences; it seemed to be an all too familiar occurrence since the crash of 2008.

She put it to one side for the moment and clicked on her desktop link to YouTube which often proved to be the catalyst for the germ of an idea. Trending that day was a video of a supposed singing cat, a semi-deranged girl ranting about her excitement at the impending release of the latest film in the Bridget Jones franchise and an iPhone video of what looked like a decapitated head on a spike. She clicked on that and ran the three minute clip.

It was indeed a man's head stuck on a spike together with a gathering crowd of voyeuristic onlookers. In fact it was the head of the man she had been looking at a few minutes earlier in the image accompanying the Reuters release.

The YouTube film was shot by a student from York University along with a sound track that declared the scene as 'awesome' before adding 'Vlad the Impaler is alive and well and living in York'. The video showed something that the police photo didn't. There was something scribbled on the forehead. It was difficult to read because the phone cameraman had a very jerky style that would not have troubled the BAFTA awards committee; as far as Caroline could determine the letters were S, O and C. Did the student do that for a laugh she wondered; were they his initials or was it done by the person who put the head there? In either case the matter needed promoting to the Do It file.

****

The mobile incident room was buzzing. Two additional detective sergeants had been assigned to the team along with three uniformed officers and two support staff.

'It appears our head belongs to a Thomas Wethersby,' said DS Sperring. 'Three callers have identified the photo as a teacher from Howden. I'll contact the school for an address.'

'That was bloody quick' said Pullman. 'The photo's only been out there for an hour. Make sure we keep a lid on the SOC bit,' he was saying when Sperring cut in.

'I'm afraid it's too late for that sir, it's gone viral. It's on YouTube; already had over a quarter of a million hits and it's been posted on Facebook. That's how he was identified so quickly.'

Pullman held his hands out palm side up in a gesture that said how the hell did that happen?

Sperring recognised the look of bewilderment. 'A passing student shot it on his phone before the scene was screened off,' she explained. 'It was online before we'd even got the photo ready; initials and all.'

Pullman shook his head in resigned disbelief. He valued his mobile phone as much as the next person but the speed at which incidents like this were broadcast was frightening; besides which, it could actually jeopardise a future prosecution.

'Forensics has confirmed the head matches the body but I don't suppose anyone's called in with the meaning of the letters have they?' They hadn't. 'Okay let's get that address and go see how our Mr Wethersby lived.'

Sperring was holding her mobile to her ear. 'On to it, now,' she said.

'Hello is that Howden Sixth Form College. ....Could I speak to the head teacher please...... Detective Sergeant Sperring, Humberside Police.... Thank you.'

She put her hand over the receiver to muffle the sound. 'He's in a meeting they're interrupting him,' she removed her hand.

'Yes, thanks for speaking to me. We ..... Yes it is about Tom Wethersby.... How did you...... I see, yes the wonders of modern technology.......I need an address for the decea... err Mister Wethersby... okay thank you, I'll wait.'

She muffled the receiver again and turned her head to Pullman. 'That's why he was in a meeting. One of the students had seen it online and both Facebooked and tweeted his friends and in seconds it was all over the college. The staff meeting is discussing what to do.'

Once again she shifted her hand. 'Yes I do.' Sperring waved the pen in her hand as if it could be seen on the other end of the line. She wrote down the address being dictated. 'Yep.... Yep..... Yep... got it thanks. Sorry ... he what......Oh I see.......when was this...... really. Sorry I didn't get your name..... Johnston, Trevor Johnston. Okay Mr Johnston I think we'd better come over to the school and have a chat with you first if that's convenient...... That's good of you..... Should be there in under the hour......yes....yes ....see you shortly. Bye.'

Sperring replaced the receiver, leaned back in her chair and blew a plume of invisible breath upwards.

'What was that about?' asked Pullman.

'Our Mr Wethersby was suspended from the college two weeks ago following accusations of having had a sexual relationship with two fifteen year old girls. It's been reported to the local nick and they're looking into the allegations.'

'Maybe someone had made their mind up that the allegations were true and appointed themselves judge, jury and executioner. Right let's get going.'

The journey to Howden SF College took just forty-seven minutes and the blue lights were only needed on two occasions; to pass slow moving farm vehicles. The college was a modern glass fronted, two storey building with an atrium tower as a central focal point and landscaped gardens to the front and sides. A driveway with speed humps led to a large car park at the rear. Trevor Johnston greeted them in the reception area of the atrium which featured an aviary and aquarium. Pullman thought it looked more like the corporate headquarters of a multi-national than a place of education. Not having children of his own he hadn't realised how much schools had changed since his boyhood days back in North London. If kids couldn't learn in an environment like this then they couldn't learn anywhere.

The head teacher escorted them to his office, continually praising the surroundings as they went. His office was a large rectangular space with a curved beech wood 'L' shaped desk, matching meeting table and six blue upholstered chairs, a matching blue upholstered sofa with a beech wood coffee table. They sat at the meeting table upon which a pot of tea was waiting.

31

'Dreadful business,' said Trevor Johnston, serving the tea, presuming that his guests would welcome a cup. 'Terrible. We thought about closing the college for the day as a mark of respect but it causes all sorts of logistical problems.'

'I take mine black no sugar,' said Pullman.

Johnston nodded understanding. 'It's very inconvenient for parents; you know travelling arrangements, child care that sort of thing. We'll be offering students counselling of course.'

Counselling, thought Pullman. If a bloody kid loses a pencil these days he's offered counselling. Just get over it. Then the expression physician heal thyself sprang into his mind. Anyway if the allegations were true then the students would probably put up bunting and organise parties. 'How long had Mr Wethersby worked here?' he asked.

'About seven years, joined us from Pontefract College when we were upgraded to college status.'

'Was he okay at his job?'

'More than okay he was excellent. He was well liked by his colleagues and most of his students get A stars and As.'

'In?'

'Modern languages.'

'And the trouble?'

Johnston explained that a student by the name of Gemma Maxwell had accused Wethersby of a serious sexual assault. She did not report the alleged attack for several days until another girl, Angela Carson, corroborated her story. Not that she was a witness; rather that she accused Wethersby of attacking her in the same manner some months previously.

'So are you saying both girls accused Wethersby of rape?'

'Yes.'

'But the second girl, the first alleged victim, didn't report it at the time?'

'No, she said that Tom threatened her with violence if she did; in any case she thought no one would believe her but when Gemma made the same accusation she came forward to support her allegation. The local police interviewed both girls. Do you want to speak to them as well?'

'Not right now, maybe later, after we've talked to the investigating officers. What did Tom Wethersby have to say?'

'That the girl, Gemma, was lazy and disruptive in lectures and that he'd warned her she would not be entered for her GCSEs if she didn't work harder and stop disrupting the classes. He said that Gemma then offered to.....' Johnston hesitated and looked nervously towards DS Sperring then down at his feet '..... perform a sex act on him if he marked her for a B+.'

'Only a B+, obviously she isn't very bright. How old is this Gemma?'

'Fifteen going on thirty. There have been stories of.... promiscuity.'

Pullman smiled at the head teacher's delicate use of language. 'Perhaps Wethersby had heard the stories and decided she was a good bet.'

'Tom is...was... absolutely adamant that the whole thing was complete fabrication; that he didn't even bother to respond to her and that he did not touch her in any way.....nor she him.' Johnston added quickly.

'What about the second girl?'

'As I said, she is Gemma Maxwell's best friend and by all accounts of a very similar disposition. Quite frankly I believe...believed Tom implicitly. He was a very dedicated teacher and took great pride in his student's success. I firmly believe that the two girls concocted the whole story however I had no choice but to suspend Tom pending a thorough investigation which I am quite sure would have exonerated him totally.'

'So you don't think Wethersby was a rapist or a paedophile then?'

'Absolutely not! Tom kept his private life very much to himself which he had every right to do. I don't even know who his friends were. He was never accompanied on any staff activities nor attended any functions; that was his prerogative. We have two other members of staff who act in pretty much the same way. They like to keep their work and personal life separate and frankly who can blame them. Tom just got on with his job. But he had a perfect CRB report and perfect references.'

Sperring asked, 'Have you carried out an Enhanced DBS since it came into being?'

'No, not for existing staff we haven't. Of course we do it for new members of staff.'

'Given the situation it might be an idea to re-check all staff; just to be on the safe side.'

'I'm confident that Tom had nothing in his personal life to require further checks,' said Johnston.

In Pullman's experience no one on earth, not even his Holiness the Pope, led a completely faultless life. Everyone has a secret or two, things they got up to in their past or things they do now that they wouldn't want shouted from the rooftops. Things that stay locked in the mind and filed deep in a mental vault. People acquired habits that others might find unusual. It was human nature. He knew he wasn't faultless.

'Okay we won't take up any more of your time. If you could just let us have his address again.' requested Pullman; DS Sperring had left it on her desk in the incident room.

'Of course.' Johnston went to his desk to retrieve a typed note of Wethersby's address, mobile telephone number, national insurance number and a copy of his spotless CRB report. He was well prepared.

'You might find this useful,' he handed Pullman a Yale door key. 'Save you breaking the door down.'

Pullman gave him a quizzical look. Johnston understood the meaning. 'He went away for a full six weeks this summer, backpacking in Asia,' he explained, 'Tom left the key with Bob Jenkins our caretaker who volunteered to look after his houseplants and cat. He asked Jenkins to hold on to it so it was never returned.'

Outside in the car Pullman said 'I'll drive; you ring the local nick and set up a meet with whoever is looking into the girls' allegations. The murder is most likely connected to that; unless we find something more at his house.'

FOUR

Tom Wethersby's house was a two up two down terraced cottage in Clipton, a small hamlet to the north of Howden. Yorkam Road, the main thoroughfare through the village, was less than half a mile long; a row of individually designed, early Victorian terraced cottages, painted in various pastel shades lined the left hand side of the road on approach. On the right were five larger dwellings of which two were thatched and one, at the end of the row, had been converted into a combined post office and village store outside of which hung a faded For Sale board; it appeared to have been there quite some time. There was no pedestrian pavement on either side. At the northern end of the hamlet a small church with a Norman style tower was set back from the road; in front, a lychgate led to an overgrown graveyard; the rear backed on to farmland.

The detectives pulled up outside Wethersby's cottage, number fourteen, directly opposite the shop. They parked, got out of the car and went to the front door; each putting on a pair of soft forensic gloves as they did so. As Pullman put the key into the lock he noticed two neatly dressed, elderly ladies, on the opposite side of the road, taking a keen interest in the strangers. Pullman nodded at them and smiled to acknowledge their presence. They turned and scurried into the shop, like mice to their hole in the skirting board. The unfolding news had obviously not reached this tiny backwater as yet.

The inside of the compact two up two down cottage was immaculately furnished in a minimalistic, eclectic style combining antique and contemporary pieces. There were two rooms downstairs plus the bathroom. The front door opened straight into the main living room.

'Nice taste,' said Pullman, 'Give him his due he was a tidy guy for a bachelor.'

'Doesn't look lived in,' said Sperring. 'It's too tidy if you ask me.'

Grey was the dominant colour of the décor with deep purple contrasting highlights. The two-seater settee in a soft mid-grey ribbed material was complimented with matching curtains and rug. A small rectangular cabin trunk had been converted for use as a coffee table – on inspection it contained spare bed linen. The TV was a flat screen model in proportion to the size of the room. The original cast iron fire surround had an electric imitation log fire and a stone hearth; open stairs led up to the first floor.

An open archway led to the narrow galley kitchen fitted with light oak units surmounted with faux marble work surfaces and chequered tiled splash backs; heavy duty linoleum in a black and white tiled pattern covered the floor on which stood a chrome pedal bin and a soiled pet food bowl. A small drop down TV was on stand-by mode and a capsule type coffee maker had also been left switched on; by the look of it Wethersby hadn't expected to be out all night. Sperring helpfully switched off both appliances. At the rear of the kitchen was a small bathroom recently re-fitted with a walk-in shower and white two piece angular ceramic suite?

Pullman experienced an unexpected feeling of melancholy creep over him; Wethersby would never see the inside of his cottage again just as Jane would never see their home again. Death was so wasteful and so final. He forced his thoughts back to the here and now.

'See if you can find his computer, bound to have one. We'll need to get it checked over if the local boys haven't done it.'

He followed Sperring up the narrow, steep staircase, making a conscious effort not to look at her pert bottom, he failed.

The main bedroom, the exact size of the sitting room below had a double bed but only one bedside cabinet, a double freestanding pine wardrobe and a single saddle back chair. The second bedroom, narrow like the kitchen beneath had been converted into a study with a small desk; bookcases covered one wall and either side of the window.

There was no sign of a PC but on the desk was a colour laser printer with a lead snaking across the surface of the desk to where a computer could have been; there was no monitor on the desk. A photographic case was sitting on a chair; it contained a Nikon full frame, digital single lens reflex camera, a 50-400mm zoom lens and a wireless remote shutter control. There were no memory cards in the case and the camera slot was also empty. A selection of other size lenses had been placed neatly on a wall hanging display unit.

The bookshelves displayed a number of academic volumes on language and social geography, assorted reference books, numerous biographies, a complete set of Shakespeare, Trollope and Dickens and incongruously Tom Clancy novels. The top two shelves were crammed with DVDs all of which, from Sperring's cursory glance, were pretty standard stuff for a man with the possible exception of Notting Hill and Pretty Woman but then she noticed that the entire top shelf consisted of Julia Roberts' films, she counted thirty-four out of curiosity. So he had a thing about Julia. Ah well at least it wasn't Judy Garland.

There were no signs of any pornographic material; nothing to suggest any kind of perversion or strange practices, excluding the obsession with Julia Roberts. In fact they both thought it strange that the cottage was so lacking in any kind of man's stuff.

'Well you'd say this guy was whiter than white from this place. In fact it's remarkable by its unremarkableness, if there is such a word.' There was now. 'Doesn't look as if there has been any kind of disturbance here; no sign of a kidnapping or struggle.'

DS Sperring agreed. 'Maybe someone has over compensated by tidying up a little too much. The printer must mean he had a home computer of some sort sir.'

'Arrange for forensics to give the place the once over.'

They left the cottage none the wiser about the man who had lived there. There was no visible personality; it was all too antiseptic. Sperring went back to the car to arrange for a forensic team while Pullman crossed the road to the shop; taking off his gloves and

38

popping them into his jacket pocket as he did so. He entered the post office to the accompaniment of a tinkling brass bell fitted above the door; activated by the door opening and closing; he was greeted with stares and silence from the mice and the aging man behind the counter.

'Morning ladies…and gentleman,' he added having spotted the old man. 'I'm DCI Pullman, Humberside Police,' he held out his warrant card but he might as well have held out a Nectar card for all the attention they paid to it. 'Have you noticed any comings or goings across the road in the past few days; anything out of the ordinary?' They didn't speak, just stood there like frightened mice. 'Did any of you know Mr Wethersby?'

'Yes,' said the old man behind the counter.

Pullman hoped the old boy would proffer some further information but that was all that was forthcoming. 'I mean did you know the deceased well?'

'Deceased!' they echoed in unison.

'Yes, Mr Wethersby is unfortunately dead. I'm sorry, have you not heard?'

'How did he die? He looked very well on Sunday; he came to church. It was Reverend Bestend. Second Sunday of the month,' squeaked mouse one.

Mouse two added. 'He always came to church, every second Sunday.'

'Are you sure he was there last Sunday?'

'Yes. Only seven of us attended and he was definitely there.'

The old man piped up, 'He went out at about ten o'clock Sunday night. He drove off in that noisy little black mini of his. I can't believe he's dead; car accident was it?'

Pullman knew the full story would eventually reach them. 'I'm afraid he was murdered.'

'Murdered,' they echoed in unison.

'How dreadful,' added mouse two.

'Was he the man they found in Bridlington? Asked the old man.

'Yes he was.'

'How dreadful,' they said in unison again.

'But you've not seen anyone strange hanging around or acting suspiciously?' Present company accepted he thought to himself.

They all agreed that they had seen nothing untoward. Pullman thanked them for their time and asked if they would inform the local police if they remembered anything else.

Sperring was on the mobile when Pullman returned to the car. 'Like something out of League of Gentlemen in there,' he said.

'That was the local nick. The DS who's handling the college case is back in and can see us now.'

'Let's get a coffee first. There's a garden centre up by the roundabout in Howden they've got a decent coffee shop. Save us having to have a cup at the nick. I'll drive; you get the boys in Brid to look out for a black mini, don't have the reg but they can get that from the PNC. It's possible he took his laptop with him.'

****

Caroline Nichols was busy on the internet. She had surfed from the Fox News site to CNN to the Bedford-Katonah Patch site which had detailed coverage of the Katonah murder.

Head Found in White Plains

The dismembered head of a man found murdered in Katonah yesterday was today discovered on the hood of a police patrol car in White Plains. The officer who found the head was returning to his vehicle, having investigated a reported break-in at the local pharmacy. It later transpired that the reported break-in was a hoax.

Police sources would not confirm that the head, which had been severed in a vicious attack (see yesterday's report), had the word Tarquin scrawled on the forehead but they have stated that DNA tests confirm that it is the head of the Katonah murder victim.

40

A spokesperson for Bedford Village police said that the investigation had been handed over to the NYPD and he felt sure that they would arrest the perpetrator very quickly so there was no need for the public to worry unduly.

Caroline scrolled down the page to find the previous day's report.

Man murdered in Katonah

The decapitated body of a man was today found in Katonah. The unidentified victim was discovered by Mr Clark Meridith, a shop owner living opposite the scene of the killing. Mr Meridith said that he was woken early by a dog barking and when he went to his window to see why he saw a Golden Retriever nuzzling the body with its snout. He immediately called the police. Mr Meridith, 57, a lifetime resident of Katonah said that nothing like this had ever happened before in Katonah "I guess it was just one of those nights. In the early hours of the morning I saw a woman so drunk she couldn't stand up and now a body with no head."

Caroline gave a wry smile that this man should compare a drunk with a vicious killing in the same sentence. Whatever next? A litter lout? Illegal parking? Would there be no end to this crime spree?

The police are appealing for anyone who may have witnessed the incident or anything else suspicious in the vicinity yesterday to contact them urgently.

So both crimes happened within two days of each other. Both were similar in execution, both victims had words written on their foreheads. She Googled Tarquin. There were over a million results available. She chose to view the Street Dictionary site which listed various modern, urban usages for words. Tarquin had five such alternative definitions listed in order of supposed popularity:

1.   An arrogant little, posh tosser who thinks he's better than others

2.   A male whom women find attractive, a hot piece of ass or too sexy

41

3. Someone you can't find again on Bluetooth once you've found them the first time
4. A rapist
5. Someone who proclaims to have magical powers but cons and assaults victims

Despite considering herself to be IT literate, she had only a vague idea what No.3 meant and as for the second offering she didn't think that finding someone sexy was a motive for decapitation otherwise she'd be after Gerard Butler with an axe. The other three were all possible motives though. She herself could think of one or two arrogant tossers she'd like done away with. The other two options were perfect rationales for revenge killings.

The search engine results page also offered her an alternative choice of word selection which was Tarquinius. Caroline clicked on the link which opened the Classical Legends site, supported by the British Museum; it covered classical Roman and Greek legends and mythology:

Definition: Lucius Tarquinius Superbus

Caroline's first take was to read the name as *super bus* as if it were some form of modern transport but instinctively she knew the pronunciation was *superb us*. She continued reading:

Also known as Tarquin the Proud, ruled from 534-510 B.C., was the last king the Roman people would accept. One of the Etruscan kings of Rome, Tarquin the Proud was the son or grandson of Tarquinius Priscus and son-in-law of Servius Tullius, whom he is alleged to have murdered. Tarquin the Proud's son, Tarquinius Sextus, raped Lucretia, the wife of his cousin, another Tarquin, Tarquinius Collatinus.

Several words in the passage were live hyperlinks. Clicking on Lucrecia brought up:

The Roman view of women was that they were the property of their husbands. Therefore an assault upon a wife was a crime against the

husband's property, much the same as burglary or vandalism today.
Lucretia's story personifies the shame felt by women victims.
She was considered a model of Roman feminine virtue. It was this
very virtue that inflamed the passion of Tarquinius Sextus, the son of,
Tarquinius Superbus, so much so that he contrived a situation to be
alone with Lucretia in private. He tried to force himself upon her but
when she resisted his attention, he threatened to strip her naked, kill
her and a naked male slave; he would then place their dead bodies in
bed, in such a manner so that it would look like adultery and joint
suicide. The threat worked and Lucretia submitted to his sexual
violation.

However Lucretia could not live with the shame and so told her
relatives of the attack. She got them to vow to exact revenge on
Tarquinius Sextus, then despite being the innocent party she
committed suicide by stabbing herself.

The article was accompanied by an illustration of a painting by
Titian depicting the scene; Caroline gave a resigned shake of her head.
It was typical of paintings of that period, painted by a male artist;
Lucretia was naked but the rapist Tarquinius Sextus was fully clothed;
nothing more than early pornography.

So the use of the word Tarquin to describe a rapist obviously
related back to Tarquinius Sextus. Although in current usage, she
wondered if the expression had been used in the same way for
hundreds of years, not that it was important. The NYPD would
probably not link the two things; they would undoubtedly spend their
time looking for a missing person called Tarquin.

At lunchtime she checked back on the Bedford-Katonah Patch
website to see if there had been an update. There had. The NYPD
were running true to form.

Do you recognise Tarquin?

NYPD have today released a picture of the decapitated head, of the
Katonah murder victim, discovered yesterday in White Plains. Police

43

are appealing for anyone who recognises the victim believed to be called Tarquin, to come forward.

Lieutenant Danny Pabloski of the NYPD said 'I know people may find the picture of the victims head gruesome but it's important that we identify him as soon as possible while the trail is still hot. At the moment we have no motive for the slaying of this unfortunate man. This was a particularly vicious crime and the killer may strike again.'

Always nice when the police convey a reassuring message to the general public thought Caroline. The picture was indeed pretty gruesome but her attention was drawn to the writing on the head. Tarquin was reasonably clear but the end of the word appeared to be blurred as if there were further letters. *I bet the' ius' has been smudged* she thought to herself. Which, if she was right, meant that it was a pretty strong message that the victim was a rapist? 'I wonder how long it will take them to work that out' she said out loud.

****

DS Peak of Howden Police was intrigued to learn that his inquiries into the sexual assault case at the college might be linked to Tom Wethersby's murder. 'Yeah as I say I don't trust either of the young ladies' evidence. That Gemma girl even tried to come on to me during the interview.'

'The headmaster said she was promiscuous.'

'Promiscuous! She's a right little tart if you ask me. Prick teasers we used to call them. If Wethersby had succumbed then she'd have forced the situation.'

'But you don't believe he did?'

'Nah; both girls submitted to medical examinations. Both are on the pill and both were infected with Chlamydia, probably still are or worse. If Wethersby had poked either one of them he'd almost certainly have picked up a dose. He was checked out at the hospital; clean as a whistle. In fact I'm not sure he used his dick for anything other than pissing.' DS Peak didn't stand on ceremony and being a born and bred Yorkshireman he spoke as he thought; regardless of the company in which he found himself. 'I reckon those two were just trying to shaft the guy for revenge, spite maybe or even just for fun; a bit of a laugh; to make them feel important. They might even have thought about blackmail. Perhaps they just wanted to get a few hours off school and to hell with the consequences. Scrubbers; the pair of them will probably end up working under a red light somewhere.'

'What did you think of Wethersby?'

'Nice enough guy. Naturally we checked him out; seemed squeaky clean. Regular church goer; not exactly an active member of the community but then you've been to the local version of Royston Vasey.'

'Royston Vasey?' queried DS Sperring.

Peak ignored the question. If she didn't know the programme, the reference didn't matter. Pullman got it though; he'd already compared the inhabitants of Clipton to those of the fictional village.

'We didn't dig too deeply but there wasn't a whisper of anything suspicious. Now the poor sod's dead. I wouldn't have surprised me if the shame of the accusations was enough to push a sensitive guy like him to suicide. Once the girls put it on the internet then the hate campaign really started. Sometimes this new social media can be anything but social. What with the bullying and piss taking; young kids can be really cruel little bastards. They think they can say what they like when they're hiding behind a keyboard or tweeting snide comments. No thought about the consequences; just a joke to them.'

Pullman stood up 'Well one thing we can be sure of, it wasn't suicide. We'll interview the girls; might get a different story now we're looking into murder. Could you, in the meantime, re-check Angela Carson's family and see if she has a relative with the initials SOC. Might as well check the same thing with the Maxwell's too.'

Sperring asked 'Did you by any chance remove a laptop from Wethersby's cottage?'

'No. I interviewed him there but had no reason to search the place or gather any evidence.'

45

They exchanged farewells before Pullman and Sperring set off on the car ride back to the mobile incident room in Bridlington.

FIVE

Wednesday 9th October

Caroline Nichols was in the process of updating the Newzferret site with details of the head found in York when an email came through with the news that the body had been identified as that of Thomas Wethersby, a teacher from Howden in East Yorkshire. She edited her article to include the updated information and to include the murder in Katonah without making any inference of a link between the two crimes.

Out of curiosity she Googled *decapitation.*

In addition to the inevitable Wikipedia entry there was a host of articles that made her realise decapitation was not as rare as she expected. To her surprise it was still the major form of capital punishment in Saudi Arabia and it appeared that beheadings there were on the increase with almost fifty having taken place in 2013 alone. Several men had been executed following summary trials; one man was beheaded for being a sorcerer after being paid to concoct a 'spell' by a jealous husband. A national television presenter had been sentenced to death for 'predicting the future' on his TV show although the sentence had at that stage not been carried out. Many of those who suffered beheading in Saudi Arabia were also crucified and displayed to the public as a general warning.

According to one newspaper report the country was considering moving from beheading to the use of a firing squad due to a shortage of skilled swordsmen. Wow she thought, now there's a great career opportunity for a budding Samurai.

There was a report of a former naval officer who beheaded his neighbour in Australia following years of un-neighbourly disputes. Another report of a Malaysian villager who beheaded his daughter for

47

having low moral standards after she allegedly had relationships with men following her separation from her husband. And an amazing story from Columbia where a football crowd beat and beheaded a referee after he attacked a player, because he refused to leave the pitch, when he was red-carded. That would certainly spice up Match of the Day she mused.

It seemed that beheadings occurred in many so called civilised nations around the world but the story that really caught her eye was from India. In an interview with a journalist from Drammens Tidende, one of the most popular tabloids in Norway, Prajit Sohoni a self-employed tour driver recounted a horrific attack he had witnessed.

Norwegian wildlife photographer, Kristine Gjøen, had been on a solo assignment for National Geographic capturing images of Bengal tigers in one of their last natural habitats. For seven days she had been staying at Tiger Lodge Hotel on Lake Siliserh near the Sariska Wildlife Sanctuary in the remote North-west region of Rajasthan, India. The monsoon season had started early; conditions throughout the region were deteriorating rapidly.

She had hired Prajit and his Land Rover Defender for the week, to run her to and fro from the hotel to the reserve. He had grown fearful that the route back to Lake Siliserh would soon become impassable; the mud track from the reserve to the main dirt road had already become awash with a torrent of rainwater.

She had stubbornly resisted his attempts to persuade her to leave. Finally his anxious pleading got through to her. Gjøen loaded up her camera kit and they set off. Fifteen minutes later they came to a fork in the road that took traffic either side of Lake Bhagha; a fallen dhok tree was blocking the right hand tine requiring Prajit to divert to the left. It was not a concern; he'd driven the route hundreds of times and knew the paths would converge in a few hundred yards, at the northern end of the small lake.

The Defender's windscreen wipers were fighting a losing battle with the deluge; visibility was down to less than fifty metres. Prajit had been squinting through the semi opaque torrent cascading down the glass, distorting his vision, when a man appeared from nowhere; he was just standing on the track like an apparition, staring at the oncoming Land Rover. Prajit hit the brakes hard, swerved around the man; skidded in the slush, lost control and came to a halt sideways in the bushes.

Before he knew what had happened, the driver's door was wrenched open; he was dragged out and viciously clubbed to the ground.

Police believe that Kristine Gjøen was then brutally gang raped by up to five men.

Prajit eventually regained consciousness and quickly realised what had taken place. His passenger was naked and sobbing hysterically. Despite bleeding profusely from the severe head wound he used the mobile phone which he kept concealed behind a custom made panel on the dash; having previously had a number of mobiles stolen, he kept the new one well hidden from view. Thankfully BSNL, the state-owned telecoms company, had not long before erected a series of relay masts between Jaipur and New Delhi; mobile communications were now possible in the National Park and surrounding area.

Prajit had previously stored numerous contact numbers in the phone's memory; keeping one hand pressed to his wound he used the thumb on his free hand to dial the Tiger Lodge Hotel. He explained that there had been a frenzied attack on their guest and that both she and he needed urgent medical attention. He gave them his approximate position but left the line open so they could maintain a conversation and allow the GPS to pinpoint his precise location. The hotel receptionist immediately alerted the police and medical services. Prajit had been unconscious throughout the attack but he knew exactly what had taken place.

When she returned to Norway Gjøen told reporters that after five hours in Jaipur medical centre, during which time every orifice in her body had been swabbed for DNA she was allowed to shower and dress herself in the fresh set of clothes the police had retrieved from her hotel. She had been questioned sympathetically by a female officer who herself had suffered a similar experience in her teenage years but at the time Kristine was unresponsive to all attempts at cajoling her into discussing the attack. Doctors had since diagnosed her as having developed repressed memory syndrome, a psychological defence mechanism preventing her from recalling the ordeal. She was still unable to discuss the actual assault.

Prajit's head wound required sixteen stitches. Forensic examination of Prajit's genitalia showed no traces of physical contact with the victim. Police questioned him at length before they were satisfied that he had not been in collaboration with the assailants. He had been unable to drive for several weeks.

Within days a juvenile, was arrested after being found in possession of Gjøen's stolen camera, but was subsequently released through lack of evidence linking him to the actual assault. The fact that he was related to a leading politician was just a coincidence, it was claimed. Three days after being released his decapitated body was found by the roadside. In this case the victims head was found alongside the body, it had been mauled by wild dogs and most of the flesh around the cheeks and jaw area had been devoured the report also stated that forensic examination showed traces of isopropanol and urethane acrylic resin on the brow below the hairline.

Caroline wondered if there would have been a forensic examination had he not been related to a politician.

The world- wide web that Tim Berners-Lee bequeathed to the world is seen both as a curse and a blessing depending on your school of thought. Caroline deemed the benefits to far outweigh any negatives; understandably so, as her livelihood depended on it. Before the web she would have needed to visit the library or telephone a friendly neighbourhood scientist to learn what isopropanol and urethane acrylic resin was. With the internet at her fingertips she could type the names into a search engine and have all the information she needed in less than a second. She was intrigued and satisfied to discover that, amongst other uses both chemicals were used in the manufacture of ink for permanent markers.

50

So, she wondered, had this victim also had something written on his forehead. Her investigative journalist instincts went into overdrive. In a little over an hour, buried deep in layers of results pages, she had found eleven more incidences of beheadings where the head had been relocated from the body and found with a message either written on the forehead, cheeks or on a wall close by. The incidents had occurred in South Africa, Indonesia, Hungary, Canada, Turkey and Holland and on five occasions in the US over the previous three years.

In ten of those cases the message was just three letters – South Africa; SVC , Indonesia; SOC, Hungary; NC, Canada; SOC, Turkey; KC, Holland; ZVC and in the US; SOC as in Britain. In the eleventh case also in the States the word Tarquinius had been used exactly the same as the Katonah murder. Surely it was no coincidence that this murder happened in Buttermilk Falls County Park less than twenty miles from White Plains where the Katonah victim's head had been retrieved. But if both victims had the same message inscribed on their heads why hadn't the NYPD tied the two cases together. Perhaps they had. Perhaps they were deliberately playing down the link for fear of starting a panic that a serial killer was on the loose; maybe they were trying to avoid triggering copycat murders or maybe they were just trying to supress the one thing that only they and the killer knew, in which case they had failed miserably.

She wrote the sets of letters on individual post-it notes and affixed them to the wipe board. The most frequently found sequence of letters was SOC so she entered that in to the search engine.

The first result was for an integrated circuit board called Systems on a Chip, she preferred vinegar; second up was the Scottish Ornithologists' Club. Unless the victims were all bird's egg thieves she ruled out this version of SOC. Likewise she ruled out The Southampton Orienteering Club and the Southampton Oceanography Club, that must cause some confusion down on the south coast. The largest entry was for Standard Occupational Classification - codes used by the UK Border Agency when assessing entry qualifications for would be immigrants. She doubted there was a job code for

51

executioner. She delved into another site listing meanings for the acronym SOC, of the two hundred or so only three seemed to have any ring of credibility in relation to her quest, she took a look at each individual site.

Firstly she visited Soldiers of Christ. That seemed a possibility but it turned out to be a devoutly religious site for young people seeking to change current world thinking to that preached in the gospels. Interestingly the banner on their site depicted an armour wearing soldier carrying a large sword, the size of sword that could easily be used for decapitation. Maybe the victims were anti-religious or considered to have sinned against God in some way. No, she'd rule them out. Although the eye for an eye saying might mean something to them, further investigation of the site clearly showed that it patently wasn't the kind of organisation that would stoop to murder for retribution.

Caroline also ruled out the School of Christ for much the same reason and Squadron of Chaos seemed to be related to computer gaming. That left Scene of Crime but as the head of the victim was more often than not, found quite some distance from the rest of the body, then that version of SOC didn't make any sense either. Besides who would need to flag up that the discovery of a decapitated head was a crime scene. The police could probably come to that conclusion without help; even the NYPD.

So after a lengthy piece of research, Caroline was none the wiser. She was deep in thought when her mobile rang. She recognised Mark's mobile number. 'Hi darling', she answered. 'Does sock mean anything to you?' she said before he could speak.

'Why? Have you found an odd one?'

'Not sock, sock S.O.C.'

After a brief silence he replied, 'Nothing, why should it? Oh, I've had dealings with the Serious Organised Crime Agency – SOCA, could it be that?'

'Only if the killer's pen ran out of ink. Anyway what do you want?'

'What I always want.'

'You know phone sex isn't my thing,' she said with a smile in her voice.

'Food! Paul and Katie have invited us round to their place tonight. Fancy it?'

'Yeah. Okay, be nice. I hadn't got anything in. What time?'

'About eight okay?'

'Fine but be home by seven, I feel in need of a little appetiser first.'

'A whole hour eh, you must be very hungry, even after the feast last night?'

'All right enough of this nonsense I'm sure you've got work to do.'

She made a kissing sound into the receiver and cut the call. At twenty nine she was two years younger than her partner Mark, with whom she had lived for eighteen months although they had been together, on and off, for a lot longer. They met at the Guardian where he was the senior crime reporter and she the court reporter. It was Mark's original idea to set up Newzferret but then unexpectedly but not undeservedly, he was offered promotion to Deputy Editor; the salary package with share options was too good to pass up. They set up Newzferret regardless; Caroline ran it but Mark took a keen interest and his salary helped keep it afloat. As well as being madly in love with Caroline he was very proud of her and the work she did, frequently regretting his decision to sell out to mammon.

****

Jeromes Café and Pizzeria, just a hundred yards from the mobile incident room, was busy, even though it was a dull overcast day. It was one of the few eateries on the front in Bridlington that remained open year round, regardless of the climate. Having consumed their late lunch, DCI Pullman and DS Sperring sat in silence, each pondering the facts of the case. He took an occasional swig from the bottle of lager in front of him; she toyed with the empty cappuccino cup she had drained more than ten minutes before.

'Nothing' said Pullman to no one in particular. 'We know diddly squat that matters.'

'We know the vic's name....'

'The what!' exclaimed Pullman. 'Don't you start with that American jargon, if you mean the victim for god's sake say victim.'

Sperring winced at her faux pas. She knew full well that her boss hated American cop shows and the idiom they used, yet still she slipped up occasionally. 'Sorry sir. We know the victim's identity; we know where and how he was killed; we know that he was accused of underage sex; we know he was suspended from work; we know that he had two thousand pounds cash in his car when we found it yesterday.'

'But it still amounts to five fifths of bugger all. We don't know who or why; that's what matters,' he said.

'The *why* could be blackmail or maybe a member of the Maxwell family believed Gemma's version of events, saw a red mist and took unwarranted revenge, father, brother, cousin, boyfriend; maybe it's both revenge and blackmail.'

'But why kill someone in Brid and dump their head in York?'

'It wasn't exactly dumped sir. It was deliberately placed on that spike and left at the courts. That definitely smacks of someone saying hey look everybody this guy was a paedophile rapist; the law wasn't doing anything so I've exacted justice.'

'The allegations weren't proven. Was there anything to prove in the first place? He wasn't charged; the case hadn't even been to court. For Christ's sake there was no justice to be exacted.' Pullman leaned back put his hands behind his head a let out a gaping yawn. 'Maybe Peak will get something we can latch on to, although I'm beginning to think that we need to look a bit deeper into those families ourselves. Anyway when I say why York, I mean why risk the journey with a severed head, presumably in a car. They'd have got just as much publicity leav... well no they wouldn't actually would they. If they'd have left it in Brid it probably wouldn't have even made the nationals. He held his hand to his mouth as if smoking an imaginary cigar and said mockingly with a WC Fields style American accent 'whoever the perp was, he wanted maximum publicity.' Sperring thought he was doing a very bad impression of Colombo. 'Have we checked out the budding film director?' he asked normally.

'Yep, a genuine student, Jonathan Elliott, so SOC wasn't his tag. Anyway he had a cast iron alibi. Just happened to be passing and thought it would be fun to catch it on his phone and post it on the net. Understandable I suppose, it's not something you see very often; even for us.'

'Okay let's get back and concentrate on the families of the two girls'

****

Dinner that night consisted of a starter of avocado and lobster claw salad, Katie's take on a beef stifado followed by a choice of crème Brule or cheese board, or in Mark's case both, together with copious amounts of wine. Katie was at pains to point out that the avocados were the first of the year's Fuerte crop flown in from the States. She made it sound as if they had been transported especially for her on a privately chartered plane. Wealth had not changed Katie; she'd always been wealthy and a snob. But a nice snob, one that Caroline could laugh with, rather than at.

The food, as always, was delicious; Katie's stint at Raymond Blanc's Le Manoir Aux Quat'Saisons, Cookery School in Oxford had proved to be a very good use of Daddy's money.

Paul, Katie's husband of two years, was the youngest ever director of the London Stock Exchange. Katie had never had a proper job since leaving University where she scraped through with a third class honours degree in French. It was rumoured that a very generous endowment from her father's global advertising agency group, Spread, may have resulted in a very sympathetic evaluation of her anticipated Ordinary Degree. In conversation she only ever mentioned that she had gained an honours degree in French, never that it was a Thora.

She once dabbled for five weeks with a position as a PR executive in one of Spread's smaller media relations agencies in Paris, thanks again to Daddy; but when she upset the Marketing Director of Banque Générale, the agency's largest client, her tenure was aborted. That was the one and only time her name had ever appeared on a salary slip. Despite being the opposite sides of the work ethic coin, she and Caroline got on famously as did Mark and Paul who met on their first day at Cambridge and clicked immediately. They had been the best of friends ever since, even taking a gap year together, back-packing their way around South America.

Over dinner Caroline had talked about her current interest in the beheadings and they had taken it in turns to guess what SOC might mean. It made a welcome change from Trivial Pursuit. Earlier in the day, Mark had taken a look at the SOCA web site and found that they had a division called Specialist Operations Centre but he could see no reason why the killer would be identifying with them. Some of the other suggestions, especially from Paul, would have made even Jimmy Carr blush but in the end they came up with nothing remotely sensible although that had more to do with the wine than their collective intellect.

'It's a fascinating piece,' said Caroline.' I think it could develop into Newzferret's biggest ever story.'

'I might be interested in it for the paper,' said Mark.

'Don't even think about it,' replied Caroline. 'Unless of course you want to pay me a nice big fat fee.'

'No seriously, like I said earlier you're onto something here that could be big news. Maybe the paper's international resources could help speed things up.'

Katie chipped in. 'I'd love to help too,' she said eagerly.

Caroline ignored the comment as did everyone else. 'Give me a few more days before you steal it,' said Caroline patting Marks hand over the table. 'Don't worry darling, I'll give you first refusal.'

Paul looked at Caroline and changed the subject. 'Have you dug up anymore on Ebingdon?'

'Don't think there's much more to dig up; seems like he just wanted to disappear.'

'Must be a reason though, surely,' said Paul. 'A man doesn't up and disappear for no reason.'

Mark answered. 'You'd think not wouldn't you but our guys haven't been able to find out any more than Caroline and I've had them out there, on expenses for nearly a fortnight, trying to track him down. We think he's in the Czech Republic now.'

'Perhaps he's suffered a breakdown,' proffered Katie pouring coffee. 'The chief executive of Daddy's company in Kola Lumper' – that was how she pronounced it –'had a breakdown last year and threw himself off a skyscraper. Apparently the pressure just got too much for him. So sad.' Katie was mistress of the inconsequential.

'DFZ's share price has certainly had a breakdown,' said Paul. 'Dropped another one and a half points today; that's about half a billion pounds wiped off the value of the company since he went missing.'

'Investors must be getting a bit edgy,' said Mark.

'Edgy! Just a tad,' said Paul raising his eyebrows. 'Could be a call to suspend share dealings.' Paul knew he could safely tell Mark that without fear of it finding its way into the paper or the information being used for insider trading. It was an unwritten and sacrosanct understanding that anything they said to each other was strictly confidential and off the record. It was a trust that neither had ever violated.

'Well I say good luck to him,' said Katie. 'It's his life. If he wants to disappear, that's up to him.'

'Look guys,' said Mark. 'We really have to get going I've got an editorial meeting at silly o'clock in the morning. Thanks for a great evening.'

'Oh you can't go yet,' said Katie. 'Paul and I have something to tell you.'

Caroline and Mark looked at Katie. Katie looked at Paul then back at her guests as a broad smile spread across her face. 'I'm pregnant!'

Caroline jumped up from the table and gave Katie a big hug. Mark followed suit.

'I don't know how it happened,' Katie said, excitement resonating through her voice.

'Didn't they teach you that at finishing school?' Mark quipped.

'Silly. I mean it wasn't planned or anything but we're thrilled to bits.'

'Congratulations. That's wonderful news,' said Caroline. She and Mark had discussed starting a family but had decided to wait a year or two. 'I'm so happy for you.' She genuinely was too.

SIX

Thursday 10th October

Trevor Johnston showed Pullman and Sperring into his office where Gemma Maxwell and her parents were already waiting. 'I'll leave you to it then. Help yourselves to tea or coffee,' he indicated towards the coffee table and left the room.

Gemma was wearing a neat school uniform, her hair tied back in a ponytail and no make-up. She looked nearer thirteen than fifteen. Innocence personified.

Pullman took a back seat in the proceedings. Standard procedure required that a female officer with Child Protection Training lead the interview. Sperring qualified on both counts, Pullman on neither.

'Hello Gemma, I'm Detective Sergeant Sperring and this is Detective Chief Inspector Pullman.' She pointed out her boss; he smiled. 'We need to clear up a few matters relating to the allegations you made against Mr Wethersby who as you know was found dead on Monday.'

Gemma nodded demurely. The butter was safe in her mouth.

'Would you please tell us in your own words what happened.'

Her father interrupted angrily. 'Look she's already told the other copper what that pervert did. Why don't you leave the girl alone?'

Sperring smiled reassuringly. 'I do appreciate that Gemma has already given a statement Mr Maxwell but this is now a murder enquiry so I'm afraid we have to start from the beginning.'

'She didn't kill the bastard but I would have.'

'Did you?' Asked Pullman.

'Did I what?'

'Kill Mr Wethersby.'

'No I bloody didn't but I'm glad he's dead for what he did.'

59

Sperring said, 'Mr Maxwell we need to interview your daughter, we are doing so in your presence as a matter of courtesy but if you continue to interrupt, you will have to leave. We are only required to have one of you here so Mrs Maxwell would be fine by herself.'

'If I have to leave then so does she,' he ranted. No control freak here then.

'If you both leave we will have to call in an Appropriate Adult.'

'What do you bloody mean an appropriate adult? I'm her bloody father it don't get more appropriate than that.'

'Yes you are appropriate Mr Maxwell and so is Mrs Maxwell and as I said, we only need one of you here, so if you interrupt again I will terminate this interview until we can conduct it without your presence do you understand?'

'Just get on with it. I gotta get back to work; this is costing me money.'

'You can leave at any time.'

Sperring turned her attention back to Gemma. She smiled reassuringly at her. 'Okay Gemma please tell us what happened.'

Gemma's story was almost word perfect to the statement she gave DS Peak. Mr Wethersby had asked her to stay behind after class to discuss her failure to complete a homework assignment. She apologised to him and said that she would catch up by the end of the week. Mr Wethersby smiled and said that if she was nice to him she wouldn't have to do the homework or any other homework he set because he would just mark his records to say it had been done to a standard that would mean a high grade for her. When she asked him what he meant by 'be nice to him', he took his capped fountain pen out of his breast pocket and pushed in and out of his mouth. She said she told him that she didn't understand. He then unzipped his fly and exposed himself and said come on Monica; she had no idea why he called her that. Then he moved closer to her and said he wanted her to give him a blow job she said she still didn't know what he was talking about. He called her a little tart and said she knew exactly what he wanted. He started to grab her by the shoulders to pull her down onto

60

her knees but she screamed out, tried to kick him in the private parts and called him a filthy pervert. He then pushed her back on the desk, pinned her down with one arm across her throat, with the other hand pulled her knickers aside and raped her.

Mrs Maxwell was crying; Mr Maxwell was fuming; Gemma was sobbing without tears; DS Sperring was expressing sympathy; Pullman was concealing his scepticism.

'What happened then?' asked Sperring quietly.

She said there were some loud voices in the corridor and he stopped raping her. He said that if she told anyone what had happened he would deny it and no one would believe her anyway and even if they did, no matter how long it took, he would find her and do things to her that she would never be able to forget. Then he just left her in the classroom, sobbing.

'There, you satisfied now you've made her go through it all again,' snarled Mr Maxwell.

Sperring tightened her lips and gave him a withering look; he shut up. 'Why didn't you report it straight away?'

'You heard her, he threatened her. Scared her half to death.'

'Mr Maxwell please, for the last time.'

'Why didn't you tell someone you'd been assaulted? Your parents, a teacher...'

'I did, I told Ange.'

'Angela Carson?'

'Yes and that's when she told me that he'd done the same to her. That's when we decided that if we said it together they'd have to believe us; for all we knew we weren't the only ones.'

'You didn't feel you could tell anyone else; a doctor maybe?

'I wasn't bleeding or nothing.'

'Had you had sexual experience before the attack?'

Gemma looked sheepish. 'A bit of kissing and that.'

'But not sexual intercourse?'

'No never.'

'So you were a virgin.'

'Yes, of course.'

The medical examination showed otherwise but Sperring didn't push it any further. If the case had ever come to court any self-respecting defence barrister would have torn her story to shreds. Sperring was simply establishing to her and Pullman's satisfaction, that Gemma was capable of lying.

'So you didn't feel that you needed to tell an adult directly, yet you both posted the allegations on Facebook and made dozens of tweets.'

'We thought we should warn the other girls.'

'Didn't you think he would find out? Surely if Mr Wethersby threatened you, weren't you still afraid? How did you cope with seeing him at school?'

'I didn't, me and Ange bunked off school, so we wouldn't have to see him.'

'What did you do when you bunked off school?'

'Just hung about really, at my house and Ange's. We did a lot of crying and just hugging each other we were too frightened to go out.'

Sperring looked at Pullman as if to ask is that enough. He nodded back. 'Okay Gemma we'll leave it there for the time being. Thank you. Sorry we had to put you through it again.'

Gemma and her parents left the office but not before Mr Maxwell had had another rant. Sperring and Pullman didn't even have time for a cup of tea before Angela Strong and her mother were shown into the room. If Gemma looked thirteen then Angela looked like her younger sibling. If she had been carrying a teddy bear it wouldn't have looked incongruous.

Angela's account of her assault by Tom Wethersby was almost identical to Gemma's except that the fountain pen became a pencil, it went into the mouth from a sideways angle pushing the cheek flesh into a bulbous shape She said she hadn't reported the rape for the same reason as Gemma but had been scared until her next period that she might be pregnant. That was a lie, according to the police doctor Angela was taking oral contraceptives. Angela was a lot more forthcoming than the seemingly demure Gemma and did not deny that she was well aware of what Wethersby had been asking of her but she wouldn't do it. She obviously had a more open relationship with her divorced mother than Gemma had with her parents but not so open that she wanted her mother to know she was on the pill. Neither did Gemma.

'After you put it up on Facebook and tweeted it did any of the other girls say anything had happened to them?'

'No. We got lots of 'likes' and some of the girls said nice things but nobody else said that the pervo had touched them. Guess it was just us. Some woman did call me and Gemma a couple of times asking if the police were doing anything about him.'

'Who was that?'

'Don't know her; think she said her name was Tizzy Fenn or something. Don't know who she was but she knew us or at least about us. Wanted to know how we felt about Wethersby; she was a right nosey cow. Gem thought she was a reporter. I just told her that I hoped the police locked him away and that he got bummed in prison. Sorry Mum.' Mrs Carson was doing her best to feign deafness.

'Did your mobile log the woman's number?'

'Don't know, anyway this is a new phone and sim,' she held up a pink version of the latest smartphone. 'My other phone was nicked; smart innit?'

When Angela and her mother had left the room Pullman said 'Pass me a tissue please, sob stories always make me cry.'

'You don't believe it either?'

'That is what my dear old granddad used to call fanny twoddle. I don't know what if anything, actually took place but their stories have been co-ordinated and well-rehearsed. And what a pain in the arse that Maxwell is, his wife's terrified of him. He looks the type that could punch someone in a bloody rage but there's no way he lured Wethersby out to Brid then chopped his head off. Peak's looking into the family alibis so we should know for sure.'

'According to their Facebook pages both girls went to a see the One Direction film three or four times while they were supposedly at home crying and hugging each other,' said Sperring. 'Don't these kids think we know about Facebook and Twitter? Christ they put their life up on the internet for all to see; they can't then lie about it. They even posted photos of themselves at the cinema and neither of them looked distraught.'

'Let's forget those two for the time being and concentrate on Wethersby's personal life. If he's a sexual predator then there must be others who had suspicions. Let's get Peak to have a chat with the previous college he taught at, maybe Johnston's checks weren't quite as comprehensive as they might have been. Let's see if he had to leave there rather than wanted to leave. The principal may have suppressed doubts about Wethersby to get rid of him. It happens. There was an incident at one of the places Jane worked; a guy who had been disciplined for sexual harassment on two occasions, he got a new job and when the other company asked for a reference Jane's company never mentioned the disciplinary issues– they didn't lie they were just economical with the truth. Happy to see him go.'

It didn't occur to Pullman that he had spoken about Jane. He had mentioned her without any feeling of sadness. Maybe the process of letting go of the past had begun.

'There are laws about that; you have to disclose pertinent facts, 'said Sperring.

'I know but what the eyes don't see etcetera; becomes someone else's problem.'

'So did Wethersby become someone else's problem?'

'Yes he did – ours. If we could find his bloody computer it would help. I wonder if he had a locker or something at the college; didn't think to ask.'

'So we just forget the rape allegations?'

'Not saying that; but we haven't got a shred of evidence to prove or disprove the accusations so until we do find something on him we can't go any further. If we could prove they're lying we could charge them with attempting to pervert the course of justice but with Wethersby dead we'd never get enough together for the CPS and even if we did, they're still juveniles; they'd just get a wrap on the bloody knuckles. Let's see if we can find out who Tizzy Fenn is; that's not even a name is it, Tizzy? Better try Tilly or Lizzie or anything else you can think of. Wonder why she was so interested. Let's see if any of the nationals have got a reporter by that name.'

Sperring said. 'I'll check Angela's phone records and see if I can get anything on her.'

On the way out of the college they checked with Johnston and were told that Wethersby did have a locker in the staff room but it had already been searched and it was empty. He thought that Tom may have emptied it when he was suspended.

****

Caroline Nichols went to her office via two stationers to purchase a wall map of the world, without success. So she ordered exactly what she wanted online with full confidence that it would arrive the next day. Her intention was to pinpoint the locations of the beheadings she had identified to see if there was any geographical pattern; that would now have to wait. Instead she started writing the various initials that had been found on post-it notes and sticking them up on her electronic computerised wipe board. Mark had insisted on buying the state-of-the-art board when they furnished the office. This was the first time it had been used; it had never even been plugged into the socket. She had no idea if the notes would help but it's what they did on TV and films so it seemed like a good idea and felt like she was being busy. The phone rang. It was Paul.

'Hi Paul,' said Caroline surprised that she should hear from him so soon after their dinner the previous night. 'What can I do for you?'

'More what I can do for you,' he replied. 'Good morning by the way. Excellent evening last night; really enjoyed it.'

'Yes so did we, must do it again sometime soon, our place next time. Congratulations on the news once again.'

'Thanks. Anyway look I had a business breakfast with an old pal of mine at DFZ this morning and he told me something that may be of interest to you but you didn't hear it from me. I'm not even sure if it's true. You may or may not know that DFZ appointed a well-known firm of international investigators to find and keep tabs on our friend Peter Ebingdon.'

'I didn't know but it seems like a good idea.'

'Yes, anyway as Mark said last night he is indeed in the Czech Republic under an assumed name but here's the bit you will be interested in; according to my pal's source in another department, the investigators believe that Peter Ebingdon isn't.'

'Isn't what?'

'Isn't Peter Ebingdon?'

'What the one in Czechoslovakia?'

'It's the Czech Republic now but that's by the by. No, the guy we know as Peter Ebingdon, CEO of DFZ doesn't appear to have existed before nineteen ninety four.'

'I don't understand?' said Caroline.

'I don't know much more except that they say his existence before then is pure fabrication; they can't find any history of his existence before he was at Edinburgh University. My pal is trying to find out more for me. In the meantime I thought that you might be able to ferret something out, which is what you do isn't it?'

'Supposedly so; I'll give it a go. Thanks for the heads up Paul. If your friend finds out anything before me, do let me know.'

Caroline spoke to Mark on the telephone when his editorial meeting was over. She recounted what Paul had told her and asked if he, Mark, had any ideas about how she might go about finding out if Ebingdon was who he claimed to be. Mark told her that if he had changed his name it could be very difficult depending on how the change was carried out. The only time he had been involved in this sort of thing was when a child killer was released on parole and the Home Office set him up with a completely new identity. It came to light eventually through an astute neighbour who recognised one of the killer's relatives when she went to visit but reporting restrictions at the time meant the paper couldn't reveal any details. Mark did also say that it was very unusual for someone who wanted to conceal a previous identity to have such a high profile position. Normally you would expect them to have a job that kept them away from the public eye. Ebingdon's photograph was frequently featured in the pages of the financial press and his big society wedding, a few years back, made all the nationals and TV; hardly the actions of a man trying to hide his identity. Unless of course he had also changed his physical appearance so much that he could readily appear in the spotlight without being recognised.

Mark came up with the idea that he would get the paper's obituary team on the case. The team of two was very good at researching people's lives and had profiles of hundreds of people ready for the day the grim reaper called them. He'd justify their involvement on the basis that the runaway may take his own life and they needed to be ready with the obituary. He said he would speak to them and depending on what they said he would get back to Caroline or they could discuss it that evening.

Caroline decided that there was no point on doubling up on Mark's efforts so she turned her attention back to the SOC conundrum until such time as he got back to her. She tried searching SVC, NC, KC and ZVC all with similar results to those she got for SOC; nothing that remotely related to a rationale for murder. She leaned back in her swivel chair and clasped her hands around her neck as if she was attempting to strangle herself; then slowly rotated her fingers to massage the back of her neck and yawned. Looking at computer screens all day was tiring on the eyes.

'What do you mean? She said out loud to the florescent yellow notes. 'What? Come on tell me.'

They suddenly spoke; it occurred to her that the letters SOC were used in English speaking countries but were different in other languages. Could it be that all the letters meant the same thing in the native languages of the countries in which they were found? That made a kind of sense to her. Maybe if she could crack one set of letters she could translate them all. She sucked her teeth and said out loud 'Aye therein lays the rub.'

She brewed herself a cup of coffee whilst she pondered the other two more recent cases in America where Tarquinius was the word used. Tarquinius the rapist, what did he have to do with it. The most likely scenario was that the men killed were rapists and that they had been 'Tarquined' by the killer as a public statement. She checked back on the reports of the Katonah murder but there was no specific mention that the victim was a convicted rapist, nor any mention that he was accused of being one. The Buttermilk Falls victim, Carl Morton, however had been tried on an indictment of first degree murder and rape but the trial was aborted on the grounds of possible faulty DNA evidence. The defence proved that the sample of DNA the alleged killer gave could have come into contact with the murder victim due to poor procedure at the forensic lab. The sample could not be re-tested because the victim's DNA had been inadvertently destroyed and the body cremated. This meant that any conviction would have been unsafe; the District Attorney's office had no alternative but to withdraw the prosecution's case to avoid Double Jeopardy should there have been a formal acquittal and subsequent new evidence.

Surely the NYPD would have tied the two cases together if there was any corroborating evidence that the Katonah victim was a rapist. That didn't explain why he had been 'Tarquined' but again, they were surely investigating that link between the two victims. She had gotten no further by the time she left the office for the evening.

On her way home, Caroline picked up some pork medallions from her favourite butchers cum delicatessen on Putney High Street. By the time Mark arrived home she had potatoes Lyonnais simmering nicely in the oven and was busy sautéing a few shallots.

'Smells good; what are we having?'

'Pork; had a good day?'

68

'Same old, same old.' He put his arms around her waist as she stood moving the shallots around the frying pan and kissed her on the side of her neck. 'G and T?'

'No thanks not sure you've got time either; this could be ready in five minutes if you will be; I'm already on the wine.' Caroline placed the medallions in the frying pan and put several handfuls of wet baby spinach in a saucepan to wilt.

'I'll be ready; I'm ravenous, no lunch today.'

'There's a surprise.'

'I'll join you with the wine then.'

He poured a glass of the Pinot Grigio that Caroline had opened and topped up her glass. 'See you've brought your work home,' he said noticing the post-it notes stuck on the fridge door. 'Any further forward yet?'

'Got a feeling I'm missing something obvious but woods and trees and all that.'

'So what are all these other initials then?' he asked having already been aware of SOC.

'I've dug up eleven other murders involving beheadings that took place over the past two or three years. Those are the initials that were written on the victim's heads, like the one found in Yorkshire.'

'And Glasgow.'

'What about Glasgow? She turned the medallions.

'They found another decapitated head but no sign of the body so far.'

'There was nothing on the news.'

'It only came through on the wire service as I was leaving the office. I expect it will make the ten o'clock bulletin.' Mark was still standing staring at the refrigerator. 'Presumably the countries you've added on the notes are where the bodies were found.' Being an ex-crime reporter as well as co-founder of Newzferret, Mark was not feigning interest in Caroline's work.

'Yeah, I'm guessing that they are translations of SOC but as I still haven't fathomed out what that stands for, I'm just going round in circles.' She removed the pork from the pan and placed it on some kitchen foil. Then she poured a splash of the wine into the pan and stirred in some cream and Dijon mustard. 'Stick a couple of plates in the oven for me. Careful it's hot; you could take the potatoes out while you're at it. Don't suppose there's any feedback on Ebingdon yet?' Caroline returned the medallions to the sauce in the pan.

'No, be at least a couple of days I would think. They're busy working on updates of Terry Grantham and Dinah McCarroll, neither of whom is expected to make it to the weekend.' Mark put the dinner plates on a shelf in the oven and put the piping hot dish of potatoes Lyonnais on the trivet then turned his attention back to the fridge door.

Caroline served up the meal.

'Looks good,' said Mark.

'Make the most of it,' said Caroline. 'I haven't bothered with desert.'

Mark's eyes widened as he realised something about the notes. 'You know what you said about not seeing the wood for the trees,' he said. Caroline nodded. 'Well, take another look at the initials.' Caroline turned to look. 'What's the common denominator?'

Caroline was looking but shaking her head at the same time.

'They all end in C; they're all in different languages but still end in the letter C,' said Mark.

'Which means?'

'That the C is probably a common language; English I expect; that means that it's almost certainly a pronoun – a country, place, person maybe; something that doesn't translate; something that's the same in any language.'

Caroline ignored the grammar lesson. 'Of course, so it could be Christ for instance.'

'Could be a lot of things,' cautioned Mark. 'This is delicious, by the way.'

Caroline didn't register the compliment, she was up from the table to fetch her electronic tablet; she returned to the table and searched for

70

the online translator whilst eating her meal American style – just with a fork.

She typed in the word Christ, then checked the Afrikaans; *Christus*, 'That works', she said.

Malay; *Christ*, 'that works too,' she said with mounting excitement.

Dutch; *Christus*, 'Yes!'

Hungarian; *Krisztus*. The bubble deflated.

Turkish; *Mesih*. The bubble burst completely. 'Damn,' she said.

'Hey, so it's probably not Christ but you'd have been bloody lucky to have hit on it straight away. We'll find it; Sherlock had his three pipe problems we've got our two bottle problem.'

He topped up both their glasses and opened another bottle.

SEVEN

Friday 11ᵗʰ October

Pullman went to sleep thinking of the case; he was thinking of the case at 6am when his ringtone sounded. He answered the call, still drowsy.

'Mmmmm,' he hummed.

'Mike?'

'Yes', he slurred

'It's Pauline Crompton.' Bloody hell! What could the Chief Constable possibly want at this time of the morning; his immediate reaction was to panic that he'd screwed up. 'Sorry to wake you,'

'It's okay ma'am, you beat my alarm by about thirty seconds. What can I do for you?'

'Could you be in my office for two o'clock this afternoon?'

Shit; sounds like he had screwed up. 'Is there a problem?'

'No, no just something we need to discuss regarding the Bridlington murder and now the one in Glasgow. I'd do it sooner but I have to be in Manchester by nine for a meeting but I'll be back for two.'

'Okay ma'am see you at two this afternoon.' They cut the phone connection simultaneously.

The first time he thought of Jane in the previous eight hours was when he opened the wardrobe and reminded himself that it was time to take her clothes to the charity shop. He'd promised himself he would do it as soon as he was ready; he felt ready. Tomorrow was Saturday, as good a time as any.

He watched the start of Breakfast on BBC while he ate his bowl of cereal and drank his coffee. The aftermath of typhoon Parahan, the most violent storm in recorded history, occupied the headlines and

72

major part of the first segment. Reports from Indonesia of more than five thousand fatalities, utter devastation and a huge humanitarian crisis put his personal issues into perspective. Here he was living in Hessle, in his comfortable detached house, eating his breakfast, full of self-pity over the loss of his wife; while in the western Pacific tens of thousands of relatives were mourning the death of loved ones surrounded by debris where there homes had previously stood; scavenging for scraps of food and filtering filthy water to boil before it was fit to drink. He recalled what his dad used to say to him in his teenage years when he got dumped or didn't get the grades he wanted: *remember there's always somebody who's got the wrong end of shittier stick than you*; his mum always added *but if that's the way the cards fall son all you can do is play the hand you're dealt'*.

He was playing the cards he'd been dealt but just wished the game was a rubber of bridge and he had a partner.

Coverage of the discovery of the head in Glasgow was no more detailed than it had been the previous night on the ten o'clock news. Pullman hoped that there would be more details when he got to the incident room. There was no further details of the find on Five Live, his chosen listening on the drive to Bridlington; no music to invoke sentimental memories.

'You're in bright and early, Lynne or did you sleep here last night?' said Pullman entering the incident room with a cup of take away coffee. 'Sorry didn't get you one.'

'You're early too sir. Did you see the news last night?'

'Yep and again this morning. That's why I'm in early. Bloody marvellous isn't it when we find out about a major crime from Huw Edwards.'

'It would have filtered through to us eventually. Anyway sir I've already been on to Glasgow SCS and they confirmed the news report; the head was delivered to Barlinnie Prison last evening. It was in a hat box and a black cab was used for the delivery. The pathologist will be carrying out a full examination of the head this morning but it looks like the vic...tim,' she corrected herself before Pullman did, 'was hit on the head prior to it being cut off although it could have been dropped on to a hard surface after decapitation. And it *did* have SOC written on the forehead.'

'Any sign of the body yet; or the identity?'

'Not yet; a bit too soon to be a copycat, so maybe we're looking for the same killer.'

'Maybe; had any joy yet on Tilly?' he asked.

'Tizzy,' she corrected him, 'and no, not yet sir. The mobile operator said they'd get both sets of phone records over as early as possible this morning but I don't hold out a lot of hope that they'll tell us much.'

Sperring's phone rang; she answered. 'Yes this is DS Sperring.' She listened intently, nodding frequently and mumbling affirmative noises. 'Right thanks for letting me know. Yes it does look like the same guy. Of course the moment we know anything. Thanks again.'

She turned to Pullman. 'They've interviewed the cabbie who described the man who gave it to him along with twenty quid note, as medium height, with a thick black beard; wearing a dark, plain hoodie and had a Glaswegian accent.'

'Didn't have a big pink plastic nose and black rimmed glasses as well did he?' said Pullman sarcastically; emphasising that the perpetrator had clearly worn a very bad disguise.

Sperring smiled briefly but carried on. 'He still has the note used to pay the fare so they're doing the usual tests on that. It was a Scottish note and pretty crisp by all accounts but they're not holding out a lot of hope that they can isolate anything specific to help identify the killer. The parcel was addressed to the Governor so as a safety precaution they had to call bomb disposal before they could open it.'

'Looks like the same MO as Wethersby eh? For court read prison but still making the same point about justice. Let's see if this victim is a nonce or rather an alleged nonce,' said Pullman. 'Tell you what, it's a good job Saville's not around or he could have found himself with nowhere to shove his cigar.'

'This means that the killer isn't necessarily local to our patch sir.'

'I'm sure you're right, Lynne. Maybe that's why our illustrious Chief Constable rang me at six o'clock this morning; she's called me back to Hull for a two o'clock meeting this afternoon. I'm guessing that someone has already decided it's a too big a fish for us to net.'

****

At the NewZferret office in London, Caroline Nichols spent the morning trying every sensible word in the dictionary beginning with C that she thought plausible without any realistic answers. Cabinet to cypher, countries from Cambodia to the Czech Republic and every plausible person she could think of from Caesar to Custer, not that Custer was in any way plausible. Everything she tried changed initial in at least one of the nominated languages; cabinet became *szekreny* in Hungarian; cypher became nol in Indonesian; Cambodia became *Kambodja* in Africaans and Czech Republic became *Tsjechische Republiek* in Dutch. She also finally understood that Czechoslovakia had become the Czech Republic twenty years earlier when it split peacefully from Slovakia.

Surnames offered the most hope with many of them remaining the same in all languages; none of them made any sense in relation to the use on the victim's head. The end result was numb fingertips and strained eyes but no progress on identifying what C might represent.

She did receive two pieces of news that were of interest. The first, via Reuters, following-up on the Glasgow killing; police said they would be making a statement at 4 pm that afternoon; the second was an announcement from the NYPD that was featured on all the satellite news channels and the local Katonah web site:

Raymond Hospic Serial Rapist
Further DNA tests have identified the Katonah murder victim, Raymond Hospic, as a serial rapist who has escaped detection for over five years. Hospic's crimes were committed in three states and

75

involve seventeen reported attacks although police think the number may be far higher.

He is known to have preyed on inebriated women leaving clubs and bars usually in the early hours of the morning. In three cases he is believed to have befriended the women whilst inside the clubs and it is thought he may have spiked their drinks with the so called 'date rape' drug Rohypnol.

A police spokesperson said: This man has eluded capture in three states over the past five years. He may well have been responsible for other attacks and whilst we would prefer to have arrested and tried Hospic at least he is now no longer a threat to women. However we do not in any way condone his murder. The person or persons who committed this act should have contacted the police with their evidence rather than take the law into their own hands. We cannot allow society to retrograde into the days of the Wild West.'

Police have linked this murder to that of Carl Morton a known sex offender who was murdered in July at Buttermilk Falls County Park; however they insist that this does not mean that the general public have any cause for concern. They would like anyone who has any information relating to either of these crimes to contact them.

Well they got there eventually thought Caroline. She remembered that the shopkeeper who reported the murder had said he'd seen a drunken woman in the early hours of the morning before the body was discovered. So Hospic was almost certainly stalking her. Did some sword swinging white knight come to her rescue? Actually it would have been a dastardly black knight carrying a permanent marker, who knew who Tarquinius was and also just happened to be over in Buttermilk Falls when that murder took place too. Surely that would have been too much of a coincidence. She wondered if there was some connection between whatever C was and Tarquinius. She searched Tarquinius online again but nothing came up to connect the two.

Over breakfast that morning Mark had mentioned, very diplomatically, that the web site had not been updated for a couple of days and that there was nothing worse than a news exposé site that had old news. His remark played on her mind while she was researching online. She decided that she really ought to put something together on what she'd found thus far and see if there actually was a story worth pursuing or if she should forget it and move on.

What exactly was the exposé here; was it that there was an international murderer who had now reached mainland UK? Was it that police across the world had failed to co-ordinate information that would have shown the existence of an international serial killer? But was it one killer? Could one person have committed all the SOC murders?

She pinned up the map that had arrived, as promised, in the post along with the office energy bill and some unwanted circulars; spread the printouts of the details of the various murders in order to pinpoint them on the map. As she did so she quickly realised that two of the murders had occurred on the same day in 2012 and another the following day. Problem was that one killer could not have been in Canada and Hungary on the same day nor could he have got to Holland by the next day from either of the other two locations. Quite clearly therefore there was more than one killer. Now if there was more than one killer who tagged their victim with the SOC letters then that meant that it was co-ordinated and co-ordination required organisation or rather an organisation to be behind it. So that would be the lead-in for her article; despite the fact that she had promised herself she would not butterfly from task to task she did just that; leaving the map she sat at the PC and typed the headline; *Organised to Kill*, then changed it to:

Organised Murder

Newzferret has discovered that, over the past three years, eleven murders have been committed across the globe that all have the same distinctive characteristics. They have all involved the killing of men who have been accused of, or convicted of, sex offences but are considered to have escaped justice. All the victims were decapitated;

all but one of the heads were deliberately left at a place at which justice is administered– court, police station, parliament building; every decapitated head had the letters S O C or the native language equivalent, written on them before being left.

These are the cases we have identified but there are sure to be many, many more; possibly hundreds that have not been reported online. A study of the dates of the incidents involved proves that the murders could not be the work of a single person. This demonstrates that the killings must be organised and we believe that the person(s) or organisation responsible goes by the acronym SOC.

The latest murders have occurred in Yorkshire, England and Glasgow, Scotland; with your help we at Newzferret are determined to identify them and expose their crimes.

Wherever you live in the world if you have knowledge of similar killings that have not made it to the international arena please let Newzferret know so that we can build a bigger picture and hopefully assist the authorities in putting an end to the killings. If you have knowledge of any organisation with the initials SOC who in anyway promote the use of violence against anyone, whether or not they are considered to be a sex offender, then please inform us by email or through the forum.

The Jimmy Saville affair has heightened anti-sex offender prejudice which Newzferret can fully understand but we cannot allow any non-governmental organisation to administer their concept of law and implement rough justice or we will descend into a state of lawless anarchy; the kind of which hasn't been seen since the Dark Ages.

The Dark Ages had an emotive ring to it so she added a sub heading to the article:

Organised Murder
Have the Dark Ages returned?

Caroline decided to run the article past Mark that night; if nothing else it would prove that she wasn't neglecting the Newzferret site. As a copy of the article was coming off the printer Mark rang her in case she was unaware of the Glasgow police statement that had just been televised. She was; she had lost track of time and missed the 4 pm start. He brought her up to-date; the Glasgow police had said they were linking yesterday's murder in the city to the murder of Thomas Wethersby in Yorkshire last Monday. The Glasgow victim was identified as Jozef Kulkinski; a Polish immigrant who was wanted by the police. Mark said he remembered the name and had looked it up in his files. In 2006 Kulkinski was arrested in Glasgow and charged with rape, grooming teenage girls for prostitution and trafficking immigrant girls. Two other men were arrested at the same time but were released through lack of evidence. Kulkinski was sentenced to eighteen years in prison but after sentencing he escaped from the prison van transporting him to HMP Barlinnie. Police believed that he had returned to Poland.

The police statement said that the killer placed the victim's decapitated head into a hat box and sent it by taxi to Barlinnie prison. The head also had the letters SOC inked onto the forehead in the same manner as that of the Yorkshire victim. They said that it was highly likely that the killings were committed by the same person and therefore could be the work of the same person. The case was being handed over to the National Crime Agency for further investigation. They appealed to anyone who may have information concerning the murder or who may have witnessed a man with a bushy black beard and wearing a dark coloured hoodie hiring a taxi in George Square to contact them as soon as possible.

****

Pullman arranged to meet DS Sperring in the bar of the Pipe and Drum pub near Beverley. It was on his way home and he'd often eaten there with Jane on special occasions. It was early, so the bar was virtually devoid of customers. He arrived first and ordered a pint of bitter and a white wine spritzer for Sperring and took them to a window table from where he had a view of the car park. His gaze wandered around the bar stirring wonderful memories of evenings spent there with Jane.

He saw Sperring parking her car; she waved to acknowledge that she had seen him at the window. As she entered the pub she signalled from the entrance that she was visiting the ladies before joining him at the table. That gave him a few more moments to clear his mind and stem the tears.

'Not been here before sir; often passed by; seems nice.'

'Foods excellent, a bit pricey, you don't get much change out of a hundred quid for dinner for two with wine but you get what you pay for in life, so they say.'

'I can safely assume you haven't bought me here to buy me dinner then?'

'You certainly can.'

Pullman told his DS that when he got back to the Priory Road headquarters for his two o'clock meeting, Pauline Crompton, the Chief Constable was waiting for him in her office along with a guy called David Overend, Director of the Organised Crime Command in the newly formed National Crime Agency in London. She introduced them and Overend explained that their Serious Crime Analysis Section, formerly part of Serious Organised Crime Agency, had identified a pattern between the murders in Bridlington and the one in Glasgow. At the time it was all Pullman could do to stop himself making a facetious remark about their astute observations but uncharacteristically he contained himself. Despite the blatant, almost identical similarities between the two murders, it was nevertheless surprisingly quick of the NCA to co-ordinate the information and to officially recognise the similarities; even more surprising given that the on-going re-organisation would certainly have caused some teething problems.

The Serious Crime Analysis Section (SCAS) was originally formed in 1998 to gather and analyse data from a network of contact officers employed in intelligence departments in every police force in the UK. Its role was to identify crime patterns that may indicate the possibility of serial killers and serial rapists at the earliest possible stage of their crime spree commencing.

SCAS analysts code the information onto a database - ViCLAS (Violent Crime Linkage Analysis System), developed in Canada by the Royal Canadian Mounted Police. The analyst's report identifies if there are grounds to believe that the offender has previously been identified. It provides a summary of the finer detail of the perpetrator's behaviour which can alert an investigating officer to less obvious aspects of the crime which may not be immediately apparent.

Because NCA was down on personnel, with dozens of its people tied up in Operation Yewtree, they desperately needed additional personnel to deal with this case in particular. It seemed prudent to approach Crompton to request Pullman's secondment to head up the murder enquiries as he was already the Senior Investigating Officer involved in the case. He would still be investigating the Bridlington murder in addition to the Scottish one but doing so under the auspices of the NCA; it really wouldn't make a great deal of difference to the Humberside Police operation. Subject to Pullman's agreement his Chief Constable had reluctantly agreed to the request even though it would temporarily leave the force without one of their most experienced officers. Pullman was delighted to have been considered for overall responsibility of the cases.

'Wow!' said Sperring, 'so you're going back to London.' She knew that Pullman had relocated from North West London to Hull eleven years ago when his wife joined the marketing department of Reckitt and Coleman.

'Not necessarily,' replied Pullman. He explained to Sperring that he was naturally considering the attachment but had made a proviso in his response; that condition being, he would go if he and she went as a team.

'Me! London. Be nice to have been asked, sir.'

'That's what I'm doing now. I didn't commit you. I'm asking you what you think. And it's not London; we'd be working out of the

Leeds regional offices. So you wouldn't be far away from that boyfriend of yours.'

'I hardly see him as it is.'

She didn't tell her boss that her relationship with Gary was extremely strained to the point where they were more or less on the verge of splitting up. In fact if they could each have afforded their own individual flats they would most probably have gone their separate ways weeks ago.

'Would I need to relocate?'

'Not if you don't want to. It's only an hour or so from Hull assuming that there are no hold-ups on the M62; it's commutable but the investigation will involve long hours as well as some travelling so they've offered an accommodation allowance if needs be.'

The move could be the motivation she needed to split with Gary. Although it might only provide a temporary solution it was a tempting situation. 'Okay, you're on,' she said. 'I'll discuss it with Gary and call you.' That was a lie. She wouldn't discuss it with her partner but would simply tell him that their relationship had run its course. He wouldn't be surprised nor would he be upset by her decision, of that she was certain.

It was an easier conversation than Pullman had expected. 'One more thing, as we'll be working closely together let's use first names Lynne, drop the sir and call me Mike when it's just the two of us.'

'That'll seem strange sir,' she said.

'Look, Lynne if we were in any other job, an office or whatever we'd be on first name terms wouldn't we?'

'I suppose we would, sir,' said Sperring having never worked in any other work place environment. She noticed Pullman raise an admonishing eyebrow. 'I suppose so, Mike.' She hesitantly corrected herself. It was going to take some time to get used to calling him Mike and she wasn't sure she wanted to be on first name terms. She had referred to him as sir from the first day she joined his team. She felt comfortable with sir. He was her superior officer; sir was what she was taught to call superior officers.

82

EIGHT

Saturday 12th October

As dawn broke and the sun rose over the horizon, the driving rain was cascading in rivulets down the French windows distorting Pullman's view of the wood pigeon persistently making attempts to get seed from the empty hanging bird feeder. The plump bird balanced precariously on a stem of the wisteria, rocking to and fro as the fragile stem buckled under its weight. Pullman was staring at the futile attempts of the bird to have breakfast but his eyes were not transmitting the image to his brain; he was looking without seeing. His mind was otherwise engaged.

Thoughts were travelling through his mind like ingredients in a pulsing food blender; no detail just a revolving blurred mess. Jane; the murders; the weather; the secondment; Lynne; Arsenal; SOC; they merged into a spinning morass inside his mind, not a single clear thought amongst them. The crash of a, gale blown, plastic watering can hitting the French doors jerked him back into reality. The blender ground to a halt. It was only then that he was conscious of the gale force winds and heavy rain. He yawned and stretched his legs out, raising them off the carpet as he did so. He sat upright thrusting his chest forward and arching his back bringing his bent arms up to ninety degrees in the process. He had been slumped in the armchair since around 2 am, unable to sleep. He hated nights; at least he had done so since Jane died. Almost two years ago the big 'C', as Jane pragmatically referred to her cancer, dominated both their lives. Forty-two was much too young to die. So many unrealised plans they had made for their future; so many unfulfilled dreams.

Death had never affected him before. He'd seen it far too frequently; he'd comforted so many grieving relatives. When his own relatives died, even when his parents passed away, he always rolled out the same old trite words; *well none us know what's ticking away inside us.*

Well Jane didn't know, not until the colonoscopy found the tumour. She had just felt tired and lethargic. Put it down to overwork. The doctor ran tests for anaemia, celiac disease, vitamin deficiency until finally, after a year; he ordered the colonoscopy and endoscopy.

Pullman remembered the condescending words of the gastroenterology nurse after the examination found the tumour; *try not to worry, think of it as the start of a long journey.*

Five weeks later the start of the journey had taken them to the oncologist's office via CT and MRI scans; he and Jane were both sitting in front of the consultant optimistically expecting him to make an appointment to whip out the offending lump when he quietly told her that she only had months to live; the bowel cancer had spread into the peritoneum and lymph nodes to the point where it was inoperable. They just hugged and cried. He, a hard-nosed copper, cried; he realised he was crying now. He shook his head and the tears scattered like a shower. He took a deep breath, wiped his eyes and pulled himself together. He reflected on the irony of the current situation; now another big C was dominating his life; the big C of SOC.

****

In Putney, Caroline was sitting at her home office PC by eight thirty. Officially it was a third bedroom but it had long since become their study cum office when at home. They could quite easily run Newzferret from there but Caroline preferred the discipline of leaving the house to go to work during the week; even though the official place of work was little more than a mile away. Mark was at his office in Kings Place having set off in the rain before first light; he was duty editor for the morning. Caroline was amending and uploading the Organised Murder article to which Mark had suggested the odd tweak or two, the previous evening. She hoped that one of the tens of thousands of subscribers would be able to decipher the meaning of the killer's tag. Mark would be home by midday; shortly after which they would set off to visit her parents in Surrey where Newzferret, and anything connected with it, would be strictly off the agenda for the remainder of the weekend.

****

Lynne Sperring was home alone. Gary had gone to the pub after she told him she wanted to split up and he had stayed out all night, not for the first time. She often told him that he had probably been a cat in a previous life; with traits like staying out, being stubborn and things he could do with his tongue. Which trait she mentioned depended on whether they were arguing or making up.

****

The NYPD detained two people for questioning in connection with the murders of Raymond Hospic and Carl Morton.

****

In Kuusamo, Finland, Olli Maarken a 56 year old foreman in the local saw mill was found dead in tragic circumstances. The safety cage on the horizontal saw, used to slice whole tree trunks into rough cut planks, had developed a fault; in an apparent attempt to resolve the issue Maarken had slipped and fallen on the blade he was operating which dissected his body in two; entering at the crown of his head and exiting through his rectum. It was the most serious accident to have ever occurred in the Finnish timber industry. A full enquiry had been instigated.

Sunday 13th October

The sun shone unusually brightly for the time of year. Prague was enjoying an Indian summer and not surprisingly the terrace seating

85

outside the Kotleta Bar, normally stacked and stored away by the beginning of October, was three quarters occupied. The number of customers was swollen by the arrival of two Brits who approached a man in his mid-forties sitting alone, gently stirring his cappuccino. They asked if they could join him. The man looked around at several empty tables then up at the men hovering over him. Before he could answer they sat down. The taller of the two spoke.

'Peter, my name is Mike Rutter and my colleague is Hugh Newman were from the Guardian newspaper.'

'I think you've got me confused with someone else.'

'I don't think so Peter. We've tracked you right across Europe.'

The man they called Peter threw some coins on the table and started to rise from his seat. Rutter placed his hand on the man's arm. 'We'll just keep following you until you speak to us. We're not here to cause you any trouble; we just want to ask you some questions. Please, five minutes.'

The man made a point of sighing deeply to show his frustration then reluctantly sat down again. He looked at both men. Were they really journalists? Did he recognise them? He didn't think so; the man who called himself Rutter was around six feet tall, slim with neatly groomed mousey coloured hair and a darker goatee beard with moustache. His questioner had a hint of a northern accent but nothing so pronounced that he could place it to a specific part of the UK. Newman on the other hand was around four inches shorter, heavy set with a polished head upon which the sun was glinting. His ears were flat to the sides of his face and his chin was prominently square cut affording him more than a passing resemblance to a shorter David Coulthard, the ex- F1 driver. They didn't look like police but they did look friendlier than the other two men that had been following him and were now sitting at a corner table taking more than a passing interest in the scene.

'The clock's ticking,' said the man they called Peter.

'We're not questioning your right to disappear without officially resigning from DFZ,' said Rutter.

86

'I've never worked at a bank,' interrupted Peter. 'Like I said you've got me confused with someone else.'

'But you knew instantly that DFZ is a bank; most wouldn't have heard of it. Peter, please, you may have shaved off the beard and tinted your hair but you're still Peter Ebingdon. You've rented an apartment off Wenceslas Square in the name of Donald Canard', Rutter snorted a stifled chuckle. 'Nice touch that, I suppose you thought that a Czech wouldn't speak French. Easier to pronounce than Mickey Souris, though.'

An almost imperceptible smile appeared on Peter's lips. He hadn't thought of calling himself Mickey Mouse; maybe next time. There was little point in continuing the pretence. Rutter's eyes looked honest, if eyes could look honest. They afforded an air of integrity 'What do you want?'

'Your side of the story.'

'There is no story. I'd just had enough of corporate politics, enough of boardroom bullshit and enough of living a life I didn't want any more.'

'What about your wife?'

'Yeah what about my darling wife,' he replied making no attempt to conceal the venom. 'We're separated; getting a divorce.'

'When we spoke to her she seemed very concerned that something had, or might, happen to you.'

'Before *she* got to me you mean,' he emphasised the she.

'Sorry? What do you mean before *she* got to you?' Rutter noticed that Peter's demeanour had changed. He looked anxious and the anxiety came through in his voice.

Peter looked furtively over each shoulder 'Does she or anyone else in the family know where I am?'

'I don't know. The bank employed a firm of investigators to find you.'

Peter interrupted him 'Presumably those two goons sitting over there.' He waved to the two goons. 'They've been on my tail for a couple of days.' Rutter and Newman instinctively turned to look. 'I thought perhaps she'd sent them.' The goons tried their best to look invisible.

'I would think the bank is keeping her informed so it could be she knows you're here.' said Rutter.

'Fuck! That's me out of here then. Nice meeting you. Not.' He rose. Rutter put his hand on his arm to stop him again but this time Ebingdon firmly shook it free of Rutter's grip. 'Good day gentlemen.'

Rutter furrowed his brow in an inquisitive manner. 'Are you frightened of your wife?' He asked incredulously.

'Frightened of my wife? My dear sweet wife, good heavens no; she's a pussy cat.' He said with heavily ladened sarcasm.

'You are aren't you?' called Rutter as Peter strode away.

Peter stopped; half turned and said 'Let's just say that our marriage has run its course. It's time to move on and if you don't mind that's just what I'd like to do. I refer you to William Congreve.'

Rutter watched Peter walk away. After a few seconds he said to Newman 'What did he mean by that?'

Without having to consider it, Newman said 'I'm guessing; Heaven has no rage like love to hatred turned, nor hell a fury like a woman scorned.' Rutter looked at him in amazement. Newman smiled 'Part of my Eng Lit degree course; William Congreve: seven year wonder or wasted talent, discuss.'

The two goons left their table and followed Ebingdon. Rutter and Newman followed the goons. All four lost their prey in the bustling crowds enjoying Prague's warmest October day on record.

That evening Rutter called Mark on his mobile; in-laws or not Mark always answered his mobile. He excused himself from the game of Rumikub they were playing; fortunately he'd just played his turn so the disruption would not interrupt the flow of the game for a few minutes. Caroline's mother was a slow thinker so they never set the timer for her turn; her frequent inability to complete her turn within the allotted time was the cause of countless heated exchanges. They let her take all the time she wanted – within reason.

Mark walked through to the kitchen listening to Mike Rutter as he went; Rutter took him through the brief conversation with Ebingdon. He explained that they had re-connected with him at the apartment building but that their taxi lost his taxi in the Old Town. He was presumably going to the airport or the station so should they keep tabs on him.

Mark thought about it for no more than a second or two before deciding that they'd incurred enough expense tracing a man who didn't want to be traced; he hadn't done anything criminal so if he wanted to disappear then so be it. He'd let the investigators spend the bank's time and money instead. Mark was however more than intrigued by Rutter's instinct that Ebingdon was afraid of his wife. Why would he say that? It was probably just sour grapes or vindictiveness but he'd get someone to take a look at the lady; looked like the storm clouds of divorce were gathering on the horizon.

On the way back to South London Mark filled Caroline in on the conversation with Rutter and suggested that she might like to look into Tamara Bell-Sampson's background while his obituary team were still trying to dig up anything on Peter Ebingdon. There had to be some reason why Ebingdon should not want his wife to find him. Putting Caroline on the project wasn't altogether for altruistic reasons. It was party conference season and the newspaper's resources were stretched to breaking point with teams in Newcastle, Birmingham and Bournemouth covering the actual conferences as well as all the fringe activity that surrounded the events now they had several journalists out in South East Asia.

The Ebingdon story looked as if it had run its course in any case so he couldn't justify assigning resources to investigating a follow up story that might just be the misdirected accusations of a disillusioned or vindictive man.

****

Pullman and Sperring spent Sunday afternoon gathering together the files on the Wethersby and Kulkinski cases in the mobile incident room, prior to vacating the mobile unit. Not that they had much on the Kulkinski murder at the moment. Pullman told Sperring that he wanted to get off to a flyer on Monday morning; in reality he just wanted to occupy his mind.

As it happened Lynne Sperring had nothing better to do. Gary, her boyfriend, had decided to spend a few days on a friends couch until Lynne had sorted out accommodation nearer to Leeds; Pullman had a very limited social life which became virtually non-existent on a Sunday since he stopped going to the pub. Soon after Jane's funeral his drinking was in danger of becoming a habit he knew would put him on a downhill path; he had the sense and willpower to curtail his excesses.

Pullman was in two minds as to whether to suggest that they rented a joint house with shared facilities but it wasn't really a serious thought. Besides it was his intention to commute from his Hessle home until he knew how long the secondment would last or they cracked the cases whichever was the sooner. There were too many memories in the house for him to consider leaving them behind just yet. Sperring was struggling with calling sir, Mike, so much so that she made a point of not calling him by any name at all if she could avoid it, not that Pullman noticed. He, on the other hand, was quite comfortable with calling her Lynne and did so on every possible occasion.

While the latest recruits to the NCA ranks were engaged in planning their move to Leeds, their counterparts at the NYPD were busy questioning the suspects in the two headless murder investigations. When it had been established that both men were un-convicted rape suspects, a police psychological profiler had suggested that the perpetrator of the crimes would most likely be a family member of a rape victim or indeed the rape victim herself. Did he really need a psychology degree to work that out? Acting on this suggestion police had drawn up a list of possible suspects and began questioning the most active feminists and outspoken rape victims.

As part of that questioning they interviewed Charlotte Gortman at her home in Belleville, New Jersey. Gortman, herself a victim of a violent sexual assault for which the assailant had not been arrested, was a known activist for the feminist movement; she was noted for voicing encouragement for vigilante action against known sex offenders on her nationwide blog. She was also a vehement campaigner for greater funding and facilities for the testing of Sexual Assault Evidence Collection Kits or 'rape kits' as they were popularly known.

With their consent every victim who reported a serious sexual assault or rape underwent a thorough examination. The examination included detailed questions on the incident as well as the collection of DNA samples, fingerprints - where appropriate, nail scrapings, urine samples, tests for STDs. The 'rape kit' was then sealed and sent to the appropriate authority for testing. And that's where most of them stayed; untested for months, even years. The backlog of tests had become a national disgrace and Gortman was just one of many campaigners who were demanding White House action to correct the situation. The kits from victims of sex offenders caught in the act, known to the victim or subsequently identified through other means were given priority testing. But thousands of perpetrators would remain at large to offend again while forensic evidence, required to match DNA samples remained piled up in underfunded and over worked laboratories. Gortman's attacker was lurking somewhere amongst the pile.

Charlotte Gortman or Charlie as she was known, stood five ten tall, weighed around two hundred pounds, with dyed auburn hair tied back in a ponytail and she had a physique that put both officers to shame. Not that she had always been that build. At the time of the assault on her she had weighed thirty pounds less with the muscle definition of a couch potato. Months of hard work in the gym and a controlled diet had ensured that, should she ever be attacked again, the assailant would rue the day.

During her initial interview she became agitated and verbally violent to the officers. She derided them for doing nothing to catch the perverts and called for the reintroduction of the death sentence for bastards who violated women. At that stage there was nothing to connect her to the murders; the officers had no reason to take any further action. As one of the officers said to his partner after the interview, 'I wouldn't want to meet her down a dark alley with my dick in my hand.'

A couple of days later , when that same officer was looking at a PC screen over the shoulder of a colleague who was researching Tarquin, he noticed that his colleague was looking at a Rubens painting, the Rape of Lucretia. He remembered seeing a defaced print of the same painting at Gortman's house; the print had been lying on the floor by the sofa. He remembered noticing that the face of the character on the left had been obliterated with black ink. It wasn't until his colleague told him that the guy on the left was Tarquinius that the cent dropped and he realised what the significance could be. Within an hour they had a search warrant for Gortman's house. They found the print still lying on the floor where he'd seen it on the first visit; the face of Tarquinius had indeed been inked out with a black marker pen.

On a bookshelf was a volume on the life and times of the Roman and his family; in the garage they found a heavy sabre sword hanging on the wall in the centre of an array of more than forty other knives and swords; they took the entire collection for forensic testing. Her dark grey UV parked on the drive was towed away to the police forensics garage.

A check on her phone records showed that over the previous few months she had made calls every day to Jessie Ansdean who lived in Secaucus, a few miles away; every day that is, except for the two days on which the murders took place. The assumption being that they were together on those days. Ansdean was subsequently arrested for questioning. Unlike Gortman her physical presence did not intimidate the arresting officers. She was the almost antitheses of her phone buddy; around five feet six tall; around one hundred and twenty pounds with short blond hair and breasts that were doing their best to escape from the boob tube she was almost wearing. Unlike Gortman she was not arrested on suspicion of murder but merely asked to go to the precinct to help the police with their inquiries. They had no evidence against her. Being friends with Charlotte Gortman was not yet a criminal offence.

Gortman was read her Miranda rights, choosing to waive her right to counsel at that time but exercising her right to remain silent; which with characteristic determination she managed to do on that occasion.

NINE

Much to Pullman's surprise there was a fully furnished office waiting for them at Bankside House on the Clarence Dock development in Leeds. In fact they could have had a choice of offices because the entire top floor of the building, occupied by several government agencies including the NCA, was vacant. The desks and chairs had been purloined from other offices but were still newer than the antiquated furniture back at their Priory Road headquarters. The building itself had been constructed in 2006 as a continuation of the waterfront regeneration plan that had turned Leeds in to a modern, centre for commerce and tourism. The primarily glass structure building afforded magnificent views of the River Aire and looked out over the Royal Armouries Museum and Roberts Wharf; it was the redevelopment that had attracted the likes of Harvey Nichols and other flagship stores of the major high street retailers, to establish outlets in Leeds city centre. These together with refurbishment of niche outlets in the Victoria Quarter, in particular, would ensure Sperring would enjoy some excellent retail therapy.

The new occupants were in the process of sorting files and booting up their computers when Sperring's ringtone broke the silence. She answered. It was her estranged partner Gary; Sperring initially spoke in hushed tones so that Pullman had difficulty hearing; then her voice became clearer as it became obvious that the call was not one of a personal nature. It was a realisation that filled her with a combination of relief and disappointment; relief that Gary had accepted the situation without any animosity or futile attempt to keep their relationship alive but disappointment for the self-same reasons. The call finished and she immediately logged on to the internet.

'That was my ex,' she said without thinking whilst entering a domain name into the search engine. If she had looked across at her boss she may well have seen his slight look of puzzlement at the word ex; he made no comment. 'Apparently the friend he's staying with has shown him a web site called Newzferret on which there's a bit about the cases were on, something about the dark ages.'

'Never heard of it.' said Pullman. He meant Newzferret; he had heard of the Dark Ages.

'Got it,' said Sperring. 'There are various news stories on it including one called Organised Murder,' she clicked on the link. 'Here we are.'

Pullman joined her at the monitor so they could read the article simultaneously. Her hair smelt fresh and clean; it was a familiar aroma; the same shampoo that Jane had used.

Apart from minor changes suggested by Mark, Caroline had posted the article as it had been written along with a picture of Wethersby taken from the student's video and the equally gruesome picture released by Glasgow police of Jozef Kulkinski's head.

'Bloody hell,' said Pullman when he'd finished reading. Then having thought for a minute, he said, 'What I don't quite get is the international connection here. It surely isn't the same killer travelling the world chopping up sex offenders or is it? Is there enough time difference between each murder for it to be a travelling psychopath?'

'Shall I contact the site and see what info they've got to back-up this story?'

'No I will, Lynne,' he used her name purposefully. 'You get us some rail tickets for tomorrow.'

'Where to?' she asked.

'London of course. Then I'll call SCAS and set up a meeting with whoever the analyst is on our team. Surely they must know about this too. Make it an early train and I'll try a fix up a meet with someone at this Newzferret web site for late morning.' Lynne had expected their first trip would be to Glasgow.

****

Caroline Nichols took Pullman's call and said she would be delighted to discuss her research with him and they arranged to meet at 11 am at her office the following morning. She immediately rang Mark to tell him of developments but he was in a meeting, she would have to curb her enthusiasm, at being asked to cooperate with police on the investigation, until she got home.

****

Pullman gave Lynne the time of the meeting; she booked the train tickets online using her own credit card. NCA's travel department was in London and she didn't have the time, inclination or knowledge of the organisation to get it booked through them. Initially she planned the journey from Leeds before realising that as they both lived in the Hull area there was no point in travelling to Leeds at that time in the morning to catch a train. She had a choice of two trains from Hull the second of which would just about get them in to Kings Cross station in time to get across to the Newzferret offices. She opted for the 7 am train for which the tickets were £230 return each but the cheaper off peak train at £154 each involved taking a train via Bridlington and changing at Doncaster although there was only 7 minutes arrival time difference at Kings Cross she knew Pullman wouldn't enjoy changing trains so opted for the earlier start.

She then suggested to Pullman that she spend some time on line digging up info on the international murders but Pullman thought they may as well wait until the following morning to see what Newzferret had and also what the analyst had to contribute. There was no benefit, in his view, in duplicating work that was already in existence. They'd find out soon enough. Instead he suggested that she concentrate her mind on identifying the Tizzy woman.

****

96

Charlotte Gortman had maintained her right to the fifth amendment throughout her questioning by good cop and bad cop, even though the frustration of both the investigating officers had boiled over into heated verbal abuse on more than one occasion. They tried telling her that Jessie Ansdean had confessed to assisting in the murder but she was having none of it. She just smiled at her interrogators which incensed them even more. Gortman was supremely confident that Jessie would not admit to anything. Ansdean knew the consequences.

The officers informed Gortman that forensic evidence showed Hospic's blood on the sabre sword found on the wall of her garage. Her fingerprints were found all over the handle and blade and traces of the victim's blood were also found in the trunk of her UV. Conclusive proof of Gortman's guilt as far as good cop Layman and bad cop Hanson were concerned and more than enough evidence to charge her with first degree murder.

At that point Gortman broke her sustained silence. 'It's not an ordinary sword; it's a Medieval Falchion Scimitar and I found it.'

The officers were initially surprised that she had spoken. 'You found it; lying on the sidewalk was it?' said Layman, the question heavy with sarcasm.

'No by the side of a path in Delfino Park.'

'Yeah sure,' said bad cop Hanson equally sarcastically, 'someone just dropped it did they?'

'Guess so.'

'And you just picked it up as a souvenir?'

'That's right. It's a replica but it'll still set you back about three hundred; I thought it would make a neat addition to my collection. You do know I collect knives and swords?'

'Well I don't believe you found it. I think you bought it and used it to chop off the vic's head but couldn't bear to throw it away.'

'If I'd done it do you think I would be so stupid as to leave my fingerprints on the weapon and not make same attempt at cleaning it and my trunk? I found it lying there, picked it up and put it in the trunk. It was pretty dark, I didn't notice any blood on it; I just thought that some punk had chucked it away.'

'Why would someone do that?' asked Hanson

'Maybe he'd just chopped off someone's head,' she said.

'Where is this Delfino Park?'

'White Plains.'

'What were you doing there?' asked good cop Layman.

'We often go there.'

'We?'

'Yes we.'

'Who's we?'

'Girls who like to have fun.'

'Dykes?' snapped bad cop Hanson.

'Oh dear, homophobic are we?'

Over the previous year Hanson had been ordered to attend two courses and take part in psychological evaluation in an attempt to cure his intolerance towards various sections of society. His bigotry was the subject of numerous disciplinary meetings during which he had been told that his attitude would no longer be tolerated. He had been left in no doubt by the NYC Civilian Complaints Review Board that if there were any more complaints filed about his behaviour towards ethnic or gender minorities he would be facing suspension; despite this, there were times when he simply could not control his vitriol. Layman was tired of smoothing over his partners abrasive comments. On more than one occasion he had personally persuaded suspects to drop threats to report Hanson to the CCRB; one day a perp would go free because of Hanson's ingrained prejudices.

Layman threw a visual dagger at Hanson. 'Are you saying that this,' he consulted his notes, 'Delfino Park it's a hangout for lesbians?'

Gortman just smiled and raised her eyebrows.

'What do you do there?'

'Exchange cookie recipes, what do you think we do there, eh?'

'Were you there with Ansdean?'

'Yes. We meet up there most Saturday nights.'

'Even in winter?' asked Hanson angrily.

'It's only fall; but we have ways of keeping warm.' She grinned knowing it would wind him up.

Layman sensed his partner was about to explode, he rose quickly and nodded his head towards the door to indicate that they should leave the room. Layman had capped the volcano in the nick of time. He temporarily terminated the interview.

Hanson and Layman left Gortman sitting in the interview room, watched over by a uniformed officer, while they stepped outside for coffee and cigarettes to allow Hanson's rage to subside. Layman also called the police in White Plains and was told by a detective in the local police department that the park was a regular location for 'Dyke Dogging'; he must have been a relative of Hanson. Layman persuaded Hanson that they should discuss the case with their boss, Lieutenant Capolski before they continued with questioning.

The Lieutenant listened to what they had to say; rose from his chair, put his hands in his trouser pockets and gazed out of the window. After a minute's reflection he said 'So we have a suspect who says she found the murder weapon when she was in the park. The type of weapon she collects. Her prints are all over it as well as the vic's blood and that's also in the trunk but that's where she says she put the blade. She doesn't clean it but just hangs it on her garage wall with the rest of her collection for all to see. We have no other forensics connecting her directly with the body or with the head neither do we have any evidence connecting her to Katonah where an eye witness says he saw a woman with long black hair, apparently drunk, in the same spot as the body was found. Gortman was a rape victim but the dead man was not the perp. So what do we have? A woman,' he emphasised *woman*, 'in possession of a sword that was used to commit a murder, for which she has a plausible if unlikely explanation. That weapon was used to decapitate a man's head in one clean swipe, takes some real strength to do that. I doubt that even you could manage that Hanson, even in one of your fits of rage. No doubt there'll be witnesses to say she was at the park that night, if we can get them to talk to us at the very least the Ansdean woman will back her up and you've got nothing at all on her except being a lesbian and a friend. Last time I looked that wasn't a criminal offence.'

He turned to face the officers, took his hands out of his pockets and placed them palm down on his desk as he leaned forward. 'I don't think we've got enough to hold her. If we got an OJ jury, we'd have no chance of getting a conviction unless we can tie her in to the actual victim or find out where she really got the sword. I'll talk to the DA but I think he'll agree.'

The District Attorney did agree; being in possession of the murder weapon alone would not be enough to convince a grand jury. Five hours later Gortman and Ansdean were released without charge. Despite the NYPDs stretched resources a stakeout team was assigned to each woman. Knowing the truth was one thing; proving it was another.

****

Pullman sat at his desk tucking into his Coronation Chicken sub, half wrapped in the bag in which it had been served. Some of the contents fell onto his desktop conveniently landing on a blank piece of paper which he screwed up and threw into his stainless steel waste paper basket. He was noted on the force for his inability to retain the contents of sandwiches whilst consuming them. Proof being the evident stain on his plain blue tie. Sperring on the other hand was the epitome of delicate eating as she nibbled on her prawn mayo, brown bread, quartered sandwich whilst checking through Angela Carson's phone records. Most of the numbers of calls received were repeated frequently. Only two numbers featured just twice. Sperring rang the first number which was answered by the receptionist at the Manor Street Surgery in Howden the second number went unanswered. A call to the mobile phone operator identified that the number was registered to The Bell-Sampson Communications Group. No individual was named as the user. She looked up the land line number for Bell-Sampson and called them. She explained to the telephonist what she wanted but was told that BSC employed over two and a half thousand people at that location and the telephonist did not have all their mobile numbers.

Sperring insisted that she wanted to speak to someone about the number and was eventually put through to the media centre which handled all press and public relations enquiries. Sperring explained the nature of her enquiry, giving the specific number and saying that the user could be called Tizzy, Tessie or even Lizzie Fenn. The Press Officer made a note of the number and name and said she would check it out and promised to get back to her within the hour.

Much to Sperring's surprise and relief the Press Officer was true to her word. She had checked out the number and it was assigned to their phone pool. She went on to explain that the company had a phone pool in something she referred to as the Comms Dock which also had laptops and tablets. Anyone going out on an assignment could withdraw a piece of equipment for use on company business. It was, she explained, impossible to tell who had used that particular phone. Once upon a time they kept stringent records but the inconvenience of doing so far outweighed the benefits; now they had a system whereby authorised users used an electronic device to release the item for use. In the nineteen months since the change of policy only one phone had gone missing and that was when one of their reporters was unfortunately killed in Syria. Neither she nor the phone survived the explosion. Upon enquiry Sperring was told that the reporters name was Hannah Montgomery and that she had never, to the best of the Press Officers knowledge, been referred to as Tizzy or anything similar.

Sperring brought Pullman up to-date; he suggested she ring them back and arrange a meeting around 4pm the following day as he had fixed a meeting at NCA for two o'clock.

****

101

At least thirteen people were thought to have died when Hurricane Hilda strengthened violently and changed direction on Sunday after becoming Mexico's third hurricane of the Atlantic storm season, following Hurricane Ingrid in September. On Saturday evening, Hilda reached maximum sustained winds of 86 mph (142 kph). The storm was centred 195 miles (315 km) east of Tampico, Mexico and moved north at 8 mph (13 km). Thousands of inhabitants were evacuated while an increasingly dangerous tropical storm Norman, which was likely to be re-designated as a hurricane, unleashed torrential rainfall that caused flash floods and mudslides. A bridge collapsed near the northern Veracruz city of Misantla on Sunday, cutting off the area from the state capital. The body of Miguel Hernandez was recovered from his car in the debris of the collapsed bridge. The roof of his vehicle had collapsed severing and crushing his head in the process. Seventeen more people died when a landslide buried their homes in heavy rains. The fact that the bridge had collapsed was a fortuitous happenstance for the killer of Miguel Hernandez. The police would not be looking for anyone in connection with his death nor would it be included in statistics being collated in London. It also brought to an end the investigation against him for a series of sexual assaults in Xalapa the state capital.

TEN

Tuesday 15ᵗʰ October

The train journey from Hull to London, King's Cross was uneventful. Pullman and Sperring agreed not to discuss the case for fear of putting fellow passengers off their breakfast. Speering alternated between reading A Song of Snow and Ice on her Kindle and playing Angry Birds after she downloaded a free update of 15 games. Pullman attempted to read the newspaper in between nodding off and staring aimlessly out of the window at the English countryside trying to think of anything but Jane. The last thing he needed was to well-up on public transport. Intermittently he stared at his own reflection, when the train entered one of the numerous tunnels en route to the capital. He tried talking to Sperring on occasion but could see he was disturbing her reading besides, apart from the job, they had very little, if anything, in common to stimulate conversation. He was after all sixteen years her senior although studying his reflection he thought he looked ten years younger than his forty five years; he was fully aware that the lack of definition in the reflection was very flattering. What did he know about his colleague? He knew she went to the gym regularly; he never worked out. He used to walk a lot with Jane but not anymore; not on his own. He really ought to get more exercise he tried to convinced himself but knew he wouldn't. Lynne went to the cinema frequently; he watched movies on satellite TV. She went to music festivals; he couldn't stand crowds or most of the music the acts played. He recalled when he was a constable on the beat and had to help police the Reading Festival. He remembered a rain sodden day when Eva Cassidy was on stage singing Fields of Gold while he was walking around in fields of mud and piss. He just couldn't see what the attraction was. In fact, he had to admit to himself, that he and

Lynne had absolutely nothing in common apart from the job and he knew only too well that building any lasting relationship around the job was a rarity.

They disembarked from the train on time at King's Cross. Headed straight for the underground and bought tickets for Putney Bridge station. They boarded a Piccadilly line train to Earl's Court where they changed to the District Line; even at 10 am in the morning the train was crowded but, having been born and bred in London, Pullman new that an hour before they boarded, the train would have been full of commuter passengers packed together like a jar of anchovies. Passengers still on the platform would have been pushing people on board so that the doors could close. They eventually emerged into the dazzling autumn sunshine with thirty-five minutes to spare before the meeting at Newzferret was scheduled.

The stroll from the underground station was straightforward; across Putney Bridge taking in the beautiful views of the Thames glinting in the sunshine; along the High Street to the junction with Putney Bridge Road where the offices were situated above a restaurant on the corner. The most difficult part of the exercise was finding the entrance door to access the first floor. They finally located the entrance but with almost twenty minutes still to go before they were due they opted for a quick coffee at a nearby café in preference to sitting in a reception.

There seems to be an unwritten law in the world of commerce which states that if you arrive early for a meeting the host must keep you waiting until the designated time even if they have nothing better to occupy their time. It's as if the person is trying to imply that whilst you may have the time to be early, they have a very tight schedule and are actually doing you a favour by seeing you at all. Games people play.

They need not have worried about being kept waiting in reception; there wasn't one. The door to the Newzferret office opened directly into a single office. Caroline Nichols was engaged on the telephone. She motioned to her visitors to enter while she closed the conversation. They did. Pullman glanced around the room; was this the extent of the company? It was certainly more functional than glamorous. One room around eight metres by ten metres housed two desks upon which there was two workstation PCs; a small round meeting table that seated a maximum of four people; a two seat chesterfield style settee and a long white laminated worktop, running the entire length of one wall, piled with magazines, multi-coloured files and sheaths of paper. They stood like naughty pupils waiting to see the headmaster. Caroline finished her call.

'I'm sorry about that. I'm Caroline Nichols and you are Detective Chief Inspector Pullman and Detective Sergeant Sperring but then I guess you know that,' she chuckled; her visitors smiled politely. 'Sorry, it's something my Dad always says when meeting someone he knows by name only. He thought it amusing and now I've fallen into the same trap.' She was talking too much and knew it. 'Please take a seat. Can I offer you a coffee or tea?' Her guests declined much to her relief as she had forgotten to buy fresh milk on her way into the office that morning. 'You said on the phone that you were interested in discussing the research behind my organised murder article.'

Pullman explained that until the second murder in Glasgow they had been investigating what they believed to be a one off local crime. Since then they had been seconded to look at both crimes and were naturally interested in her assumptions that the murders related to similar murders in several other countries. It would help them enormously if they didn't have to duplicate her research and may even save lives if it helped to speed up the investigation. He didn't tell her that SCAS was working along the same lines.

Caroline explained that her interest started with a murder in the States in which the victim had had the word Tarquinius written on his decapitated head. A quick look on the net came up with another murder in the same area with the same message. She explained who Tarquinius was, along with the urban usage of his name. She then discussed how it was quite by accident that she happened to be researching decapitation when she picked up the on the SOC murders in numerous countries then of course when the Glasgow murder happened it all seemed to come together.

Most of the victims were either known or suspected sex offenders which as the victims' heads all bore the same initials probably meant that the rest were too. She asked if the Yorkshire victim was a known sex offender. Pullman simply said that he was not without any further elaboration. He did however agree with her that there was no way that the methodology was coincidence and unlikely that it was copycat killings because of the wide geographical spread involved. She felt sure that there was more to it than that but so far hadn't come up with any answers except that she thought the C of the initials used must be the same in any language and was therefore probably a proper noun.

Her visitors listened intently. Pullman explained that it was early days in the investigation and at this stage they could not clarify anything for her nor could they add any sensible comments to her assumptions. They were unaware of the two murders she mentioned in America and although the word used was different it was, in his experience, very unusual to have such similar MOs without there being some kind of connection. It was certainly something they would need to take into account in their investigations. It was difficult for Pullman to sound knowledgeable because she currently knew far more about the cases than he did, a situation he would put right with some haste. They thanked Caroline for her co-operation and for the disc containing the relevant information that she had prepared for them prior to the meeting.

ELEVEN

The meeting at the NCA's Serious Crime Analysis Section was not until 2 pm so with two hours to kill they decided to have an early lunch. Neither of them was very hungry having had breakfast on the train so they popped into The Swift; a bar and restaurant directly opposite the Newzferret office. Being just before noon there were only seven other customers in the place. The decor was an eclectic mix of wooden tables and benches constructed from reclaimed timber; blue and yellow metal chairs and tables in the main bar; at one end three steps lead up to another communal seating area. It had the feel of an establishment that was no doubt popular with the in crowd most evenings. Pullman's footsteps echoed on the polished oak floor as he approached the centrally positioned bar, which was also clad in reclaimed timber. The list of beers on the chalk board behind the bar also gave the specific gravity of each type. He really fancied trying the Brooklyn but at 5.2 per cent gravity and it being lunchtime and he having two more meetings that afternoon he prudently opted instead for the 4.0 per cent of the Yokima Red. Speering only wanted an orange and mango juice. They had decided that they would not eat but Pullman could not resist the lure of the house burger he saw waft past him on the way to an even earlier customer. He returned to the table with the drinks and little change from a twenty pound note. 'You sure I can't tempt you to a burger?'

'Certain, thanks.'

'So what do you make of our Caroline Nichols then?'

'Seems okay, mind you if that's all she does for a living, then I don't know how she keeps the proverbial wolf from the door.' said Sperring

'It was clever of her to spot the Tarquinius thing though.'

107

'I did do a bit on him during my degree. There were several members of the same family with the same name but a different epithet like Sextus or Superbus, I think. It's a long time since I studied it.'

'Time to do a refresher course then, Lynne. Be interested to see if our wonder boys at SCAS have homed in on that too.' He took a draw of the Yokima Red. 'Blimey that's got meat in it. Bloody good job I didn't go for the Brooklyn.'

Not having seen the chalk board herself Lynne Sperring had no idea what he meant. They continued the chat while Pullman devoured the towering burger that was delivered to him with a portion of lightly spiced potato wedges and a pot of green relish. He had to eat the stacked burger with a knife and fork, not having been born with the jaw hinges of a yawning hippopotamus.

When they had killed sufficient time they grabbed a taxi to the NCA and upon arrival were shown to the separate mini reception of the SCAS section. A fresh faced young man greeted them. Richard Pointer had been at the SCAS division of the now defunct Serious Organised Crime Agency since leaving Durham University in 2006 and was now, at the age of twenty-nine, a Senior Crime Analyst.

Until two months ago he and his colleagues at SCAS were working out of the Police Training College based in a historic Jacobean mansion, Bramshill House in Hook, in the picturesque Hampshire countryside. Now, following the rebirth of SOCA as the NCA they had relocated to the less picturesque environment of central London. The college was closed and the magnificent four hundred year old house, set in three hundred acres of landscaped gardens and grounds, was put on the market for £25m. The buyer would no doubt be a person of unspeakable wealth — a Russian oligarch, an Arabian oil billionaire or a Premiership footballer.

Pointer's case load had a number of current assignments including the headless murders in which he had taken a very keen interest. He loved his job and did it well. As part of the NCA he received all relevant information that came in from the International Crime Police

108

Organisation (Interpol) covering one hundred and ninety member countries and from Europol the agency that co-ordinates criminal intelligence specifically across twenty-eight EU Member States and in other non-EU partner states such as the USA, Canada, Australia and Norway. The NCA's prime brief was to work with national law enforcement agencies in combating organised crime, drug trafficking and, increasingly, in preventing terrorism. So it was that Pointer too had compiled a detailed folio of murders across the globe that had similarities with the recent cases in the UK. He had been busy that morning creating a PowerPoint presentation outlining his findings to show his visitors.

At the end of the presentation Pullman was having extreme difficulty in keeping his eyes focussed. Whilst Pointer was very animated and proficient in his presentation it contained too many statistics to retain Pullman's interest, falling asleep in stuffy meetings was an old habit of his; in addition to which he was beginning to regret succumbing to the temptation to sample half a pint of Brooklyn before he left the bar at lunchtime.

'Thanks Richard that was extremely interesting.' Pullman managed to sound genuine. It was a well-practised skill. He half turned to Sperring. 'So Caroline Nichols was right; there have been dozens if not hundreds more SOC murders across the globe.'

'Ah you've spoken to Caroline Nichols have you?'

'Yes this morning; she wrote an article on the murders so we thought we ought to interview her. You know her?'

'Yes I do and I was on her news site this morning, I saw the article too. Caroline and I were on the same law degree course at Uni but after a year she dropped out and went to Sheffield to study journalism. Bright girl. I tried to persuade her to join us a couple of years back.'

'No success then?' Pullman regretted saying it even before he'd finished. If Pointer had been successful she'd be there not at Newzferret. 'Sorry stupid thing to say.'

'Not really, I did succeed until her boyfriend un-persuaded her and set up the web site instead. Anyway back to the matter in hand. So to summarise — your two murders are the latest in a chain of murders going back over five years. Not until this department was formed did we have the official capacity to pull all the information together. Now we have done that, there is a distinct pattern which we originally referred to as the SOCrates Paradigm; you know how we like to wrap things up in neat parcels and give them fancy names.'

Sperring made her first contribution to the meeting. 'Socrates didn't have his head cut off, he died from poisoning.' It was the second time in one day that her degree in Ancient History had been useful.

'You're right of course but in his younger days he was a stonemason and legend has it that one day in a fit of pique over criticism of a statue he was working on, he chiselled off the head. So initially our best guess was that SOC referred to the philosopher. But now we have identified the sexual assault connection we will have to find another name for the paradigm because history would tell us that he was as straight as the proverbial arrow. The allegations against him of corrupting youth referred to mental corruption not physical. Anyway we are actively working on deciphering the meaning of the three letters because we believe that they hold the key to whom and why.'

'Can we have copies of all this?' requested Pullman.

'Of course.' Pointer inserted a memory stick in a USB port and copied over his PowerPoint presentation. 'This is a copy of my presentation. Within a couple of days they will have configured a VPN for your workstations in Leeds so you will have direct access to all my files on this case. The unique password is SOCrates in upper and lower case with the O being a zero.'

Pullman took a sideways glance at Sperring and she nodded to indicate she understood the password. 'Have you come across the murders in New York that follow the same MO as our murders but use the word Tarquin or Tarquinius on the forehead?'

'No, tell me more.'

Pullman went through the story as Caroline Nichols had told it to them earlier. 'It seems too similar to your Socrates paradigm to simply be a coincidence.'

'I agree at first thought although it's a big world out there so anything is possible; I'll take a look and see if we can find any connection.'

'That'll be useful. One final thing. We're going to see someone at BSC, the broadcasting people; I believe they are somewhere round here, any idea how far?'

'They're in that big pointy tower you can see through the window behind me.'

Pullman looked past Pointer through the window. He felt stupid that he had been facing it for the past hour and a half without realising. 'Ah you mean the big pointy tower with the huge red neon BSC logo on top.'

Pointer smiled. 'That'll be the one.'

They exchanged farewells and both agreed to keep the other up to-date with anything relevant to the case. Pullman wasn't sure that the day hadn't so far posed more questions than provided answers but it certainly felt more of a challenging investigation than simply being involved in the murder of a schoolteacher from Yorkshire.

****

Global House, the London headquarters of the Bell-Sampson Communications Group was indeed a big pointy tower that could have been architect designed for the 22nd century let alone the 21st. It seemed to be constructed entirely of glass and chrome defying the laws of physics and gravity; the numerous moving walkways and escalators could easily have been used as a backdrop for a futuristic science fiction film. The vast entrance cum reception area was the size of a tennis court. An enormous electronic map of the world with the locations of BSCG offices illuminated in sparkling green LCDs dominated the wall behind the reception station. They announced themselves to the receptionist who entered their names in a computer; it obviously confirmed the appointment and issued two, self-adhesive visitors name badges. Sperring applied hers to her lapel and Pullman put his inside his breast pocket until he noticed the withering look from the receptionist. With the facial expression of a naughty schoolboy he retrieved the badge and affixed it to the outside of the pocket this satisfied the receptionist.

'When they say global they mean global,' said Pullman studying the map. They took a seat in what looked like an airport departure lounge. Pullman picked up a copy of BSC World the monthly house magazine. He flipped through the pages while Sperring checked her mobile for messages.

Laura Green greeted them inside five minutes. She was younger and shorter than Sperring had expected, probably about twenty-five years old Sperring estimated. She didn't really know why she thought the Press Officer would be older or taller; just the mental picture she had built up from their brief telephone conversation the day before. Laura Green wore a short floral patterned smock over black jeggings; her mousey blonde hair was neatly tied back in a ponytail. Sperring introduced herself and DCI Pullman, handing over a business card as she did so. Green reciprocated, introducing herself as Deputy Head of Media Relations.

'What exactly is it that I can help you with? She asked Sperring.

'As I said on the phone, we're trying to trace the user of this telephone line.' Sperring held out a piece of paper on which she had written the mobile number. 'It's a woman by the name of Tizzy possibly Lizzie Fenn, we think.'

Laura Green took the paper, looked at it and saw that it was the same number and name Sperring had given her over the phone. 'I have checked and it is definitely one of our pool lines. Let me show you.'

She ushered them through to another glass walled room, the words Communications Dock were etched into the glass door. Everything in the building seemed to be constructed of glass; Pullman hoped he wouldn't need to use the loo while he was there.

'Right, this is the Comms Dock. As you can see we have a pool of communications equipment,' she swept her arm around in an arc to point out the array of mobile telephones, laptops and tablets on the black glass counters and tables. 'Not just mobile phones. The dock operates like a library really; any authorised member of staff can borrow any piece of equipment at any time.'

'And you told my sergeant that you don't keep tracks on it,' said Pullman.

'Well no and yes, in a way we do. We know who has any one piece of equipment at any one time but we don't keep historical records. What happens is that authorised staff have a Xingot, with an X not a Z. Don't ask me why it's called a Xingot I've no idea, just some name dreamed up between the marketing department and HR.'

She held out her hand to show her personal Xingot, a rectangular piece of black plastic with a domed centre hump. 'You place it in the lock and it releases the item.' Green demonstrated the methodology. It was something along the lines of the electronic tags that supermarkets put on bottles of spirits and which have to be removed at the checkout or the tags on the more expensive clothing items in chain stores.

'Your Xingot is then locked there for as long as you have the equipment so we know who has the item out on loan. When the item is returned, the lock releases the Xingot.'

'And these are coded to individuals,' said Pullman.

'Correct. Security has an electronic reader so that should an item go missing then they can identify the Xingot.'

'And you say there's no historical record,' queried Sperring.

'No; before the Xingots we had a computerised log but some people simply didn't fill it in but now we know who *currently* has the item but not who has *ever had* the item. By the way, Detective Sergeant, I've checked with HR as to whether we have a Tizzy or Lizzie Fenn on the staff and they say not. There's a Samantha Fenn and Gordon Friend, and we have an Elizabeth Brent she is sometimes called Lizzie but none of them have access to the dock. HR can't come up with any other suggestions that might be your Tizzy Fenn.'

'Okay thanks for that.' Sperring was disappointed but not surprised. She asked an obvious question. 'Tell me, why doesn't everyone have their own phone or laptop?'

'I'd be surprised if there is an individual member of staff who doesn't have their own private phone of course but for business use this method saves the group millions in hardware, in admin and in.... how shall I put it.... errors on expenses claims.' Green could see that Sperring was still a little puzzled and that Pullman too had a questioning look on his face; she hadn't noticed that it was his natural expression and had been there since he arrived. 'Worldwide the group employs over forty thousand people, of which some seven thousand work in the field, some of the time but not all of the time, they require to use phones, laptops et al for purely business purposes, if the company supplied them all individually it would cost millions and they would need upgrading, go missing when people leave the company etcetera. This way is more economical and cuts down on admin, it honestly works very well. And it's not a taxable benefit for the employee.'

'I'd have thought that a company such as yours could have devised this Xingot system so that it kept a record of every log out permanently'

'You'd think wouldn't you.'

'Okay,' said Pullman cutting to the chase, 'we know that one of your pool phones was used to make the two calls we're interested in but you're telling me it could have been any one of seven thousand members of staff.'

'No. That's the worldwide number. Here we employ two and a half thousand staff of which approximately four hundred have access to the pool.'

The reduced number was a relief to Pullman but was still an enormous haystack; he had neither the budget nor the manpower to

114

search for that particular needle but he had no option other than to follow it through.

'I'd like a list of those four hundred people please,' he said.

'I'll get it run off for you but it'll have to wait until tomorrow, I'm afraid. The whole HR department closed early today for a training seminar; I'll send it to you.' She checked the business card that she had in her hand there was no address. 'If I had your address that is.'

Pullman explained that they were between offices and that the card was temporary. He took out his notebook, wrote down his email details and the address of Bankside House and handed it to her. They said their farewells on the way to the exit. Green collected their name badges before they disappeared through the revolving doors. It had been an informative if not entirely productive day.

On the rail journey home Pullman did a lot of thinking and dozing. Sperring killed a lot of little green pigs.

TWELVE

Wednesday 16th October

Lynne Sperring did not realise that it was 1.30 am until she partially rolled off the settee on which she had fallen asleep just before midnight; she awoke with a start. Her lap top was still logged on to the mythological history page she was studying before Morpheus had overwhelmed her with his soporific charms. She and Mike Pullman had arrived back in Hull ten minutes late; they popped into the Mercure Royal Hotel for a very swift night cap before going their separate ways. Pullman would have preferred to stay longer but there was no legitimate reason to keep Sperring talking besides which he was driving. She made a quick detour to the Peking Palace for a takeaway before arriving home at a little before 11pm. The chef's special recipe rice and Kung Po Chicken was devoured as if she hadn't eaten since breakfast – which she hadn't because the buffet car on the return train was out of commission; no reason was given and no alternative was offered.

Sperring had eaten whilst viewing numerous web sites on Roman and Greek mythology. It was almost eight years since she'd studied the subject but the names and stories came flooding back as if it were only yesterday. She refreshed her memory bank on Tarquinius Sextus, his rape of Lucretia and the resultant formation of the Roman Republic; scrolled through page after page, that switched from Roman mythology to Greek mythology and back again until something, just short of the paranormal made her come to rest on a page covering the Greek Errinnyes or Erinyes or Eumenides also known as the Furies.

In Greco-Roman mythology the Erinnyes or Furies were goddesses of vengeance. As with many mythological stories there are many and

116

varied versions of their origination. Hesiodos, the Greek didactic poet, wrote that they were the offspring of Gaea (Mother Earth) and were conceived from the blood of Uranus after he was castrated by his son Cronus. Other versions of the story place them as the daughters of Nyx (the Night) or the Titans Cronus and Eurynome. They were perhaps seen as personification of curses or the ghosts of murder victims.

Euripides, the classical Greek tragedian, was believed to be the first person to state that there were three females in the group. This could have been in one of his many plays and been a convenient method of reducing the cast numbers. Subsequently writers, taking his lead, named them Allecto ("the Angry"), Tisiphone ("the Avenger"), and Megaera ("the Envious"). Their home was at the entrance to Tartarus, that hellish place deep in the Underworld; a dire place in Hades where the souls of the condemned were exiled and from where the Erinnyes ascended to earth in pursuit of the wicked. Others call their home Erebus, the darkest depths of the Underworld, where, the Erinnyes would hold those unfortunate souls who had yet to atone for their sins, relentlessly tormenting them.

Because everyone was terrified of these avenging creatures, mortals rarely referred to the Erinnyes by that name, for fear that they would invoke their wrath. For that reason Orestes, one of their unfortunate victims is recorded as calling them Eumenides, the 'Kindly Ones' or 'Solemn Ones', in an attempt to appease them.

Nothing would divert them from their pursuit. No amount of pleading, no sacrificial offering, and no begging could dissuade them, or protect the hapless object of their persecution; if ever they felt that the criminal would escape them, they called upon the goddess Dike (Justice) for assistance in their unequivocal pursuit of strict justice.

As awareness of them grew so too did their reputation, the Erinnyes (Furies) became the personification of revenge, vindictiveness and retribution

Depictions of their appearance were mainly that of hideous winged creatures swathed in black robes sometimes with snakes entwined in their flowing locks. Often they would be shown with glaring red eyes sometimes dripping with blood, or having the repulsive appearance of Chiroptera in the form of giant vampire bats or occasionally having the heads of wolves or slavering dogs.

Quite often they were depicted alongside a large flock of flying Harpies, who were disgusting, heinous, vulture-like female beasts feared and loathed in equal proportions by mankind. Harpies were often said to assist the Erinnyes in punishing those unfortunate souls who had angered or displeased them.

Apart from pontificating that these creatures were possibly the inspiration behind the Dementors in the Harry Potter novels, there was something in this piece that was nagging at her subconscious. Something she was looking at but not seeing. That's when she had made the mistake of closing her weary eyes in an effort to concentrate and was in a deep sleep as she hit the floor. Then at that waking point when she landed on the rug, the Eureka moment hit her; she suddenly saw what it was that was staring her in the face. Her immediate reaction was to call her boss and she picked up her mobile before coming to her senses and deciding against doing that at gone 1.30 am. Being her boss he may well feel able to call her at that time of the morning but it wasn't prudent for her to disturb him except in an emergency which this wasn't. Anyway maybe she was being over eager to justify her thoughts. She would print off the page and let Pullman read it in the morning to see if they had the same train of thought.

She was her desk by 7.30 am having grabbed a few hours disturbed sleep and a coffee and breakfast bap on her way in. Mike Pullman arrived two minutes later with an identical combination 'Great minds.' he said waving the bap towards her.

'Sir,' she said and grimaced, 'Mike.' Sir still sounded right to her. 'I think I may have found something. Take a look at this and see if anything jumps out at you.'

She handed him the print that she had run off in the early hours of the morning. He read it slowly and deliberately whilst consuming his breakfast bap. She watched him reading with anticipation 'Shit!' he blurted out.

'You've seen it.' Sperring said her voice full of excitement.

'No. I've spilled half the contents of my bloody roll on the paper.' He scraped off a little egg yolk with a ruler and dropped it into the wastepaper bin; half the contents of his roll might have been more than a slight exaggeration. 'Never mind I can still read it,' he continued. 'Ah!' he said 'I see, Chiroptera; you think that could be the elusive C word.'

Her euphoria turned quickly to bewilderment. 'No,' she replied with a pained expression her face. 'Chiroptera are bats. There's nothing in any of the MOs to suggest that the murders have anything to do with bats. Read it again.' It was as near to an order as she was ever likely to bark at Pullman; he obeyed without hesitation. When he'd finished he still hadn't seen whatever it was she thought she'd seen.

'Tizzyfenn,' she mumbled.

'Tizzy Fenn? What about her?' he asked.

'That's not what I said but it's what you heard isn't it? What I said was Tisiphone,' she waited for his reaction.

It was a slow burn as it dawned on him. 'You think that Tizzy Fenn is Tisiphone,' he looked back at the notes, 'Tisiphone the avenger! Brilliant, that's well spotted. If you're right.' He said qualifying the statement unnecessarily.

For over two hours they went over the evidence and discussed the hypothesis that somehow the modern day version of the Furies or at least one of them was connected to the killings. Furies was the name Pullman had decided to settle on, finding the word much easier to remember and pronounce than the Greek equivalents.

'But only Superman and Santa Claus can fly,' said Pullman facetiously. 'Tisiphone can't be all over the world, she can't be in more than one place at a time.'

'Who's to say there's only one? said Sperring. 'Or maybe she has a flock of Harpies working for her.' Now she was being facetious.

'But that doesn't solve the SOC riddle, does it? There's nothing here to connect the Furies with anything resembling SOC. It doesn't solve anything on the Tarquinius problem either.'

Sperring was quick to respond. 'I think we're looking at two separate and distinct cases. I'm beginning to think it's a coincidence that both killers have come up with similar MOs and are using different tags to get their point across. In fact that's it,' she said, 'the American cases involve Tarquinius a known rapist and the men that were killed turned out to be known rapists. Maybe our killer is using the initials of a rapist too.'

Pullman rubbed his eye with the side of his index finger and yawned. 'So we need to identify a rapist at some point in the timeline of history who has the initials SOC.' He took an intake of breath and blew it out with puffed cheeks. 'Well that'll be a walk in the park.'

'Who knows we may strike lucky.'

Pullman looked at his watch, it read 10.20 am. 'I'm going to call Pointer and fill him on your theory; let's see if he's got any bright ideas. You call Caroline Nichols and do the same.'

Sperring gave him a quizzical look. 'Yes Lynne I know she's a journalist and she's not in the job but as Pointer said, she's a bright girl and it'll do no harm to have her two-penneth thrown into the mix. Your brilliant hypothesis might trigger something in her thoughts.'

THIRTEEN

Peter Ebingdon instructed the taxi to double back and drop him in Wenceslas Square at Mustek metro station. He was sure that they had lost both the journalists and the goons but was determined keep them off his tracks. He took the metro train to Florenc where he walked across to the bus terminal and bought a one way ticket to Vienna. He had decided to take the bus on the grounds that his followers would no doubt expect him to fly or take the train. He boarded the big yellow single decker bus and slumped down in the plush blue seats next to a very attractive blonde woman in her mid-thirties he guessed. Not that he had any intention of talking to her or anyone else on the journey. He didn't want to be remembered. The journey took just over five hours and the attractive stewardess kept him topped up with fresh hot coffee throughout the trip. At the Lassallestrasse terminal in Vienna he left the bus and hired a car for the onward part of his planned journey to Graz in southern Austria.

Several toll roads and two hours later he arrived at the Ibis Budget Hotel in Graz. At forty Euros per night it was cheap and cheerful but clean, tidy and, as most guests were transient, it was unlikely that he'd see the same person two days running; just as he wanted it. The hotel receptionist was welcoming but not intrusive, had she have been, Ebingdon would have told her that he was a lecturer visiting the Graz University of Technology. He prepaid for five nights in cash. He left his valise in the room and returned to the coffee shop in the lobby area where he sat and studied each new arrival. Most were couples, some of whom had probably only recently met and would go their separate ways in an hour or less; that suited him just fine. He did the same the following day until he felt satisfied that he had evaded the attention of the British newshounds and the goons.

That Wednesday afternoon the weather was dull but dry. Feeling safe to venture out, Ebingdon left the hotel to walk over the Kepler

121

Bridge, down through Stadt Park and into the old town. He was in need of female company having been celibate for several weeks, no problem for most men on the run but an interminable time for a man with his libido and insatiable appetites. Bar Sporgasse, lurking in a dimly lit back street looked to have the kind of ambiance and facilities he was seeking. It did.

****

Richard Pointer's counterparts at both Interpol and Europol got back to him within twenty-four hours with a list of murders covering similar MOs to the SOCrates paradigm. Pointer's database file was now populated with more than one hundred and seventy cases that could be related to those under investigation in the UK. The earliest identifiable incident occurred in 2008 right up to two days after the Glasgow murder. The latest incident happened in Finland where a timber mill worker was thought to have had a fatal accident by falling into the saw he was operating; after he deliberately disabled the safety guard. Police investigations revealed that the man, a widower and grandfather, was accused by a thirty-two year old woman of raping her when she just nine years old, the woman came forward after the reported an attack on another young girl in the same village bore the similar hallmarks to that of her own assault. Since the mill worker's death several other women had come forward with accusations against the man. Police revealed that the letters SOC had been daubed in blood on the casing of the saw machine; presumably, Pointer concluded because there had been insufficient writing space on either side of the divided head.

Pointer concurred with the hypothesis that the initials were being used as an international symbol of retribution and as such it was likely that world-wide recognition would be promoted by the perpetrators through online and telephonic channels. Therefore the answer lay somewhere out there in the ether. He decided to talk to his boss about two potential courses of action.

Gerry Hannington, NCA Director of Intelligence agreed to Pointer's request to seek the help of his expert colleagues in the National Cyber Crime Unit's Computer and Internet Forensic Team to assist him in the search to identify the significance of SOC; the key factor in the investigation. The day-to-day main role of CIFT was to interrogate computer hard drives to uncover criminal activities and internet fraud; however Pointer felt that their expertise in understanding all things internet related could throw up something that he and the investigating officers had not considered. He wasn't wrong.

Gerry Hannington definitely did not agree to Pointer calling in a freelance Symbologist to help on the case but Pointer did so regardless. The young analyst's thinking was they were all assuming that SOC was English but that wasn't a given; it could easily be Latin or maybe Greek. It was the use of the word Tarquinius in the American murder cases that implanted that thought in his mind.

Miriam Dennaby, fifty-seven year old freelance symbologist and noted academic, had written several books on the subject and had taken part on many TV panels during programmes that discussed the work of author Dan Brown. Pointer thought that she would bring a fresh viewpoint as well as a classical bent to the table. So despite his boss's veto he called her.

****

In discussion with CIFT officers, their view was that SOC could be the initials of some form of organisation, just like WHO, IMF or even SCAS if it came to that; a thought that Pointer had already considered. An alternative was that it could be the designation of a domain name (something that Caroline Nichols had already examined) either for all three letters or SO plus .com; the C being the c of com (which neither Pointer nor Caroline Nichols had examined).

'Can we run a search of domain names then for those that contain SOC and SO.com?' asked Pointer.

'Yes we can,' replied Tom Nerbis, 'the only slight problem, Richard, is that is since 1985 there have been more than one hundred million dot com domain names registered. We can speak to Verisign who control the registry in the US and see if they can develop an algorithm to segment those that begin with a word beginning with an S and then filter those with the OC but even if they can, the possibilities could run into millions.'

'Okay let's do it then,' said Pointer dispassionately.

'I wish it were that simple, besides which, we are only assuming that it is a dot com URL. If it turns out to be SOC dot something else then it's a game changer. In the UK, the Nominet register has more than ten million dot co dot UK addresses and then we've got all the other designations from dot org to dot TV etcetera. It's the same situation in every country on the planet. Even if we're right and it is a domain name, we can't be sure it was registered in the UK or the States.'

'Right so it's a big ask but we have to start somewhere and who knows we may hit oil.' So that was Pointer and Sperring who were both placing their hopes on lady luck.

'We'll do a quick scoping analysis to see if we can work out what's involved and put together some sort of time frame.'

Pointer sighed. 'Scoping studies are all very well Tom but while you're deciding on a course of action people are continuing to be murdered so as fast as you can guys, please.'

****

DCI Mike Pullman and DS Lynne Sperring were seated at their desks in Bankside House each deep in their own thoughts.

'Lynne, I'm sorry to argue against part of your hypothesis but I think we could be looking at this from the wrong direction. If this Tisiphone was the avenger and the one who could be calling herself Tisiphone now, is a modern day avenger then unlike Tarquinius, SOC wouldn't be the initials of an attacker but the initials of a victim meaning that the killings are carried in the name of the victim. Does that make sense?'

Sperring puckered her lips and nodded partial understanding.

Pullman continued. 'We know that there must be more than one person doing the killing but it doesn't mean we've got hundreds of Tisiphones out there. We might have another Charles Manson on our hands although it's more likely to be a Charlene Manson; a woman or women enticing others to murder at their behest, in this case sex offenders, in the name of someone who was raped.'

'Yes I'll go along with that,' said Sperring. 'Which means the probability is that Tisiphone is using the internet to spread the word. Maybe social media - Facebook or Twitter perhaps or even a dedicated website.'

They were both silent for a minute or two whilst they each thought of the implications of that line of thinking and how they might follow it through. Tisiphone might be located anywhere in the country. On the other hand she may not even be domiciled in the UK; she could be operating from anywhere on earth. Was there a latter day Alecto and a Megaera working alongside her? Were they calling themselves The Furies or one of the Greek alternatives? Why the beheadings? There were no implications in the myth that the Furies beheaded any of their victims, and what was the connection with SOC?

Once again another chain of thought posing more questions than answers. Pullman was happy. Questions occupied the mind. Answers needed thinking about.

FOURTEEN

Thursday 17th October

Faustus Socinus or Sozzini as it was in Italian and his Uncle Lelio rejected the traditional Christian doctrines such as original sin, the belief that every being is born with an inbuilt instinct to do wrong, (for some Adam and Eve and the temptation with the apple is the embodiment of the original sin concept) They also rejected the divinity of Christ and the Holy Trinity believing that those who follow Christ's virtues will be granted salvation.

Caroline Nichols was reading notes emailed by her uncle the Very Reverend William Basewell. It was in response to her email asking him if he could think of anything in the scriptures or Bible teachings that could be connected with the initials SOC in relation to murder or physical assault; she felt uncomfortable using the word rape in conversation with her uncle, even in electronic conversation. He prefaced his response with a caution that his thoughts were tenuous to say the least and he doubted that Socinians, as followers of this belief were known, would interpret the concept as an eye for an eye and promote the murder of criminals.

His other option was that it was the initials of Simon of Cyrene the man who was plucked from the crowd of onlookers and forced to carry the cross at the crucifixion. It could be that this killer believed he was bearing the cross of Jesus and therefore doing Jesus's work. Alternatively that person or persons may believe he is obeying the law according to Deuteronomy 22:23-27

(23) "If there is a betrothed virgin, and a man meets her in the city and lies with her, (24) then you shall bring them both out to the gate of that city, and you shall stone them to death with stones, the young woman because she did not cry for help though she was in the city,

126

and the man because he violated his neighbour's wife. So you shall purge the evil from your midst.

"But if in the open country a man meets a young woman who is betrothed, and the man seizes her and lies with her, then only the man who lay with her shall die. (26) But you shall do nothing to the young woman; she has committed no offense punishable by death. For this case is like that of a man attacking and murdering his neighbour, (27) because he met her in the open country, and though the betrothed young woman cried for help there was no one to rescue her.

If this was the case then one would expect the victim to be murdered as well unless the killer was assuming that in this day and age a woman would cry out in the city but it is highly likely that her cries would go unanswered. Good Samaritans were few and far between in today's world; most potential rescuers preferring to turn a blind eye than become involved. That was all he could suggest but he told her he would keep thinking and if anything else occurred to him he would contact her.

That the killer was tagging his victims with his identity, believing himself to be Simon of Cyrene was stretching the imagination to breaking point; if that was the case why were the victims all sex offenders? It was certainly the only semi-plausible explanation she had so far. She turned her attention to the notes she made during Lynne Sperring's telephone call the previous afternoon. The Tisiphone hypothesis was sound and had evidence to support it. There was not, and would never be, any connection between the Furies and Simon of Cyrene so she could rule him out as well as Faustus Socinus. She emailed her thanks to Uncle William and promised to stay in touch. She didn't bother to print off the email nor did she think it worth mentioning Uncle William's information to the other parties.

****

Pointer's decision to disobey his boss and bring in Miriam Dennaby delivered in spades. In this case her expertise in unravelling the mysteries of symbols was of little value however her detailed knowledge of classical mythology would prove to be priceless. He took her telephone call with eager anticipation.

'I have given considerable thought to your SOC conundrum and its relationship to the cases you outlined. I cannot find any symbolic meaning to the letters but I believe that I may have identified a possible rationale for the letter C which dates way back to the Romans and Galatians. Are you familiar with that period of history?'

Pointer was not familiar with any period of history having failed the subject at GCSE much to the disappointment of his father Simon, who, at the time, was Professor of History at Southampton University and his mother who was an assistant curator of the V&A in London.

The young Richard believed that his father, like so many history teachers, had it easy. Once learned it was a subject that never changed. History may repeat itself, so they say, but what has happened stays happened. Very little history, if any, is ever re-written. Simon Pointer earned his living teaching the same thing year after year to new students who were hearing it for the first time. Unlike geography teachers who have to keep up to-date with a changing world or those who taught science, politics, business studies and especially those who taught computer technology for instance, history teachers had it made.

In his rebellious, teenage years Richard found history to be as dull as he found his pedantic, boring father. Simon put his son's disinterest down to an unhealthy obsession with Blur and the whole Britpop scene at that time in the mid to late 90s. Richard still had no great interest in history, neither did he have any lingering interest in Blur. As far as Richard Pointer was concerned anything that is reputed to have happened before the industrial revolution was of no consequence to his or anyone else's life in today's high tech world. As for the Roman period how much was fact and how much was fiction. As an atheist he considered the big story of the time to be a great work of 'faction'. Romans crucifying a man who claimed to be the son of a God, there were quite a few Gods around at the time, may well have been fact but embellished in the retelling to the point where the man they called Jesus had magical powers. To his mind a man who could turn water into wine and could even walk on water, was an illusionist. They were the kind of stunts that the magician Dynamo did these days on television to the amazement of onlookers. Would this magician's feats be considered 'miracles' in a thousand years hence; most probably not? It was fact that Dynamo is seen to be doing what he does but fiction to suggest that he possesses supernatural powers as was written about the man from Galilee. In a thousand years Sherlock Holmes, Oliver Twist and the Scarlet Pimpernel amongst a myriad of fictitious characters could well be considered to have existed and academics may well debate the existence of Middle Earth and Hobbits. There were dozens if not hundreds of different religions around the world – to his mind they couldn't all be right. Besides which most of the major conflicts throughout history have been caused by opposing religious beliefs. People and events become folklore over a period of time. Burke and Hare, those well-known body snatchers whom folklore tells stole bodies from graves, didn't. They were just plain, simple murderers who killed unsuspecting victims and sold their bodies to medical science.

Pointer had spent many hours in his youth discussing religious beliefs with Andy Parsons who ran a youth club. Parsons and his wife were devout Christians, who argued their case but did not impose their beliefs on the boys. Pointer and a small group of the boys, who regularly attended the club, were often invited back to the Parsonage, as the boys called Andy's house, for Sunday tea. The boys were well aware that they would be subjected to religious instruction but Mrs Parsons made exceedingly good cakes so an hour of religious ear bashing was a small price to pay for a plateful of cupcakes. The teatime discussions did nothing to deter Pointer from his journey to atheism but they did show Pointer not to disrespect those who chosen to believe in the Bible stories nor those who chose to make a living from them. So did he have an interest in ancient history, whether or not it was fact or fiction?

'No, modern history is my thing,' he lied, trying to demonstrate empathy with her broad interest.

'Such a shame; ah well, let me explain.'

Pointer gave an inaudible sigh. The thing about experts is that they seize upon every opportunity to prove they know more than the next person; never more so than when they are pontificating on a subject which is considered to be academically beyond the average layman. Despite her innate ability to simplify her subject into the vernacular, Miriam Dennaby, was no different. Pointer knew it would be like listening to his father.

'During the Galatian war of 189 BC, the wife of Ortiagon, one of the three princes of Galatia which is now the central region of modern day Turkey, was captured along with others when the Asiatic Gauls were defeated by the Romans under Gnaeus Manlius Vulso. Her captor offered her up to Ortiagon for ransom. Now there are conflicting reports as to the status of the man responsible who is generally believed to have been a centurion. A centurion by the way is often thought of as a mere foot soldier but was actually the commander of a roman century which was a cohort of one hundred men originally but later was reduced to eighty or even as low as sixty'

Get on with it he thought to himself; just get to the crunch. This was like lectures from his father during his childhood. He'd never been in the mood for a history lecture then any more than he was now but he remained silent and patient.

'Now the centurion in whose hands she was held hostage, raped her, possibly more than once, before he handed her back to collect the ransom. The arrangement was that he would meet a party of Gauls representing Ortiagon on the banks of a river which divided the two camps, hand her over in exchange for a small fortune. Unfortunately for her captor, when the exchange was made she immediately called for the Centurion to be slaughtered. One of her rescuers reacted immediately and cut off the centurion's head with his sword.'

Pointer began to see that this diatribe was leading to her telling him that the C stood for centurion but continued listening, interjecting with the occasional affirmatory grunt.

'Now the wife picked up the head and took it home with her. When she got back to her husband, she threw the head at his feet, he was taken aback and apparently said, 'Ah! my wife, it is good to keep faith.' or words to that effect. She replied 'Yes, but it is better still that only one man who has lain with me should remain alive.' Miriam stopped talking.

After what seemed like an interminable pause Pointer asked, 'Are you telling me that the C stands for centurion?'

'Good heavens no.' she said in a tone of a headmistress admonishing a stupid pupil. 'Here we have a woman who was raped and her rapist was decapitated as punishment; the point is that her name was,' she paused for effect, 'Chiomara.'

'Key o mara is spelt with a C I take it?' he queried.

'Of course,' she replied with obvious disdain that he should even ask the question.

'Brilliant! Chiomara; sounds good to me. You could have solved the puzzle, Miriam. I don't suppose you know where the SO fits in?' he asked hopefully.

'That I don't know but I'm sure you can work that out for yourself.'

'I'm sure we can.' he replied 'That's brilliant,' he repeated. 'I'm very grateful to you Miriam; let's hope Chiomara is the key.'

'It's a perfect fit. It makes absolute sense. Whoever is committing these crimes is doing so using Chiomara as the focal point for justice and revenge. Don't you agree?'

Pointer did agree. What he failed to accept was the total authenticity of the story. Who was around at the time to record the events and conversations? Assuming that there is some validity in the tale it would almost certainly have been retold, perhaps recounted several times, like Chinese whispers, before some scribe, poet or philosopher of the time wrote it down for posterity. Then over time more academics retell the tale and it becomes 'fact'. An alternative version could be that Chiomara was a willing participant to sex with the Roman soldier and when she became pregnant offered him money to take her home which he did. After he delivered her safely back to her homeland she gave him the money but the soldier was mugged and had his head chopped off - a little extreme but not unheard of given the ferocity of the time – wondering how she was going to explain the pregnancy to her husband she seized the opportunity and made up the story of her virtue being dis-honoured. She then delivered the head to her husband knowing that it was the head of the one person who could disprove her allegations. If that version had been written at the time it would now be taken as fact.

It was the continual questioning of received wisdom that had steered Pointer into joining SCAS where he got paid to indulge his natural instincts never to accept anything at face value. Not that on this occasion it was an issue. Whatever the facts of the matter, the tale of Chiomara certainly existed so there was some credence that the chain of killings could be based on the story, whether it was factual or not.

He called the investigating team to give them the information on Chiomara. It was received by both Pullman and Sperring with genuine interest and controlled excitement that the key had been found. Pointer then turned his attention to another case he was analysing.

FIFTEEN

In Leeds DCI Pullman and DS Sperring were simultaneously surfing the internet looking for a potential web site that linked to Chiomara and might provide a catalyst for murder. Although they were duplicating the search neither of them were able to progress with other lines of inquiry until this particular riddle was solved. On one search engine alone there were over fourteen thousand entries. They each read the pages that dealt with the story that Pointer had outlined to them in order to get a better handle on the lady in question. Each scanned through page after page of entries on Chiomara butterflies, on social media entries variations of the same theme, page after page of duplicated entries until they both landed on the same site hidden deep in the bowels of the pages returned by the search engine. At first glance the Sisters of Chiomara web site index page struck them both as being a religious order of nuns but as each opened the entry, there before them they realised was the answer they had been seeking.

The Sisters of Chiomara website looked as if it had been professionally designed or at least designed by someone who had more than an amateur's basic ability. The site was primarily designed in black and white using the simple Helvetica typeface giving it a clean, almost clinical feel. Under the title of the site was the sub heading:

United in avenging violence against women and seeking justice.

A menu bar had an index for: *About Us; News; Rapists; Perverts; Paedophiles; Heroines; Forum.* There were logo hyperlinks to a Facebook page in the identity of Alecto Furie and a Twitter feed as #megaerasoc.

It was little wonder that Sperring's and CIF's searches for SOC on both had not delivered results. Sperring and Pullman simultaneously clicked on the About Us tab to find an editorial signed by Tisiphone.

'Tisiphone!', exclaimed Pullman. 'What's she got to do with the Sisters of Chiomara?

'No idea.'

Pullman looked across to Sperring. 'That reminds me, have we had that list yet from our friend at BSC? Sperring shook her head. 'If it doesn't arrive in tomorrow's post give her a boot up the jacksie will you. We need that.' He turned his attention back to the web site.

The editorial read:

The abuse of women by men cannot continue to go unpunished.

For too long our male dominated world has failed to deliver justice to female victims of violence, sexual abuse and rape. Police and law enforcement agencies worldwide along with prosecutors and judges fail to take the required action against those that commit these crimes and those that promote them through pornography in all its forms.

You have the right to dress as you want; to have freedom of thought and movement and the right to decide your own moral code. You should no longer be intimidated by deviants and perverts who are unable to control their satyriasis and no longer should you tolerate inaction by authorities who fail to protect and uphold the rights of women.

Take unilateral action to invoke justice for your sisters where no justice has been forthcoming. Now is the time to be strong; to fight back; to take action. Rapists deserve to spend eternity in Hell.

Join us, the latter day Furies and let us all take inspiration from Chiomara, the Galatian Princess, who decapitated her rapist assailant during a time of male barbarity towards women. You are still living in a time of male barbarity towards women; nothing has changed in more than 2000 years but collectively we the Furies can

134

lead you, the Sisters of Chiomara to avenge the violation of women across the world.

Tisiphone

Links: Chiomara   The Furies   Lucretia

Apart from an outright call to kill rapists that diatribe was as blatant an incitement to murder as Sperring had ever come across.

'Have you read the welcome page yet?' she asked Pullman.

'Just finishing,' he replied. 'Quite a vitriolic little piece,' he said when he'd finished, 'but does it break any laws sufficiently to warrant prosecution? Need to check that out with the CPS.'

Part 2 of the Serious Crime Act 2007 includes three offences of intentionally encouraging or assisting an offence; encouraging or assisting an offence believing it will be committed; and encouraging or assisting offences believing one or more will be committed.

Section 59 makes incitement to commit a crime a criminal offence. No doubt the flames would have been stoked by comments on social media sites which have been known to whip up frenzied activity such as Britain's inner city riots of 2011. Social media is quite frequently cited as the catalyst for suicides and the incitement to commit acts of terrorism throughout the world.

'But before we worry about that,' he said, 'we need to find out who these self-proclaimed Furies are. I don't suppose that'll be very easy either.' Pullman suggested that Lynne continue reading the site whilst he started the ball rolling with CIF on locating the authors and sources of the Facebook page and the location of the Twitter feed. 'This is a bigger job than you or I have the knowledge to do. I'll talk to Pointer and see what we can sort out.'

Pointer said that he didn't have the authority to involve any more personnel; Pullman would have to speak to David Overend, Director of Organised Crime Command to whom he had been seconded. Pointer said he would email Pullman a contact list.

Sperring went through the Sisters of Chiomara site section by section:

135

News

The tab opened a drop down menu which had two options; Crime News - this section contained page after page of reports of alleged rapes and sexual assorts from all over the planet. There were quite literally hundreds of them which more or less ran in chronological order. In many cases the alleged attackers were named and shamed whether or not police had made an arrest, charged or released anyone or exonerated the accused. The second option was surprisingly entitled Retribution – and featured countless postings concerning the unsolved murders of many of the men featured at some time or other in the first section.

Sperring clicked on the Crime News tab. She scrolled through the reports until she located a report on the allegations made by Gemma Maxwell and Angela Carson against Thomas Wethersby. The story read:

Rapist Goes Free

A paedophile teacher who raped two 15 year old girls in their classroom has not been charged by police due to a 'lack of evidence'. The rapes took place at Howden Sixth Form College in East Yorkshire where Thomas Wethersby preyed on the girls over a period of 6 months. Loner Wethersby abused his position of trust to commit his heinous crimes and has left the innocent children traumatised and psychologically scarred for life. Wethersby of 14 High Street Clipton has been allowed to walk free to commit further sexual assaults because of the CPS's unwillingness to believe the distraught girls. How many more times will this monster rape before a victim is believed and he is held to account for his crimes. We must not let one more girl suffer at the hands of this evil creature.

Wow, thought Sperring, that's how to crucify an innocent man. No ambiguity there. No implication of doubt; no concerns with facts or indisputable proof; just get the bastard. Even gave his address; but was this one story enough to incite someone to take the law into their own hands? It was certainly a story that could possibly push someone with homicidal tendencies over the edge; to go way beyond the law but were vitriolic rantings of an anonymous vigilante enough to incite someone to murder?

Sperring continued to scroll through; attempting to locate an article on Josef Kulkinski and found what she was looking for way back in an entry dated April 9th:

The Vilest Man in Britain

Polish immigrant Josef Kulkinski is a sexual predator, rapist, child prostitute trafficker, drug dealer, blackmailer and murderer but he still walks free on the streets of Britain. This vile creature was sentenced to 18 years imprisonment for his crimes, yet police let him escape while being transported to Barlinnie prison, in Glasgow to begin the jail sentence that would keep him off the streets. The police have made no attempt to recapture this piece of filth which begs the question; who is being paid to keep it that way? Someone must know which sewer this rat is cowering in. It's time he was made to pay for his crimes and time to make sure he can never repeat them. It is time for retribution.

The piece was accompanied by three photos of the fugitive, two of which showed him with accomplices. Again the article did not actually say go out and kill this man — but it might just as well have done because that's what the murderer presumably took it to mean. Locating Kulkinski had obviously not been easy if it had taken almost 9 months for the murderer to strike. Sperring didn't know, nor could she have known, that the time had been spent getting close enough to the target to carry out the crime.

Josef Kulkinski had gone into deep hiding after he escaped from the security van taking him to prison. The escape had been made easier by Gerry McCarty the officer in charge of the vehicle who yielded to threats to his family by the Pole's henchmen. No violence had actually been inflicted on the family members but McCarty had been shown photos of the thugs alongside his wife and children to demonstrate how easy it would be to harm them. Following the trial there wasn't a single person in Glasgow, indeed the whole of Scotland, that didn't know what violence Kulkinski was capable of inflicting personally or ordering to be done from the confines of a prison cell. McCarty complied as instructed and got a severe beating in the process; carried out to convince his colleagues, police and the public that he was not involved in the escape. They were all convinced at the time and remain convinced to this day. He still bore the scars on his face and chest from the assault. Kulkinski took a great deal of sadistic pleasure from his work.

The Pole's mini crime empire continued to flourish even though he himself remained out of the public eye. Police raided several of his clubs, brothels and gambling dens without success. As they shut them down so, like weeds, another sprang up. Still the child prostitution, trafficking in Eastern European women and drug dealing continued unabated. He considered himself untouchable but two women had other ideas.

Avril Jura and Tanya Belman as they called themselves became lap dancers at one of Kulkinski's dens of iniquity named the Kicius Club in the Bridgeton area of Glasgow; Kicius being Polish for pussy. Situated in a three storey warehouse building it was furnished with black vinyl chairs and settees set out around small tables in private booths. Drinks were available from an unlicensed bar providing bottled beer, spirits and overpriced inferior sparkling wine posing as Champagne. The club did not adhere to the national smoking ban but the clientele were not the type to complain. On the first floor were the working rooms. The second floor had been purposely left empty in order to create the impression that the rest of the building was vacant.

The third floor had been expensively converted into a luxury penthouse style apartment for Kulkinski with a private entrance and a private exit that led to the rear of the building. A corner of the apartment had been partitioned off to make an office area which contained an array of CCTV screens allowing him to keep an eye on the goings on below. The main living area was furnished with a white leather U shaped sofa configuration facing an unpainted red brick wall on which a fifty inch plasma TV had been mounted. The bedroom was dominated by an enormous Emperor sized bed, winged by two bedside cabinets displaying oversized solid brass bedside lamps. A wet-room had been installed to the left of the bed and a walk in wardrobe to the right. The wall space over the bed was filled by a lithograph of Made in Heaven by Jeff Koons on which the artist's head had been replaced by an image of Kulkinski himself.

During the conversion a false wall had been installed along the windowless side behind which was a two metre deep space providing a priest hole where he could conceal himself in the event of a police raid. Kulkinski never left the apartment. He had confined himself to a five star prison cell with all mod cons and a stream of women on tap until the day he would be able to walk the streets again.

The Kicius Club was frequented by men from all walks of life seeking sexual gratification for their perverted fantasies. For them the club was not just providing a rich seam of perversion at which they could mine their desires, it was a veritable Klondike. For the right price Kulkinski provided every sexual deviance known to man including on one occasion so called 'snuff' sex for a group of six slavering men who quite literally, over a period of forty-eight hours, continuously gang raped and tortured a young Serbian girl to death. Her charred remains were found on Glasgow Green two days later having been dumped there by the Pole's 'cleaners'. Collectively the customers had paid nine thousand pounds to commit rape and murder; it was very lucrative for Kulkinski but he never let it happen again; not for altruistic reasons but because if it became too popular it would deplete his livestock. He did, however plan to make additional money selling the video tape they were unaware was being made of their horrendous crime; after he had finished blackmailing them that is.

Jura and Belman had cover girl looks and Baywatch bodies and they knew how to use both to great effect; Kulkinski had watched the girls perform their routines several times via the CCTV, before he gave instructions for them to be brought to his apartment, as the girls had hoped he would. They made themselves special to the Pole and virtually lived with him in the apartment for several days until they had gained his confidence; after almost week of satisfying their host's sexual cravings they decided the time was right to fulfil their goal.

Jura and Belman went on a shopping trip ostensibly to buy some new sexy lingerie and to buy him a special surprise. When the women returned that evening they were carrying several bags from fashion stores and Belman had a brand new hat in a large round hat box. Kulkinski, who was preparing to take his habitual 6 o'clock shower, asked where his special surprise was, Tanya Belman told him that he'd get it after his shower. As planned Jura joined him in the wet-room; she was prepared to be with him one last time.

Kulkinski came out of the wet-room he was naked save for a towel wrapped around his waist. Belman posed provocatively at the foot of the Emperor sized bed; dressed only in her new blue silk lingerie; a lacy transparent bra, matching thong and suspenders with lace topped stockings. Kulkinski was pleased with what he saw and dropped the towel to the floor, saying it was time for his special surprise. Jura had emerged from the shower and carefully picked up one of the solid brass lamps. Belman said the surprise was behind him; as he began to turn Jura brought the lamp crashing down on his skull; he went out like a light.

They rolled his lifeless body onto the bedside rug and dragged him through to the living area. Jura opened the concealed entrance to the priest hole that he had shown them during one of their many vodka marathons and between them they dragged him and the rug into the space. Once inside Jura retrieved a folding camping saw from the hat box and they took turns in sawing through his neck; when the sawing commenced he was merely unconscious, not dead. It took them almost ten minutes to sever the head completely during which time they vented their repulsion of their victim with a series of foul mouthed tirades. Job done, they wrote SOC on the brow of his head before placing it in a plastic bin liner and putting it in the hat box. They then closed the priest hole and each took a shower to rinse off the copious amounts of blood from their bodies. After dressing they left via the private exit taking the hat box with them along with the master copy of the 'snuff' video that the Pole had taken pleasure in making them watch. They had no idea when, if ever, his body would be found neither did they care. Kulkinski, the team of private builders who had since returned to Poland and the two women were the only people who knew the secret bolt hole existed.

Jura and Belman returned to their own flat on the other side of Glasgow. Belman slipped into a pair of jogging bottoms and matching hooded running top; she strapped her breasts down with a sports bra. She then fixed a bushy black beard in place with make-up artistes adhesive and Jura drove to George Square where Belman hired a taxi to deliver the hat box and contents to Barlinnie Prison; in the deepest baritone voice she could muster she told the cabbie it was a present ordered by the prison Governor for his wife's birthday.

The two women were confident that as long as they kept their own counsel no one would ever know the facts surrounding the killing of Josef Kulkinski.

Did his death make any difference to the world in general? No. The day he disappeared his entourage assumed he'd become disillusioned with life in the apartment and decided to skip the country with the two women. A day later when his head was found and his death confirmed, a short and bloody battle for control of the late Pole's organisation ensued; a new boss emerged and it was business as usual.

****

The Retribution tab of the web site opened with 'hot off the press' news of the death of Josef Kulkinski. Sperring noted that it was reporting the death of Kulkinski as if it was by natural causes. As she read other reports she realised that none of the reports in this section mentioned the word murder or killing unless it was a direct quote from

141

a police media statement. There were reports from Malawi, Singapore, New Zealand France, Belgium, Thailand and Macedonia then she found the case of Thomas Wethersby in Britain. It simply stated:

Tuesday 8th October
The decapitated body of Thomas Wethersby the British teacher who raped two 15 year old pupils in his charge was found yesterday in the coastal town of Bridlington in East Yorkshire, England. The head was located outside the law courts in the nearby city of York and bore the identifying initials SOC.
Transferred to Tartarus.

Sperring checked back over the previous reports and noted that each one specifically mentioned decapitation; the SOC initials and ended with Transferred to Tartarus or a variation. That seemed to be a very clear message as to how the murders should be carried out by describing the key identifiers and finishing with their ultimate destination in Tartarus; the home of the Furies in Hell.

SIXTEEN

Friday 18th October

Sperring had exhausted the midnight oil studying the Sisters of Chiomara web site. She had been copying numerous pages and articles and pasting the information into new Word documents to create her own more easily accessible files.

She created a potential targets file from relevant postings concerning men cited as being responsible for sexual assaults on women from the non-contact psychological assault of stalking to violent rape. In most postings the allegations were unsubstantiated but nevertheless identified the accused by often quoting names and addresses; in some instances adding an image. Her rationale was that if they could identify the prime targets of attention then maybe they could avert the escalation from libel to murder.

The SCAS analysis of the newly gathered additional reports of SOC cases had highlighted clusters of murders around various cities and conurbations across the world. It stood to reason that there was a greater propensity to kill in those highlighted areas; so if they concentrated on cited potential victims in those locations they could possibly work with the local police to watch and guard the targets with the aim of apprehending the culprits in the act.

Amongst the targets was an Indonesian tuk tuk driver alleged to have assaulted a British tourist on her way to the airport; a South African businessman accused of child rape; a group of Malaysian men from the same family accused of the multiple rape of two Australian backpackers; a serial paedophile in Germany; and several allegations against mainly Afro-Caribbean and Hispanic men in the USA.

In the absence of a chat room facility on the site it was the Forum that provided the most evidence of incitement to murder as well as

143

statements of intent to murder. The section was prefixed with a disclaimer by the anonymous web master: *the views expressed in the forum are the private postings of individuals and do not necessarily represent the views of the Sisters of Chiomara. We reserve the right to remove any posts that we feel are unsuitable.*

From the language and subjects used by the forum users there was obviously very little that the site deemed to be unsuitable. Following one thread led Sperring through pages of posts calling for the death of a serial rapist in the city of Xalapa in Mexico. The posts were explicitly calling for an avenger to kill Miguel Hernandez who had thus far escaped justice. Those messages were answered by a post attributed to someone signing herself Vengador claiming that she had been a victim of the man, she called Diablo, and that he had been executed for his crimes by herself and her brother. Sperring cross referenced the claim against the list of killings in Mexico that Pointer had produced but there was no mention of the murder claimed to have been carried out by the self-proclaimed avenger. The list wasn't definitive, of course but it crossed Sperring's mind that maybe some of the claims were more likely to be statements of bravado than fact. However it appeared as if Tisiphone believed the claim because the last post in the thread was attributed to her and simply read:

Miguel Hernandez; Transferred to Tartarus

****

On her way to the office Caroline Nichols had decided that she really had to stop butterflying once and for all and clear one thing at a time before flitting on to the next subject. The previous day she had been actively working on the Peter Ebingdon disappearance. She was looking at the home life angle and promised herself that before she spent one more minute on the SOC story she would complete the research on Ebingdon; she kept her promise.

Having pretty much drawn a blank on Ebingdon's background she chose to come at the problem from his wife's angle.

144

Until her twenty-fifth birthday Tamara Bell-Sampson had an unenviable reputation as a habitual party animal. Her outrageous behaviour at nightclubs in every major city and at international social events was the stuff of legends. Now at the age of just twenty-nine years old, the woman who was once widely regarded on the social scene as an airhead was the Chief Executive Officer of BSCyber the digital communications arm of BS Communications Group wholly owned by the Bell-Sampson family. To the socialite scene she once represented the face of a spoilt little rich bitch but within BSCG she was now highly regarded by almost everyone who worked with her. Tamara's understanding of the world of digital media was considered second to none as indeed was her work ethic. She had driven the company from a minor player in internet communications to fourth behind Apple, Google and Microsoft with an estimated value of $230 billion; an estimate that the family neither confirmed nor denied but which US revenue sources believed to be accurate. The company's growth had come mainly from emerging economies with healthy market shares in Asia, particularly the Indian sub-continent, Central and South America and in South Africa where they were the dominant brand leader. Tamara had achieved this on her own abilities the fact that she got the job because she was the only child in the family was incidental.

Caroline had little difficulty in digging up reams of media coverage concerning Tamara's business and well publicised social life but found it much more difficult to uncover details of her home and family life, particularly her early life in South Africa. Information on the WikiPeople site, which would need verifying, said:

Tamara Bell was born on the 2nd April 1985 at the Monument Hospital Cape Town South Africa to Anna Marie Bell born 2nd January 1968. Father not stated.

Anna Marie Bell married George Ronald Sampson on 12th July 1992 at Marylebone Registry Office, London, England taking the name Anna Bell-Sampson.

Education: Tamara Bell-Sampson attended Parlettes Preparatory School 1992 – 1996 Sherbourne Girls School 1996 – 2003 Imperial College London 2003-2004.

Married Peter Ebingdon on 18th August 2004.

Currently CEO BSCyber a division of the global Bell-Sampson Communications Group.

If this information was accurate then Caroline now knew that Tamara was born in South Africa and her mother was just seventeen years old at the time; that sometime between 1984 and 1992 they moved to the UK and Anna Marie married George Sampson. Could he have been the father? Tamara went to private schools and ultimately University but only stayed for around one year. Knowing her current reputation it was quite possible she was sent down for some reason.

Caroline logged onto the BSC group website>About Us>Our Founder. There was to be found a brief potted history of the now global conglomerate:

Our founder George Sampson started the Mighty Sampson Video Production Company in 1982 in studios in Wardour Street in the Soho area of London, to produce music videos for the fledgling MTV music channel. Such was the success of the video productions that Mighty Sampson soon moved on to produce TV shorts and commercials for leading international advertising agencies.

Within 5 years the company had grown exponentially with studios in New York, Los Angeles and Cape Town and gained a reputation for outstanding creative and production quality. During this period the company changed its name to Sampson Productions and turnover had grown from a few thousand pounds to over £10 m ($16m) per annum.

In 1989, Anna Marie Bell, CEO of the Cape Town office, moved to the UK to run the organisation alongside the founder.

In 1991 George Sampson was quick to spot the commercial potential of the new phenomenon that was the World Wide Web and created a division of the company he called Universal Web.

In 1992 George married Anna Marie Bell and the company changed its name, once again, to Bell-Sampson Communications.

146

In 1993, when the World Wide Web was free for everyone to use and develop, BSC was ready to launch a browser application under the brand name WWWOW! That would compete directly with Microsoft's Internet Explorer. Concurrent with this development an Internet Service Provider (ISP) division was formed as WebLynka, now used by tens of millions of people around the world to access the internet. Subsequently the browser was also branded as WebLynka.

Today the Group, which remains a privately owned family business, operates more than 180 companies in over 31 countries across the globe; employs almost 40,000 people world-wide and has a turnover in excess $230 billion (£144 b).

Well that seemed to verify some of the WikiPeople site information and explained why Anna came to London. They were probably getting it together in Cape Town before she moved. So George probably didn't go to South Africa until he set up the studio out there which meant it was unlikely that he was Tamara's biological father.

Caroline typed Anna Marie Bell into the search engine and the results were instant.

Anna Marie Bell (born 2nd January 1967) former South African athlete who took British Citizenship in 1984 in order to compete at the Los Angeles Olympics. She won a silver medal in the 400 m hurdles. She retired from athletics for medical reasons in October of the same year. [See Bell Family Tragedy]

In 1992 she married George Sampson and became Chief Operating Officer of BSC Group based in London. She has a daughter Tamara.

Caroline clicked on the Bell Family Tragedy link. It was short and to the point:

Roland Bell, his wife Amanda Bell and their 11 year old son, Russell were killed yesterday (February 21st) when the vehicle in which they were travelling careered off the road between Wolmaransstad and Klerksdorp, South West of Johannesburg. Police are trying to establish why Mr Bell, a wealthy businessman from Cape

Town, and his family were travelling to the predominantly black area. Anna Bell, their surviving daughter, who won the silver medal in the 400 metres hurdles at last year's Los Angeles, Olympics for Great Britain was staying with relatives in Mossel Bay when the accident occurred.

Caroline wondered why Anna had taken British Citizenship; it didn't take long for her to ascertain that in 1984 South Africa was still practicing apartheid and was banned from taking part in the Olympics by the United Nations from 1962 until the 1992 games. She had a vague recollection of an athlete called Zola Budd doing the same thing. She checked the dates of the Los Angeles, Olympics to find that they took place between July 8th and August 12th in 1984. Tamara was born on the 2nd of April the following year which meant that Anna Marie may well have been pregnant during the time the games were taking place. No wonder she had to retire on 'medical grounds' and pregnancy might also explain why, fortunately for her and her unborn child, she wasn't travelling with her parents when they were killed.

SEVENTEEN

The video conference call was set for 11 am Pointer and his colleague, Tom Nerbis, from CIFT at the London end with Pullman and Sperring responding in Leeds. After the obligatory salutations they got down to business.

Pointers opening remark was, 'That's quite an interesting site.'

'You could say that,' was Pullman's response.

'Probably the most blatant incitement to commit murder I have ever come across,' said Nerbis.

'And me; makes Abu Hansa seem like a voice for moderation. The problem as far as I'm aware,' said Pullman, 'is that website content is illegal if it threatens or incites hatred of a person or a group of people. If Sisters of Chiomara incited violence based on race, religion, sexual orientation, disability or transgender then it could be considered to be committing a hate crime. But, and it's a big but, do rapists, perverts and paedophiles fall into any of those groups? I'm not so sure. If doesn't could we make a prosecution stick?'

'So what can we do about it?' asked Sperring of no one in particular.

'Well I guess we can try and close it down and find the owner while we debate the finer points of the law,' said Pointer.

'How do we do that?' asked Pullman. 'This technical stuff is way over my head I'm afraid.'

'Over to you Tom,' said Pointer.

'Well we've done the easy part; we've traced the registrant of the domain name through the Whois records. It was registered way back in two thousand and five by a Geheim Schatten with an address in Dusseldorf. Any of you speak German?'

'I can count to ten, recite the days of the week and tell you that I don't speak German - Ich spreche kein Deutsch,' said Pullman.

149

'That's about the extent of my linguistic ability too,' said Nerbis. 'I am however reliably informed by a colleague that Geheim Schatten can be translated as secret shadow.'

'Nice alias. What about the address?' asked Pointer.

'Doesn't exist,' replied Tom Nerbis. 'The thing is there's an organisation called ICANN – Internet Corporation for Assigned Names and Numbers – that oversees each company operating as a domain name seller. Those companies are required to ensure that they hold accurate records of the owners of domain names so that you or I can check them out on the Whois database. To comply with the requirements, all those registration companies have to do is contact the owner – that's the original person or organisation that registered the name – supposedly on an annual basis and ask them if the details are correct; if they are then the owner needs do nothing.'

'Pullman understood something for once. 'So am I right in saying that no one really checks up if the details are still correct; they just take registrants word for it.'

'Yep, that's right but the real problem is no one checks if they were right in the first place.'

'So we've got little chance of finding the true identity of this Geheim Schatten then.'

'More chance of finding the Holy Grail.' Said Nerbis

'Okay that's a blind alley so is there anything we can do?'

'Well under RIPA we can, in theory, do quite a lot.'

'Sorry to interrupt,' said Sperring. 'Ripper is?'

'The Regulation of Investigatory Powers Act 2000; R, I, P, A.' Nerbis replied with a hint of subdued surprise in his voice that Sperring needed to ask the question.

'Yes of course, sorry it just didn't flick the switch,' apologised Sperring. Pullman was glad Lynne had asked because it hadn't connected with him either and he wasn't going to risk losing face by asking the question. Problem was that there was so much legislation brought in by successive governments and the EU it was just not possible for a general police officer to keep abreast of every law which came into being especially those involving technical cyber-crimes. Nor was it possible to remember every acronym.

'But you said in theory?'

'That's right,' said Nerbis, 'Under RIPA we can demand that the internet service provider, in this case Weblynka, supplies us with the full details of the site operator's location, contact details etcetera but whether that's meaningful depends on how sophisticated the operator was when the site was established. We've had instances where the site has been routed through so many proxy servers that not even the originator knows where they started from.'

Pullman had heard the term proxy servers before but had no idea what they were and what effect they may have on the investigation; as he probably wouldn't understand the explanation either he just nodded to indicate understanding where there was none.

Nerbis continued. 'We occasionally hit a brick wall when the ISP is in a country that doesn't adhere to international protocols and the ISP just puts up the shutters, just won't listen to the request. Ironically when the shutters go up it's normally in a country with a restrictive regime that controls and monitors the internet usage of its citizens in any case.'

'So are you saying that if the service provider is in a country that doesn't like us it can just put up two fingers and tell us where to shove our request?' said Pullman.

'Unfortunately that's right. Unless the issue is threatening world peace or involves international terrorism in which case we can to try to persuade the UN to apply pressure through diplomatic channels; especially if it's a threat to our friends on the other side of the pond. That's between these four walls by the way.'

Pullman wanted to say that it was between eight walls but instead asked Nerbis, 'Does that apply to Weblynka?'

'No it's one of the good guys but it doesn't mean we'll be able to locate the operator with any less difficulty.'

'Where are we with the social media sites?' asked Sperring.

'They too have to give us the information but to register with them you really just need an email account. You can supply a false name and address and have an email account that again bounces all around the planet. You'll have no doubt seen a movie or two where some boffin is sitting at a computer trying to locate an online address and you see a screen with red lines pinging all over the globe, well that's how it is for us in reality. So none of this will be easy but we'll do our best. If that doesn't work we'll ask for an interception warrant so that we can examine the contents of all communications going into and out of the internet and social media accounts. Alternatively we can demand that Weblynka fits our monitoring equipment to do the job.'

'Aren't all emails and search engine enquiries automatically monitored?' asked Sperring.

'Good heavens, no. There's only so many emails that GCHQ can read in a day,' answered Nerbis with his tongue planted firmly in his cheek.

'Why is it then that when I send an email about something specific like, say, I email my long lost aunt that I'm buying a new sofa, the next time I go to send an email I get a pop-up on the screen for sofas. Are you telling me that my emails aren't being read?'

'Not by humans they're not. All the search engines and email providers have robots or spiders that crawl over your emails or search entries and pick up key words so that they can….,' Nerbis made speech quote marks in the air, '…send you information relevant to your needs or interests. That's how they make their money.'

'Back to the matter in hand, gentlemen,' said Pointer bringing the session back to order. 'CIFT are doing their bit to trace sources, I'm doing my bit in continuing to gather data on these crimes and you, as the investigating officers, are hopefully gathering the evidence from the web site etcetera so that when we do finally identify the culprit you can make a prosecution stick.'

Sperring informed the meeting of her current process of intelligence gathering. Pullman said he was working alongside Lynne and was sure that they would be ahead of the game when the shit hit the fan. It wasn't quite the right expression to use but the group understood his meaning.

Nerbis said that his team would continue working over the weekend. He suggested that Pullman and Sperring journeyed to London on Monday morning to meet a colleague and discuss what they had managed to pull together in the two days. It was agreed that they would catch the first available train.

****

Mark arrived in the Newzferret office unannounced and much to Caroline's surprise, 'What are you doing here?'

'Wait till you hear what I've got to tell you,' he said.

'Couldn't you have called me? Not that I'm not pleased to see you. How comes you can leave the paper?'

His meeting had been cancelled. It was a slow news day and besides which he couldn't wait to tell her what the paper's obituary team had stumbled across. 'Will you stop asking questions and listen,' he said. 'I came over here because what I've got to say can't be risked over the telephone and certainly not on email. We can know it but we mustn't repeat it or we'll have…'

Caroline interrupted him abruptly. 'What is it?'

'Peter Ebingdon, who, as we now know, isn't really Peter Ebingdon was actually born Robert Langdon Cruickshank West,' he paused for effect, 'he's the cousin of……' he looked at her with a come on have a guess look and holding his hands out, palm upwards.

Caroline realised immediately. 'From your implied drum roll I'm assuming it's not Timothy or Mae so I'm guessing it's Fred.'

'Give the lady a cigar; he's the cousin of Fred West. Apparently the Langdon comes from his paternal grandmother's maiden name and the Cruickshank from his mother's maiden name.'

'If my middle names were Langdon Cruickshank or I was the relative of sadistic murderer I think I might have wanted to change my name too.'

153

That wasn't the sole reason Bob West changed his identity. His cousin Fred West was one of Britain's most notorious serial killers. Over a period of twenty years he was accused of torturing, raping and murdering at least thirteen girls and women although he told police the count was up to thirty victims. He was aided and abetted by his second wife Rose who was also charged with killing Fred's four year old daughter from his first marriage. The couple were brought to justice in 1994 after Gloucester police began an investigation into claims that Fred had abused and subsequently murdered his own daughter, Heather. A murder that both he and Rose initially denied but police investigation and some digging in the garden discovered her remains, and those of other victims, buried under the couples patio; Fred later confessed to ten murders.

Bob West was initially implicated in the crimes but he denied ever being involved. His fingerprints and DNA were found at the house but this was explained away by him having stayed there on numerous occasions. There was no forensic evidence linking him directly to any assault or murder and the CPS agreed that in exchange for giving evidence against Fred and Rose he would be given immunity from prosecution and a completely new identity.

It was a win-win situation for the CPS because they would never have enough evidence to proceed with a prosecution against him. Fred was charged with eleven murders and then a twelfth but hanged himself in prison before he came to trial. Although his cousin never had to give evidence the CPS kept to their side of the bargain and in January 1995 Robert Langdon Cruickshank West disappeared without trace. He was not called to give evidence at Rose West's trial at which she was given a whole life prison sentence for ten murders.

Mark said, 'There was no evidence to implicate Bob West in the crimes but there's no smoke without fire as the saying goes. I'd be amazed if he could have been in that house and not known what was going on.'

Mark was an impressionable twelve year old boy when the case hit the headlines and influenced him in his choice of career as a crime reporter. He had since covered several major serial killers including the notorious Harold Shipman, the Manchester GP convicted of fifteen murders. An official report later concluded that the deluded doctor had killed between two hundred and fifteen and two hundred and sixty people between 1975 and 1998. At his trial in 2000 Mark was a reporter at the Manchester office of the Guardian working alongside his mentor Bill 'Sniffer' Jackson the papers senior crime reporter. Mark enjoyed his current job, most of the time, but he still maintained a keen, some would consider unhealthy, interest in serial killers and secretly held a desire to be a modern day Poirot or Holmes. Over the years Mark had collected dozens of books on exponents of multiple murders, from Jack the Ripper to Steve Wright aka "The Suffolk Strangler" an Ipswich taxi driver who killed five women over a six week period in late 2006. The SOC murders and the intrigue around Bob West/Peter Ebingdon were riveting diversions for Mark.

'As I said, we can't use the information because of the new witness protection laws and probably the personal privacy laws too although I haven't checked that out with our lawyers yet. Neither must we spread the information, at least not in any way that's attributable to us.'

Caroline gave him a naughty child look as if to say maybe I might not be able to contain myself.

He recognised the look. It was one she had used many times before to get her own way. 'No seriously; we can't use the info; we might get away with it if it was deemed to be in the public interest but I'm not sure that just exposing him for the sake of it would meet the criteria. So do not, repeat not, do anything until we can at least get his side of the story. I'm serious.'

'And how do you propose we do that?'

'I propose that you and I have a romantic weekend in Austria.'

'That's a nice idea,' said Caroline, 'but to what end.'

'That's where he is.'

'I thought he was in Czechoslovakia.' Would she ever get used to calling it the Czech Republic?

'He was but Paul's contact at DFZ told him that our man is now in Graz in southern Austria, so do you fancy a weekend break?'

EIGHTEEN

Saturday 19th October

British Airways flight BA0696 touched down on the runway at Vienna as scheduled at 10.50am local time on Saturday morning. Mark had booked the only two seats available on the flight. They were the more expensive business class which he had wanted to avoid given that the airtime was less than 3 hours and he was paying for them out of his own pocket. But they would be tax deductible.

Mark's original thought was that they could take an internal Austrian Airline flight down to Graz but the flight times meant that the next scheduled departure was at 17.25pm that afternoon; the previous flight having departed half an hour before their Airbus A320 was scheduled to land. Whilst it would have been nice to have spent some time in historic Vienna he wanted them to get to Graz as quickly as possible as he had no idea how easy it would be to locate Peter Ebingdon.

Of the three onward travel options of bus, train and car hire he opted for the flexibility of the latter. It took them no time at all to clear customs. They had only taken hand luggage which meant that they avoided the bane of all air passengers - hanging around at baggage reclaim waiting for the carousel to spring into life.

It took less than half an hour to sort out the car hire before they were on their way down the A2 toll road en route to Graz. The journey involved a little over two hours non-stop driving to cover the two hundred kilometres plus a further twenty minutes to locate the Hotel Weitzer where Caroline had booked a room online. She booked it despite, or maybe because of, the hilarious translation of the room and facility descriptions. This was probably more to do with the online translator than the hotel itself but nevertheless it amused her immensely. They parked in the multi-storey next to the hotel and had a light lunch after checking into their clean and comfortable room described on the website as; *there is bathroom with bath and separate shower, comfortable seating areas, exotic plants and a mute servant, annoying clothing from Keeps body. All this as I said in addition, that is the equipment to the Classics.* It had lost a little in translation.

They had struck lucky with one of only two rooms in the hotel with a balcony overlooking the Schlossberg. It was now 3.10 pm and the Hotel Ibis, where they had been reliably informed Ebingdon was staying ,was a little too far away to get to on foot so they called a cab for the six minute journey by road. Neither of them had ever met Peter Ebingdon but they had his photo on their smartphones, taken by Mark's colleague Rutter when he met Ebingdon in Prague.

They couldn't enquire at reception for his room number because they had no idea what alias, if any, he was using so they opted to sit in the coffee bar in the hotel lobby from where they could see the entrance and the lifts. Not many guests moved through the lobby, neither were there many other customers in the coffee lounge which made their presence all the more noticeable. Mark had displayed growing impatience throughout their wait and the copious amounts of caffeine were doing little to calm his agitation. Caroline killed time by surfing the net on her tablet courtesy of the hotel's free Wi-Fi point. By 6.20pm they were getting fidgety as too was the hotel receptionist who approached them to enquire if there was anything she could get them. Mark explained their prolonged caffeine intake by saying they were waiting for a friend to arrive. They hadn't expected the receptionist to ask who that might be but she did. Thinking quickly Caroline said their friend had not yet made a reservation but had told them that he was planning to stay at the hotel so they were waiting in the hope that he would show up.

Outwardly the receptionist appeared to accept their explanation and said that she hoped their friend arrived soon as they only had a few rooms vacant. Inwardly she was suspicious and asked security to keep an eye on them; there had been occasions in the past where members of the public had tried to use the lobby as free accommodation. Security was a sixty-eight year old retired bus driver with a prostate condition; he spent more time in the toilet than he did watching Mark and Caroline or anyone else for that matter.

It was 7.20 pm, just ten minutes before the cut-off point they had set themselves, when Peter Ebingdon emerged from the lift. Having told the receptionist that their friend hadn't arrived they could hardly acknowledge Ebingdon. They waited until he reached the revolving doors of the exit before they waved goodbye to the receptionist and gestured, by tapping their watches in unison that they were giving up on their friend. The receptionist called to them that if they would like to leave their names and a contact telephone number she would, tell him that they had been waiting. They felt obliged to comply with her suggestion and invented a name for him. By the time they had done that and got outside Ebingdon was at the end of Neubaugasse turning right onto Keplerstrasse. They chased after him but he had disappeared by the time they rounded the corner. Mark thought he caught site of their quarry in the back of a white 878 taxi as it drove past but he wasn't positive.

At least they knew he was staying at the hotel. They got a cab back to the Weitzer to enjoy the Wiener schnitzel that they had both been looking forward since they landed. What else would one have when in Austria? Mark had the authentic veal recipe but Caroline chose the pork option. She hadn't eaten veal since early childhood when she discovered that it came from baby cows. The fact that the calves were born to keep the milking cows producing hadn't made any difference to her then nor did it now. For a time she had dabbled with being a vegetarian, even a Vegan while at university but the lure of the bacon butty and the burger proved too irresistible. For some reason she ate pork, lamb and beef without any qualms but she still retained a resistance to veal. Mark on the other hand would eat his grandmother if she was sautéed in breadcrumbs.

The following morning they showered and dressed. They made coffee from the equipment and ingredients provided and consumed it on the balcony whilst watching small boats bobbing along on the Schlossberg. The couldn't quite make up their minds if it was the coffee making facilities or the mini bar that was the 'mute servant' mentioned on the web site. Neither of the items had much to say. After breakfast of ham, garlic sausage, boiled eggs and croissants they walked to the Ibis Hotel arriving at 8.45am. It was a dry bright morning with crisp clean air that invigorated them both. They ventured warily into the hotel and were relieved to see that there had been a change of personnel. A male receptionist was on duty and the security man was perhaps thirty years younger than his colleague on the night shift.

Caroline sat at a vacant table facing the lifts. Mark went to talk to the receptionist. He thought he would pre-empt any concerns the staff may develop by explaining their reason for being there. He didn't give the real reason of course. Caroline had ordered coffee which arrived as Mark returned to the table. 'He says we are welcome to wait as long as it takes, which I sincerely hope isn't too long.' It wasn't.

They both had their eyes fixed on the lift doors when Ebingdon walked past in the opposite direction on his way to the reception for his key, having just entered the hotel. This time Mark dashed over towards the reception and as their quarry called the lift he stood next to him and was joined by Caroline. Fortunately the receptionist was otherwise engaged with a guest objecting to the cost of the adult film channel being itemised on his bill.

Caroline glanced at their prey. He looked seedy, almost debauched. His crumpled clothes gave him the appearance of a man who had been out all night, which he had. His appearance was not helped by the dishevelled hair and a six o'clock shadow, which was rapidly becoming a full eclipse; he had an aroma of cheap perfume mixed with whisky and perspiration. He was carrying a large cardboard cup of coffee sealed with a white plastic lid. The lift doors opened and the three passengers entered. They briefly caught his reflection in the mirrored rear wall of the lift. Ebingdon stood at the front of the lift guarding the panel indicating the twenty floors of the hotel, his face to the wall. He pressed the button to light his fourth floor destination then looked over his shoulder at the two other passengers standing behind him and gestured a hand towards the buttons as if to say which floor would you like me to press?

'Four's fine thanks,' said Mark picking up on Ebingdon's meaning.

With the closing of the lift doors the intensity of their quarry's aroma grew stronger. Instinctively Caroline and Mark held their breath, looked at each other and wrinkled their noses with distaste.

Mark, trying desperately not to inhale said, 'Been out all night then Peter?' There was no reaction from Ebingdon. 'Would you prefer it if I called you Robert?' asked Mark.

Ebingdon ignored the question as if it wasn't directed at him. Unseen by Mark, Ebingdon's eyes flicked from side to side as he controlled the urge to turn and face the questioner.

'My name is Mark Carver and this is Caroline Nichols we run a web site called Newzferret, you may have heard of it.' Mark saw no advantage in mentioning his Guardian connection; this was unofficial as far as the newspaper was concerned.

Ebingdon still made no acknowledgement; the lift doors opened and without looking at them he stepped out into the fourth floor corridor, turning right towards his room. Mark and Caroline followed hot on his heels.

'I don't want to cause you any problems,' said Mark as they walked along the corridor.

'Then fuck off,' said Ebingdon.

'Look we know who you really are and unfortunately it won't be long before the rest of the media do too. All we want is your side of the story before the tabloids start making up their own stories.'

'What part of fuck off didn't you understand?' said Ebingdon with as much menace as his tired body could muster and swinging his arm round towards the couple. Caroline thought she was going to get the coffee thrown at her and raised her arms to protect her face.

Mark was not intimidated. 'It's not our intention to put any of this on line; we just want to be ready with the truth in case someone prints a load of fabricated bullshit.'

Ebingdon reached his room, swiped his key card in the lock and went inside closing the door behind him, leaving Caroline and Mark standing forlornly in the corridor.

Caroline called through the closed door. 'Really Peter we're honestly here to help if we can.' There was no reply from inside. Caroline said 'Think about it, if we found you it's only a matter of time before someone else does.' She gave a shrug of resignation towards Mark and he reciprocated.

'When you're ready to talk we'll be in the lobby,' she said. They turned to walk back down the corridor when Ebingdon's door swung open. They took it as an invitation to enter.

Ebingdon was sitting on the edge of the bed. 'Why can't you people leave me the fuck alone?'

Once inside Mark closed the door. 'Peter you can't expect the public not to be interested in why the head of a merchant bank should want to disappear.'

'The public don't give a shit. They don't know who I am and they don't care; only you parasites care. I'm just an ordinary guy who's had enough of the corporate rat race and wants some time away from the merry-go-round. Can't you just leave it at that?'

'But you're not just an ordinary guy though, are you,' said Mark.

'You don't seem to think so,' Ebingdon swivelled his head wearily and rubbed the nape of his neck. His head bowed towards the floor he said, 'Go on then tell me why I'm not an ordinary guy.'

Mark explained. 'We know that you are Robert West; that you changed your identity in nineteen ninety five for reasons which we don't need to go into; that you have built a remarkable new life in the past twenty years; that you have run away from it all and that you don't want your wife to find you.'

It was the last eight words that caused Ebingdon to react. 'Is this some kind of shake down?'

'No,' said Caroline, 'as Mark says we just want to understand your life. Yes we are journalists but we believe in the truth, you might find that hard to believe following Levinson but it's true.'

She sat down on the bed next to Ebingdon and felt that, with anyone else, it would be an appropriate moment to put a re-assuring arm on his shoulder but his body odour was making her feel nauseous besides which the thought of touching this man suddenly gripped her with a feeling of revulsion. A feeling she couldn't shake off; she realised in that instant why the real him would not be accepted by society at large. There would always be a lingering doubt as to his past; what did he know; what did he do? He must have been aware that the public reaction would not be favourable. No wonder he was resolute in protecting his true identity.

'We have nothing to gain by revealing your past. Anything we write you can read and approve before it goes online. I promise you that it will only be used if, and when your true identity leaks out or when....' She was loathe to say the final few words of the sentence.

Ebingdon finished it for her. 'Or when I'm dead,' he said. Caroline did not reply. 'How do I know you won't leak it anyway just so you can use the story?'

Mark was surprised by Caroline's promise. Fortunately she had used the singular pronoun rather than the collective which left him out of the commitment. 'You don't,' he said, 'but we have nothing to gain by doing so, if as you say, the public have no interest in you.'

Caroline stood up and stepped over to open window the window 'Not only might the readers have no interest in you but an exposé of your identity would not be deemed to be in the public interest.' She drew in a lungful of fresh, cool air.

Ebingdon reflected on the situation. What had he got to lose? If he didn't co-operate they might just dig deeper to mine a richer seam. If his change of identity did leak out it would just stir up a lot of suppressed memories and public animosity; it would be another irritant to Tamara. He had hoped this day would never arrive. He stood up and took a deep breath. 'I need some breakfast. Give me twenty minutes to shower and change and I'll meet you downstairs in the coffee shop.' He could see that Mark was looking a little doubtful. 'I will.'

He did; he smelled a whole lot better too. They made small talk about Austria, Graz and the Newzferret website while Ebingdon finished his breakfast and Mark finished his second breakfast of the day.

Caroline showed Ebingdon her hand held digital recorder, it was about the size of a mobile phone. 'Do you mind?' Ebingdon gave a non-committal shrug of his shoulders; she took that as approval, switched it on and placed it in the centre of the table waiting for him to speak.

'Okay... erm where to begin. If you're telling me the truth you'll know why I changed my name.'

Mark said. 'We are and we do but if you don't mind me asking, why did you spend so much time at the house?'

Ebingdon took a moment or two to compose himself. 'Yes why indeed? Hindsight is a wonderful thing but as far as I was concerned it was just my cousin's house, if I'd had any idea what was going on I would not have stayed there.' He leaned forward across the table. 'When you stay with relatives do you wander around their house spying on them? Do you ever wonder that they might have someone chained up in their garden shed? Of course not; they're relatives, why would you?' His pent up anger at being doubted began to materialise, his facial muscles tightened. 'In twenty four years nobody thought to ask Josef Fritzl if he had a secret basement; if he was keeping his daughter prisoner. Did they? No of course not. And the guy in the States who kidnapped three girls...'

'Ariel Castro,' offered Mark, he was very familiar with the case.

'Whoever; did his brothers suspect anything?'

'Not according to them or the police,' said Mark.

164

'Exactly, so why does everybody assume I knew what was going on. I didn't.' He drew a deep breath to calm himself down.

Mark asked, 'You didn't think anything was suspicious, people were disappearing?'

'If your parents or any relation told you that your second cousin had gone to Devon to work, wouldn't you just accept that? You wouldn't say - prove it - would you? Devon wasn't exactly the other side of the world from Gloucester so why should I question what I was told. It was only after everything came to light that I started to remember events that suddenly had a different interpretation. Things that were said took on a different meaning and I realised that I must have been around when some of those things had taken place. I'd actually helped Fred mix some concrete when he was laying the patio.' He stopped talking and took a deep breath as if to free the memories from his mind.

'Were you living in Gloucester at the time?' asked Caroline.

'No, I was staying with my coach at his home in Stourbridge…'

'Coach?' queried Mark.

'Athletics coach. I'd been jumping for Birchfield Harriers, the Birmingham club, you've heard of them?' His inquisitors nodded. 'I'd been with them since I was fourteen which was a bit awkward as my parents lived, and still do live, in Folkestone; well my mother does, Dad died about fifteen years ago.'

Mark wanted to ask why he was training in Birmingham it was a fair way from Folkestone but he let it pass.

'So it was felt to be to my advantage to stay with my coach's family when I was sixteen in preparation for the Olympic selection trials, he acted as my chaperone as well. The triple A were very keen that anyone under the age of eighteen had a chaperone.'

'Did you make the team?'

'Yeah,' he said dismissing the feat with undue modesty, 'youngest ever British long jumper to take part.'

'When was that? Asked Caroline, she'd been reading up on the games just two days prior to the conversation.

165

'Eighty four, eighty eight and I was selected for the ninety two games but events overtook me and I was dropped like a sack of King Edwards. I had a good time in Seoul and would have loved to have taken part in Barcelona but it wasn't to be.'

'And did you like Los Angeles?'

'I didn't make the cut there. I was a bit too young; it was my first time at an international meet and I have to admit I didn't really do myself proud. Anyway that was all a long time ago.' He looked down at his stomach and gave it a pat. 'As you can see I'm not in such good shape these days; too many corporate lunches.' He paused, flicked his eyes from side to side, as a memory stimulant. 'Where was I?'

'You were saying why you visited the house,' Mark reminded him.

'Oh yeah, Gloucester is only an hour away from Stourbridge so I used to go down there just for a break from training and from Gerry's strict regime, he was a hard task master. Fred would let me have the odd beer.' Ebingdon seemed to be getting more relaxed with the situation and feeling relieved to be talking about the past.

Mark asked, 'What was it like inside the house?'

'I'm not going to discuss it any further. It was twenty five years ago and those days are long gone. I am a different person now, quite literally. Anyway I shouldn't have been blackmailed into giving evidence, there was nothing linking me to those crimes. Then Fred committed suicide so I didn't have to give evidence in the end but I was still given the new identity. I went to live in Edinburgh. I had a nose job; my ears pinned back, changed my hair colour, grew a beard and wore plain lens glasses. Even my own mother didn't recognise me when I attended my father's funeral. That's my greatest regret; I couldn't attend the funeral as myself. I had to watch my mother grieving without comforting her, without supporting her. Now it's too late; she's in a care home suffering from dementia – doesn't even know her own name. I've been there and talked to her, she thinks I'm one of the carers when I'm there and forgets I've been the moment I leave.' He looked genuinely sad as he looked down at his empty coffee cup.

Mark and Caroline remained silent while he regained his composure.

'As I said I moved to Edinburgh. I had already been studying business management at Aston Uni for a couple of years so I enrolled at Edinburgh and finished up with a first class honours degree. I wheedled my way on to the graduate trainee programme at the Royal Bank of Scotland and was rapidly promoted up the RBS management ladder eventually moving to London to join the board of DFZ and the rest as they say is history.'

'What about your marriage? When did you meet Tamara?'

'Ah, yes my marriage; not one of my better decisions.' He said with feeling before taking a deep breath to brace himself. 'I met Tam, Tamara, in two thousand and one at some business function or other; think it was a CBI do, no, no it was a garden party at Buck house the first time I met her, then I met her again at the CBI do. She was so young and vivacious; I suppose I was flattered that she found me interesting enough to date. I thought I could tame her rebellious streak. It was a little strange the first time I went to meet the future in-laws because I'd already come into contact with her mother through athletics.'

'She competed at the eighty four Olympics.'

'Mmm you have been doing your research. Yes she joined the GB team after getting British citizenship. The story didn't quite make the same headlines over here as Zola Budd but then Anna wasn't supported by a national daily. Her defection for want of a better word, sort of slipped under the radar.'

'Did you meet her in Los Angeles as part of the team?'

He looked down at the table. 'Not that I recall. The track athletes tended to stick together as did we field athletes. My relationship with Tam raised a few eyebrows at first, me being about the same age as her mother and Tam being just turned eighteen. Mind you I was only thirty five myself; it's only as one gets older that the age gap becomes more apparent.'

Ebingdon drained his coffee cup and went to the buffet counter for a refill. Mark took the opportunity to nip to the toilet. Ebingdon returned to his seat and when Mark returned he resumed where he had left off.

'Her mother was very attractive too; they could easily have been taken for sisters. Tam and I saw more and more of each other. Anna was not happy about it, to say the least but the more she tried to dissuade Tam the more she stuck her heels in and decided that we should get married. Yes, *she* decided; it was like I was on a fast moving conveyor belt and couldn't get off. At that time she was studying computer technology or something along those lines at Imperial College. After the first term she left and we got married. It should never have happened. You obviously know about the parties and the binge drinking and there were recreational drugs but we managed to keep her short experiment with hard drugs away from the media.' He looked at each of his companions and asked, 'We did didn't we?'

Caroline said, 'It was common knowledge but as it was quite a short period it never seemed worth reporting. She was doing enough other newsworthy stunts at the time.'

'Yes she certainly was, I couldn't keep pace with her. She went out sans Peter, as she put it, frequently; sometimes she'd be gone for days at a time. No doubt there were affairs or flings but by that time our marriage was more or less over, if indeed it ever really started. Then suddenly she decided to stop socialising; to resurrect our marriage and start a family. It was if someone had turned off a tap. Instant.' He clicked his fingers. 'Just like that; to this day I don't know why.'

'Caroline tried to sound concerned. 'But you didn't.....have children I mean.'

'No. It was great fun trying, Tamara was a great ....' He curtailed the sentence. 'But we weren't hitting the target, as it were. Tamara was impatient so last year we went to a Harley Street clinic; one that the family had used for years; we did all the usual tests and each of us had a full MoT. The results showed that she had POI, Primary Ovarian

Insufficiency; her ovaries simply didn't produce eggs. Once we knew that, I didn't need to look at my results. I have this thing about not wanting to know if I'm going to die; couldn't cope. If I've got something fatal the coroner can tell my descendants at the inquest when I'm not listening.'

He averted his eyes from Caroline and looked down to his left at nothing in particular 'But I was completely unprepared for what happened next; she had another complete change in personality. She became verbally violent towards me said things like she would cut my balls off and boil them in oil if I ever came near her again. She wouldn't let me comfort her, not even touch her. The vitriol got increasingly more macabre. I couldn't understand her attitude; it wasn't my fault she couldn't conceive yet somehow I became the focus of her anger and frustration. She buried herself in her job twenty four seven almost to the point of obsession. BSCyber took over her life. Her days were spent online and her nights too. I tried to see her on several occasions but it was like approaching an angry Cobra; she hissed and spat venom, so I had to leave.' He raised his eyes towards Mark, 'I moved out, took an apartment in the Barbican but she kept threatening me until the situation deteriorated so much so that I had to get away from it all before she carried out one of her threats. I prefer my testicles raw. That's why I'm here and that's why I don't want her to find out where I am.'

He sat back in his seat looked up at the ceiling and exhaled forcefully. 'That's all folks. There you have the potted life story of Peter Ebingdon ex CEO of DFZ Global.' Silence reigned while Mark and Caroline absorbed the story. Caroline switched off the recorder.

Mark broke the silence. 'What will you do now?'

'Pretty much up to you I guess. With your permission I'd like to stay Peter Ebingdon, I'd like to stay as far away from the family as I can and I'd like to stay alive.'

'You don't need our permission.'

'Perhaps permission is not the right word, I need you to forget this meeting; forget what was said and forget where we are. Do you think you could do that for me?'

'As I said at the outset, we will not repeat a word unless someone else prints or broadcasts inaccurate information, in which case we will only use what you've told us today to put the record straight.'

'I'll hold you to that. Now if you'll excuse me I had a late night last night and I intend to have another tonight so I need to go and study the inside of my eyelids.'

Ebingdon stood up and shook hands with Mark and then Caroline who again felt the same feeling she had experienced in the bedroom earlier. She excused her noticeable shudder by complaining of a chill draft; in reality she couldn't get past the real person behind the mask. Ebingdon made his way to the lifts; Mark paid the breakfast bill and Caroline felt an overwhelming need to visit the ladies room to wash her hands.

Peter Ebingdon entered the lift alone, pressed button 4 and stood looking in the rear mirror; as the doors silently closed behind him. A broad, smug smile spread across his face. God he was good at this. He had convinced the police of his innocence all those years ago, he was sure he had now convinced his latest interrogators.

Without any spoken agreement to do so Caroline and Mark walked back towards their hotel on auto pilot. They had strolled several hundred metres without speaking, each mulling over the interview in their own minds until the silence was broken by Mark. 'Well what do you think?'

'He gives me the heebie geebies,' said Caroline. Mark gave her a questioning look. 'Because I know who he is, deep down I can't help thinking that there's more to this than he's telling us. There's no logical reason but I just don't buy the story; something's telling me that he's not telling us the whole truth.'

'Your feminine intuition again, I suppose.' Mark put his arm around her shoulder and gave her a comforting hug as they walked. 'Tell you what let's forget him for now. We'll have a wander around

170

the old town, a nice romantic dinner and an early night.' He gave her a telling wink. 'We've got an early start back to Vienna in the morning.'

Caroline stopped walking, put her arms around Marks waist and rubbed noses Eskimo style. 'Would you mind if we went to Vienna this afternoon and found somewhere there to stay tonight. The rest of it sounds like a very good idea though.'

She did not want to spend another night in the same city as Peter Ebingdon. Mark didn't have a problem with the suggestion. At that time of the year they shouldn't have a problem finding a hotel and they might just get there in time for a fleeting visit to the Hofburg Palace. In any case they would have had to check out of the Weitzer at silly o'clock in the morning to get back to Vienna airport in time for their 7.40am return flight.

So that's what they did.

NINETEEN

Monday 21st October

Pullman and Sperring were sitting in Pointers office anxiously waiting to get the meeting started. They had caught the earliest train down to London at the behest of the SCAS analyst to discuss the results of the CIF team's efforts over the weekend. Pointer was pouring four coffees including one for Tom Nerbis who was running a few minutes late; as he poured he updated the investigating officers on the current situation with the murder tally. A further seventeen had been identified that fell within the so called SOCrates paradigm. Of those nine were cold cases and eight had occurred within the previous week, two in India, one in Bangladesh, two in Nigeria and three in Moldova.

Tom Nerbis arrived with lap top in hand and a colleague in tow. 'Morning everyone; let me introduce Colin Mahone, one of my colleagues. He's going to explain where we're up to so far.'

Pullman and Sperring introduced themselves whilst Pointer poured a fifth coffee. And Nerbis connected the lap top to the projection system.

'Over to you Colin.'

Colin Mahone was short. Maybe five feet maximum thought Pullman who at first hadn't noticed the hump on Mahone's back, a condition caused by congenital kyphosis; an abnormal development of the vertebrae during foetal development. He had grade one cropped hair and a patchy attempt at a goatee beard. His white shirt was unbuttoned at the neck and he was wearing a tie with a Windsor knot almost as big as his head, the tail of the blue and red striped tie finished halfway down his chest. Here was a man who had no interest in how he looked; he'd grown up being ridiculed by his peers for his

172

lack of height and his hunched appearance. He'd listened to taunts of *'the bells, the bells'* and *'hey Quasimodo where's Esmeralda?'* for as long as he could remember. The jibes had hurt deeply during his childhood and adolescence but as he matured he had come to terms with the situation and had long since ceased to care what anyone else thought about his appearance. He compensated by having become a British Chess Grandmaster whilst at university and by being exceptionally good at his job. He could have been an international Grandmaster or maybe even World Champion but his fear of flying, motion sickness and loathing of being buffeted in crowds restricted his ambitions to home territory. Standing at the table to operate the laptop he was still shorter than those seated.

'Okay lady and gentlemen. Whoever it is that's behind the Sisters of Chiomara web site they have a very sophisticated network of proxies and firewalls.'

'You said whoever is behind the site, so we still don't know then?' said Pullman.

'No Mike we don't and it's possible we won't be able to find out either. We will discover the operator's location, we will discover the source but we will not be able to identify the specific person responsible. That will undoubtedly come down to your skills as a detective to identify the actual culprit.'

'We're in trouble then,' said Pullman with a self- deprecating smile.

'The master server is somewhere in Indonesia, which as you know consists of some seventeen thousand islands.' He wagged a finger in the air, 'But we have narrowed it down to an area between Sumatra and East Timor. Which is easy to say but a hell of big area to search as you can see from this map.' He brought up the map on the screen 'As Corvus corone would know it's about two and a half thousand miles between the two places.'

'Who's Corvus Carone?' asked Sperring much to Pullman's relief once again.

'Not who, but what; it's the Latin name for the crow. The distance is two and a half thousand miles as the crow flies,' said Mahone very pleased with his superior ornithological knowledge. Being able to manipulate conversations to include facts which he knew but others didn't and had no reason to know, was one of the few pleasures he had in life.

Sperring had saved Pullman's face once again as he had assumed Mahone was referring to a contemporary of Columbus or Magellan.

Mahone continued. 'In turn that means that we are currently examining an area of some four million square miles. Not something you'd want to cover on foot.'

No you'd get wet you supercilious prick thought Pullman then immediately felt guilty that he'd mentally insulted the diminutive expert.

'In any case finding the server will not necessarily find the culprit. The site could just as easily be managed from Papua New Guinea as Sumatra.'

'So all of this you're telling us is a waste of time,' said Pullman.

'Absolutely not; the server is buried deep within Weblynka one of the world's largest ISPs. It takes an extraordinary level of access to achieve that complexity of concealment; I'm of the opinion that someone with inside knowledge and senior authority within the Weblynka Asian network is the most likely operator of the site.'

Pullman thought for a moment; he had to risk the chance of humiliating himself. 'I'm no expert but why couldn't someone with the level of access you refer to, be able to operate from downtown New York, Beijing or Milton Keynes for that matter?'

Mahone's brow furrowed as he thought for a moment or two while he digested the suggested locations. 'No reason at all. My thinking is simply that as we've narrowed the proxy server down to that region then the most likely scenario is that the originator is there too but you could be right the operator could be right on our door step for all we know. In fact it could even be me.'

174

'No,' said Pullman, 'our man is definitely a woman.' He realised how ridiculous that sounded as the words left his mouth; he smiled at his own stupidity. 'What I mean is the person we're looking for is a woman or women. The whole Furies thing, the Sisters of Chiomara the vitriolic language used. This is definitely about misguided belief that these murders are justifiable retribution for injustice to women.'

'What about the social media sites, have we got anywhere with them yet?' Sperring directed her favourite question at Mahone.

'The accounts use false names and addresses and false email addresses but once again all connected to a patchwork of servers and locations involving Weblynka. Facebook and Twitter both offered to take down the sites but we've told them not to.'

'Good. That would have tipped off the culprit. We need to keep them operating until we locate them.'

'That's what we thought too.'

Pointer leaned forward and rested his elbows on the table, his fingers interlocked in clench fists under his chin. 'Could I make a suggestion Mike?' It was a rhetorical question, he continued without waiting for a response. He released his two index fingers from the interlocked mesh and tapped them on his lips. 'I'd like to repeat my response to a question you asked me the very first time we met.' Pullman looked at him with head cocked to one side waiting for the big reveal. 'Take a look out of the window.'

Pullman remembered. 'At the big pointy tower?'

Sperring smiled. 'Of course BSC own Weblynka.'

'They do indeed. Colin was right, the culprit could literally be right on our doorstep,' said Pointer.

Pullman was suddenly angry with himself for not placing greater emphasis on the phone calls made to Gemma Maxwell and Angela Carson. In the euphoria of finding the Chiomara connection, the website and the social media accounts he'd side lined the one concrete fact they had; someone with access to the BSC comms dock made those calls. That person called themselves Tisiphone and that would undoubtedly be the same Tisiphone that ran the web site. What a plank he was! They hadn't been into the office since Friday so it was possible that the list had arrived in the mail but now it had taken on an even greater priority. 'Lynne shoot over to our friend Laura Green at BSC and get a copy of that list, in fact get two and don't take no for an answer.'

Sperring rose from her chair and left the room. An imaginary light bulb illuminated over Pullman's head. A thought had suddenly occurred to him, without explanation to the meeting he jumped up from his seat and he chased after his DS.

'Lynne. Lynne.' She stopped in the corridor and turned to see her boss approaching her rapidly with the swinging gait of a long distance race walker. He ran the last few paces so would have been disqualified. 'I've had a thought; there are about four hundred names on that list, we can't possibly interview them all agreed?' Sperring nodded emphatically. 'So get a breakdown of their movements in October. We'll make the initial assumption that whoever made the calls did so from the UK, probably made them from the office. Anyone who was out of the country when the girls received the calls is unlikely to be on our list of suspects that should narrow down the field a bit.'

'Okay, on top of which, we're only interested in the woman on the list anyway so that narrows it down even further,' added Sperring.

'With a bit of luck there'll only be one name left.' He wished.

Lynne turned to continue her walk.

'One other thing, it would make sense for us to work down here for a day or two. Do you have any problem with that?'

Sperring shook her head. *As long as we have single rooms she thought.* 'No', she said.

'Okay. I'll get that sorted, you get the list.'

Pullman's temporary boss David Overend was in Poland with John Hickson, Director of the new Border Policing Command setting up an NCA office out there. They were then going on to Nigeria, Vietnam, China and Albania where further offices were being established; the idea being an attempt to stop people trafficking at source. General consensus was that it would be an exercise in futility. With Overend out of the country, Richard Pointer agreed to have a word with his own boss to find some temporary desk space for the investigating team. Wi-Fi internet access was not an issue nor was hardware. Something that could be an issue was hotel accommodation so Pointer arranged for the NCA travel section to make the necessary arrangements for two, budget priced single rooms, which in London, at short notice, was not going to be easy.

Pointer looked wistful. 'It's a pity we aren't still located in Bramshill we had over three hundred bedrooms in that house and some vacant staff cottages; could have put you up there for as long as you liked. Loved it down there; a nice easy fifteen minute drive to the office from home in Basingstoke. Now I have an hour and a half on the train and a tube ride too.'

A change of clothing was the only other issue. Pullman was in need of a couple of new shirts and a new suit too if it came to that; he'd only bought a few casual clothes since the funeral and colleagues were beginning notice that he was not keeping up his normal standards of sartorial elegance. Sperring should get by with only having to buy a blouse and maybe some underwear he decided on her behalf. They would manage; it wasn't much different from working through the night on a case and they'd both done that often enough in the past without worrying about their appearance. It wouldn't be the first time he'd washed his jockey shorts and socks in the hand basin then placed them on a radiator to dry overnight. The hotel would supply the shower gel and shampoo so they'd just need to pick up a toothbrush and a tube of toothpaste each.

A sandwich lunch arrived on a stainless steel trolley pushed by a middle aged lady in a white hygiene coat and white pill box style hygiene hat.

'I wish we could get SOCO to deliver our lunches in Leeds,' Pullman joked. 'Mind you we'd probably get spleen rolls and grilled brains.'

177

That was a nice pleasant image to put out there prior to lunch. The pusher unloaded the contents of the trolley into the centre of the meeting table, leaving the thermal coffee jug and tea pot on the trolley alongside several bottles of still mineral water and the cups. She seemed pleased with the display and asked if they required anything else. A quick scan of the sandwiches, wantons, samosas and bowl of fruit before them resulted in negative response from the four men. They thanked her and began filling their side plates before she had left the room.

'Been meaning to ask you Richard, if you'd dug up anything on the Tarquin murders in the States that we mentioned at our first meeting?'

'It would appear that there is nothing to dig up. The two murders have a similar MO but are quite separate. Our friends over the water say that they are pretty sure the two women they arrested committed the murders and that they were working together, alone, if you get my meaning. As I said earlier there have been a number of SOC murders in the States so I reckon the killers were just stamping their own identity having possibly got the basic idea from Sisters of Chiomara.'

'Do the NYPD know we've identified the web site?'

'We certainly haven't told them and frankly I see little reason to do so yet; makes a change for *us* to have something to keep from *them*.' It wasn't just payback time for all the occasions when the police authorities in the States, including the FBI, have kept information to themselves but Pointer really didn't feel there was any mileage in broadcasting the information at this stage of the investigation. The fewer people who knew they were on the trail of the Sisters of Chiomara the better; it would be very easy for the operators to shut up shop and disappear without trace.

'They're very sparing with the sharing of information.' said Nerbis joining in on the conversation. 'The special relationship,' he almost hissed the words, 'seems only to be special in one direction. I've lost track of the number of times we've worked tirelessly to uncover an internet trail to an organised crime syndicate only to find the FBI,

LAPD, NYPD or some other bloody PD have been camped out on the site days or weeks before us.'

'Perhaps now you're the National Crime Agency they'll give you a little more respect.' said Pullman.

'*We*,' corrected Pointer.

'Speaking French now?' Quipped Pullman.

'Now *we* are the NCA. You're on the team too,' Pointer reminded him.

'Pro tem for this one case only,' replied Pullman.

'Is that what they told you?' said Pointer letting out a slight chuckle through his naval cavity. 'Trust me, now they've got their claws into you you'll soon realise that you are part of the team; as long as you don't mess up of course.'

'And we won't let you do that.' said Mahone without turning his attention from his laptop which he hadn't ceased playing with since the meeting began.

Pullman had definitely not considered the secondment to be permanent but would he have any real objections if it was? Probably not, he usually went with the flow. It could actually be good for his mental state. Enough people had advised him to get away from the memories in Hessle. Was London the answer? Jane's family still lived here. He'd grown up in the suburbs and they both had friends around the area. It was as much home as anywhere was ever likely to be again. Deep down he knew that he would find it incredibly difficult to sell their house but maybe the time was right. His instincts were telling him that it was too soon to leave the memories behind but maybe the events of the past couple of weeks were meant to be. Future cases would no doubt be a lot more interesting than investigating car thefts; small time drug dealers and the occasional suspicious death that usually wasn't. He didn't know if they would want Sperring or what she might think about it if they did; she was intelligent, ambitious and a good detective in her own right so there was no reason to think that she'd pass up on the opportunity. He decided he wouldn't mention it for the time being.

Pointer interrupted Pullman's thoughts. 'Got you thinking has it? Pullman just smiled in reply.

Sperring returned within the hour to join them for what remained of the sandwich lunch. Her choice was Hobson's. Fortunately she quite liked egg mayonnaise and rare beef with Dijon mustard. She had two copies of the printed list of the four hundred and seven people who had access to the phone pool together with a copy of the file on a BSC branded memory stick. She gave a copy to Pullman and showed him the stick. 'I thought it would be a good idea to have the info on editable file as well, so we can manipulate the data,' she said.

Pullman nodded appreciation and raised his thumb in the time honoured manner; he couldn't speak because he had a mouthful of crisp green Gala apple. 'But I haven't got the list of personnel movements through October. Laura was very reluctant to get it done to the point of being obstructive. So I told her that if it wasn't available to me by four pm I'd get a warrant and we'd remove all of their personnel records. She changed her tune then and said it would be ready if I went back at four.'

'So you'll be there at three thirty then.'

'Absolutely,' replied Sperring.

****

The return flight from Vienna got them into Heathrow at 9.40am. They took the Piccadilly line underground train rather than a taxi. At a mere five pounds, the cost of the tube train was anything from thirty to fifty pounds cheaper depending on how long they would have been standing idle in stationary traffic with the meter running. A fiver each got them to their destinations in under an hour. Caroline disembarked from the train at Earls Court and changed to the District line for Putney; Mark carried on the journey into King's Cross from where he could walk up York Way to his office.

Caroline called in at home first to shower and change. It had been an early start and she didn't want to travel with damp hair, so she forewent showering in the hotel. They had avoided discussing their

180

interview with Ebingdon during the rest of their brief stay in Vienna. Mark got a very clear sense that Caroline was reluctant to do so. Not wishing to upset her and spoil his romantic ambitions he decided to drop the issue from the conversation. It worked.

They did however discuss the subject whilst waiting for their flight when they could do so in relative privacy of the Air Lounge at Vienna airport, over a complimentary coffee and croissant. Caroline took the opportunity to once again express her unease with Peter Ebingdon. 'It's not that I've got anything concrete, it's just a general feeling. Call it intuition if you like but there's something about him that I just don't like or trust.'

'So you said, nobody likes bankers these days.' quipped Mark.

She ignored the comment. 'I can't quite put my finger on it but.....'

Mark said. 'If it's his background then you know what they say – you can choose your friends but you can't choose your family.'

Caroline wasn't condemning the man for his family connections. No one should be held accountable for the actions of relatives or tarnished with the same brush but still she felt that there was more to this man than he was letting on or that she had so far discovered. Whilst they hadn't discussed it the previous night, at any length, she had thought about it and had determined that she would carry out further investigation into his past.

'I'm trying hard not to prejudge him and I know you think women's intuition is fluff and nonsense but it's worked for me in the past.'

'Oh yes, when?'

'When I met you darling,' she smiled and patted his hand. 'Despite all the terrible things people said about you and my friends trying to dissuade me from seeing you, my intuition was that under that gruff exterior was a man I could love.' She was winding him up and he knew it well enough not to take the bait. 'I'm sure I'll find him in there one day.'

'I must admit that it does seem strange that a grown man, a high level businessman to boot, should be so afraid of his wife that he would skip the country rather than face up to her or get a divorce. That bit I don't get.'

'Exactly why would he do that? He must be independently wealthy so I wouldn't have thought it was a financial issue. If he was intimidated by her close proximity he could take out a restraining order, he could even hire himself a bodyguard if it came to that. I don't know what he's hiding but I'm sure there's something and I intend to find out what it is,' she said with a firm tone.

'I don't doubt that,' said Mark. 'Don't doubt it for a single moment.'

She started to carry out her intention as soon as she booted up her PC on entering the office. The issue niggling her went way back to the 1984 Olympics. Ebingdon said that he didn't really know Anna Bell at the time. This despite the fact that they were pretty much the same age, were both new to the British team and would have travelled together. Surely the team would have mixed. Athletics was athletics whether it was field or track; there wouldn't have been any delineation between the two as far as the team management was concerned. He admitted that he "hadn't really done myself proud." What did he mean by that? Was it just his poor performance or was there a Freudian admission of something else? She surfed the net for any information about the Los Angeles games; there were thousands of pages covering the event but a quick skip through the page indexes showed that most just covered the Zola Budd change of citizenship and paid scant attention to that of Anna Bell; there was some coverage of the actual games themselves; the results of the numerous events but nothing that was anything out of the ordinary which could shed light on her anxiety.

She called Mark explained her failure to find articles of interest and asked him if it was possible he could search the papers archives and see if there were any reports relating to Ebingdon and Anna Bell at those Olympics. He reluctantly agreed to put someone on to it even though he felt that he was now beginning to over use the papers resources for what was really a Newzferret story. He just hoped there might just be a story in it for the paper at the end of it all.

Within an hour Caroline received an email from Mark. It read:

Struck lucky. Attached is an article we ran way back in 84. Can't find any follow up articles.

Disgrace at Olympics

The British Olympic team have dismissed reports that a number of our young athletes were involved in an alcohol fuelled party in the athlete's village at the Los Angeles games. Rumours circulating suggest that athletes from a number of competing nations including the USA, Canada and Germany were also present at the party which, according to one source, developed into "a Bacchanalian orgy reminiscent of ancient Rome". Simon Honeydew, the recently appointed British team manager said "We believe that the conduct of a few of the younger athletes did fall below the high standards we expect. We are talking to all those concerned and will deal with the matter within the terms of our disciplinary procedure."

If Peter Ebingdon or rather Robert West, as he was then, had been involved in the party then his admission that he hadn't really done himself proud was somewhat of an understatement.

TWENTY

The hotel in which Pullman and Sperring had been booked was part of a national chain; the kind of budget hotel guests stay at for one or two consecutive nights at most. The style of the hotel buildings changed dramatically from city to city but this was by far the grandest Pullman had visited. Occupying a prime position in Pimlico in London's Victoria area it was a five storey Georgian building. The interior décor was very familiar to Pullman; he and Jane had frequented the hotel chain on many occasions. The familiarity did nothing to help him have a restful night sleep.

He met up with Lynne Sperring in reception; neither of them took breakfast each settling for a large mug of coffee before setting off on the walk to their temporary office. It was a cramped windowless room with just sufficient space for a desk, chair and laptop each. Pullman looked around the rabbit hutch and was not a happy bunny; he'd put convicted criminals away in better accommodation than this. Hopefully he and Sperring would only be in the cell for a few days. If nothing else it was a great incentive to get the case cleared up at the earliest opportunity. He booted his laptop, placed the memory stick into a USB port and opened the Excel file titled Communications Dock Authorised Users. The file contained two documents; a list of names and a separate file of contact details.

Sperring booted up her laptop and inserted the memory stick containing the assignment schedule of the Comms Dock users that she had eventually picked up at 5.35pm the previous evening. They both saved the respective files to their hard drives before starting to manipulate the data.

The list of users was in alphabetical order; some with full forenames others with just initials before the surname. Pullman scrolled down the list eliminating all the male names. This left him with sixty-three female names and two that he judged to be ambiguous – Chris and Gill; Chris could be Christine or Christopher and Gill could have been pronounced like the girl who went up the hill with Jack and therefore be female or like the breathing organ of a fish in which case it would be a male. He thought that it was sure to be a female but didn't want anyone to slip through the net at this stage.

He read out the names to Sperring who checked them against her information. After a little under an hour they had whittled the list down to fifteen possible suspects who were female; had both access to the pool of phones and were not away on assignment at the time of the calls to the girls in Howden. In the process they also eliminated Gillian Scott who was, after all, a female. Pullman printed off two copies of the list.

'Right here we have our final fifteen. And in a few minutes we'll have the addresses of each one. Now while I'm doing that can you think of any other criteria we can use to reduce the list a bit further?'

The address list wasn't linked to the alphabetical file so he had to copy and paste each of the fifteen contact details.

As requested Sperring was thinking, with little success. Obviously they would run a criminal record check when they had the addresses sorted. The girls hadn't mentioned if Tisiphone had an accent or regional dialect but until they interviewed those on the list, they wouldn't know either.

Pullman interrupted her thoughts. 'As well as a DBS run a check to see if any of them have reported being assaulted – if Tisiphone is bearing a grudge then the likelihood is she's been a victim.' Pullman spoke whilst he studied the list again. 'I've just realised something, Laura Green isn't on this bloody list and we know she's got a widget, ingot thing.' He found her contact details and phoned her.

'Hello Laura, DCI Pullman here. Fine thanks. This list you supplied, I notice you're not on it.'

He listened then said in his best head teacher voice. 'I see, right when I asked for a list of everyone who had access to the phones I meant everyone including managers. So would mind emailing me a complete list of additional people including managers, post room boys up to the Managing Director; everyone means everyone. No, I want it now. Could I remind you Ms Green that this is a murder enquiry and I would appreciate your co-operation. That's very kind of you. I look forward to receiving it,' he replaced the receiver and banged his fist on the desk. 'Jesus H Christ' he exclaimed. He mimicked a female voice. 'I didn't think you would want senior people, are we suspects then?' In his own voice albeit slightly raised in volume. 'I think she's being deliberately obstructive. Check her out first.' It was more in spite than expectation. Then, through clenched teeth, he uttered 'Damn.' He picked up the phone and hit last number redial.

'Hello, it's Mike Pullman again, I forgot to ask you to include personal contact details as before. Thanks', he hung up and as he did so the phone rang immediately.

'If this is her with an excuse…' he let the intended threat fall silent. 'Hello. Yes it is. Oh hello Miss Nichols what can I do for you? Have you, well I'm always willing to listen to something interesting, fire away. Oh, okay of course we can but are you sure it's not something we can do over the phone? A recording. Okay, your place or ours?' He remembered his surroundings. 'Tell you what we'll come to you if that's alright. We're in London for a day or two actually so any time you like. Okay sure why not?' He checked his watch. 'Shall we say twelve thirty? We'll bring you in a sub then we can talk over a bite.' It wasn't chivalry, not having had breakfast he knew he'd be hungry by midday. 'Great…. erm… what would you like? Consider it done. We'll see you at twelve thirty then. Look forward to it.' He hung up and said to Lynne Sperring, 'That was Caroline Nichols she wants to talk to us about something that might have a connection to the case. Can't do any harm besides I hate being cooped up in this bloody airless rabbit hutch.' He had been in that bloody airless rabbit hutch for less than two hours.

****

There was a steady drizzle in Graz as Peter Ebingdon put his valise in the boot of the Mercedes 210 he had hired that morning. The past twenty years or so had taught him not to trust anyone, especially journalists; he certainly didn't trust those particular journalists not to leak his location. He should have known that a man in his position couldn't just disappear without interest from the media. He should have handled it better. Just resigned; waited a week or two until the interest subsided, which it surely would have done, and then he'd have been free from the pursuit of the media and the bank's investigators. Dumb thing to do in hindsight but why they needed to find him was beyond his comprehension. Everything was in order, he'd committed no felony, no fraud; had done nothing wrong that anyone knew about. The bank's trading position was better than it had ever been thanks to his stewardship. Yes he should definitely have handled it better. Now even his past might catch up with him. Bloody stupid.

He planned to drive south along the A9 to Slovenia then take the A1 via Ljubljana to Triest on the Adriatic Coast. A journey time of around three hours, travelling at around one hundred kilometres an hour which, provided the drizzle did not transpose into heavy rain, was well within the realms of possibility. He stopped at the first petrol station he saw; filled the fuel tank, bought a vignette for the Austrian tolls knowing that he'd have to stop and purchase another when he crossed over the Slovenian border. He also bought a bottle of water and some Paracetamol for his throbbing head. A very heavy night of drinking and adult activities that he called fun but others might call torture had left him with the mother of all hangovers. He'd have to watch out for police vehicles and observe the speed limits because if stopped he would be sure to fail a breath test and a subsequent blood test. The fine was affordable but time in custody was something he wanted to avoid. It would take several more hours for the alcohol in his blood stream to be absorbed so he would have to concentrate for the entire journey; the drink drive laws in Slovenia were every bit as stringent as those in Austria.

He sat down in the car seat very gently; his Gluteus Maximus was very tender and the skin red raw from the flagellation inflicted by the dominatrix. She had been very proficient at her job. Probably the best sadist he'd experienced in a long while. The nape of his neck was also chafed where she had over-tightened the gimp mask he wore throughout the session. He was so engrossed in his thoughts and in the lingering pain that he hadn't noticed the black Audi A7 with tinted rear windows that had been with him since he left the car hire office.

****

Pullman handed Caroline Nichols her BLT sub as requested then opened his chicken mayo baguette and pushed the filling further into the centre using the paper bag to protect his fingers. Sperring had a Brie, bacon and grape sub with extra crispy bacon. Their host had prepared a percolator of coffee and suggested that they eat before they got down to the purpose of the gathering but inevitably the conversation swung round to their common interest – SOC.

'Can I assume I'm right in thinking, that you know what SOC stands for by now?' asked Caroline.

'Do we?' said Lynne Sperring, beating Pullman to the question due to him having just bitten off a mouthful of baguette.

'Well I know, so I'm sure you also know that it stands for Sisters of Chiomara.'

Pullman's brow furrowed as he swallowed. 'Did you work that out or did someone tell you?'

Caroline smiled knowingly. 'Come, come Detective Chief Inspector, we journalists never reveal our sources, you should know that.'

Someone must have leaked it to Newzferret. Pointer? He knew Caroline; would he have informed her? Pullman thought it unlikely to be Nerbis or Mahone. Maybe Caroline Nichols knows Miriam

188

Dennaby. No, it was sure to have been Pointer. Whatever, it was only professional curiosity, her knowing would make no difference to his investigation; in fact it might help.

The journalist put her lunch to one side. 'No doubt you have had your experts crawling all over the site.' Pullman made no comment or facial movement to signify confirmation or denial just carried on eating his baguette. Caroline continued regardless. 'Being a mere mortal I have only been able to find out that the site is hosted by WebLynka. I'm sure by now you know a lot more about them than I do however I have a chain of thought that you might not have latched onto yet.' Once again there was no verbal response from either Pullman or Sperring. The only visual response was Pullman leaning his head slightly to the right to signify he was listening. 'Does the name Peter Ebingdon mean anything to you?'

Pullman closed his eyes to help him think. 'Merchant banker who disappeared a few weeks back,' he said.

'That's the guy. Mark and I, that's my partner, have met him and interviewed him.' She involuntarily shuddered at the thought of Ebingdon. 'Sorry about that but for some reason he makes my flesh crawl anyway that's beside the point. He's done a runner because he is in fear of his wife.'

'You said wife; did you mean life?' asked Sperring.

'No I meant wife but yes he is in fear of his life because of her.'

'I see,' said Pullman, 'and you think this has something to do with the SOC case?'

'I do. However we promised Ebingdon that we would not repeat what he told us to anyone but you're not just anyone are you? You're a policeman investigating a murder and if you insist I tell you then I couldn't refuse, could I.'

Pullman understood what she was saying he smiled. 'Miss Nichols I am investigating a murder case and I must insist that you tell me everything you know about Peter Ebingdon.'

'Very well DCI Pullman if you insist then I have no choice. The first part of what I'm going to tell you is fact, the second part is just a hunch, call it feminine intuition.'

'The floor is yours,' said Pullman.

'Peter Ebingdon is not his real name, he changed his name from Robert Langdon Cruickshank West.'

'So would I if they were my middle names.'

'That's what I said when I heard them. Anyway he's the cousin of Fred West and I'm sure you know who he was.'

'How did you find that out then?' Pullman was curious.

Caroline smiled. 'As they say at PM's question time – I refer the right honourable gentleman to my previous answer.'

She went on to explain the reasons behind the name change.

'I remember the West case very well; I was at Hendon Police College at the time. Horrendous, the case not Hendon,' he added for clarity. 'Incredible really that something like that can be going on in a normal urban location and nobody realises. But crimes like that usually surface eventually. What makes you think that he's related?'

She played the recording to them. Pullman and Sperring listened intently as they finished their lunch and drank their coffee.

'Witness protection's worked well then. So what's your intuition?' asked Pullman.

'I'll get to that in a moment. Do you know his wife Tamara? Pullman said he didn't think they did but there couldn't be too many Tamaras about whom Caroline would consider of interest to the case so it was no surprise when she said, 'She is Tamara Bell-Sampson; the only daughter of the Bell-Sampson family and Chief Executive Officer of BSCyber, a division of their communications empire.'

Pullman turned to Sperring 'Damn it. She wasn't on the bloody list either.'

'What list is that?' asked Caroline.

Pullman thought for a moment, looked in Sperring's direction with an expression that implied what he was about to say may seem unethical but bear with me. 'Caroline the rest of this conversation is strictly off the record, strictly; do I make myself clear?'

Caroline confirmed that she understood and agreed not to repeat to anyone but pleaded for Mark to be an exception to what they discussed from here on in, he was her partner both personally and in Newzferret. At first Pullman didn't want her to discuss the conversation with her partner but he knew from experience that it was an impossible ask. She wouldn't be able to keep it to herself any more that he could keep some case details from Jane during their marriage. He was unaware that her partner was also Deputy Editor of a national daily newspaper; he might have thought twice had he known.

Pullman told her about Tisiphone's calls to the two girls. He told her that they had traced the calls to a pool phone at BSC and that they were in the process of interviewing everyone who had access but that Tamara, along with other managers, had not been included on the original list; she was certain to have access to the phones. So this meeting could well have saved them hours of time on unnecessary enquiries. Tamara had suddenly and unexpectedly become a suspect.

'Anything else?' he asked rising from his chair.

'Yes my intuition.'

Pullman apologised and sat down.

'You've heard what he had to say on the tape about the medicals and the reasons for not having a family but I don't believe him. His body language was all wrong. You had to be there to see his eyes; there was something in them that told me he was lying. I was the court reporter for a national daily for a few years and got to know when a witness or a defendant was lying; it gets to be a kind of instinct and hardly ever wrong. I feel strongly that there is more to him than meets the eye. Why would she have been so antagonistic towards him? Surely it wasn't a reaction to her inability to conceive – it wasn't his fault. I think that there's something else involved here. As I say I can't prove anything; it's just my intuition but it's normally pretty good.'

Sperring said 'Female intuition is a very under-rated gift as I frequently prove to my male colleagues.' She gave Pullman a knowing look.

'Did Mark get the same vibe?' Pullman asked.

'Despite all those years as a crime reporter, Mark has the intuition of a water buffalo. No he didn't get the vibe but then he doesn't know when we're having an argument either.'

Sperring snorted trying to contain a chuckle.

'Not that we argue very much so the poor man hasn't had much practice. No really, I think you need to check out Ebingdon's story.'

'To be honest, I don't see how this implicates him in the SOC cases except through his wife's possible connection but we'll check it out just to be thorough.' He stood up again. 'Can I keep this disc? I assume you've got the original'. Caroline nodded. 'Thanks for thinking we'd be interested. How was Austria by the way?'

'Beautiful, we've promised ourselves we'll go back there one day.'

'Not been myself but I hear Vienna is stunning.' He felt sad for a fleeting moment. Vienna was one of those capital cities he and Jane had planned to visit.

****

Pullman checked his emails as soon as he returned to the office. Laura Green had sent the additions to the list. He read through the seven names. 'Surprise, surprise Tamara Bell-Sampson isn't on the list.' He immediately picked up his mobile and called Laura Green. She was not at her desk so they put a call out for her on Pullman's insistence.

While he was waiting Sperring said 'I was thinking sir, all the people on this list are correspondents, photographers, cameramen etcetera but what about the techies, the ones who set up the Xingot system and maintain it they must have access too.'

She was right of course and Pullman was even angrier now with Laura Green even though he now only had Tamara directly in his crosshairs. When she eventually came to the telephone he tore into her and before ending the call left her with the clear understanding that if he discovered one more person who should be on the list but wasn't he would charge her with perverting the course of justice; it was an idle threat but one he enjoyed making.

Sperring mockingly admonished her boss. 'I hope you haven't gone and upset her again. She is pregnant you know.'

'Is she? I didn't notice. She's old enough to look after herself.'

Pullman wanted to arrange to speak to Tamara but didn't want to ask Green for contact details having just threatened her; he redialled the main switchboard. He was put through to Tamara's PA who told him that her boss was in a meeting. Could she ask what it was in connection with; he told her it was a routine matter to do with the disappearance of her husband. That was common knowledge and a perfectly feasible reason for the interview. The PA said that she would talk to her boss when she came out and get back to him with some possible dates. Pullman told her that he didn't want dates he wanted to see her by noon the following day at the latest or at any time in between.

Pullman checked in with Colin Mahone to see if he had moved any further forward. He hadn't. All Mahone could do was confirm that whoever was operating the site definitely had full access to the WebLynka system. The depth of hidden layers to the web site route could only be achieved by someone inside the organisation he reiterated. He told Pullman that it was like mining at the moment; he was down at the coal face chipping away and would eventually hit the main seam. It wasn't very PC but Pullman had a mental picture of Mahone crouching in a low tunnel with a pick and shovel in his hands singing Hi Ho with the rest of the dwarfs. It was an image that projected onto his mental screen on several occasions during the remainder of the day and would be a feature length two reeler when he was trying to get to sleep that night.

True to her word the PA got back to Pullman within the hour; Tamara would see him at 2.30pm tomorrow afternoon. What part of before noon tomorrow didn't she understand? He didn't respond to the obvious put down, he could bide his time besides he didn't want to seem so anxious that it would spook Tamara. He agreed to the time and to the place being her office.

In the meantime Lynne Sperring had been on the police computer system trying to check up on Ebingdon but access to the files on Robert West was denied; leading her to believe that the story of his identity change was true. There was no other reason to deny her access to the files had he just been treated as a suspect or ordinary witness. She knew she would not be granted access so there was no point in applying besides neither of them was convinced his identity had any bearing on the case.

There was a missing persons report filed by DFZ but apart from his name it was merely marked NFA – No Further Action – although within the force most officers replaced the Further with another seven letter word.

She contacted the British Olympic Association and UK Athletics but neither party could shed any light on events concerning West at the Los Angeles Olympics other than to have a record of medal winners. She was put through to the Chief Executive of UK Athletics who explained that although they had taken over seamlessly from the British Athletics Federation in 1999 they had not kept files on matters of disciplinary action or reviews prior to 1992. To be expected really, twenty years was a sufficiently long period to keep such files, particularly on matters that might place competitors and the association in an unfavourable light.

Census checks found no other Ebingdon family members other than the not so happy couple. Checks on ancestry sites failed to locate any past family members. It appeared that the name began and, given the fertility problems, would end with Peter.

Sperring didn't want to contradict Chesney Hawkes but Peter Ebingdon was the one and only.

TWENTY-ONE

Wednesday 23rd October

Pullman entered the familiar reception area of BSC Towers alone. He had decided that this interview did not warrant both he and Sperring attending. His decision was based on the belief that Tamara would be more at ease if not confronted by two interviewers for what he was trying to portray as a routine matter. The neon lights were still twinkling on the map behind reception but the receptionists were now seated behind a brand new high tech chrome and glass barrier guarding the inner portals of the communications empire. He was asked to take a seat and told that Miss Bell-Sampson's PA would be with him shortly.

He took a seat where he could see the lifts, they were constructed of glass on the exterior of rising columns, so could actually be seen from anywhere in the reception area. He sat and glanced around whilst reflecting on the receptionist referring to Tamara as Miss Bell-Sampson. She could have dropped the Mrs Ebingdon, since the marriage rift but more likely she had never used her married name in business. As he waited he mused that many married women chose to retain their maiden names in their chosen careers. Many successful business women and celebrities were unknown by their married names.

Somehow the names Angelina Pitt, Lauren Bogart or Elizabeth Hilton/Wilding/Todd/Fisher/Burton/Burton/Warner/Fortensky didn't quite have the same ring as Jolie, Bacall or Taylor. On the flip side, would Margaret Thatcher have had the same gravitas as a world leader if she had chosen to remain Margaret Roberts? Eva Braun never had the opportunity to be known as Eva Hitler; which was probably a good thing for her. Would history remember Anne Boleyn quite so well if she had changed her name to Anne Tudor? Jane had chosen to become

195

Mrs Jane Pullman when they married rather than remain Jane Bullock. Now she was the *late* Mrs Jane Pullman – no he wasn't going to allow himself to go there.

He tried to change his train of thought and immediately Mahone sprang into his mind. It was an image he couldn't shake off. He picked up a copy BSC World magazine he'd read on his previous visit and began flipping through it when he noticed a Titian haired, thirty something nearing the ground floor in the lift; she stepped out and walked towards him. She looked as if her pillar-box red skirt had been sprayed on and her crisp black shirt fitted in all the right places; now that was a better vision. She introduced herself as Gretchen Sarcophagus; at least that's what her surname sounded like to Pullman who felt it too impolite to ask her to repeat it. Gretchen would suffice, if the situation arose where he had to call her anything at all.

Gretchen asked Pullman to follow her as she set off, hips swinging, Beyonce like towards the lifts. It was then that that the realisation of what was coming next hit Pullman; he was going to ascend in a glass coffin.

He had an abject fear of heights. As a child his mother had instilled in him that he suffered from vertigo which she, like most people, wrongly classified as a fear of heights. As he found out in later life vertigo has nothing to do with heights per se; you can suffer the dizzy spells associated with vertigo whilst standing in the kitchen. What he had was acrophobia which caused him to panic and perspire when at any height above a few inches; even standing on a chair to change a light bulb was, for him, a terrifying experience. As a child he had a recurring nightmare in which a second him floated out of his body and experienced extreme anxiety as it looked down on the first him. The anxiety expanded as the lower him looked up at the elevated version; complete panic ensued as he fought the force of levitation to return to his body before he woke up or he knew that he would be dead. Whether it was the frightening dream that caused the acrophobia or vice versa he had no idea but fortunately he no longer experienced the problem; in fact he could no longer recall at which point in his life it had stopped.

The panic he felt getting into the lift was real enough. Beads of perspiration bubbled from his brow; his throat dried up and he couldn't swallow. A hot flush wafted over him; his breathing rate increased and he closed his eyes in an attempt to both control the fear and to avoid looking down from the lift as it reached the fourteenth floor. They left the lift much to his relief and walked the short distance to the office; as she turned to usher him into the room she noticed his predicament for the first time.

'Are you alright Chief Inspector?' she asked with genuine concern.

'I'll be fine,' he croaked, 'must be something I ate.' It was an excuse he had used many times before in similar situations.

'Would you like some water?'

'Wonderful, yes please.'

She went to a state-of-the-art water dispenser that was lit up like Cape Canaveral in launch mode. 'How would you like it; hot, room temperature or ice cold?'

For Christ's sake as long as it's wet who gives a shit is what he thought in his tetchy state of mind. 'Cold would be perfect,' is what he politely replied. She bade him to take a seat but he chose to stand, in a minor show of pointless childish defiance.

The outer office was clearly created by some minimalistic trendy designer, not very functional but beautiful to look at just like the lovely Gretchen, seated behind a desk top that appeared to have no visible means of support. Set into the glass wall opposite the floating desk was a horizontal row of digital timepieces covering eleven time zones. It was 09.30 am in New York, 20.30 at night in Jakarta and 17.30 in the evening in Moscow. Oddly enough none of them showed the current time in London. He checked his watch it showed 14.31pm.

His thoughts were disrupted by a buzzer sounding somewhere in the room; Gretchen stood up and beckoned him towards the door of the inner office. He followed her through the portal then she turned and left the room.

The first thing Pullman noticed about Tamara was the big shock of natural blonde hair cascading over her shoulders. She was standing with her back to him waving her arms in the air doing palates or something similar; then he realised that she was actually standing in front a huge transparent screen and was actually dragging data into place with her finger tips and opening other screens within the screen. It was the sort of high tech wizardry that he thought only existed in the minds of Hollywood set designers employed on futuristic blockbusters.

Pullman couldn't make up his mind if her extremely slender body was natural or the result of an eating disorder. He'd only seen the rear view thus far but it was certainly the kind of body seen on a catwalk during London Fashion Week. She was wearing blue denim jeans moulded to her bottom with legs that were tighter fitting than airline compression socks; it was surely a physical impossibility to squeeze her ankles through. He imagined that she detached her feet and screwed them back into her legs when the jeans were on. The alternative, he mused, was that she had worn them since childhood and had grown into them. Whatever method she used to get into them, one thing was certain they cost more than the suit he was wearing, probably more than his entire wardrobe. A white shirt disappeared into the waist of the jeans but there were no visible signs of what happened to it after that; no tell-tale lumps or bumps showing through the denim and absolutely no VPL. The wide gold belt around her waist sparkled in the glow of the screen. Her height was deceptive due to the stilts she was wearing; the fact that women can walk in such creations was an eternal mystery to him. Jane wore similar shoes on occasion but only those occasions when walking or dancing were not involved. Jane could no doubt have bought half a dozen pairs for the price of those that Tamara was wearing.

Without turning her attention from the display she said, 'Inspector, please take a seat, I won't be a moment.'

He ignored the demotion, anticipating, from past experience that it was part of the verbal game in which he was about to participate. He'd had the occasion to interview many top business people during his career; some had been pleasant but the majority, for some reason which he was never able to fathom out, were obnoxious. They adopted the attitude that he was an ignorant plod and it was demeaning to converse with him. He hoped that Tamara wouldn't be amongst them.

He took a seat and perused the office. Her desk was made from what looked like a single piece of natural grey slate. It was the size of a championship snooker table; at least two inches thick and rested on six chromed columns, three on each of the short sides. It looked so heavy that they must have erected the building around it; he most definitely would not have wanted to be part the delivery team that put it in situ. Despite its vast surface area there were only four cordless telephones on the desk, each resting in a charging cradle; a laptop and a picture frame but he couldn't see the subject of the photograph from where he was sitting. The walls were adorned with several abstract paintings one of which he could clearly identify as a seascape the others could have been produced by hallucinating chimpanzees. Dotted around the office were numerous wood and stone tribal artefacts; a carved mask with a spear, a three feet high African elephant roughly hewn from some sort of hardwood, a granite sculpture of entwining natives and several pots; presumably a reference to her country of birth. A round glass topped meeting table and four single pedestal red upholstered chairs completed the furnishings.

Tamara ignored Pullman for as long as she thought would be irritating but not so long that it could be construed as ignorance; she did not want to appear rude but neither did she want to speak to him about her husband or anything else if it came to that. 'What can I do for you? She eventually asked, turning towards him; the front view lived up to expectations. She looked even more stunning than she did in the images he'd seen.

Pullman ignored the question. 'Very high tech set up.' He indicated the computerised screen which was now blank save for a rotating BSC logo. 'This sort of stuff is way above my head but you obviously know your way around it.'

'I've had a bit of practice,' she replied.

'Yes I hear you're quite an expert in the field. I'm told there's nothing you don't know about the internet and all this digital media business.' Pullman was trying to engage Tamara in general conversation. He hoped she would drop her defences and reveal more about the woman rather than the businesswoman.

'As you are no doubt aware I run our BSCyber division so I've picked up little bits here and there,' she said with dismissive modestly. She sat down behind the expanse of slate and ran her left hand through her hair and closed the laptop with her right. Tamara brought the conversation back to topic. 'You told my PA that you wanted to discuss Peter Ebingdon.'

Not my husband, not even just Peter but Peter Ebingdon as if he was just someone she simple knew rather than the man with whom she had shared a marital bed. Interesting thought Pullman; she obviously doesn't think to highly of the man. He tried to continue the general conversation. 'Oh, I think you're being a bit too modest about your career; from what I've been told you are regarded as the first lady of cyber space.' He hadn't been told that at all, he was just hoofing it, desperately trying not to confine the conversation to her husband.

'As much as I would like to discuss my life story with you Inspector, I'm afraid I have a very busy schedule so I would appreciate it if you would get to the point of your visit.' She sat back in her chair. 'Neither we nor his employers have officially reported him as a missing person so I don't see why you're interested in him. Has he committed a crime?' She had the kind of confident self-assurance that comes from a wealthy background and a privileged up-bringing.

'We are investigating that possibility. Do you know where your husband is currently?'

'I am reliably informed that the man you refer to as my husband is somewhere in central Europe. Where exactly I neither know nor care, our marriage was over a long time ago.'

'But you're not divorced?'

'I don't see that our marital status is any concern of yours.' They were not divorced because her husband was demanding half the value of BSCyber as a divorce settlement; a demand to which she and her parents were refusing to accede. Their respective lawyers had argued long and hard with no ground being conceded by either side. Negotiations had reached an impasse but she wasn't about to enlighten Pullman on their private battle. 'Look inspector, he simply decided to take off under his own volition. He left his job and his friends, not that he had many, to hide from reality. He chose that course of action and if, and when, he returns that will also be his choice. As I said I have no interest either way.' She said it with conviction and never diverted her eyes from him at any point.

'What can you tell me about your husband's background?'

'Nothing.' Sharp and to the point.

'What about his family?' persisted Pullman.

She shrugged her shoulders. 'Didn't have any. He was an only child and his parents were killed in a plane crash when he was six or seven, I think. He was born in Leamington Spa but following the accident he was raised by his grandparents in Edinburgh, where he went to University; they have both long since passed on. His grandmother had a long running dispute with other members of the family and never saw them; consequently neither did he.'

Pullman could see that the witness protection people had obviously put a very convincing back story together. 'None of his family came to the wedding?' he asked already knowing the answer.

She sat forward causing her hair to fall over her eyes; she pushed it back into place. 'Only two friends from his university days and a handful of work colleagues attended.'

If there was one thing Pullman prided himself on it was his ability to judge when a suspect was lying. On this occasion he had no idea;

she was either a very accomplished liar or she really didn't know Ebingdon's history. As an ex-addict she was probably a very good liar; people with an addiction, be it drugs or alcohol, tended in his experience to be able to conceal their problem and deny its existence even to themselves; although he wasn't sure if that applied to Tamara. He thought about it and recalled that in her rebellious years she had actually paraded her excesses; wore them like a badge of honour so she didn't need to be an accomplished liar. On the other hand why would she know the truth of his past? He'd have no reason to tell her. Pullman was developing the view that Tamara was actually, even now, unaware of her husband's true identity.

'You were quite young when you married,' he said.

'I don't see what that's got to do with anything? I don't think I want to continue this meeting.' There was a hint of anger in her tone.

'I'm just trying to get a handle on the man. We haven't been able to trace his history so I'm trying to piece together a profile. I really do appreciate your help.' He looked at her with his best pleading face. They stared at each other across the desk for a few seconds. He could see she was unsure as to whether or not to answer so he pushed on. 'You were nineteen I believe.'

Tamara took a deep breath. In the few seconds of silence between them she had decided that the only way to get rid of her inquisitor was to answer his questions or at least those that she wanted to.

'Yes I was nineteen. I admit now that I was a spoilt cow. I wanted everything my own way and my parents indulged me. Except that they were totally opposed to my relationship with Peter. They just didn't like him; wanted me to stop seeing him. The more they opposed the relationship the more I flaunted it. So I decided that we would get married. I was just being a bitch. They couldn't say no to their little princess in the end so Peter and I had a lavish society wedding, a luxurious honeymoon and they bought us a house. Once I'd got everything I wanted of course, I didn't want it any more. It was like opening a Christmas present, I got bored very quickly; realised that I didn't actually want it very much and stopped playing with it.'

'But you stayed married.'

Tamara was now in full swing and was unburdening herself as if talking to a shrink. 'Pride I suppose. I couldn't let my parents be right not after they spent so much against their better judgement.'

Pullman of course had listened to the Ebingdon tape so he knew that according to him Tamara suddenly changed her mind and wanted a family. He was intrigued to know why but didn't quite know how to phrase a question. He didn't need to worry.

'Then two of my friends got pregnant and I got jealous. As ever my must have mentality took over and I got back with Peter so that he could get me pregnant. I didn't want him, I just wanted to have a baby; without considering that a baby is for life not just for Christmas. But it never happened, a fact for which I am now eternally thankful of course.'

'Why didn't it happen?' he couldn't believe he'd just asked that question; neither could Tamara judging by the look on her face.

'That's rather personal. I'm not sure you need to know that.' She said with indignation. It was extremely personal but she was in full flow and answered him regardless. 'Medical reasons. By then I'd gone off the idea anyway. I grew up I guess; decided to concentrate on a career and went back to finish my degree. After just a few months we drifted so far apart that we needed binoculars to see each other.' She sat back in her chair again, looked up at the ceiling then back at Pullman. 'There are you satisfied now or would you like to know my bra size too?'

Instinctively he looked at her breasts and realising he quickly averted his gaze but not before guessing 34 c. She was about the same size as Jane had been. Jane's breasts flashed through his mind, she was standing naked in front of him; it felt wrong on every level. He re-focussed.

'You've been very helpful. Can you think of any reason why he would want to skip the country?'

'To get away from me I would think,' she said candidly. 'We rowed whenever we met, he wouldn't agree to an amicable divorce and to be perfectly frank I threatened to cut his balls off.'

And boil them in oil remembered Pullman.

There was a pregnant pause.

'Now if you'll excuse me I have a business to run and meetings to attend.' She stood up and walked towards the door. Pullman had to react quickly or the meeting would be over with no result.

'In the course of running your business have you come across the Sisters of Chiomara on the internet?' he asked waiting for a tell-tale reaction.

She stopped and turned towards him with a look of puzzlement on her face. 'The sisters of what?'

'Chiomara. The Sisters of Chiomara,' he repeated.

There was no abnormal reaction; she shook her mop of blonde hair and simply said 'No. Why, should I have done? Is that some religious order that Peter's involved in?'

So now he had played his trump card and had either been over trumped or just out played. 'Their web site is hosted on WebLynka so I thought you might have come across it.'

Tamara laughed spontaneously. 'Inspector, WebLynka hosts tens of millions of web sites across the world, we have tens of millions more who have email accounts with us and the WebLynka search engine receives in excess of five hundred million hits every single day of the week; do you really expect me to have seen every one? You might have heard that I'm good at what I do but even I'm not that good.' She laughed again.

Pullman felt embarrassed at his apparent naivety. He thanked her for her time and was escorted back to reception by Gretchen.

****

It was raining all over continental Europe. The windscreen wipers of the Mercedes were at full speed from just south of Graz all the way to Ljubljana where Peter Ebingdon stopped for a fresh bottle of water and to empty his angry bladder of the one he had already consumed. He found a small cafe ordered an espresso coffee on his rapid way to the toilet. The relief was palpable. He returned to the serving counter, downed the waiting coffee in one mouthful, paid and left. Three doors away he bought a cheese and ham baguette from a small to eat in the car, which he had purposely parked under trees in the main square; the canopy of the evergreens provided respite for the overworked windscreen wipers.

The attentive passengers in the black Audi parked on the other side of the square went unnoticed by their quarry.

Heavy rain continued to fall all the way to Triest where it petered out into a fine, persistent drizzle. He drove around the congested back streets looking for a suitably anonymous place to stay. He found the B&B Rosetti in the Via Genova running from the Piazza del Ponterosso towards the Adriatic. An outdoor market was in full swing in the Piazza; the place was thronging with locals and late season tourists. Ebingdon managed to squeeze the Mercedes into a tight space in the narrow road outside the B&B. He grabbed his valise from the boot, locked the car and entered the Rosetti. From the exterior it promised to be the kind of run down establishment that he was seeking. The interior more than measured up to expectations.

A tiny, dimly lit reception area was deserted. The scant furnishings had seen better days – probably pre-war days. A faint aroma of a wood fire lingered in the air. He noticed a brass bell on the counter which he rang. There was no immediate response; he was beginning to think he had made a mistake and half turned to leave when an elderly rodent like man emerged from a curtained off area behind the small, dusty reception counter. He was wearing a stained grey cardigan over a faded cream shirt; thinning lank hair was greased back and curled over his collar. The man slithered over to the desk rubbing his hands together either to ward off the cold and damp or in anticipation of the money that might be coming his way.

'Benvenuto,' said the rat. 'Ti piacerebbe una stanza?'

205

'Good afternoon,' said Ebingdon.

'Ah, English,' the old man smiled revealing teeth that had never troubled a dentist. 'Welcome, would you like a room?'

In a previous existence the answer would have been not on your life but it was now the kind of seedy place that not even his worst enemies would consider him patronizing and, as that was just who he wanted to hide away from, this place would be ideal.

'Yes, please if you have a vacancy.' Ebingdon knew what the answer to that would be; he was just being unduly polite. 'Five nights to start with; if you can manage that.'

The sound of a cash register rang in the old man's head. 'Certainly sir it is not our busiest time of the year.'

Ebingdon took out his wallet, placed his fingers on the wad of notes inside and said, 'How much?'

Kerching. Kerching. 'Un centinaio di euro – one hundred Euros.'

'For five nights, yes?'

'Yes but it is for the room only. Unfortunately we had a fire in the kitchen so we cannot do breakfasts until the assicurazione – the insurance – pays to have it repaired. Also we cannot do any refunds; once you book it is confirmed. No refunds. You understand?'

Ebingdon understood. If he had to move on quickly he wouldn't be worrying about a few Euros. As far as the fire was concerned it made any difference to his plans; he had no intention of eating there in any case but it explained the smell of burnt wood. If this was the state of the public area he didn't want to imagine what the kitchen hygiene had been like. He was sure that it would be the kind of mess that would even defeat Gordon Ramsey. The dishevelled appearance of the manager, who would no doubt treble up as the cook and waiter as well, together with the aroma of spirits on his rank breath would have done little to encourage his appetite. He paid the old man with two fifty Euro notes.

The man removed a key from below the counter, 'stanza numero sette,' he said handing over a key attached to a three inch square piece of wood with the number seven painted on it. 'It is our best room'.

The old man pointed to a fading sign on the wall at the bottom of the stairs indicating that rooms three to seven were in that direction.

'Grazie,' said Ebingdon. He picked up his bag and climbed the stairs.

The rodent disappeared from whence he came.

The bedroom was everything that Ebingdon was expecting; shabby un-chic. At one time it had no doubt been tastefully decorated but that was in a different era now it just looked very tired to the point of exhaustion. At least it had an en suite; he looked inside the bathroom to find a small bath with a wall mounted shower over one end, a wash basin and to his dismay, a squat over toilet that was just a tiled square on the floor with a central drainage hole. He'd forgotten that those things had ever existed. Just a couple of nights he promised himself then he would find somewhere better. It wouldn't be a difficult task to improve on that dump.

He looked out of the window overlooking the Via Genova below; the light rain was still falling. A cafe in the small parade of shops looked inviting; compared to his current surroundings a Dickensian workhouse would have looked inviting. He was still completely unaware of the black Audi that had managed to park a120 metres away thanks to a departing white Fiat van. It slotted in between a row of other parked cars in the narrow street by gently nudging the bumpers of the Mercedes in front and the Fiat behind.

The space afforded a perfect view of the entrance to the Rosetti. The brunette sitting in the driver's seat was on her mobile phone, deep in conversation. Her passenger had walked down to the Rosetti to check which of the ten rooms was occupied by the latest arrival.

As she approached the entrance Peter Ebingdon came out, eyes set on the café opposite. He checked for on-coming cars in the one way road, crossed quickly to dodge the rain and entered the café. She slipped into the Rosetti entrance and rang the brass bell on the counter twice; eventually the rodent emerged.

My friend has just booked in,' she said giving him a nice smile. 'Could you tell me which room he's in please?'

The old man stood motionless looking at her like she was a piece of cheese he was unsure about eating in case the he sprung the trap.

Thinking that he may not speak English, she said in her best Italian. 'Il mio amico è appena arrivato. Quale stanza è lui a.'

The rodent remained silent; he rubbed his hands together as if washing them with soap which he evidently didn't do too often.

She got the message and handed over a twenty Euro note. It was more effective than WD40 in loosening his tongue immediately. 'Room seven,' he said. He watched her leave then turned and disappeared behind the curtain.

Armed with the information she made her way back the short distance to the parked vehicle, opened the passenger door and got into the car. The rain drops were glistening in her hair and on her jacket, her spectacles immediately misted over.

'Room seven,' she said.

Her co-passenger informed the party on the other end of the line and closed the call. When the passenger had demisted her spectacles the Audi drove off, turned first left along the Via San Spiridione and disappeared into the traffic. Mission accomplished.

TWENTY-TWO

London was shrouded in a damp mist and failing light as Pullman left the pointy tower. People were, as ever, scurrying in all directions; going to business appointments, meetings, job interviews, shopping and beating the rush hour traffic on their homeward journeys. Pullman was going back to the bloody airless rabbit hutch of an office. The short stroll across the square chilled his face; his warm breath billowed in smoke like plumes as it hit the cold of the air. He may as well have been back on the promenade in Bridlington.

He was not at all happy with the results of his interview. He hadn't expected a resolution there and then. He hadn't expected Tamara to be sitting there in a Sisters of Chiomara tee shirt shouting death to all perverts. He hadn't expected her to stand up put her arms out horizontally in front of herself, waiting for the handcuffs and say it's a fair cop guv, I'll come quietly. He didn't really know what he had expected but he had hoped it would be more than he came away with.

'How did it go?' asked Lynne, as he slouched into the office, carrying a plastic cup half full of vending machine coffee.

'Look at this,' he said holding up the plastic cup. 'Half the coffee, if that's what they call this khaki liquid missed the cup.'

She asked him again.

He thought about his answer. 'Either I'm losing my instincts or the woman deserves an Oscar. I don't think she knows Ebingdon's real identity and I got zero reaction when I mentioned Sisters of Chiomara. If she's telling porkies, her body language says different.'

'So you don't think she's operating the site?' asked Sperring.

He was hesitant with his reply. 'Difficult.' Pullman parked himself on the edge of Sperring's desk with his legs straight and crossed in front of him He thought for a moment. 'She's more than capable of doing it and she has every means at her disposal with which to do it but like I say, if she is involved then she's a bloody good actress.

Unless Tom Nerbis or Mahone can come up with some concrete evidence I don't see how we'll be able to prove nor disprove her involvement.'

'I've had a thought sir.' Pullman audibly sucked his teeth. She couldn't decide if it was because she'd had a thought or because she hadn't called him Mike. She had decided to call him sir regardless of his wishes; she felt comfortable with that decision. 'Don't know why I didn't think of it before; I could get involved in the Sister of Chiomara web site forum.' Pullman's brow furrowed. 'Post some comments or pick up on a thread and see if I can interact with some of the other contributors. If there are little conspiracy groups maybe I can infiltrate them, find out who they are then maybe it might lead us to the top.' She looked at him for approval. He thought for a while and sucked his teeth again. She added. 'If not the top then at least to a murderer or two.'

'Okay go for it but be careful we don't need any accusations of entrapment. Don't write or say anything that could be construed as incitement or do anything criminal.'

Sperring looked hurt that he felt he had issue a warning.

Pullman spotted her reaction. 'I know you won't but it's not too different from actually going undercover. I know it's online and initially anonymous but I've seen undercover officers get so deep and involved that they forget why they're there and who they really are. It's a form of Stockholm syndrome; you could get so involved that you become one of bad guys or in this case one of the bad women. Just be careful, that's all I'm saying and keep me informed all the way.' He stood up, looked into the coffee cup and pulled a face full of distaste. 'This really is disgusting.' He went and sat at his own desk. 'Oh, she told me that the break-up of the marriage was due to her not really loving him but marrying him to spite her parents because, in her own words, she was a spoilt cow; the parents by all accounts hated the sight of him so she got married to annoy them. She says that the split came because she matured from a hedonistic socialite into a sensible business woman. Talking to her you wouldn't doubt it.' Without thinking he sipped his coffee again. 'And it's bloody cold.' He hesitated as to how to dispose of the plastic cup, there was no plant to water so he settled for standing it upright in the wastepaper bin. 'Lynne, see if you can find out the name of the Harley Street clinic that carried out their fertility tests; I think we need to take a look at the results for ourselves.'

'Why's that?'

'She was talking freely but when she came to that bit she just said that they couldn't have children for medical reasons.' He made quotation marks in the air and immediately hated himself for doing it.

'That's true isn't it? She probably was too embarrassed to tell you the exact diagnosis.'

'I don't think so, I think she would have said I couldn't have children or I couldn't conceive or something like that; I got the feeling that it wasn't her problem. I think she would have said if it was. So let's see if our friend Ebingdon was telling our journalist friends the truth. I certainly don't think we should take his word for it.' He flipped up the lid of his laptop, thought better of it and closed the lid again.

'Lynne I won't be at the hotel for dinner tonight; thought I might pop over to see Jane's parents, do you mind? He had decided on the visit whilst walking across the square.

'Of course not sir I can get on with this besides it will be better to be doing it at night, more normal.'

'You could come with me if you like.'

'That's kind of you sir but I'll be fine. I'm sure you'll have plenty to talk about.'

Pullman checked the time it was 4.10. 'Right I'm going to push off.'

The office door opened and Richard Pointer rushed in. 'Have you heard?'

'Heard what?' asked Pullman.

'Another body's been found; on Hampstead Heath; same MO.'

That news put an end to Pullman's plans for the evening. Secretly he was relieved. He felt he ought to visit Jane's parents but he knew it would be tough. Her mother had been in a worse state than him at the memorial service.

There had been several more SOC murders reported from around the world but this was now the third on home territory in a little under two weeks.

'The Yard is sending a car for you in a few minutes.' said Pointer.

****

The London rush hour traffic was building steadily requiring the Vauxhall Vectra emergency response vehicle to use the blues and twos to assist in weaving through the queues of stationary vehicles. Although the police neehnah horns had long since been replaced by pulsating, directional high pitched warning sirens Pullman, like many of his colleagues still nostalgically referred to them as the blues and twos. The speeding vehicle narrowly missed a bendybus as it turned onto Victoria Street sped along Grosvenor place at the rear of Buckingham Palace gardens then through the chicane that was Hyde Park Corner past the underground station and on to Park Lane.

This was all familiar territory for Pullman. 'Have you been through Mayfair before Lynne?' He asked Sperring.

'Yes but I was only two at the time. My mother bought me down to Andrew and Fergie's wedding so I don't remember anything. I've been down to the West End since for shows and Gary and I did the London Eye a couple of years back. Do you miss the bright lights?'

'To be honest I don't. It's all changed so much anyway, hardly recognise the place,' he said with nostalgic glance out of the window.

As the car flashed past the Dorchester and Grosvenor hotels the blue hazard lights reflected in the buildings and Pullman reflected on his early days in the job. As a young uniformed officer he'd spent much of his time walking the streets of London's West End. He had been on crowd control duties at events at the glitzy hotels and at

212

heated demonstrations around Speakers Corner particularly during times of political turmoil. Free speech was a wonderful institution but there were always plenty of folk who gathered around the soapbox orators shouting them down. Some people considered the only views worth airing were those that coincided with their own.

More blue lights were strobing on parked police vehicles parked alongside Marble Arch while police were attempting to clear the area of vagrant Romanians sleeping rough.   It had become a daily occurrence. The ERV braked violently as it manoeuvred around the west side of Marble Arch throwing Pullman across the back seat; a kamikaze hire car driven appropriately enough by an oriental man decided to turn on to the one way Cumberland Place in the wrong direction. Inside the ERV the air was bluer than the lights. The police driver had to ignore the situation and drive on up the Edgware Road to Maida Vale then left on to St John's Wood Road; left at Lords Cricket Ground on to the Finchley Road. They were heading in the general direction of Kilburn where Pullman was raised as a child; he hadn't been back there for more than twenty-five years. He'd spent many happy days on Hampstead Heath with his parents and latterly with teenage friends. The memories of picnics at Kenwood House; sunny days paddling in Whitestone Pond; hanging around the fun fair when it visited at Easter made him smile inwardly.   They were happy carefree days, when the simple things in life were so much fun. Now he was going back to look at a dead body. Who would have thought?

At Swiss Cottage the car took the right hand B511 fork up past Hampstead tube station before taking the right fork along Spaniards Road. The murder sight on Sandy Heath was visible on the left as the car came to a halt. The six mile journey had taken just nine minutes.

The gathering gloom was made worse by the mist that had descended further; almost to the level of low cloud. A portable lighting gantry rig had been set up to illuminate the murder scene for the SOCO team. Beams of halogen light they emitted were diffused by the swirling mist, giving the whole scene an eerie horror film appearance.

213

The victim's body had been discovered lying in thick bushes making it impossible to erect a tented structure. Instead a series of white screens constructed of diamond shaped panels with a blue band running their length had been erected to screen off the site from the assembled spectators. Crime scene blue and white 'Police Line Do Not Cross' tape had been strung around the scene providing a further thirty metre barrier to the rapidly multiplying number of onlookers, journalists and photographers that were arriving. Personnel in white Microgard forensic suits where moving to and fro in all directions. Pullman and Sperring approached the tape, showed their ID to a uniformed female officer who lifted the tape as high as it would flex enabling the two detectives to duck under. They walked up to the screens and peered over; a forensic scene investigator standing, head bowed staring at the pathologist examining the body, looked up and said, 'Sorry but you're not allowed up here'.

Pullman showed his ID again. 'DCI Mike Pullman,' he said. 'I'm the SIO.' The FSI nodded acceptance then waited for Sperring to do the same.

Pullman said 'Can we get suited and booted?'

The duty pathologist, a tall broad man of Afro-Caribbean descent in his mid-fifties with tightly curled hair that looked as if it had a coating of hoar frost, was kneeling next to the corpse. He stood up and said to Pullman, 'I shouldn't bother. It's been here for a while, there's fox prints, dog paw prints, foot prints from the mob that were here prior to our boys arriving so you needn't worry about contaminating the scene. I'm Tony Gooding by the way.'

Pullman nodded, 'Okay Tony; what have we got? Pullman walked around to the other side of the screen. Sperring stayed put.

'Male IC3 by the name of Tyrone Bennett age twenty seven lived about five miles away in Stoke Newington.' Pullman gave the pathologist an inquisitive sideways glance. 'I'm not clairvoyant,' Gooding held up a plastic evidence bag containing a wallet. 'He wasn't robbed. All his details are in the wallet; you've no doubt already noticed his head has been cut off; as far as we can see that's not located within ten feet of the body. With all the animal prints around the body it might easily have been carried off.'

'Has anybody run a check on him yet?' asked Pullman.

'Not sure Chief Inspector. I know the Yard has been informed.'

Pullman turned to Sperring. 'Get some gloves on then examine this wallet and go and run a check on the victim.' She took the bag and went back to the car.

The corpse was bent over in a kneeling position with his hands by his side and the neck resting on the ground. His trousers and jockey shorts had been pulled down and were trapped under his shins. Pullman looked at the man's anus and did a theatrical double take then gave Gooding an exaggerated quizzical look.

'Ah, you've spoiled my little surprise,' said Gooding. 'Yes you're right he has an object inserted into his anus. I don't want to remove it until we get the body back to the lab but I would say that it is a large, solid glass dildo. The killer could have been a proctologist but as it's not a standard NHS approved anal probe, I doubt it. I'll refrain from saying that it must have been a pain in....'

'Yes please do.' said Pullman before the pathologist could finish the sentence. 'What are the chances of prints?'

'Provided gloves weren't worn there's every chance; the burial chamber shouldn't have destroyed them.' He smiled at his description of the dead man's body cavity. Pullman didn't.

Pullman considered the situation. At least this murder had an unusual element which might give it another dimension. It was possible that the killer had made a mistake and left fingerprints. Robbery patently wasn't the motive. Was this a homosexually motivated murder? Was the decapitation an incredible coincidence? Unlikely he thought and it couldn't have been done to cover up his identity or they would have removed the wallet. However if this murder had taken place a while ago why had the head not yet been found; the others had been left in view within a few hours of the crime. He ruled out co-incidence in his mind; this murder was going to prove to be inspired by the Sisters of Chiomara web site, of that he was sure.

DS Sperring returned to the crime scene accompanied by DI Reid of the Metropolitan Police Homicide and Serious Crime Command. Sperring explained that she met DI Reid on her way back to the car. He had just arrived having been assigned to the investigation. Introductions were made all round.

Sperring said 'Looks like we've got number three sir. DI Reid can explain.'

DI Marvin Reid, known to his friends and colleagues as Hank was one of the archetypal new breed of fast tracked detectives; smartly dressed, university educated, articulate and ambitious. 'The vic,' Pullman let it go, 'Tyrone Bennett had just been released from Belmarsh prison having served only thirty months of an eight year sentence for the rape of a twenty six year old mother of two in Kensington Gardens four years ago.' He reeled it off as if he had memorised the notes. He had.

'How the hell did he get released?' enquired Pullman.

'He claimed at the time that he paid the alleged victim for sex which she emphatically denied. She was apparently a perfectly normal housewife and mother with no record and no hint of anything else. In fact by all accounts she was made out to be Mother Teresa's guiding light, she was so pure. Since then she has been arrested and charged with soliciting and prostitution; it turned out that she'd been at it for years. So five months ago the Bennett family started appeal proceedings and last month the appeal court found the original verdict to be unsafe.'

'I bet you Met boys were delighted.'

'Wasn't my division sir. Apparently officers from Sapphire were waiting outside the court to re-arrest Bennett on other charges but he managed to evade them somehow and disappeared into the undergrowth as it were.'

'Ironically that's where he ended up. What were the other charges?'

'There has been of a series of rapes and sexual assaults on women in the Stoke Newington, Islington and Hackney areas; could have been as many as forty over a five year period. The first attack was on the manageress of an electrical chain store late at night. The perp broke in and raped her in the store room; after that the media nicknamed him The Comet; bit inappropriate really cos he disappeared without leaving a trail.' His straight face revealed that he was making no attempt to be humorous. 'When he was arrested in connection with Kensington rape no one at Sapphire thought to check his DNA against the other cases because the MO was different and it was off patch.'

Pullman was aware that Sapphire was a unit of the Metropolitan Police with specialist officers whose role is to investigate rapes and other serious sexual violence as well as supporting victims.

'They're dealing with about three and a half thousand rape cases every year in London sir, so the check slipped through the net. He'd already been sent down when the matches were finally made. The CPS decided that it was not in the public interest to take him to trial on those. I suppose by public interest they meant the public purse but once the appeal started they reopened the file and lo and behold no assaults matching his MO had been reported during the three years while he was inside. They decided they'd prosecute on ten other counts.'

'What was different about the MO then that caused them to overlook Bennett?' asked Pullman.

'The rape in Kensington was normal vaginal penetration but all of the other attacks involved anal penetration or attempts at anal penetration'

'That explains the dildo then.'

'Sorry sir?'

Pullman explained the discovery that had come to light after Sperring had left the crime scene. 'So maybe Bennett was telling the truth about the last reported attack but if she was on the game why report it as rape?'

217

Reid explained. 'They were caught in the act by an officer of the Royal Parks Operational Command Unit; the victim started screaming rape and Bennett legged it but got picked up a mile away. Normally working girls want the cash up front, she only had a fiver in her purse and you don't get laid for a fiver, well not in London. Bennett on the other hand had plenty of cash on him about a hundred and seventy pounds I believe. So everything was supporting her allegations.'

Pullman shook his head in bewilderment. There were more and more command units and operational divisions formed every year to the point where there would soon be an individual command unit designation for every officer employed in the job. Royal Parks Operational Command Unit? Ludicrous. Couldn't coppers just be coppers without belonging to yet another unit with another layer of bureaucracy and management? There weren't enough hours in the day to do the job as it was.

TWENTY-THREE

Thursday morning 24ᵗʰ October

As Wednesday became Thursday Pullman and Sperring were still in the office, both feeling extremely tired. Eyes that had been focused on display monitors all evening were strained and sore. Pullman decided it was time they called it a day; they were now being very unproductive and hoping that some flash of inspiration would miraculously come their way. The Metropolitan Police had assigned a team to work under Pullman on the latest case and he had spent some time preparing his briefing set for 9am tomorrow which had now become today.

Broadcast media had transmitted news coverage of the discovery of the body extensively through the night on news channels and internet sites and undoubtedly the press would feature the story when the morning editions hit the streets. The official police statement had not mentioned the identity of the body; they would not release that information until they had informed his family which they would do as soon as they had a positive ID. Although there was little doubt that the body was that of Bennett, without a head and without results of DNA or fingerprint checks they couldn't be absolutely certain. Just because the victim was in possession of Bennett's wallet it was not proof positive. There was always the outside chance that the murderer had planted the wallet; as unlikely as that was.

Bennett was not exactly flavour of the month with the Met but he was afforded the same rights as anyone found in similar circumstances.

DS Sperring was unable to find any mention of Tyrone Bennett on the SOC site so she and Pullman decided to implement her plan to become a contributor to the forum. She posted:

Another scumbag off the streets

219

Sisters have you seen the news of the body found on Hampstead Heath well I can tell you that the world is rid of another piece of shit. They'll find out who the bastard was soon enough but I know who he was and what he'd done. He won't fucking do it again.

Rat Catcher

Sperring had kept the post short with enough venom and use of the vernacular to be in keeping with the general tone of the forum. It was purposely worded to not imply she had committed the crime in the hope that the actual perpetrator would react and claim responsibility. There was also nothing inaccurate in the post.

****

The police incident room had been set up overnight in a training room at Stoke Newington police station; a modern, purpose designed building on the High Street. A team of local uniformed officers and four plain clothes detectives, two local and two from the Metropolitan Police Homicide and Serious Crime Command, one of whom was DI Reid, were present when Pullman and Sperring arrived, both clutching mugs of coffee, and Sperring, a thin light blue A4 pocket file.

Being a training room it had already been set out classroom style. Pullman took position at the front and introduced himself and DS Sperring to the assembled gathering and asked them to introduce themselves in turn although he did warn them that he probably wouldn't remember their names first time round.

'DI Marvin Reid, Homicide and Serious Crime Command.'

'DS Rachel Grant, also with the HSCC.'

'DS Rajindar Patil, Hackney CID.'

'DC Peter Rankin, Hackney CID.'

Then the seven uniformed officers stationed at Stoke Newington announced their names.

While that was going on Sperring had removed a sheath of laser printed images from the folder and affixed to the smart board with blue magnetic discs. Introductions completed, Pullman began the briefing.

'On Monday the eleventh we,' he pointed to Sperring and then to himself, 'were investigating the murder of a local schoolteacher called Thomas Wethersby whose headless body was found on the prom at Bridlington – that's on the East Yorkshire coast for those of you who have not ventured further north than Watford. The following day his head was recovered outside York County Court, with the initials SOC written on the forehead in black marker pen.' He indicated the appropriate image that Sperring had put on the board. 'We were working on the premise that it was a local murder and trying to identify the significance of the letters. I'll come back to that in a minute but don't start trying to guess; you won't succeed. As most of you will know on Thursday the fourteenth another severed head was found, this time outside Barlinnie prison in Glasgow. The body from which it had been detached has not yet been located. This head also had the initials SOC written on it.' He indicated the picture of Kulkinski's severed head. 'So the astute amongst you will recognise the similarities between the two MOs as did SCAS at our newly formed National Crime Agency. Because DS Sperring and I were investigating the first murder we were seconded to head up the inquiries into both cases. For reasons which I will come to in a minute we are currently working out of the NCA offices here in London. For me it's a return home; for DS Sperring it's a chance to visit Harrods.'

He paused for a swig of coffee and a reaction to his humour which was not forthcoming.

'Yesterday, as you know, the body of Tyrone Bennett was found five miles away on Hampstead Heath. The PM is happening as we speak so we are awaiting confirmation but it will prove to be him, of that I have no doubt. This victim also had his head cut off. The head has not yet been found but I am confident that when it is, it too will have SOC scrawled on the forehead. The head found in Glasgow was that of one Josef Kulkinski a low life Polish illegal immigrant responsible for people trafficking, drug dealing, child abuse and prostitution in the city. Tyrone Bennett was a multiple rapist on the run.'

He took another mouthful of coffee.

'So it doesn't take a genius to see that we are looking at a serial killer; right?' There was a general nodding of agreement and a few affirmative mumbles from the audience.

'Wrong! The murders were committed by different killers acting under a unified cause.'

He took another mouthful of coffee while that sank in.

'Why do we say that, well there are two main reasons; firstly an SCAS analysis shows murders with the same MO have been happening right across the world over the past few years, the timings of which show that they could not have been committed by one person. Secondly we now know that SOC stands for Sisters of Chiomara,' he looked at Sperring and said, 'You fill in the rest.'

She wasn't expecting to speak but was happy to do so. She swapped places with Pullman and put a picture of the web site home page on the board. 'This is a screen shot of the site. It's a little small I'm afraid but....'

'Excuse me DS Sperring,' said DS Patil, 'we can get the actual site up on the screen, if that would help.'

'Sure.'

He went to the board and activated the screen, touched an icon on the right hand side and brought up Internet Explorer then turned his head in Sperring's direction expectantly.

'Oh, it's www dot sisters of Chiomara' all lower case, she spelled out Chiomara as Patil entered it into the browser. 'Dot com.'

He pressed enter and the site opened instantly. 'It's an active screen so just touch the buttons as you want.'

Sperring went through the site explaining who Tisiphone, Megaera and Alecto were; she showed sample pages of the rogue's gallery. She indicated that entries for Wethersby and Kulkinski had been crossed through with a wide semi-transparent red cross on which the words

Transferred to Tartarus was inscribed. She explained what Tartarus was.

Pullman was studying the reaction of the team. Expressions ranged from incredulity to bewilderment. He smiled inwardly; it did seem a bit fantastic, in the removed from reality sense of the word.

'So far I have not come across any mention of Tyrone Bennett except for this; she showed them her entry on the forum page and let out a slight exclamation as up popped a response to her posting. She quickly explained that in order to try and stir the culprit into responding she had posted her comments.

The response read:

Rat Catcher

Did you really know the worthless fuck was Tyrone Bennett had he violated U2. Well whatever the fucking pervert has got what he desveres he screamed when his arse got split. it will keep happening until we bury all his kind if the law won't give us justice then wheel take justice for ourselfs . keep going sisters.

Pendragon

It wouldn't win a Pulitzer Prize or a spelling bee but it was just the response Pullman and Sperring had hoped to achieve; he also hoped that Bono had fully recovered.

Pullman stood up and addressed the room. 'Perhaps I ought to mention, in case it hasn't hit the grapevine yet, that he screamed when his arse got split refers to the fact that the killer had inserted a glass dildo into the victim's rectum. It also answers the question as to whether it was inserted pre or post mortem; dead men don't scream.'

It flashed through his mind that dead men don't scream would make a great title for the book he promised himself he'd write one day but knew he never would.

He pointed to the screen. 'So there is Bennett's killer, Pendragon, or at least one of them. We think that there must be at least two in each case in order to carry out that strength of attack. Oh and yes, we do think the killers are women. Excuse me just a minute.'

He turned towards his DS. 'Lynne get on to Mahone at CIFT alert him to the response and see what he can do and while you're at it see if they've had any success yet with the WebLynka trace.'

He turned his attention back to the classroom. 'We'll assign tasks in a while but as DS Sperring had been dealing with that it made sense to get her to sort it.'

No one vented any dissent. 'Okay let's pull together some of the relevant facts and maybe some not so factual points for consideration.' He looked along the front row. 'DC Rankin, would you mind being the scribe?' He didn't mind. Pullman silently congratulated himself for remembering the DC's name. Rankin went to the white board next to the smart board and chose a medium width black marker, removed the cap and stood poised for the first of Pullman's points. 'Let's just get all these thoughts down, we can mind map it later.'

He began to reel off a series of bullet points:

'Victims are all sex attackers or alleged sex attackers.'

'Vigilante justice is the motive.' He pointed to DI Reid and DS Grant. 'That's presumably why you two have been assigned to the team; it's both a murder and a form of manhunt and therefore falls well within your Command's remit.'

'SOC website is the catalyst for the murders.'

Rankin was struggling to keep pace with the bullet points.

'We need to identify the operator of the website.'

A uniformed officer at the back raised his hand to ask a question. Pullman acknowledged him. 'Yes constable.'

'Couldn't we shut the site down, sir?'

'Yes constable ....?' Pullman tilted his head waiting for a name.

'Brannigan, sir.'

'Yes, Constable Brannigan you are right, we could, but our thinking is that while it's running we can hopefully use it to our advantage to tempt the killer out in to the open. Like the response you've just seen. Leaving it open is probably not going to make a lot of difference to the murder rate over the next few days. If there is anyone else out there planning a revenge killing then the chances are that they have already laid plans. Okay?'

Brannigan nodded acceptance of the answer and was relieved he hadn't made a complete fool of himself. Pullman had put him down gently; he was grateful for that.

Pullman had completely lost his train of thought but it had given Rankin the chance to catch up. Pullman read the board notes. 'Yes, we need to investigate the murders with conventional methods.' He held a hand up to Rankin and motioned him to cease writing. 'As you will find out during this investigation I am an old style copper, all this internet stuff is important but there is no substitute for getting out there and digging. At the end of the day we will hopefully be able to bring charges against the web site operator for incitement to commit murder but whoever we find responsible it will still be very difficult to prove incitement because they are very careful not to actually instruct anyone to specifically go out there to kill. What we need to do is find the people responsible for the physical act of murder. That's where groundwork comes into its own and so do you. We will find Bennett's killer through the efforts of this team. Right?'

He paused for a moment to let the message sink in and for the agreement to build.

'We need to know who this Pendragon is; maybe CIFT can tell us maybe not, but the contents of that forum post would suggest that she is local and probably one of Bennett's victims. Let's interview everyone who reported an attack including the woman he says he paid, you never know it could be a revenge attack by her or someone close to her. I know that's a lot victims to interview as well as family and friends but there's no alternative. I also want to know where he's been hiding for the past two weeks. He lived with his mother, her flat was checked out and he wasn't there; it was kept under surveillance but he didn't show. Someone must have been harbouring him and we need to know who and where. SOCO didn't find a mobile but he may have had one. Who doesn't these days? I would expect it to be pay-as-you-go but check out the phone companies anyway.'

Pullman's stream of ideas had come to a log jam. He puffed his cheeks out and drummed his lips together while he racked his brain for anything he'd missed. He threw it open to the team.

'There must be something I've forgotten'.

'DI Reid spoke first. 'His records show that he attended the One Jesus Gospel Church, we could check out the congregation there.'

Another one of the uniformed constable chipped in. 'That's less than half a mile away sir.'

'Yeah good, let's do that. Anything else?' Heads shook negatively and team members looked around at each other. There appeared to be no further thoughts. 'Okay, I don't know your individual strengths so I want you to get together, under DI Reid here, to allocate the tasks. If there are any issues I'll sort them. Constable Brannigan, unless you or anyone else has any objections, I suggest you take on the Collator's role.' No objections were lodged.

TWENTY-FOUR

The One Jesus Gospel Church was previously a place of worship for Baptists and was situated about six hundred metres further down the High Street from the Police Station towards Dalston, Kingsland. It was set back from the pavement with a grassed lawn to the left of the paved entrance area looking from the road; black painted railings and a small low hedge determined the boundary. The main part of the building resembled a miniature church with a high pointed gable facia inset with a stone arched window with five sections filled with harlequin patterned glass panels. The entrance was a heavy, wooden double door surrounded by stone set into a side wall abutting a recently completed block of flats. Above the door was a sign written in a Gothic typeface reading One Jesus Gospel Church above that was an outdoor, movement sensor activated, security light. To the left of the door was another sign featuring the hours of worship and other meetings that took place on the premises. A smaller brass engraved plaque declared that the Pastor was John Oyelude. The diminutive chapel was dwarfed by the huge Aziziye Mosque to the left with its ornate light and dark blue tiled facia and Corinthian style entrance; the oldest Turkish Islamic Mosque in London being converted in 1983 from a disused cinema originally opened in 1913. The two contrasting places of worship were indicative of the diverse multi-cultural nature of the local community and the changing usage of the buildings.

Ladybird Bennett had cared for the church for over 30 years. For most of those years she had never missed her turn to prepare the church for worship or community meetings. She did not consider for one moment that her missing son was sufficient reason not to serve

God on that Thursday morning. At 8.30am on the dot as usual she turned the key in the brass lock of the oak door and stepped inside, she hung her dark brown overcoat on the peg inside the vestibule, placed her red hat over the top, unwound the scarf from around her neck and stuffed it into a pocket of her coat and went straight to the kitchen.

Ladybird Bennett always started Thursdays with a cup of tea; she filled the electric jug kettle to the minimum water level and switched it on, she did not believe in wasting electricity by boiling more water than was necessary. She knew that by the time she had retrieved the trug of cleaning materials from the broom cupboard the kettle would be in the throes of billowing steam into the air before switching itself off. She popped a tea bag into her Jesus Loves Me mug stirred and squeezed the bag before spooning it out and depositing it in the pedal bin under the sink. She picked up the trug in her right hand and carried her mug of black tea with the left hand. She shuffled into the chapel, turned down the central isle past rows of wooden pews towards the altar.

She always started with the altar upon which stood a large golden crucifix; Jesus deserved to be polished first she always said. As she passed the front two rows, her attention was drawn to something on the far left of the altar. Her son Tyrone was at the back of the altar watching her approach; her initial surprise quickly turned to motherly anger.

'Tyrone you bad boy; is this where you've been hiding? How did you get in here? He did not reply. She stepped closer. 'Why didn't you come home? You know I.....' she realised something wasn't right. Tyrone wasn't behind the altar; he appeared to be poking his head through the altar. Then she looked in horror as she saw the red stain that had spread across the altar cloth and emanated from Tyrone's head; she gasped in horror and collapsed in a heap onto the front pew. She said he son's name over and over again. Tyrone was silent. Then maybe through divine intervention it hit her that here was the missing head from the body they found on Hampstead Heath. Last night and again that morning she had said prayers for the poor soul murdered so savagely. Now the realisation had hit her that she had been praying for her own son. She wept tears of anguish as she stumbled her way back along the rows of pews to the small office where she gathered herself together sufficiently to call the police.

****

Haringey Mortuary, a converted and extended park keeper's cottage, was situated in the grounds of Bruce Castle Park. Pullman stood behind the glass screen of the viewing chamber with DS Sperring along-side him. They had just arrived in time to observe the final stages of the post mortem of the Hampstead Heath corpse. Doctor Marcus Capton, the chief pathologist, had taken charge of proceedings. Pullman assumed that his assistant behind the surgical mask was Tony Gooding who had attended the crime scene. He was certainly big enough. Capton looked up as they approached the window.

'Nice of you to join us; Detective Chief Inspector Pullman I presume.' He had a voice for upstairs rather than downstairs.

'When you've seen one you've seen them all,' replied Pullman. 'Watching cadavers being opened up has never been a particular pleasure of mine, only the results are of any interest to me.'

'As you weren't here throughout I suppose that means I'm going to have to go through my findings again.' said the pathologist as if talking to a naughty, inattentive child.

'DS Sperring and I would appreciate that very much,' replied Pullman. Trying not to sound too condescending he added. 'It would be an enormous help to us in our attempts to apprehend the perpetrator.' He came across as sarcastic to the point of rudeness as far as Capton was concerned. Pullman on the other hand knew this was the first and possibly the last occasion that he would meet the pathologist even so he felt a twinge of regret at not being a little friendlier. 'My apologies Doctor Capton that may have sounded a little rude, it wasn't my intention. Can we start again?'

Capton accepted the apology and began running through only the findings that really weren't visually obvious. 'The man had been dead for between eighteen and twenty four hours. I am unable to determine the cause of death until we have found and examined the head but cause of death might be decapitation; it does tend to have that outcome. He was exactly twenty six years of age and his name was indeed Tyrone Bennett.'

'So you've had his DNA and fingerprint results back then.' Now who was playing games?

'Yes about fifteen minutes ago. His last meal was pizza with pepperoni sausage. He had no alcohol in his blood nor was there any trace of proscribed drugs in his system although there were several needle marks on his right arm, stomach and upper thigh.'

'Heroin?'

'No insulin; he was a diabetic'

'Dr Capton, I've apologised for getting off on the wrong foot so I would appreciate it if you would tell me the pertinent facts in a professional manner.' Pullman said, keeping the words *you pompous prick* to himself.

Now Capton apologised and kept the rest of the conversation straight forward and on a professional track. 'There were minor lacerations to both wrists indicating that the deceased had been bound at some stage; the marks are consistent with handcuffs. Several canine hairs were found in his nostrils and lungs. There were numerous signs of interference by unknown fauna.'

'Is it possible that was the source of the dog hairs.' asked Pullman, immediately wishing he hadn't. For the dog hairs to have reached the lungs they would have needed to be breathed in through the mouth or nose. For that to have happened, his head would have needed to be attached. Ipso facto the hairs entered the lungs while he was still alive. 'Forget I asked that,' he requested.

Capton held up the dildo like a prize in a tournament. 'This was the item that had been inserted into the deceased's anus and up through the rectum. It measures twenty five centimetres in length, that's ten inches in old money, and such was the force with which the insertion had been carried out that it had split the Sigmoid Colon at the top of the rectum. It would have been a very painful experience. There were two partial fingerprints and one full thumbprint on the glass; those have been sent for matching.' He saved the best until last. 'One thing that you might really like to know is that his penis has been removed. The blood and wound analysis would tend to indicate that this was removed while the deceased was alive.'

Pullman involuntarily clenched his groin and rectum and grimaced at the thought of losing his manhood. Memories of the pain he felt when a cricket ball, delivered by 'Wicky' Wickham, the schools fastest bowler, hit him at full speed in his wedding tackle came back in an instant. He'd never forgiven Sparky, the PE teacher for making him open the batting without wearing a box. Having it cut off just didn't bear thinking about. Whoever Pendragon was, she would have given Dr Mengele a run for his money.

Capton agreed to email the post mortem report that afternoon. Pullman thanked him before he and Sperring left. On their way back to the car he got a call from Rachel Grant in the incident room; the head had been found by the victim's mother at the church where they worshipped. DI Reid had gone down there and SOCO were on the way. Now too were Pullman and Sperring.

****

The whole of Stoke Newington High Street is a red zone. The double red lines, rather than the normal yellow lines, indicate that there is no stopping at any time for any reason. The road immediately outside the One Jesus Gospel Church was no exception and in addition it was a bus bay but no matter, police on police business can ignore the red zone. Pullman did, he parked immediately behind the Forensic Service van and another Mondeo that turned out to have been parked there by DI Reid.

231

Inside the church a forensic scene investigator was busy examining the area around the altar and another was dusting for prints around the broken window in the single unisex toilet. They were both dressed in forensic overalls and overshoes as was DI Reid who was watching them at work. As Pullman and Sperring entered the church Reid told them that Mrs Bennett was in the kitchen with a WPC; he explained how she had found her son's head and told them that the killer's access to the church had been gained through a toilet window. They went through to the kitchen and Reid returned to observing the scientists at work.

Pullman and Sperring introduced themselves to the grief stricken woman. Lynne Sperring made them all a cup of tea; in the spirit of the new team ethic Sperring delivered a cup to Reid.

'Ladybird, that's a pretty name isn't it,' Pullman said softly, 'and unusual,' he added.

Her head was bowed, she was dabbing at her eyes with a damp tissue. She nodded gently without looking up the look of grief chiselled into her wrinkled face. 'Yes I suppose so, sir.'

'Were you named after Lady Bird Johnson, the American President's wife?'

'I don't think so unless she had sisters called Butterfly and Honeybee too,' she spoke very softly and still had a strong West Indian patois.

'Really, your parents had some imagination then.' Pullman thought he saw a slight nod of her head.

Sperring re-entered the kitchen and sat down next to Mrs Bennett.

Pullman spoke to Sperring 'Mrs Bennett has sisters called Butterfly and Honeybee' Sperring looked dubious. 'No really she has,' He reassured her. This was no time for cracking jokes. He was trying to make the grief stricken mother feel more at ease but he'd have to get around to asking her a few questions shortly. He need not have worried; once she started rolling all he had to do was sit back and listen.

'Had,' said Mrs Bennett, 'God called B three years ago; she is with our Lord now.'

'Is Butterfly still alive?'

'That was Butterfly; we called her B for short, she thought Butterfly was a silly, childish name. Honeybee was just Honey.'

'I see. Is Honey in Britain too?'

'No she is three years older than me. Last year she and Samuel, her husband, went back to Barbados to wait for the Lord to call her too. She is very ill. She had no family of her own. I have my children so I stayed here. My husband left us in nineteen eighty eight just before Tyrone was born. They said that because of my age he might not be born normal. I wouldn't let them do tests; if the Lord wanted him to be all right he would be but Tyrone's father William couldn't cope with another child, not one that might not be perfect so one day he just disappeared, walked out on us and we have never seen him to this day.'

'I'm sorry,' said Sperring. 'It must have been a difficult time for you, being alone like that.'

'The Lord Jesus was with me. He is always with me. I had my other children to look after so I just got on with it. And Tyrone was a beautiful, healthy, normal baby. William would have been proud of his only son.'

'Your other children were girls?' asked Sperring needlessly. No, I had two cows and a goat was not going to be the response.

'Yes three; two are living in Germany now, only Yvonne is here, she lives in Tottenham. Not far away, she visits her mother every week. She's a good girl. She comes to church when she can.'

'Does she know about ...' Sperring hesitated.

Mrs Bennett shook her head and sobbed. 'Who would do such a thing to my boy? What kind of a monster is he? Tyrone was a good boy, he looked after me. He couldn't have done those terrible things they said he did. He's a good boy; he's always been a good boy.'

'Is there some way we can contact your daughter? I'm sure she'd want to be with you,' said Pullman.

Mrs Bennett took a business card from her handbag and gave it to Pullman; he glanced at it and passed it to Sperring who raised her eyebrows when she saw it was a card for a beauty salon called Scissor Chicks.

'Is that where she works?' asked Pullman.

'It's her own business. She has three girls working for her but she works very hard herself. I'm very proud of her.'

Mrs Bennett was very proud of all four of her children. 'Yvonne always took care of her little brother when I was out at work, they were inseparable. Her heart will be broken.'

Sperring left the kitchen to arrange for the daughter to be informed and if necessary driven down to the chapel.

'I know it's a very difficult time Mrs Bennett but we want to catch the person that did this terrible thing to your son, as quickly as possible. I have to ask you if you can think of anyone who might want to harm Tyrone.' Pullman could think of dozens of people but he knew what the answer would be form Ladybird Bennett.

'No. He was a good boy; a popular boy. He had lots of friends.' Would she ever have considered Tyrone to be a man, if had outlived her he would always be her little boy.

'Do you know where he'd been staying since his release?'

'He called me twice. I wanted him to come home but he said he couldn't. He said the police were watching my home; that they wanted to arrest him for other crimes that he hadn't done. He was very frightened.'

'So you don't have any idea who was harbour......where he was staying?'

'He wouldn't tell me in case the police questioned me but he said he was safe; I don't think he was far away. Did you?'

Pullman asked. 'Did I what?'

'Did the police want to arrest my son again?'

'There were some questions we wanted to ask him but that doesn't matter now. What matters is that we find the person responsible for his death. So anything you can tell us that might help us to do that would be really useful.' Pullman maintained the soft, sympathetic tone.

Mrs Bennett thought some more and sobbed some more but in the end she could not throw any light on the investigation. She refused to be driven home and would not leave the church until she had prepared it for use. Pullman arranged for the WPC to stay with her until her daughter arrived.

DI Reid was looking agitated when Pullman eventually walked through to join him in the church. 'Sir you have to see this.' he indicated for Pullman to follow him to the altar. The head was now in a plastic exhibit bag on the altar; alongside it was another exhibit bag that Reid picked up and showed to Pullman.

'What the hells that,' he asked peering at the contents.

'It's his dick.' said Reid. 'It was stuffed down his throat.' Pullman winced. 'Tell you what sir he was a big boy; probably choked to death on that black beauty' Pullman gave him very stern look of admonishment.

'Sorry, sir,' apologised Reid.

'The pathologist said that his penis had been amputated while Bennett was still alive so your supposition could well be right, even though it was crudely put. Don't let me ever hear you say anything like that again DI Reid. Understood?' Reid apologised again.

'I'm going back to the station; when you've finished here come back to the incident room.'

It was not meant to be a deliberate racist comment. Pullman was unaware that Reid's wife was of mixed race and they spent a lot of time with her parents and their extended family both in the UK and on holidays in St Lucia. When they were together, both sides of the family joked about stereotypical white and black characteristics; none of the comments were derogatory; they all took it in good part and no one took offence or became defensive. He quickly decided that it was neither the time nor place to mention his family culture to the DCI; it would be like trying to defend his comment and that would only make matters worse.

The forensic team were in the process of wrapping up their investigation of the crime scene and removal of the exhibits including the altar cloth.

Pullman went over to the fingerprint specialist and said. 'Before you go, check the gate between here and the mosque next door. It's the only access down the side to get to the toilet window.'

Pullman left the chapel and joined Sperring at the car.

Reid took his mug back to the kitchen; nodded towards Mrs Bennett who didn't avert her gaze from the floor; rinsed out his mug under the cold water tap and left it in the sink. He went through to the small office next to the kitchen and searched around the desk until he found a contact number for Pastor Oyelude. He called the number and explained to the situation to the Pastor; told him that Mrs Bennett was still at the church and that they had contacted her daughter. He suggested to the Pastor that he contact a glazier and have the window repaired. The pastor said that he would attend to it immediately and then go to the church. DI Reid informed the WPC and left her to watch over the grieving mother pending the arrival of her daughter.

****

The weather front that had been circulating over central mainland Europe moved on leaving a front of high pressure in its wake. There was a clear blue sky over Trieste which belied the chill from the Bora blowing across the Adriatic towards Albania and lowering the temperature on what, in a photograph, would have appeared to be a perfect summer's day.

Peter Ebingdon felt it was time to buy a heavier jacket than the thin summer weight garment he was wearing. He knew nothing about Triest when he chose it as his next destination. It was just a place on a map that would give him access to the Adriatic or transport links to Croatia, Bosnia and Herzegovina and all places east if he needed them. Alternatively it would afford him access to the whole of Italy and through into the rest of Europe.

As he wandered around the streets, window shopping, he was taken by surprise at the size and beauty of the city; he was spoilt for choice for cafes, bars and restaurants; he figured that he could stay there for months and never need to eat at the same place twice. He'd visited Rome and Venice on business and for vacations on several occasions but the sheer scale of the Piazza dell 'Unità d'Italia made it probably the grandest square he'd ever walked across. Much grander and spacious than St Mark's Square in Venice but then the last time he was in St Mark's Square there was standing room only; he'd got tired of trying to fight his way through the throng of tourists.

This beautiful Piazza was dominated by the Palazzo del Municipio, the City Hall, designed by Giuseppe Bruni in 1875; he stood admiring the magnificent clock tower with its two bronze statues, which according to the information board were called Michez and Jachez, who diligently strike the bell to announce the hour every hour throughout the day and night; lovely to hear whilst having coffee perhaps but not so pleasant if you were staying at a hotel within earshot, particularly at noon and midnight. Ebingdon wandered in and out of various boutiques and designer shops. None of them had anything that took his fancy and some of the clothing was priced even beyond his pocket. Eventually he ended up at Godina, a department store on the Via Carducci. He was just blown away by the sheer enormity of the place. He was a reluctant shopper, Tamara had had to drag him kicking and screaming into stores in Milan and Madrid on more than one occasion, but he'd never seen a department store on this scale anywhere else in the Europe. Amongst isle after isle of Armani, Hugo Boss and almost every other designer label he could think of he found what he was looking for; a stylish dark blue padded jacket lifted by a discrete flash of red on one shoulder. He wasn't so keen on the price but he'd had enough shopping for one day so he paid for it and left the shop wearing it; he felt warmer already.

He didn't need the benefit of his purchase while he sat inside the Café Pirona enjoying a mouth- watering almond flavoured pastry and a cup of creamy coffee. He'd been attracted to try it by the picture of

237

the author James Joyce dominating the window display. As he found out inside the café Joyce was reputed to have conceived his classic work Ulysses whilst frequenting the establishment, situated just a few doors away from where the author was living at the time.

Whilst Ebingdon drank his cappuccino he decided not to spend another night in the Rosetti. He would go back to the hotel pick up his bag and get the hell out of there. Ebingdon was extremely pleased he had made his purchase when he stepped out of the café into the chill Bora that had increased in strength during the hour he had sat inside. He raised the collar of the jacket against the wind, stuffed his hands deep into the padded pockets and set off back to the Rossetti.

As usual the small reception desk was unmanned when he arrived; he'd retained his door key for that very reason. He climbed the two flights of stairs to his room, slipped the key into the lock opened the door and stepped inside the room. The shock caused him to step backwards sharply, 'What the hell are you doing here?'

TWENTY-FIVE

Thursday Afternoon 24ᵗʰ October

Pullman asked DS Sperring to drive the car back to the police station; she would be back there in two minutes. It was all of six hundred metres so he decided to walk. The extra three minutes it would take would give him a little more mental digestion time.

Pendragon obviously thought that God would be the best judge of Tyrone Bennett hence leaving his head at the church rather than at a place of justice as with the other two murders being investigated and the majority of those occurring overseas. Leaving the head at the church was a big mistake on the killer's part. Whoever it was must have known that Bennett attended that particular church; it was not purely by chance that it was chosen. Ipso facto the killer was known to Bennett; their first break on any of the three UK cases. The sister, Yvonne, doted on her brother so there was a high probability that she would have harboured Bennett after his flight from the arresting officers at the court. But surely the local police or Sapphire would have kept her house under surveillance as well as the mother's house; that needed checking out. That's all the time he had to think during the short walk.

He popped into the bagel shop opposite the police station to get something for lunch. He avoided the hanging salami, pastrami, black pudding and anything else of a similar shape and ordered a bagel with his favoured chicken mayo filling, a Danish pastry with an apricot filling and coffee to go. As he came out of the shop he could see Sperring on the opposite side of the road at the corner with Victorian Road, craning her neck anxiously back in the direction from which he'd walked. She was clearly wondering where he'd got to. He crossed the road at the lights and came into her line of vision; she was relieved to see him.

'Sir, CIFT have got a bit further with tracing the email post from Pendragon they say it was from a PC that's part of the Haringey Council system. Also they know for sure that the trail from SOC does lead directly back to BSC headquarters here in London. So your friend Tamara is back in the frame. I thought you'd like to know before we got back to the incident room.' She thought that he should announce the news to reinforce his stature as being in charge.

'So we have a lead to Pendragon on a PC owned by Haringey Council of which of course there's only one.' he said sarcastically. 'It would be nice and simple if it does turn out to be Tamara that's running SOC but it could be one of the laptops in the so called comms dock that was used. I'll call Tom Nerbis and see what he thinks, can you see if we've received the PM report yet, if not give it a chase.'

Pullman called Tom Nerbis at CIFT for advice on proceeding with the investigations at BSC. Nerbis suggested that they would need a simultaneous raid on the communications dock to impound any laptops in the dock as well as retrieving the machines out on loan and confiscating Tamara Bell-Sampson's laptop. CIFT had the same authority as Her Majesty's Revenue and Customs when it came to power of entry and confiscation of goods, provided they were within the scope of their remit. Nerbis set the wheels in motion.

****

They waited a few minutes for DI Reid to arrive, he apologised for keeping them waiting. Pullman was seated at a table to the side of the classroom eating his bagel, he stood up swallowed the contents of his mouth and announced that there had been one or two developments that DS Sperring would tell them about. He sat down again and got on with his lunch.

Sperring's courtesy to her boss hadn't been accepted then. She informed the team that the Computer and Internet Forensics Team had uncovered an email address for Pendragon and were waiting for the ISP to get back to them with contact details.

There was also good news in the search for the originator of the SOC site in that they had traced the source back to the BSC building in London but that was as far as they could go. To identify the actual computer used they would need to physically examine every machine until they produced the forensic evidence from the hard drive.

Pullman finished the bagel and washed it down with half the rapidly cooling cup of coffee, he stood up and moved centre stage.

'We'll decide what to do about the Pendragon information when we get the contact details, my bet is that it will be a local address but it could be elsewhere. CIFT will get a warrant through the NCCU to seize and examine Tamara Bell-Sampson's computer, discretely in case she's not responsible and we warn off the real culprit but at the moment all roads lead to her. We're awaiting the fingerprint check on the dildo and there were prints at the chapel. They should match up with those but if the killer is known to us the likelihood is that they would have worn gloves, so I'm not holding out a lot of hope that they'll be much use for identification purposes.' He walked back to the table to get the coffee and brought the cup back with him. 'That brings us to Bennett and this morning's little show. The killer left the head in the One Jesus chapel which tells us what?'

DS Grant answered. 'That the killer knew he went to that church.'

'Correct, which means?'

DS Patil said 'That he's local.'

'That she's local,' corrected Pullman. 'I still believe that the killer is a woman or rather women, I don't think a lone woman could have physically carried out these murders, certainly not Bennett's. I apologise if that sounds sexist,' he added. 'I think it's important that we find out where he was holed up because if the killer, we'll use the singular for the time being, managed to either kidnap him or entice him to somewhere she could bind him up then she had to find him first; if she did it we can too.'

DI Reid spoke 'I stopped on the way up here sir to check what the surveillance arrangements were for the family; they had a team covering the mother's house and a team covering the daughter's house twenty four seven and he didn't show.'

'Do you know if they watched the daughter's shop?'

'I wasn't aware she had one sir.'

'We only found out when we spoke to the mother this morning. The daughter has a beauty salon called....' he looked to Sperring for the name.

'Scissor Chicks.'

There were one or two knowing looks amongst the team. 'It's in Tottenham, Lynne has the business card. The mother says that...' he looked to Sperring again.

'Yvonne.' she looked at the business card she had fished out of her pocket 'Bennett.'

Either she hadn't married or was using her maiden name.

Pullman continued. 'Yvonne Bennett doted on her younger brother so it's more than possible that she would have harboured him and no doubt helped him to get away from the court. She would definitely have thought that her brother was innocent of all charges and would have done anything to protect him. She's probably at the chapel now comforting Mrs Bennett. We'll give them a couple of hours 'til she gets her mother home and settled before we interview the daughter; in the meantime I want you DS Grant, to visit the shop — before the daughter returns — and see if anyone remembers seeing Tyrone Bennett in or around the place during the past couple of weeks.'

Sperring's mobile rang she left the room to answer the call.

'DS Patil see if there is any way we can trace where the dildo was purchased. DC Rankin have we found out if he had a mobile yet?'

'The mobile operator is getting back to us,' he checked his watch, 'within the hour they said; by two pm.'

'Keep behind them, in the meantime check for CCTV coverage of that part of the High Street. Uniform team get out there with the mug shot and see if anyone saw Bennett in the last forty eight hours. One of you go to the mosque next door to the church and see if anyone saw anything suspicious last night. The killer gained access to the toilets from a gated side entrance between the two buildings; if it's kept locked maybe the killer had to climb over it. I've had it dusted.'

Sperring re-entered the room. 'Ah, Lynne you go to the daughter's salon with DS Grant.'

****

The one way section of Via Genova between Piazza del Ponterosso and Via San Spiridione was little more than one hundred and fifty metres in length; cars were parked on the left and a row of motor cycles on the right. These together with fenced off seating areas around two cafes added to the narrowness of the thoroughfare and contributed to an increased the sense of congestion. On this Thursday afternoon it was completely blocked to traffic and pedestrians. Dark blue Alfa Romeo159s of the Carabinieri formed a barrier at either end of the street and armed officers were diverting traffic and preventing pedestrians from entering the street. Parked in the Via Genova was a dark blue Carabinieri Land Rover and two light blue Alfa Romeos of the Polizia Locale. A Range Rover and an ambulance were parked at the rear of the vehicles. Two officers of the Polizia were stationed either side of the entrance to the B&B Rossetti between the fruttivendolo's display of ripe tomatoes and melons and the macellai's counters of fresh meat.

Onlookers had gathered at either end of the street and in the doorways of the shops and cafes; residents were peering out of windows above the outlets observing events in the street below. They watched as the Scena del Crimine officers in their white forensic overalls with Polizia Scientifica emblazoned on their backs, entered the building carrying shiny, ribbed aluminium cases.

On the second floor of the B&B Rosetti, Inspector Messio Balzaretti stood to one side to allow the SDC forensic team to enter room number seven. Peter Ebingdon's body was slumped against the wall; head to one side, chin resting on his blood soaked blue padded jacket. Behind him a trail of smeared blood ran from just below a faded print of a Canaletto street scene to where he had fallen. His eyes were open, blindly staring at the floor to his right. On his forehead, shakily written in black marker pen, were the letters SOC.

Balzaretti didn't need the forensic experts to tell him that the man had been shot in the chest at close range; the gunshot wounds were plain to see. He perused the room. It had not been ransacked; everything seemed to be where he would have expected it to be.

An SDC officer wearing white latex gloves examined the man's coat pockets and retrieved a credit card sized wallet from the right hand side pocket. He carefully opened it and flipped through the clear vinyl compartments, stopping at a driving license.

'Peter Ebingdon. English,' he said.

'He did not register. It would seem that no one registers here,' said the Inspector. 'The manager obviously did not check his ID.'

In the hotel reception area the aging manager was being interviewed by Deputy Inspector Marco Gilardino. 'Can I see your register, please?'

'Unfortunately the register was destroyed in the fire and I haven't yet replaced it. I asked the man to write his details on a blank piece of paper but he refused. I tried to insist but he got angry,' he lied unconvincingly. 'I was going to report it this morning but I was feeling unwell.'

The smell of booze on the manager's breath was only just evident over the aroma of his body odour and another stench which the policeman took to be emanating from the old boy's feet. No doubt the old fool felt unwell most mornings, thought Gilardino. 'Was he with anybody?'

'No but a woman did ask after him soon after he went out.'

'Can you describe her?'

'I didn't pay her much attention.'

'Try.'

The old man spoke slowly as he recalled her description. 'I'd say she was average height, light brunette hair with a dyed blue streak across the front and down to her left ear,' he demonstrated with his hand. 'She was quite attractive. I think maybe mid to late twenties.'

'What was she wearing?'

'A black jacket which was wet because of the rain and she wore small dark rimmed spectacles.'

'Italian?'

'No. She had a foreign accent but I don't know where she was from.'

'Did she go to his room?'

'No she just asked if he'd checked in and then left.'

'Did you tell her what room the man was in?'

'No she didn't ask,' he lied again. 'She just left.'

Through the half drawn curtain Gilardino could see the TV and sofa and a bottle of cognac on the floor and guessed that the old guy would spend most of his time in there. The old man described the visitor pretty well considering he'd said there was nothing remarkable he remembered about her. Allowing for his advanced years and his liquid habit he'd remembered quite a lot. 'Not bad for someone who didn't pay her much attention. You'd better not be lying to me,' said Gilardino. The old man shook his head nervously.

Gilardino wasn't to know that the rat man had conveniently forgotten to remember that she had paid him twenty Euros for the number of the room or that the guest had paid him for five nights in advance.

He didn't forget that he'd had caught site of the rear view of a woman leaving the hotel earlier in the afternoon, he just didn't want to get involved with more questions. It wasn't the same woman with the blue streak so it would be of no use to the police he decided.

Gilardino asked 'Are there any other guests staying?'

'Yes two rooms but they are out at the moment.'

'And I suppose they refused to give their registration details as well.' The old man just gave a shrug.

In the past five years or so no guests at the Rosetti stayed more than one night; some even checked out shortly after seeing their rooms. That's why rat man always made it clear to guests at the check-in that there were absolutely no refunds and why he never took them to their rooms. He hadn't noticed that the other guests had taken their belongings with them when they left but he'd given up noticing that, years ago.

'I might need to talk to you again,' said the Deputy Inspector. There was no point in him telling the proprietor not to go anywhere. He certainly wouldn't be leaving the country.

Gilardino shook his head and turned to leave. As he did so the old man noticed that the master room key was not on the hook under the desk where he normally kept it. Another thing he decided not to tell the Deputy Inspector.

A team of uniformed police officers spent several hours interviewing apartment occupiers in the Via Genova as well as all the shop and café owners and the customers who had been netted inside the police cordon.

No one could recall seeing anyone or anything suspicious in the street and could not recall seeing anyone entering the Rosetti, except for a waitress at the café who watched Ebingdon going into the building after having a coffee.

Later that day a forensic report was issued. The deceased had been shot three times; twice whilst standing and once when slumped; that bullet had passed through the body and was lodged in the wall behind the victim. After elimination of Ebingdon's fingerprints and those of the manager and his sister, who was employed as a chamber maid, there were no other prints. No footprints were identified. According to the receipt found in the wallet, the jacket worn by the deceased had been purchased that morning at Godina; there was nothing in the deceased's personal effects that were of any interest.

The report from the hastily arranged Post Mortem followed shortly after. The gunshot wounds were made with a .38 handgun possibly a Baretta Pico. From the angle of entry two of the shots had been fired from a seated or kneeling position from a distance of two metres; the third at point blank range from a standing position after the victim had fallen to the floor. The victim was already dead when the third bullet struck. As identity had been found on the body the details of age and ethnic origin were already known. There was nothing else of significance worth Balzaretti's attention.

Balzaretti and Gilardino discussed the reports; so this Englishman was shot by a ghost waiting for his return to the room. Being a ghost would explain how the killer managed to walk through a locked door; then disappear without being seen. If it hadn't been for the aging sister of the owner entering the wrong room the body may not have been found for several days. It was not the kind of establishment that changed the bed linen every day.

Deputy Inspector Gilardino informed Europol who in turn informed the NCA in the UK in order that the victim's relatives could be informed. Due to Ebingdon's relationship to Tamara Bell-Sampson, who was being monitored by SCAS they were informed of his death.

****

Richard Pointer immediately informed Mike Pullman; by eight o'clock that night he was trying to contact Tamara to inform her.

Pullman was told by her housekeeper that Tamara was out of the country on business. He enquired if she could be contacted and was told that after visiting BSCyber's , German office she intended to take a few days break, possibly skiing in the Alps and was due to check in with the office the following day. Until then she was out of contact. He requested her parents contact number which he was given.

His suspicions were aroused. Ebingdon had been shot dead in Italy and his wife, of whom he was afraid, was out of the country and apparently couldn't be contacted; this was beginning to sound more than co-incidence. He arranged for a photograph of Tamara to be emailed to the Italian police to see if anyone recognised her in the vicinity of the murder and to check identity at border crossings.

He rang the number he had been given for Tamara's parents. Their housekeeper informed him that they too were away enjoying a long weekend at their chateaux outside Rhiems. Pullman did not push it any further; chances were that someone in the BSC Group would pick up on the story on a news channel and contact them. In any case he doubted that the Bell-Sampsons would give a toss that he was dead. Perversely the news of his death might just make their weekend perfect. Ebingdon had no other relatives to inform.

Pullman called Caroline Nichols at Newzferret to let her know of Ebingdon's murder; he left a message on her voice mail.

The Italian police made no mention of the letters on Ebingdon's forehead nor did Pullman have any reason to ask. It did not even occur to him that it might in any way be related to the other murders.

TWENTY-SIX

DS Grant and DS Sperring drove to Tottenham and paid a visit to Scissor Chicks. During the drive they broached the subject of the name of the salon; scissor chicks was a slang term for lesbians and considered derogatory by some but obviously not by Yvonne Bennett. That's assuming she was aware of the significance of the name which referred to a sexual position adopted by two women engaging in mutual stimulation. If she hadn't been aware of the sexual connotations when she opened the salon she would surely have become aware by now; they had to assume that the business was targeted at the lesbian community. Cautiously they checked with each other that it wasn't a group to which either of them belonged. It wasn't. Lynne Sperring had casually mentioned that she was in the process of breaking up with her long term partner Gary and Rachel Grant had made it known that she and her fiancé Simon hoped to marry the following year.

Externally Scissor Chicks looked like any other hairdressers and beauty salon to be seen on any high street in the country; glass entrance door, framed in natural aluminium, abutting a single plate glass window affording a clear view of the interior; they could see two stylists busy with customers.

Sperring and Grant entered the shop and were greeted by the third stylist standing behind a bust high counter on which sat a telephone and a small notebook computer. Her skin was a translucent shade of peach from too much time spent on a tanning table; heavy make-up had been applied to her cheeks, eyes and lips and her teeth looked as if they would glow in the dark. Her finger nails were patently false, each decorated in a distinct pattern, different from the adjoining nail – these were hands that never went near the washing-up. Bleached blonde hair towered above her crown in a convoluted bun.

'Good afternoon ladies, welcome to Scissor Chicks. I'm Sinead, what can we do for you today?'

The two detectives showed her their ID and a look of anxiety spread across the acting receptionist's face.

'I'm afraid the owner isn't here at the moment. She's had a family bereavement; we're not expecting her back today.'

Sperring spoke first. 'We know; is there somewhere we can talk in private please?'

'We can use a nail booth or go upstairs to the flat,' said Sinead.

'There's a flat upstairs?'

'Yes we use part of it as a staff room.'

'Let's do that then.'

Sinead lead the way through the salon. The two officers took in the décor as they followed her. The shop stretched back about fifteen metres; it was tastefully decorated in an art deco style with fancy mirrors in front of the three stylist's chairs; two of which were occupied one by an attractive young woman of mixed race and one by the white orc's sister. A row of four sinks for shampooing ran along the wall opposite the chairs, alongside each sink was a free standing domed hair dryer. Display posters showing various hair styles linked to products from some of the UK's leading hair and beauty brands decorating the wall space; pre-recorded musak was playing softly in the background. About half way down the length of the salon an area had been partitioned off to form three nail treatment cubicles; in the centre of the rear wall a curved archway was hung with a beaded fly screen that appeared to lead through to another section. Sinead held the fly screen back behind her but let it slip as the visitors walked through; to their surprise they stepped into a fully stocked sex shop display area. The wall to the right was festooned with samples of dildos in various shapes and sizes, colours and materials; some battery operated, some attached to leather or vinyl cod pieces. Boxed sales stock was stacked beneath the display. The wall in front of them displayed an assortment of leather gimp masks from full head coverings with zips and rings attached to simple masquerade style eye masks. A selection of erotic DVDs was on a floor standing revolving rack. To their left were racks of garments in a kaleidoscope of colours and fabrics. Most of the display was absorbed through their well-honed peripheral vision as they continued through another door and up a flight of stairs to the flat above. Sinead settled them down in the staff kitchen and offered them a drink which they declined.

'This is about Tyrone's murder isn't it? said Sinead astutely.

Sperring nodded and took a flyer. 'We understand that Yvonne's brother Tyrone had been staying here for the past few weeks.'

'Yeah, since he was released.'

Sperring hadn't expected it to be that easy; it took her a moment to react. 'Ah, right. Did he have any visitors while he was here?'

'Don't think so; he stayed up here most of the time which seemed a bit odd considering he'd was innocent and been freed. Eve, Yvonne, said it was to avoid the newspapers because they were trying to do a deal to sell his story to one of the nationals; reckoned there could be few quid in it.'

'Did he spend any time in the salon; meet any of the customers?' asked DS Grant.

'Oh Yeah, right bleeding barney there was one day. He was sitting at one of the sinks having a coffee and talking to Eve while she did a customer's hair. I was in booth three at the time doing a client's nails, she was getting married the next day so we had her and her maid of honour in; then in walks Karen's eleven o'clock takes one look at Tyrone and starts ranting at him; calling him a rapist and a pervert; that when they locked him up they should have thrown away the key. Tyrone was gobsmacked told her to shut her effing mouth and eff off. Then she called him a worthless fuck and punched him in the face really hard, she was a big butch girl too; we seem to attract them here.'

'What happened then?'

'Tyrone went for her; he grabbed a pair of curling tongs and said if she didn't eff off he'd shove 'em up her arse. She kneed him in the balls; she could look after herself that one could. I wouldn't like to get

251

on her wrong side I can tell you. Tyrone fell on the floor. It all happened so quickly really. Eve shoved a pair of scissors at her face and told her to get out or she'd stab her in the throat. The woman said something about not knowing how Eve could defend an effing scumbag like that and he deserved hanging then stormed out. I wanted to call the police but Eve said no.'

'Do you know who this woman was?'

'She'd been here a few times. I'd have to check the appointments on the computer.'

'Okay, before we go downstairs could we take a look at the room Tyrone was using?'

'I don't know. Don't you need a search warrant or something for that?'

'I just wanted a quick peek; save me coming back that's all.'

'I don't suppose it matters now he's dead.' She showed them along the landing to a bedroom.

The room looked like an entire university of freshers had been having a party; there were piles of empty lager cans on every surface; pizza boxes and polystyrene food containers, some with festering contents, littered the floor; the bed looked as if someone had been wrestling an alligator on it; red topped tabloids were strewn around one side of the bed. A combined TV and DVD player was on the sideboard alongside three porno DVDs. DS Grant moved them with the tip of her pen they were graphically entitled 'ANALgesics', 'Back Passage to India' and 'DP Orgies'. All reflecting Bennett's deviant preferences. Grant sniffed and screwed her nose up as if there was a foul smell in the room.

'Bleeding state in here, ennit,' observed Sinead.

Sperring and Grant just nodded and made affirmatory noises. All in all there were definitely signs that a struggle could have taken place in the room or a twister had blown through it; forensics would need to be called in just to be on the safe side. They left the room and went back downstairs where Sinead checked through the computerised appointments log.

'Let me see it must have been a Friday 'cos of the wedding the next day; here we are that's her, just say's Lu, spelt L U.'

'No surname?'

Sinead shook her head. 'Most of our clients book just using their first names.'

'Contact details, telephone number anything like that?'

'No but she must be local cos, as I say, she'd been in here a few times and I've seen her about.'

'Could you give me a description?' asked Grant.

Karen joined them. 'Who we talking about?'

'The bitch that had a go at Eve's brother in here.'

'Yeah she was right out of order; you wouldn't think she was a librarian, always think of them as being quiet mousey types.'

'A librarian; you know where she works?' Sperring asked hopefully.

'Yes at the library up the High Road right opposite White Hart Lane. I take my Kylie there, she loves her books. My Kylie says that she reminds her of that woman in that film, you know the one where the little girl does magic in school.'

DS Grant helped out, 'Matilda; Miss Trunchbull.' She'd been a big Roald Dahl fan in her childhood.

'That's it Mrs Crunchball, that's the one.'

'Look thank you, you've been a great help.' Sperring gave Sinead a card and asked if she would contact her if Lu came in again or if she thought of anything else that might be useful. Sinead said that she wouldn't dare come in again because Eve had barred her.

The two detectives left the salon. Walked a few paces to be out of sight from the shop and stopped.

Grant said 'What do you reckon Lulu, Louise?'

'Lucy or maybe from the description it's Luke.'

Sperring rang Pullman. She brought him up to date with the conversation she and DS Grant had just had. She suggested that SOCO should go over the bedroom in the salon. Pullman agreed and said he'd sort it. She told him of the rumpus at the salon and the

253

possible suspect and said that she and DS Grant would pay the library a visit if that was okay with him. It was. Pullman was hopeful that they were getting somewhere but a little pissed off that somehow he was drifting into a supervisory role rather than being out with his DSs at the sharp end. That was a situation he'd have to correct. He was the SIO after all.

Sperring and Grant drove the short distance along the High Road to the library directly opposite White Hart Lane the home ground of Premiership football club Tottenham Hotspur and parked in a side road. The library building was designed back in the sixties and may have been trendy then but was now looking dated from the outside. The visual appeal of the odd patterned brick and tile façade wasn't improved by the sprayed on graffiti. Inside was a different picture.

The décor was light, bright and clean with polished laminated flooring with stylish red upholstered seating under a huge central hanging up-lighter. Beech wood shelving units housed thousands of books; each unit clearly marked with the genre of fiction or reference works. There was a music section and a DVD selection. Leading off from the left of the main library area was a computer room with ten PCs all of which were occupied. There were just three people perusing the book shelves before the two detectives entered. They wandered around first in the hope of seeing Lu but no one matching the description was around; they went to reception where a neatly dressed middle aged librarian was seated behind filling in a form of some description. They introduced themselves and asked if Lu was around.

The very polite and softly spoken woman informed them that Janet was on sick leave but was expected back the following Monday.

'Sorry I think you misheard; we want to speak to Lu.'

'Yes Janet Luman. She likes to be called Lu but I prefer to call her Janet. She doesn't like that so I've taken to not calling her anything if I can avoid it,' she explained. 'Janet's been on sick leave all week; probably a virus there's a lot of it about at the moment.'

They asked for Janet Luman's address and after a little hesitancy and some degree of stern persuasion the librarian reluctantly retrieved Janet's contact details from the computer.

DS Grant asked. 'I notice you've got a computer room; can anyone use it?'

'Oh, yes every library member can access them; it's completely free you know. No need to book. Officially, use is limited to an hour but if there's nobody waiting then we turn a blind eye.'

'I assume they all have internet access.'

'Yes of course. People come in to search for jobs, accommodation, information for school projects, that sort of thing.'

'What about this computer?' Grant indicated the one the librarian was using.

'No I'm afraid not; this and the other office PCs are restricted to the system only; they don't have internet access. If I need to use the internet then I use my home PC but I have used a library machine once in a while.'

'And Lu, Janet would she use them?'

'Too often I'm afraid. Mr Thomas has had a word with her on more than one occasion.'

'Mr Thomas being the manager?'

'The Chief Librarian,' she corrected Grant. 'Would you like to speak to him?'

They declined the invitation; thanked her for her help and bade her farewell.

When they returned to the car Sperring rang Pullman again; while she was doing that Grant entered Janet Luman's postcode in to the satnav. Pullman instructed them to wait until he got there before they questioned Luman; if she had committed the murder, and she sounded more than capable of doing so, then she may be in possession of dangerous weapons and might resist arrest. He knew both DSs were more than capable of dealing with most situations nevertheless he didn't want to take any chances; besides he wanted an excuse to get out of the incident room.

255

They gave him the post code and arrange to meet him outside Luman's house. The satnav indicated the house was less than eight minutes away, in the event it took them seven minutes and took Pullman a further twenty to join them outside the three storey Victorian house that had been converted in to two flats. The label on the doorbell showed that flat 2b Luman was on the upper floor. Pullman pressed the bell push and waited just a few seconds before pressing again. The bell was not audible from outside so they had no idea if it was working. After what he considered was a reasonable time lapse he rang the bell for the bottom flat.

The door was opened, as far as the security chain would allow, by a throw-back to the 1970s flower power era. He had shoulder length tangled locks hanging from beneath a greasy leather Stetson; a beard reaching the middle of his chest, waxed into a point topped by a handlebar moustache. He was wearing bright red corduroy trousers faded at the knees and a grubby, white patterned waistcoat over a lightweight denim shirt. Pullman ignored the familiar aroma of cannabis wafting towards him.

'Don't want nuffink fanks?' said the man attempting to shut the door which was being jammed open by Pullman's size eleven shoe.

'Good,' said Pullman, 'then you won't be disappointed, Mr Junkin.' Pullman presumed that was his name as it was scribbled on the bell push label.

'How d'ya know me name?'

Pullman ignored the question. He held up his ID and said. 'It's not you we've come to see. It's Janet Luman upstairs.'

'She ain't in.'

'If you'd kindly open the door we'll check that for ourselves.'

'Don't fink so, mate; you ain't got no right without a warrant; you got a warrant?'

'No Mr Junkin but if you'd like us to get one I can come back and search your flat as well but I'm sure you don't want the expense of flushing your supplies down the toilet, do you?'

Junkin pulled a pissed off face at being coerced, silently mouthed a few expletives and reluctantly released the chain from the holder.

'Thank you,' said Pullman, 'very good of you to co-operate.'

Junkin stood back so that they could enter and climb the stairs to Luman's flat. 'Like I say she ain't in, she's hardly ever in.'

The three officers stopped so that they were standing in an ascending formation on the stairs looking over the bannister rail. 'Any idea where she's gone,' asked Sperring with restrained frustration.

'Down the Pendragon; I expect, she spends most of her time down there.' The three detectives exchanged glances up and down the tier.

'Pub. Club?' asked Sperring.

'Club; lesbian club. I went with them once, not that I'm gay or a woman if it comes to that but I thought it would be a giraffe, not my sort of place though; full of muff munchers; sorry ladies.'

'None taken,' said Grant, 'you said you went there with them, who's them?'

Lu and her latest partner, Singapore Sling; leastways that's what I calls her. Kai Ling is what she calls herself; comes from Singapore, attractive girl considering.'

Pullman asked 'Where will we find this Pendragon Club?'

'Down the High Road behind the George and Dragon pub,' he replied in a tone that implied everyone knew the location of the club.

'Right Mr Junkin we're going to go now but we will be back with a warrant not that we need one to search premises where we have reason to believe there are drugs; you and I both know we have reason so you've got an hour or two to get rid of your stash. See you later.'

Sperring said 'Since when have you given advanced warnings?'

'Just wanted to piss him off a bit more; I can't be arsed to deal with him we've got bigger fish to fry.'

'Yeah she sounds like a great white, sir,' said Sperring.

'Piranha,' said Pullman, 'Tears men to pieces.'

TWENTY-SEVEN

Evening Thursday 24th October

Before they got in the cars Pullman called Brannigan and arranged for six uniformed officers to meet them at the club. He hadn't seen the layout of the place so he wanted to be prepared to cover multiple exits if necessary.

Pullman took the lead as the two cars drove slowly along the High Road looking for the George and Dragon public house; he saw it on the opposite side of the road standing on the corner of a cross roads; it was newly painted in cream and red with signs on both sides of the building visible from the road reading the George and Dragon Fine Ales. The signs were in gold lettering on a black background and a large swinging sign depicting the inevitable armoured figure with a lance fighting a fire breathing dragon was hanging from a gibbet over the main lounge bar entrance.

He needed to turn right at the traffic lights. Pullman indicated right and angled his car so that it impeded the progress of the vehicles behind; his colleagues followed suit in their car which was two behind his, causing several other cars behind them to sound their horns with impatience. Neither car wanted to activate their blue hazard lights concealed in the front grill and in the rear bumpers. The traffic lights changed colour allowing Pullman to pull across to the smaller side road and park. It took another sequence of lights and more tooting of horns before his colleagues could do the same and pull up behind him. There was a narrow side entrance between the pub and a bank which led to the rear via a wrought iron gate. On the gate was a skilfully hand painted sign depicting a white swan entwined with a dragon; the two creatures were disproportionately of similar size which was necessary because the swan was attempting to devour the dragon.

Pullman was standing on the pavement talking on his mobile as DS Grant's car pulled up. He ended the call and jumped into the rear seat. 'Right we'll hang on for the uniforms then the three of us will go in. I can't believe it'll be very busy at this time of the afternoon so we should be able to spot Luman given that by all accounts we're looking for Matilda's nemesis.'

Sperring said. 'I checked in on the way here sir, figured she'd probably have a record and she did; couple of convictions for affray; a couple more for d&d and another for committing a lewd act in a public place.' She held up her smart phone so that Pullman could see the screen, 'They sent me her mug shot.'

Pullman looked at the screen. 'Bloody hell the descriptions were on the money; should spot her alright.'

A white police transit van and six uniformed officers wearing stab vests disembarked. Pullman got out of the car and spoke to the sergeant in charge. Within moments the officers were deployed at the front saloon bar entrance to the pub; the side entrance to the same bar and two either side of the small gated entrance to the rear of the property.

DS Grant and DS Sperring got out of their car and locked it before following Pullman through the gate and round to the entrance to the club. Externally it was constructed of unpainted red bricks with a frosted glass double door in a peeling wooden frame, set back a metre from the front elevation. A replica of the swan and dragon sign was fixed to the wall above an overflowing wall mounted cigarette butt bin; a sign reading Private Members Club was affixed to the return wall. Six aluminium beer kegs were stacked, in a pyramid formation alongside the building with complete disregard for health and safety issues; a large blue commercial refuse collection bin with a yellow lid was in the corner of the small area adjacent to the club.

Pullman guessed that at some stage in the pubs history this extension had been a function room or possibly a dining room or may be a snooker room. At this point in history it was the place where he hoped to find the woman they suspected of murdering Tyrone Bennett.

The double doors of the club opened inwards; Pullman led the three detectives as they entered and took in their surroundings. Around a dozen members were in the club and all of those who were seated without exception looked up or turned their heads to stare at the new arrivals. It was a scene reminiscent of a spaghetti western; all that was missing was Sergio Leone's theme tune; instead the room was filled with the sound of I Was a Fool by Tegan and Sarah.

A couple of cover girls dancing in a close embrace on the circular dance area to the right of the bar ignored the new arrivals and everyone else if it came to that; they were in a world of their own.

Pullman's pupils rocked from side to side like those of an autocue novice; the bar person had enough metal in her nose, lips, ears and eyes to explode the detectors at Heathrow; part of a multi-coloured tattoo was visible on her neck above the collar of the black shirt she was wearing. Behind her, a row of optics was hanging; the rear work surface carried dozens of bottles of less called for spirits and wines and at the furthest end a double Gaggia coffee machine was nearing the end of its brewing cycle. Two forty somethings were seated at a table in the far corner; one had an Elvis Presley quiff piled above her high forehead; her companion had curly mousey hair with a single, thin red highlight both were wearing white shirts. Seated on a bar stool, now with her back to them had to be Luman. She was alone but there were two drinks on the bar.

Pullman walked towards her followed closely by his two colleagues. 'Janet Luman?' he asked and got silence in response. 'Are you Janet Luman?'

There was no doubt that it was her; the mug shot was flattering. Luman turned her head enough to look into her inquisitor's eyes. She was a caricature of what 'disgusted of Tunbridge Wells' would consider to be a lesbian. Pullman estimated she was five seven maybe eight; difficult to tell while she was seated. Weighed around 15 stones of solid muscle, no fat; she obviously worked out. Grade one hair, unplucked eyebrows, no makeup. Two ear piercings in each ear; she was wearing a white open neck collarless shirt with a feint vertical pinstripe design and partially rolled up sleeves, unbuttoned black leather waistcoat studded with badges of various organisations and a pair of ill-fitting blue denim jeans. Her right wrist was adorned with numerous coloured bangles; her left wrist carried a heavy stainless steel watch and a chunky silver coloured chain link bracelet. She wore red leather Doc Martin boots. In twenty seven years on the job Pullman had come across countless members of the LGBT community. He had no axe to grind; he genuinely did not judge anyone by their race, creed or gender but he was close to making an exception in Luman's case. She was using her appearance to make an extreme statement; *I'm a dyke don't fucking mess with me.* Pullman could almost smell the testosterone oozing from her pores.

'I'm Lu,' she said with utter contempt. 'Who the fuck are you?'

'Detective Chief Inspector Pullman and this is Detective Sergeant Sperring and DS Grant.' Luman's expression of contempt didn't flicker. 'We'd like to ask you a few questions.'

'Didn't know it was quiz night,' said Luman. Kai Ling returned from the ladies cloakroom, surprised to see the gathering around her friend; she sat down on her bar stool without saying a word.

Pullman ignored the retort. 'Could we go to a table please?' It wasn't a question, it was a request.

'You can do what the fuck you like. I'm staying here and finishing my drink.'

'We can continue this down the nick if you'd prefer; makes no odds to me.'

Luman thought about it for a few seconds then picked up her drink, got down from the bar stool and sauntered across to a vacant table doing a very passable impression of the honey monster. She motioned to Kai Ling to stay put. Two of the remaining seven couples left the bar including the couple in the far corner and the dancers; a table of three stayed to watch the floorshow. Pullman and Sperring followed

261

Luman to the table. DS Grant stayed to talk to Kai Ling. It was a one way discussion Kai Ling appeared to speak little or no English.

Pullman sat opposite Luman. 'How are you feeling? Asked Pullman. Luman furrowed her brow. 'I hear you've been ill' Luman shook her head. 'Oh, I thought you were on sick leave.'

'I am,' said Luman 'doesn't mean I'm ill; we're allowed ten sick days a year so I took some. Everybody does it.'

'So what have you been up to on your sick days?'

'Aren't you supposed to give me that spiel about my rights?'

'We're not arresting you Janet,' he called her that on purpose to get her hackles up, 'simply asking for your co-operation in answering some questions. If you don't answer them I might have to arrest you in which case DS Sperring will read you your rights. Fair enough?'

Luman faked a yawn to demonstrate her disinterest.

'So what have you been doing on your days off?'

'This and that; spent most of the time at home with Kai.'

'Mr Junkin in the flat below you seems to think you're hardly ever in.'

'That spaced out junkie; doesn't know what fucking day it is most of the time. He doesn't even know if he's in or out himself let alone where I am.'

Pullman thought that was probably true. 'What do you and Kai do when you're at home?'

Luman just smiled and gave him an exaggerated wink.

'Where were you last Tuesday?'

'I've told you at home.'

'All day and all night?' asked Pullman.

'I don't know; I don't keep a diary. Might have gone to the shops or come down here.'

'Didn't go for some fresh air on Hampstead Heath by any chance?' Pullman was watching for a reaction; he saw a definitely flicker in her eyes.

'Do you know Tyrone Bennett?' She shook her head.

'You go to the Scissor Chicks hairdressing salon don't you?'

Luman gave a non-committal shrug.

'You had an argument with Tyrone Bennett there two weeks ago. It's on their CCTV,' he lied.

Luman still remained silent. Pullman withdrew his notebook from his inside pocket, flipped it open and referred to non-existent notes.

'You called him a rapist, a pervert and a worthless piece of shit.' He closed the notebook and returned it to his pocket. 'You punched him in the face and kneed him in the groin. Surely you remember that.'

Luman took a deep breath. 'He was all of those and more,' she said through clenched teeth.

'Was; so you know he's dead then?'

'No.' she reconsidered her reply. 'Yes; I heard it somewhere.'

'Funny we haven't released his name yet. He was only identified this morning.'

'Must have heard it on the Tottenham grapevine then; news travels fast around here.'

'Did you just hate Bennett or do you hate all men?'

'I don't like perverts, rapists and Detective Chief Inspectors,' she said.

'We already know that from your posts on the Sisters of Chiomara web site Janet or should I call you Pendragon?'

'Don't know what you're talking about,' she said with noticeably less conviction than previous answers.

'I'm surprised that an educated woman like you is so poor at spelling or was that done on purpose? He got no response.

Luman looked over at Grant speaking to Kai Ling. 'What she talking to her for; she hasn't done nothing.'

'That means she has done something,' said Pullman

'Oh dear are you from the grammar police', she said sniffily 'Did I make a double negative; I'd better watch my Ps and Qs.'

Pullman smiled inwardly. He could tell that underneath the bravado and the attempt at being streetwise, Luman was an educated woman; presumably she'd have to be to qualify as a librarian. The tone and language of the Pendragon post was obviously an attempt to distance her real life persona from the personality portrayed in the message.

'Janet you threaten and physically assault Tyrone Bennett; he ends up murdered on Hampstead Heath; you've no alibi for the day he died and you frequent a club called Pendragon.'

'What the fuck does that prove,' she said.

She was right, it proved nothing; all circumstantial. He was sure that she would be giving nothing away that would enable him to make an arrest there and then. He needed to keep her talking long enough for the search warrants he had arranged earlier, to be executed. One was for searching her flat and the other for the impounding and forensic examination of the computers in the library.

'Do you possess any sex toys?' he asked.

'Up yours,' she snapped back at him; and no doubt she would have done, given the chance.

'You see one was found at the scene of the murder and we managed to get three prints from it. They're being checked as we speak. Are any of your toys missing, I wonder? Maybe the prints aren't yours; maybe you got Kai Ling to use the dildo. Maybe…

'I've never used a dildo with Kai,' she snapped at him. 'Prefer plastic to glass anyway.'

Pullman smiled he had wanted to make her angry and put her off guard; he had succeeded. 'Glass; did I say it was glass?'

Luman put her index finger and thumb to the corner of her lips and moved them from one corner to the other as a clichéd gesture to indicate that she was zipping-up her mouth; she glared at him in defiance.

Pullman knew they had the right person all he had to do now was provide sufficient proof for a prosecution. He stood up, 'Janet Luman I am arresting you on suspicion of murdering Tyrone Bennett on or about Tuesday October fifteenth.' He nodded at Sperring, 'Read her, her rights'.

He quite expected Luman to resist arrest but she sat there expressionless and motionless as Sperring went through her well-rehearsed routine. The uniformed officers were summoned to escort Luman and Kai Ling to the transport van and take them to the police station. The three detectives remained behind. Pullman checked in to make sure the warrants were being executed. They were. He then went over to metal mickey behind the bar; he smiled at her. 'I know we're not members but do you think we could have three coffees please.'

She gave a very pleasant smile in return. 'My pleasure, I'll make you my temporary guest members.' Grant and Sperring joined him at the bar and Sperring drew up a third stool.

The girl behind the bar asked 'Have you arrested the pit bull then?'

'Let's just say she's helping us with our enquiries.'

'Good,' she said putting ground coffee in to the two chromed brewing compartments. 'She's bad for business.'

'Really,' said Sperring, 'why do you say that?'

'She drinks too much and when she's drunk she's violent and abusive to other members. She's got a foul mouth on her.'

Pullman had made the uncharacteristic mistake of judging this girl by her looks; she was pleasant, nicely spoken and articulate. 'Why don't you bar her or revoke her membership?'

'The governor won't do it; just avoids the issue; think she must have the negatives as they say.' She served the first two cups of coffee to Sperring and Grant together with a small jug of milk.

'Was the pit bull, as you call her, in here last Tuesday?'

'Unfortunately she's been in every night this week.'

'With her partner Kai Ling?'

No. Today's the first day Kai's been in for a couple of weeks. Don't know why she's with that thing. She's a pretty girl much too nice for...,' she finished mid-sentence in case the guests sensed her envy. 'You asked about Tuesday, that's the night the she was in here with two Rottweilers. Right pack they were; had a few drinks; really pumped up, one of them was flashing a pair of handcuffs; must have been going to one hell of a party.'

She served Pullman his coffee. 'Were they here long?' he asked.

'Left about eight I think, maybe quarter to; something like that.'

'Didn't say where they were going or order a taxi I don't suppose.'

'No they had a van.'

Pullman was about to ask if she got the number but waited.

'When they left I went out for a smoke there were no other members in by that time; the three of them had cleared the place. I was outside and watched them get into a big blue van. I had to laugh it had a sign on it saying Uther's Mobile Dog Grooming; how appropriate was that.' She laughed again at the memory.

It never ceased to amaze Pullman how the breaks came in an investigation. If he hadn't fancied a coffee he probably wouldn't have questioned the barmaid; she wouldn't have mentioned the van and he would have been unaware of Uther's Dog Grooming Service. As it was by nine o'clock that evening they had located the owner impounded the van and arrested Amanda Reeves and Terri Scholes on suspicion of being Rottweiler's.

By midnight forensic teams had found traces of Bennett's blood on clothing in Luman's flat; traces of Bennett's DNA on a pair of handcuffs in Luman's bedside cabinet; a Shibazi brass handled meat cleaver, in the spare tyre well of the blue transit van; it had more than enough traces of Bennett's blood and Terri Scholes fingerprints; Amanda Reeves thumbprint on the glass dildo along with a partial of Janet Luman. And the boys from CIF had found Luman's Pendragon post on the hard drive of computer number two in the library. All-in-all there was more than enough evidence with which to charge all three and more than sufficient for the CPS to proceed with a prosecution.

They decided not to charge Yvonne Bennett with perverting the course of justice for harbouring her brother; they would find it difficult to prove that she knew her brother was going to be re-arrested after his release.

DI Reid checked out Kai Ling's claim that she was in Singapore on the day of the murder. Her alibi was watertight and she was subsequently released.

Pullman reflected on a job well done by the team and hoped that his colleagues in Humberside and the Glasgow police would have as much success in their respective investigations. All that remained now was to find the source of the SOC web site and the killer of Peter Ebingdon.

Piece of cake.

TWENTY-EIGHT

Friday 25th October

Pullman was not happy being back in his windowless office at the NCA headquarters in central London. He had enjoyed his couple of days of real policing and felt satisfied with the outcome of events.

Richard Pointer breezed in. 'I hear congratulations are in order; didn't take you long.'

'Things just fell into our lap really. One of those rare cases you come across where all the pieces of the jigsaw fall into place.' Sometimes mixed metaphors make the point. 'She was a cocky bitch.'

'So I gather,' Pointer smiled knowingly.

Pullman got his drift and shook his head. 'I mean she was arrogant; almost as if she didn't care about getting caught. She threw down the breadcrumbs and we just followed the trail.'

'Maybe she's looking forward to the rich pickings inside, eh?'

'Tell you what, she'll try and rule the roost in Send or Bronzefield or wherever she ends up. They'll need to allocate the three of them to different prisons cos if they gang up, woe betide the other inmates and the prison officers if it comes to that; she is one nasty piece of work.'

'We've had several reports of arrests being made around the world since we circulated the web site information; seems like that has triggered a lot more internet investigations and highlighted suspects in all walks of life. Could be that the Sisters of Chiomara website's days are numbered.'

'Do you know if CIFT are having any joy at BSC? That's where the answer lies.'

'Not spoken to anyone this morning but they went in yesterday and confiscated all the equipment and closed the communications dock. Absolute furore, BSC top brass went ballistic said they couldn't run the operation without the equipment; they threatened a monumental law suit so our top brass got involved; we had to rethink and check as best we could on site and release each machine as soon as it was checked; wasn't ideal but it sufficed and kept BSC happy…ish.'

'But no joy yet?' asked Pullman.

Pointer shook his head. 'Also that Tarquinius business in New York you asked me to look at; well I have and I'm sure there's no direct connection with our SOC cases; seems incredible but I'm absolutely certain that the MOs are pure coincidence; no association between the two. The NYPD have re-arrested their two prime suspects; they're not looking for anyone else in connection with the two murders.'

'Good that was a complication we didn't need,' said Pullman with a degree of relief.

Sperring entered the room; she exchanged good mornings with Pointer.

'What have you got?' asked Pullman.

She was tempted to say a stinking headache from sleep deprivation; but as Pointer was still in the room she let the opportunity pass. She confined her response to matters that had come to light on the other murders while they were wrapping up the Pendragon case and handing over the tidying up to DI Reid and DS Grant.

Before she started, Pointer excused himself and left the room.

Using the notes in front of her, Sperring told Pullman that Glasgow police may have a breakthrough in the Kulkinski case; two women had been detained in the act of attempting to kidnap a man by the name of Ross McGregor a local used car dealer; the women were held overnight and were currently being questioned; Glasgow CID would get back to her if there was any news.

Equally exciting news was that a laptop had been retrieved from a water filled drainage ditch on farm land behind the church in Clipton; the farmer was using a small Caterpillar digger to clear the ditch; the laptop was caked in mud and badly water damaged but he handed it in to the police in Howden they sent it up to Hull for the computer forensic experts there to attempt a hard drive retrieval. They were still working on it but confirmed that the owner was Thomas Wethersby.

'Excellent,' exclaimed Pullman. 'Wonder how the hell it ended up in a drainage ditch? So progress on both fronts, excellent,' he said again. 'Anything else?'

'We've had all the background checks returned on the fifteen names on the list from BSC, nothing to worry us there; the odd caution for d and d and a bit of domestic but nothing to suggest a link to SOC.'

'Do something for me; go back through the list and check that we haven't missed anything there would you.'

Sperring nodded, ignoring the fact that it was him that eliminated most people from the list; then she asked, 'Any progress on Peter Ebingdon?'

'Not yet but if Tamara Bell-Sampson doesn't get back to me by lunch time I'll contact Europol and see if they can trace her, just in case she tries to skip. I sent a picture of her to the Italian police but I've not heard back from them yet. Oh, another thing Lynne, I was thinking we ought to go home for the weekend. I don't know about you but I could do with some more clothes and there are one or two things I could do with sorting out in the house.'

He had come to the decision that it was definitely time to clear Jane's wardrobes. She had quite a few little black numbers, sparkly tops and winter coats so with both Christmas and winter looming now would be a good time for the charity shop to take them into stock. On top of that he simply didn't fancy spending the weekend in their hotel, as comfortable as it was. Furthermore Jane's parents had invited him for the weekend after he cancelled the visit. He wanted to avoid that scene so he had told them that he had been ordered to return to Hull.

DS Sperring jumped at the idea of a weekend at home. Much to her surprise Pullman volunteered to speak to the travel department and organise things. She booted her laptop and opened the Excel programme containing the list of male staff with access to the laptop pool. As before she checked all the names against their whereabouts and filtered the list down to eleven targets; it was a laborious and tedious job; at one point she actually dropped off to sleep, it was only the sensation of falling off her chair that woke her up.

She went to the vending machine in the corridor and dispensed herself a cup of black liquid that purported to be brewed from fresh Arabica beans. One sip told her it that it was more likely brewed from baked beans but hopefully it still contained enough caffeine to give her a lift. She continued reading through the list of twelve names.

Abdullah Yusef Alman
Michael J Gorman
Hugh Lambert
J D Mortimer
Rob Noughton
Isaac Rabinz
S A Sealy
K L Sheng
Ken Smith
D R Trungby
Sam Warner
Jake Zimmerman

She guessed at their various nationalities, for amusement more than anything. She's been to school with a Michael Gorman but she knew he'd been tragically killed in a jet-ski accident in the Maldives while on honeymoon so this Gorman was not the same man she knew She remembered that Zimmerman was Bob Dylan's real name and had a vague feeling that Sam Warner was one of the founders of Warner Bros film studios; she was tempted to Google it but overcame the temptation. She started to cross match the names against the contact details to prepare the final list for checking on the PNC. Fortunately the contact details gave the full names and not just initials; when she got to the eighth name on the list and her eyes nearly popped out of her head. She picked up her mobile and called Pullman she had no idea where he had disappeared to, for so long, and this was important. Pullman answered. 'Sir I'm in the middle of checking the

271

full list again and you were right there is a great big elephant marching across the room.'

'What are you on about Lynne,' asked Pullman.

She wanted to say that his arbitrary decisions as to who were men and who were women on the list were flawed. She thought it but didn't say it. 'One of the names on the list is K L Sheng not a he but a she; full name Kai Ling Sheng; she's their Singapore correspondent.'

'Bloody hell how did we miss that?'

'Two days ago sir the name would have meant nothing to us, nothing at all.'

'You've got her address I take it?'

'Yes sir, she lives in Wood Green a stone's throw from Tottenham.'

'Okay get on to DI Reid and get her picked up. Well done Lynne.' Pullman deserved the plaudits; it was his idea to check back on the list but then again he'd missed it in the first place; she'd graciously accept praise while it was being offered; it infrequently came her way.

No sooner had Pullman cancelled the call than his phone rang again; it was Tamara Bell-Sampson.

'Good morning inspector, I understand you wanted to speak to me. If it's about Peter then I already know.'

'Where are you?'

'On my way back from Val d'Isere, thought I'd have a long weekend skiing but there's light rain and very little snow; the forecast isn't promising so I thought I would return home; I suppose there'll be some arrangements to make.'

From his previous conversation with her, he hadn't expected her to be exactly distraught at her husband's death but he was sure she'd have stayed out there if there had been snow. Ebingdon's death sounded like a mild inconvenience.

'I know this is a difficult time for you,' yeah right, 'but I do need to talk to you at the earliest opportunity.'

'I expect to be back in the office by about five this afternoon, shall we say about six just in case I'm delayed?'

Bollocks, he screamed silently. He just got tickets for the 19.40 train that evening; he might just make it but for safety he'd have to re-book. Lynne could still travel on that train though.

'That's fine thanks. See you there at six'.

He was surprised that she had not tried to avoid a meeting; she wasn't over eager on the last occasion. Perhaps she was being extra co-operative to make it appear as if she had nothing to hide. Before he saw her he needed to find out if the Italian police had managed to find a witness who recognised her at the hotel Rosetti; could she have got from her German meeting to Triest then back to Val d'Isere in the time available? Was she actually at Val d'Isere?

He got the travel department to alter his train tickets then went to the rabbit hutch to look at online maps and distances to and from the three locations. It was nearly seven hundred kilometres by road between the ski resort and Triest; no way could she have driven that distance both ways in the time even in her Jaguar F-type V8; especially given the adverse weather conditions right across Europe. There was no direct route by rail; commercial flights would have involved two changes and car travel in addition. There was an outside possibility that she hired a private plane or hired a contract killer; neither was beyond her capabilities or her pocket but both were a bit fanciful. He decided to leave it for the time being; if after he met her he felt unsure then he would get Europol to check it out on the ground but his gut instinct was telling him that she wasn't involved. That made him question why he was seeing her at all.

Pullman sat back in his chair, closed his eyes and took a couple of deep breaths to clear his mind. 'Lynne have we had the medical report yet from the Bell-Sampson's clinic?'

'Next on my list' she lied, having completely forgotten about it with the events of the past day or two. She hoped that the clinic would be co-operative because there was no way she'd get a court order on a Friday. She'd have difficulty finding a judge who wasn't on the golf course or at the Garrick Club.

'I'm off to Harley Street; do you want me to bring you a sandwich back with me?'

'Yes please, chicken however it comes. Lynne sorry to ruin your weekend but I'd like you to come with me to BSC this evening.'

'I thought you'd never ask,' she said.

'Well the way our luck is running you never know we might get a confession from her and you're so much better at reading the rights than me.'

She took the underground to Regent's Park; guided by the GPS app on her smart phone she walked along Marylebone Road before turning left down Harley Street. Unfortunately for her she chose the wrong end of the street; the clinic was situated at the southern end near Cavendish Square. Ten minutes later a discrete brass plaque engraved with The Harley Private Clinic told her that she had reached the right address; she entered through the arched double doors her shoes echoing on the marble tiled floor. A receptionist dressed in a light blue suit, white blouse with a light blue and red diamond pattern; hair neatly tied back in a bun greeted her. She was the antithesis of the last receptionist she had spoken to. Sperring showed her ID and asked for Doctor Bream with whom she had made an appointment en-route.

She was requested to take a seat and offered coffee which she accepted; the one from the vending machine could have been decaffeinated for all the stimulation it had on her cognitive powers. No sooner had the coffee arrived than so too did Doctor Bream, introduced himself and sat next to her.

'To what do we owe this honour?' He said in an accent befitting the second cousin of a second cousin of the Royal household.

Sperring explained that she was investigating the murder of Peter Ebingdon and that they would be grateful if he would release his patient's medical records along with those of his wife as they were relevant to their enquiries. Bream spouted all the usual platitudes about patient confidentiality; the Access to Health Records Act 1990 and how much he'd like to help but couldn't do so without the patient's consent. Sperring reminded him that the patient was dead and couldn't give his consent also that General medical Council guidelines stated that he could, and should, release the records to assist the police in solving a serious crime and that crime didn't get much more serious than murder. He was still resisting; Sperring was getting nowhere until she used the National Crime Agency name and said that it would avoid their involvement; the need to get a court order and the arrival of noisy police vehicles arriving to execute the order.

Client confidentiality seemed to take a back seat to the effect of adverse publicity. He conceded; half an hour later she left the clinic with full copies of the medical records of the husband and wife.

Sperring was very tempted to read the medical records on the tube train ride back to the office but resisted; the train was crowded for that time of the day so privacy was impossible. She bought lunch before returning to her desk. She sat down and opened the medical files. Tamara's records went back to her teens; notes on her drug and alcohol addictions and treatment were there along with records of contraception provision, inoculations for overseas travel and an abortion in 1999. Sperring was surprised by that revelation because according to the Ebingdon interview he had claimed that Tamara couldn't conceive; perhaps that was as a result of the abortion. No, he had claimed that it was caused by a condition she couldn't recall the name of it but which meant Tamara didn't ovulate; as far as Sperring could determine there was no mention of such a condition on her file. And if she knew she couldn't conceive why was she taking oral contraceptives?

She opened Ebingdon's record; there were only two entries the first of which dated back to 2002, presumably around the time of their wedding. He'd had a full medical conducted at the clinic; Sperring guessed it would have been for life insurance purposes. The second entry was in 2012 and was a fertility assessment.

Pullman came into the office 'You've got them then; anything interesting'

275

'Two minutes sir,' she said without looking up from the records. Pullman sat down and impatiently drummed his fingers on his desk before reaching for the bag on his desk; he looked inside, gave a nod of approval and returned to drumming his fingers.

'This doesn't make sense,' she said.

TWENTY-NINE

Just as Pullman was about to close down his laptop in preparation to leave the office to walk the short distance across the square to BSC tower he received incoming mail.

'Result' he exclaimed punching the air.

Sperring looked across at her exuberant boss.

He paraphrased the email as he read it out.

'They've charged the two women in Glasgow for Kulkinski's murder. Avril Belman and Tanya Belman; both denying murder but forensics have matched prints to some found on the inside of the hatbox; ah it seems that they are sisters; Avril was using the name Jura for some reason.'

'Wonder why they didn't want to be seen to be related,' said Sperring.

'At the house they shared they apparently had a DVD of a violent sex attack by six men on a young woman who is seen to die during the assault. It was filmed at Kulkinski's club. They've identified the men, one of whom was Ross McGregor, the man the Belmans tried to abduct yesterday. There were stacks of notes and plans to kidnap and murder all six of the participants. They've also found the black beard and wig together with several other disguises and they've got a positive ID from staff at the Kicius club; the women had been lap dancers there. Two more sisters bite the dust. Also the CID is in the process of interviewing all six men in connection with the rape and murder of the unidentified girl in the DVD.'

'Fantastic. Result all round then.'

'Yeah, got Kulkinski's murderers; prevented the possible murder of six other men as well as getting those guys for the murder of the girl in the film.'

'A nice little haul then sir. Any sign of the body?'

'Doesn't say; so I'm assuming not.'

If they could get a result from Wethersby's murder on their home turf it would complete a very productive fortnight.

****

At 6pm sharp, Gretchen showed them into Tamara's office; she then collected her raincoat from the chrome coat rack, picked up her bag and left for the weekend.

Tamara was seated behind the slab of slate talking on the telephone. Pullman nodded acknowledgement towards a middle aged woman sitting at the round meeting table with her arms resting on papers in an open file and fingers interlocked. She was smartly dressed in a green and white dress with matching green shoes. Tamara ended her call and rose to greet Pullman. She was wearing the same style jeans as before but with a pale pink blouse on this occasion.

'Good evening inspector may I introduce you to my mother.'

Pullman nodded towards her again. 'Good evening I'm Detective Chief Inspector Pullman' at last a chance to correct Tamara. 'And this is Detective Sergeant Sperring.'

'Hello, I'm Anna Bell-Sampson,' she said with a polite smile and a lingering South African accent. 'I hope you don't mind me being here but we have some urgent business matters to discuss.'

Pullman couldn't think of a reason why he should mind. 'Not at all; in fact it might be helpful.'

'I'm intrigued,' Anna said.

'So what can I do for you this time inspector.' asked Tamara. Pullman's ploy hadn't worked. 'Please, do take a seat.'

The visitors sat at the meeting table with Anna; Tamara pulled up the visitors chair by her desk and sat down, facing the table but keeping her distance from it.

'I presume it's to do with Peter's murder,' Tamara said; there was no inflection of sadness in her voice.

'That amongst other things,' said Pullman. 'Pity about the skiing.'

Tamara smiled. 'Yes but there'll be plenty of other occasions.'

'Possibly,' said Pullman. 'Is Val d'Isere far from Triest?' He knew exactly where it was but wanted to see her reaction to the question. There was none.

'I've really no idea, geography is not my forte. I know where our offices are around the world but we don't have one in Triest. Do you have any idea what Peter was doing there?' she asked.

'I was hoping you could tell us.'

'Absolutely no idea. I haven't spoken to him for weeks.'

'I have.' Said Pullman, it was artistic license. 'He was in Graz in Austria last weekend. He implied that he was hiding from you; said he was frightened of you.'

'Frightened of me? What on earth for? Might be frightened of my lawyers but he had no reason to be frightened of me. Ah, I see so you're here because you think I found him and killed him.'

Pullman raised his eyebrows and looked at Tamara. 'Did you?'

'I'm not a modest person inspector; I consider myself to be reasonably clever but even I can't be in two places at once. If you would care to check with the Hotel Vida in Val d'Isere you will find that I was there all day yesterday. We had lunch followed by an indoor Petang competition; all got very drunk and carried on until the early hours. There are at least thirty witnesses to that.'

Pullman believed her. This wasn't one of those Agatha Christie plots where the killer can nip out for ten minutes, commit the crime and return unnoticed. It would take a tad longer than ten minutes travelling between the hotel and the murder scene. That just left the contract killing on his list of possibilities and he wasn't serious about that.

'On our last meeting I asked you if a web site called Sisters of Chiomara meant anything to you.'

'And I told you it didn't; nothing has changed.'

'You also said that your decision not to start a family with your husband was for medical reasons.'

'That is correct.'

'Would tell me what those medical reasons were please.'

'As I told you at our last meeting inspector, I see no reason why that is any concern of yours. It's a private matter.'

'Your husband said it was Primary Ovarian Insufficiency.'

She glanced at her mother. 'What the hell is that?'

'Mrs Ebingdon we......'

'Please don't call me that; I am Miss Bell-Sampson or Tamara.'

'Miss Bell-Sampson, your medical records state that there is no reason why you can't conceive. You do not have POI; never have.'

'What makes you think I had this decease or whatever it is? I am only too well aware that I can conceive.'

The medical records of the abortion were testament to that.

'Did you actually see your records or discuss them with the clinic at the time?'

'No I was away in the States my mother took care of it while I was out of the country.'

Anna looked down at the table and tightened the grip on her fingers.

'Mother? You told me Peter was HIV Positive; you said the report showed he would develop full blown aids.'

Anna looked up resolutely and spoke softly. 'It was for you own good darling. I couldn't bear the thought of that man being the father of my grandchildren. He wasn't good enough for you. So I told you that and I told him that you couldn't conceive.'

'Well it worked didn't it; I threw him out. How could you? What gave you the right?' Tamara's eyes welled up and she put her outstretched fingers on her temples and cupped her palms around her cheeks a perfect pose for Edvard Munch; for a moment her complexion paled too. Her emotions were suddenly in turmoil; her own mother had told her a lie to stop her having children. 'So he could have fathered my child. And because of you I thought he'd been screwing around.'

Pullman leaned forward and looked at Anna. 'That's not the whole truth is it Mrs Bell-Sampson,' he said.

Anna looked down and a tear dripped onto the glass surface; she sat in silence as the droplets began to stream. 'I don't wish to discuss it.'

Tamara pleaded with her 'Mother, what is the whole truth? Did he have aids or not?'

Anna said nothing; just sat and stared at her own reflection in the glass.

'Shall I tell her Mrs Bell-Sampson?'

Anna remained silent.

Pullman decided to continue. 'There is nothing in the medical report that indicates Peter was HIV positive quite the opposite; he was very healthy. However amongst other checks, the clinic carried out DNA analysis and found that you and Peter were a match.'

'A match for who?' asked Tamara.

'Each other.'

Tamara looked at him with total incredulity. 'That can't be; I thought the odds of two people having the same DNA were millions to one.'

'The odds are a billion to one unless those people are related.'

'But we were only related by marriage. We weren't re.... are you saying that we were related?'

'Yes you were blood relations.'

'I don't believe you; we couldn't have been related.'

Pullman looked at Anna, urging her to speak before he had to. She did.

'He was your father.'

Tamara screamed 'What! No I don't believe it; my father he couldn't be my father he was my husband; no, no this is some horrible nightmare.' Tamara stood up and paced the floor. 'Why are you doing this to me? This can't be true. You're saying my husband was my father. Oh god, please no.' She stopped pacing and turned to her mother. 'You knew. Oh my god did he know? Did the man I was trying to have children with know he was my father?'

Anna didn't answer her daughter so Pullman answered for her. 'I don't know for sure Tamara,' said Pullman, 'we suspect he did but I guess we'll never know.'

Tamara almost staggered to a wall unit opened the drop down door and poured herself a brandy which she downed in one swallow before pouring a refill.

Pullman's mobile rang. It seemed like an opportune moment to take the call while the news sank in. 'Excuse me' he said.

The Italian police superintendent on the other end of the line told him that they had a positive ID of the Bell-Sampson woman seen at the B&B Rosetti. She was also caught on camera at Triest airport and on CCTV outside the Credem offices on the corner of the Piazza del Ponterosso. Pullman listened, only interjecting with an affirmative grunt when necessary. The Superintendent was texting over a picture taken from the CCTV. Pullman thanked him and said that he would get back to him within 30 minutes. He went into his messages and opened the picture file. He looked at the picture and showed the screen to Sperring.

Tamara drained the brandy glass; she was trembling with rage and indignation. 'My god the things we did together. It's disgusting, I feel sick. He couldn't have known.'

Anna looked up at Tamara with tears in her eyes. 'He knew. He'd known since you introduced him to us. I didn't recognise him but he recognised me. I didn't know until I saw the medical report. There was no other explanation; so I confronted him; he just laughed at me. He said he enjoyed screwing his own daughter; said it ran in the family.'

'My god, why didn't you say something? Why didn't you tell me? That bastard screwed me knowing I was his daughter, that's incest, it's depraved and you didn't think it was important.'

'I don't know why. I just couldn't tell you; I knew if you thought he had HIV you'd stop sleeping with him so it didn't seem so important. I needed time to think things through. I had your fath... my husband to consider.'

'Mrs Bell-Sampson where were you yesterday?' asked Pullman.

'I think you know where I was.'

'I know that you were in Triest; I know that you were at the Rosetti and I believe you shot and killed Peter Ebingdon.' Anna looked at her daughter.

'No mum, no, please dear god no.'

Anna looked at her daughter through tear filled eyes. 'I'm so sorry darling.'

'If you'd told me the truth I would have killed the bastard myself.'

'No it had to be me, no one else.'

She composed herself as best she could. 'That vuil vark raped me.' She tensed at the memory. 'It was in Los Angeles, in the Olympic Village: I was just seventeen. Even now I can see the wild look in his eyes; filthy pig is an insult to pigs, he was the devil himself. You must understand; it was the first time I had been away from my parents; I was not much more than a child. I was pressured into going to the party that night by my team mates who hadn't made it through the first round. I've regretted it ever since. I put it out of my mind and took part in my events anyway but when I returned home I was horrified to find I was pregnant; in the end when I couldn't hide it any longer I told my parents that I had been raped, not in Los Angeles but by a man from Joburg when I was doing a promotional tour after the games. I even made up a description.'

Tamara sat silently staring at her mother.

'I thought it wouldn't matter because no one got arrested for rape in South Africa at that time, unless they were black. But my father couldn't rest, he wanted to take me up to Joburg to find the man but obviously I couldn't, in the end I left home but it didn't stop him; he became totally irrational; he packed my mother and brother in the car one day and took off on a hopeless quest to find the man. They were killed in a car accident.'

Her breathing shuddered at the memory.

'It was West's fault,' she saw Tamara eyes question the name. 'Robert West; that's who the vile creature was before he, for whatever reason, changed his name and his face,' she explained. 'I have tried so, so hard to forget, to get on with my life, to protect you from the truth but three weeks ago he said that if we didn't agree to his divorce demand's he would tell the world. I couldn't let that happen, darling. I'm so sorry.'

Tamara moved slowly towards her mother and put an arm around her shoulder to comfort her. Both women were tearful.

Pullman tried hard not to feel compassion for Anna; she had committed murder; there could never be an acceptable reason for that. The ironic thing was that Ebingdon had more to lose by going public than the Bell-Sampsons. It might have rocked their business for a while but it would have withstood the scandal; Ebingdon on the other hand would have been reviled for ever.

'Mrs Bell-Sampson are you aware of the Sisters of Chiomara?'

She shook her head.

'Then would you mind telling me why you wrote the letters SOC on Ebingdon's forehead?'

'I'd been planning to kill him for some weeks; had him followed wherever he went. I needed to know where he was when I had built sufficient resolve to do what I had to do. I read articles about murders. There were several recently that were being attributed to a serial killer who wrote those letters on his victim's, not just here but across other countries, so I thought that maybe the police would think it was the same person.'

Pullman thought it ironic that in the context of the SOC case her plan was accurate; Ebingdon qualified for inclusion.

'In those murders the victims were beheaded.' said Pullman.

'I know but I couldn't do that, I'm not a murderer,' she sighed 'well actually I am, aren't I.'

Tamara squeezed her mother's shoulder and affectionately rested her head on her mother's. They cried together.

Pullman composed himself; 'Anna Bell-Sampson I am arresting you for the murder of Peter Ebingdon.'

As usual he motioned to Sperring to complete the formalities.

284

THIRTY

Loose Ends

Having arrested Anna Bell-Sampson, Pullman realised that he hadn't arranged a police station at which she could be formally charged; he thought about calling the Yard but instead called DI Reid and explained the situation. He asked Reid to arrange for Mrs Bell-Sampson to be taken into custody; Reid readily agreed and arranged for uniformed officers from West End Central police station to pick her up.

His second call was to Caroline Nichols at Newzferret; as promised he gave her the exclusive on the arrest and the medical details behind the motive. The story went online that night and in the first editions of The Guardian the following morning; the rest of the press covered it with their second editions. Caroline and Mark kept their word; they did not publish the story while Peter Ebingdon was alive.

On the following Monday at a specially convened court hearing at Southwark Crown Court Anna Bell-Sampson pleaded guilty to murder and was remanded in custody pending trial. Bail was denied.

George Bell-Sampson officially retired from the BSC Group and handed over the reins to Darrel Newman the deputy CEO. Tamara remained as CEO of BSCyber but was considered too young and inexperienced to take overall control of the group. Neither she, nor anyone else attended the committal of Peter Ebingdon at the Crematorio di Tergeste; she didn't even have the body flown home.

****

Paul and Katie had a healthy baby girl; Emily Louise, 6lbs 4oz.

****

The Computer Forensic team at Hull police headquarters salvaged the hard drive from Thomas Wethersby's waterlogged laptop discovered in Clipton. What they found revealed the murdered schoolteacher to be a sexual predator more than capable of the acts of which he had been accused by the two schoolgirls. His hard drive was populated with over eight hundred indecent images of young girls assessed as being between the ages of twelve and sixteen. Several of the images were of girls from his school; they were not pornographic but some had been taken with the zoom lens during PE lessons and others during summer months when the girls were relaxing, uninhibited on the college playing field. Accusations that Wethersby was a paedophile were slightly inaccurate the photographs showed him to be a Hebephile; Wethersby had an abnormal interest in young pubescent girls.

The majority of the images were taken at various unidentifiable locations in the UK with a small minority of files clearly having been taken somewhere in Asia. He had accessed numerous pornography sites but none of the images had been downloaded from the internet; quite the opposite in fact; all had been uploaded to his laptop by Wethersby himself or someone with direct access to his computer. In some of the images adult feet and parts of unidentifiable body shapes lead them to the conclusion that the images were taken as part of an international Hebephilia ring.

Several emails that he had attempted to delete from his Microsoft Outlook file were still on the hard drive. Many of these accused him of acts of perversion; being a paedophile; a rapist and a sexual deviant. Many of which had been received prior to the Gemma Maxwell allegations. A drill down on these showed that without exception they had been sent from cyber cafes and other public access computer locations and would almost certainly prove to be untraceable to an individual or individuals. The hard drive was handed over to officers involved in Operation Yewtree to form part of their on-going enquiries. The murder of Thomas Wethersby would, for the time being, remain unsolved.

****

Kai Ling Sheng was detained at Heathrow's terminal five whilst waiting to board flight BA011 to Changi International in Singapore; she was taken to Stoke Newington police station where she was questioned by DI Reid and DS Grant.

In near perfect English, she openly admitted founding and running the Sisters of Chiomara web site. She further admitted that she signed herself Tisiphone on the site and volunteered the information that friends in Singapore were the originators of the Megaera twitter account and the Alecto Facebook account. She also agreed that she was the person who made the mobile calls to the Yorkshire schoolgirls but only to verify facts not to incite revenge.

She totally denied inciting others to commit murder, arguing that she merely published information that was already in the public domain and provided a portal and a forum whereby others could air their views; she was not responsible for the sentiments expressed or for the conduct or actions of any visitor to the site. She did not volunteer the fact that her brother and a cousin were the technical wizards behind the hidden layers of the site nor that one was Technical Director of BSC's Asian operation and the other was a Chief Programmer in the organisation. Neither did she volunteer the fact that her mother and sister had both been the victims of rape or that her mother had subsequently committed suicide having been unable to come to terms with her ordeal. The police need not know the motivation behind the creation of the web site.

Despite outward appearance she insisted her relationship with Janet Luman was purely one of platonic friendship and joint interest in the deliverance of justice for victims of sexual attacks. She had similar relationships with both women and men in various countries who sought justice. She had no idea that Luman had committed murder neither did she in any way encourage or facilitate her actions.

Kai Ling was an accomplished liar.

CIFT had already gone through the SOC web site with a proverbial fine tooth comb; to see what, if any, crimes had been committed by the site owners. The CPS decided that it would be extremely difficult to execute a prosecution. There were dozens of sites on the internet that exposed paedophiles, sexual attackers, drug dealers and criminals in general. Even the Metropolitan Police had a 'most wanted' web site. National newspapers frequently published lists of suspects in any manner of criminal genres. The fact that others had used the identity of the site to identify their actions was not something the operators could control. The Crown Prosecutor deemed that SOC was doing little more than those sites and that it was unlikely that a prosecution would be successful. They would however continue to monitor the site for future actionable criminal intent and require the ISP, WebLynka, to apply pressure on the site to tone down the content.

There was no need for Kai Ling Sheng to seek the sanctity of the Ecuadorian embassy just yet.

****

Avril and Tanya Belman were indicted for the murder of Josef Kulkinski; however if their fate had been determined by public opinion they would have both received sainthoods.

In addition they were both charged with the attempted abduction of Ross McGregor while they were supposedly taking a used car for a test drive. They were also charged with conspiracy to commit murder.

McGregor was subsequently arrested along with the other five club members; all of whom were charged with rape and murder. The Crown Office and Procurator Fiscal Service reluctantly reduced the charge to manslaughter in return for guilty pleas by the perpetrators. They sought the maximum sentences with a minimum of ten years on each count.

****

Six weeks after they were released by the NYPD, Charlotte Gortman and Jessie Ansdean were arrested by the New Jersey State Police; they were caught on CCTV whilst in the act of depositing the

289

head of their third victim on the steps of the court house in Newark. They were subsequently charged with all three murders after Ansdean turned state's evidence in return for the slightly lesser charge of being an accomplice to murder on the grounds of intimidation by Gortman.

****

DCI Mike Pullman declined the offer to make his move to the NCA in London permanent and returned to his duties and memories in Hull. DS Sperring also remained with Humberside Police.